PENGUIN BOOKS

ACT OF DARKNESS

This is Francis King's fir
Action (1978). In the i
collection of short stories
fiction works, *E.M. Forst*
his childhood in India,
official. While an under
three novels. Then he
successively in Italy, Greece, Egypt, Finland and Japan, before
retiring in 1964 to devote himself entirely to writing. For the
past four years he has been drama critic of the *Sunday Telegraph*,
and he reviews fiction regularly for the *Spectator*. He is a former
winner of the Somerset Maugham Prize and the Katherine
Mansfield short-story prize. He has also edited and introduced
Writings from Japan by Lafcadio Hearn, which is published in
the Penguin Travel Library.

Francis King has been active on behalf of writers. A founder
member of Writer's Action Group which was active in the final
battle for PLR, he is President of English PEN.

Act of Darkness has received immense critical acclaim on both
sides of the Atlantic: *The New York Times* wrote, 'On one level it
is simply a terrific mystery story with a slippery, enticing plot
... a darkly luminous parable about innocence and evil, guilt
and redemption ... *Act of Darkness* not only possesses the
immediacy of a good thriller but also feels like an intimate,
personal work'; Graham Swift in the *Sunday Times* said,
'Recalls *A Passage to India* in setting and form ... whether read
as a detective story or as a powerful exploration of character
and motive, *Act of Darkness* will not fail to impress'; Harriet
Waugh in the *Spectator* stated, 'His novel, on one level, is a who-
done-it so carefully plotted that it fulfils the highest criteria of
the genre. However, it would be ludicrous to slot it into the
bookshelf under that heading as it possesses an emotional
charge and breadth of vision which places it in the forefront of
this year's novels. It is also highly enjoyable'; and Melvyn
Bragg commented, 'Francis King deserves the widest possible
readership. He is a master novelist.'

FRANCIS KING

ACT OF
DARKNESS

PENGUIN BOOKS

Penguin Books Ltd, Harmondsworth, Middlesex, England
Viking Penguin Inc., 40 West 23rd Street, New York, New York 10010, U.S.A.
Penguin Books Australia Ltd, Ringwood, Victoria, Australia
Penguin Books Canada Ltd, 2801 John Street, Markham, Ontario, Canada L3R 1B4
Penguin Books (N.Z.) Ltd, 182–190 Wairau Road, Auckland 10, New Zealand

First published by Hutchinson & Co. (Publishers) Ltd 1983
Published in Penguin Books 1984

Made and printed in Great Britain by
Cox & Wyman Ltd, Reading
Filmset in Baskerville

To
the memory of Alex Kellar
1905-82
in gratitude for that rare thing, an act
of totally disinterested kindness

CONTENTS

I
OMENS

PETER

The six-year-old boy, Peter, Pete, Peterkin, Petal, Pet, sprawls on his stomach, chin propped on hands, and stares down at the copy of the *Illustrated London News* in an attempt to decipher what is written below the photograph of the Indian Army officer whom he has always known as Uncle Jack.

Uncle Jack, his mother's brother, was to come and visit them on leave across hundreds of miles of desert and jungle from one side of the continent to the other but then, mysteriously, he never came.

The child entered the drawing room and the voices of everyone, previously so agitated, fell strangely silent. 'Take him to his room,' his father ordered and at once his grandmother rose from the sofa and grasped his hand in hers with a brisk 'Come along, Peter!'

Two nights later, unable to sleep and with Clare, the governess, away on her evening off, Peter crept down the stairs and heard his mother's low, gasping, terrifying sobs coming up from the darkened hall below him. The dining room door creaked open and, crouching now on a step as he peered down through the banisters, he first saw his father, Toby, stiffly erect in a yellow wedge of light, and then heard him ask with that impatience which always honed his voice when one of the family did or said something unpredictable or unwelcome: 'What is it, Isabel? What's the matter? Why have you left the table?'

Then Peter's half-sister, Helen, was also there, the taffeta

11

over her bony shoulders glistening like mother-of-pearl and one cheekbone, her head turned sideways, glistening above it, and she too began: 'What is it, mama? What is it?' Peter always called his mother mummy; but to Helen she was never anything other than mama.

'I suddenly came to think . . . He might now be . . .'

'Come. Come!' Toby's first 'Come' was tender, his second rough.

'What's the use, mama? One has to . . . accept.'

'Yes. One has to accept.' After that torrent of weeping, the voice was arid. 'Yes.'

Peter saw his mother, Isabel, in her black evening dress, the four panels of its skirt picked out in a diamond pattern in jet, move out of the darkness. The back of her right hand was pressed to her right eye as though something painful were lodged in it. Then he saw his father put an arm around her shoulder and gently propel her into the dining room, where the overhead light would be twinkling with a wattage so low from the generator that one could see its fiery filament, where old Mrs Thompson would be seated, her hands resting on the edge of the dining-table while she stared straight ahead of her, and where the two white-coated Indian servants would be standing motionless and silent, waiting to serve the entrée in its silver dish above a spirit-burner.

'When is Uncle Jack coming to visit us?' he began persistently to ask his mother, remembering the sunburned face with its jutting nose, thick moustache and blue, blank eyes. The face would look down at him, Peter would squirm and scream, as Uncle Jack demanded, his hands everywhere: 'Are you ticklish then? Are you?' Isabel, frowning across at them, would eventually exclaim: 'Oh, do leave him alone, Jack! You'll only over-excite him,' in that same voice, dry and sharp, which she would so often use to the governess, Clare.

'Oh . . . I don't know. He's gone away. Far away.'

At that, his mother would rise from her chair or, if it were night-time, from the edge of his bed, as if she could suddenly no longer bear his proximity to her.

'Gone from India?'

'Yes, gone from India. Oh, you've asked me all this before and I've told you all this before!'

Then, one evening, when yet again he put the question, she did not rise from the edge of his bed but instead bunched her lips and bit on them, her head turned away, before she told him: 'Don't ask that again. Please. He's gone forever. He won't come back.'

'Forever? What does that mean?' But, strangely, he had known all along that Uncle Jack had gone forever. He knew what it meant.

'He's gone to . . . heaven,' she mumbled in a turbulent mingling of grief at her loss and embarrassment at having to use the ghastly euphemism.

'Heaven?'

The bull-terrier bitch, which he had always thought of as his, staggered a few steps, sat down with a bewildered look on her face, and then toppled over. Blood trickled out of one of her nostrils. Her sides heaved briefly, caved in. Clare snatched at his hand and tugged at it so hard that it hurt him, as she removed him from the verandah. He knew. He knew all right. He was not surprised.

Now his mother suddenly enveloped him, going down on her knees by his bed, her white, plump arms around him and her face to his chest. She smelled of lavender, bitter and strong. 'We'll see him again,' she whispered, even more desperate to convince herself than him. 'One day. Promise.' He stiffened and then, all at once frantic, began to struggle free, as though this woman, her hair dishevelled and her eyelids inflamed with unshed tears, were clutching at him in a futile effort to save herself from drowning.

Dead. Death. He knew those words. The gardener and the 'boy' who helped him lugged the bitch between them up the winding path and out of sight and then, later that afternoon, his father, Toby, led him up to where the earth, newly thrown up, glistened. 'She's there,' Toby said. 'She's sleeping there.' Toby was unnerved and exasperated when the child began to scream, his mouth wide open and his cheeks scarlet under the dripping branches – he was so jumpy, so sensitive, what would become of him? Then the child pointed. On the earth an immensely fat, blueish-pink worm, like a lump of gristle, wriggled upwards. Silent and rapt, the child stared, stooped, knelt; extended a hand; stroked with a forefinger; then, with a little shudder and gasp, picked up the worm and, head tilted to one side, examined it as it curled impotently first in one direction and then in another. 'Put that down!' Toby shouted.

Dead. Death. He knew the words. He even knew how to spell them. He was good at spelling.

'Why did he go to heaven?' he now asked. He knew that he must not say dead or death to his mother. To his father, to his grandmother, to Helen or to Clare he might do so.

'Because, because . . .' With grave, pitiless curiosity he watched that familiar bunching of the lips and the tears slowly welling along the lower eyelids. 'Because . . . he was tired. He went to sleep. He was tired.'

'Might I go to sleep and also . . . ?'

'Of course not!' She towered above him, the woman whom he imagined to be getting fat, like the ayah, and whom he did not know to be pregnant. She was angry now, no longer grief-stricken and embarrassed. 'You're far too young, far too young.'

'Uncle Jack wasn't so old. How old was he?'

'Thirty-five, nearly thirty-six.'

'Was he older than you?'

'We were twins. You know we were twins.'

'I never knew.' And, truly, he hadn't. But for some reason this made his mother even angrier. 'Of course you knew!' she shouted at him, as she shouted at him when, having disobeyed her, he pretended ignorance of what she had told him to do or not to do.

When next he was riding with Helen, he on the squat pony with the tufty coat of a donkey, and she on the gelding which really was their father's, he asked her too: 'How did Uncle Jack die?'

14

Helen hesitated, looking out from her eminence, over the trees to the lake below. Then she shrugged, as though it were a matter of little concern to either of them. 'Some kind of fever. I don't know. He fell ill. Died. Quickly. Like that. No pain.' Peter always knew when people were lying to him. She was lying.

. . . Now the boy, Peter, Pete, Peterkin, Petal, Pet sprawls on his stomach and, with one stubby finger tracing the letters, attempts to read what is printed below the photograph of the dead man whom he loved. There is another photograph, similar to the one before him but larger, on the chimneypiece. Its *art nouveau* frames makes it appear as if some exotic liana had suddenly solidified to silver while it was wreathing itself about the face staring with blank, blue eyes, two sepia shadows in the photograph, into the ferocious sun above the bowed head of the unseen fellow officer with the Box Brownie in his hands.

A gust of rain whips the window, disintegrating the fine cobwebs of moisture clinging to it. The boy screws up his eyes – one day he will have to wear glasses, Toby is always saying with that suppressed irritation which his son's physical shortcomings arouse in him. Clare and Helen have gone out for a walk, in their belted raincoats and the hoods which they pull down low over their foreheads. His father has gone away for two or three days, on one of those journeys which he is always making to one of his farms, businesses or hotels, and his bearer, Muhammed, has gone with him. His grandmother, old Mrs Thompson, sits alone at the window of her bedroom, working, as so often, at some knitting. His mother is resting, as she often rests these days, a white, plump arm behind the luxuriant dark hair uncoiled from its knot and her belly mountainous under the sheet which drapes it. The ayah is also asleep, cross-legged and leaning against the door which opens out from what was once called the playroom and is now called the schoolroom, on to the verandah. From time to time the rain spatters her sari, her bunched, greying hair or her wrinkled face, but she is unaware of it or indifferent to it.

15

He reads in puzzlement, then he reads in mounting horror. He cannot make out all the words but he can make out enough of them to know how his uncle died. There was a private soldier who wished to be corporal but the colonel of the regiment denied him his promotion; and so the soldier, a Gurkha, sharpened his *kukri* and resolved to kill the colonel. The colonel was summoned to a conference in Simla and the soldier, unable to kill him, killed Uncle Jack, the major, instead. The soldier stabbed Uncle Jack in a frenzy, over and over again. He went on stabbing him long after he was dead. Eventually, it took four men to prise open the hand in which the handle of the *kukri* was grasped so tight that it seemed to be embedded there.

As the storm now lashes the window, with a din as of gravel hurled against it, the boy reads the stiff, glossy page of a magazine which has spent three weeks in the hold of a liner and three days in a sorting-office in Bombay and three more days on a train before the postman has trudged up the hill with it in his satchel, to be scolded by the bearer because he has let the rain dampen its cover. The boy feels horror rising within him, as in the past he has felt his gorge rise after too rich a meal, until he has screamed out to one of the women of the household: 'I'm going to be sick, I'm going to be sick!' With the horror, there is also fear and, yes, despair, as though the stiff, glossy page contained confirmation of all that he has already believed in his inmost heart and yet has tried not to believe. *That's it, yes, that's it. That's how it happens.* He stares down, the pupils of his eyes dilated, his nostrils wide and his mouth half-open, as though he were trying to cry out 'Help me, help me!' into the gale hammering at the window and had been paralysed in the effort. He has often before looked at pictures in the *Illustrated London News* and, hard though it has been, has even read some of the captions beneath them. *Their Majesties, King George V and Queen Mary, visiting the Star and Garter Home for Incurables* . . . (Skirt, stiffly pleated, all but brushes the ground, toque, parasol). *Miss Jean Forbes-Robertson, who will once again this Christmas* . . . (Peter Pan is transfixed, a sombre, huge-eyed moth, against a backcloth of whipped-cream clouds). *Champion of the Year at Cruft's* . . . (A pekinese bitch wrinkles her muzzle, feather-duster tail flaunted proudly high).

'Oh, oh, oh!' The boy sets up a weird keening. He has an over-mastering desire to wet himself, perhaps to do even worse.

The door behind him opens and there, thrusting her swollen belly before her and a plait of thick, dark hair lying like some furry creature over her left shoulder and arm, stands Isabel, her large teeth gleaming out of the shadows.

'What are you doing in here?' she asks angrily, because he is not allowed in the drawing room unless one of the grown-ups takes or calls him in. Then she sees his face, puckered and white, and the paper, smooth and shiny, on the carpet before him. None of them has yet read that copy of the *Illustrated London News*, it arrived only that morning. After dinner, she or her mother-in-law or one of the girls will pick it up and, bored, will turn its pages and later her husband, back from one of his farms or businesses or hotels, will demand irritably: 'How did you manage to make these pages so grubby?' He always likes to read every paper or periodical or book before any of them. That is how it should be but that is not how it will be now, because Peter, Pete, Peterkin, Petal, Pet has got in before them. She stares for a moment at this frail, precocious son of hers, her only child, who often seems to her to resemble some plant, sappy and green, forced in the gloom of a potting shed. She stoops and, her Chinese wrap swishing about her, snatches at the magazine which he is now clutching and jerks it away. At that, he gives a single, piercing scream, as though she had tugged out a *kukri* embedded in his hand. But tears, not blood, well out and flow, fatter and faster.

She sees the photograph of the twin brother, with his nail-bitten, nicotine-stained fingers and his thin sinewy torso above long legs, whom she loved almost as a lover and whom she has mourned and is still mourning and will go on mourning almost as a husband. She, too, like the boy, feels

17

horror rising within her; but her horror is not for that deed of frenzy, the knife smashing again and again into the already lifeless body and the blood spurting and the soldier grunting with each successive lunge, since all that has long since grown familiar to her in sleeping and waking nightmares, but rather for the intrusion, as of armed marauders exploding into the room in which she lies cradled alone in her grief, of so many unfeeling eyes staring down, as her son's feeling ones have been doing, at the photograph and the sensational account beneath it.

Suddenly she is furious. 'You shouldn't be in here! You're not allowed in here alone! You know that! Where's that bloody ayah? Ayah!'

The boy wails as his mother snatches him up in her arms. The drunken Scots doctor of the hill-station has warned her to be careful, she has already lost more than one child, she must not exert herself, she must rest. But she does not think of this.

The ayah, one cheek with a pleat in it where it has been pressed against the door-jamb, now jogs into the room on her flat, bare feet, her elbows tucked in close to her sides. She stifles a yawn, puts up a hand to tuck a wisp of grey hair into the untidy bun on the nape of her neck.

'What is it, memsahib?' she asks in Hindustani.

Isabel scorches and shrivels her with her gaze. 'Why did you let him come in here? Why don't you keep an eye on him? Can't I trust you for a single moment? You know Miss Clare and Miss Helen are out!' Her Hindustani is fluent.

The ayah cowers, a hand over her eyes, as though to shield them from a light so brilliant that they can barely look into it. But all Isabel's attention is now for the boy, whom she is holding above her mountainous belly, his face, warm and wet with tears, pressed into one side of her neck, while his hand clutches at the sheaf of hair over her shoulder. 'There, there, darling. There, there, Peter, Pete, Peterkin, Petal, Pet.' She rocks him as though he were still a baby. 'That's the trouble of being so clever that you can read absolutely anything at the age of six. There, there!' He emits a hiccoughing sob. 'You

18

had to know sooner or later.'

The two girls have returned from their walk and now stand in the doorway behind the ayah, their belted raincoats and their hoods dripping water, and their faces seeming to the boy, now gazing at them over his mother's shoulder, to be mysteriously transformed. He stretches out a hand first to one and then to the other, but neither of them moves.

'What's all this about?' Helen asks.

He stops crying abruptly when he hears her. It is not like a voice that he has ever known.

He is a beautiful child. Everyone – army officers, tea-planters, missionaries, civil servants, even those who sense something effeminate and, yes, not quite wholesome about him – agrees on that. His face, with its long, dark lashes, its pointed, dimpled chin and its skin so soft and so translucent that it seems as if a mere touch might break it and cause the blood to seep through, has about it a vulnerable girlishness. It is not only his mother who feels, when she holds him in her arms, that if she were to squeeze him too tightly his fragile limbs might snap. His hair is so blond that in certain lights – under the coppery sheen of an imminent thunderstorm or in the orange circle thrown by the drawing room standard lamp with its bell-like, beaded shade – it acquires an unearthly pallor, making his mother call him 'my changeling'. Unlike other children, he is always clean and neat, washing his face and hands deliberately with a large sponge in the bathroom which, like his bedroom, he shares with Clare, even when no one has told him to do so. He fusses if the ayah has not cleaned his shoes or brushed the mud off his shorts. He does not like the feel of wool against his skin and his eyes water, as though he were about to cry, when a comb is jerked and tugged over his scalp or his nails are cut.

He has always been a happy child, even if so solitary, with few white children in the small hill-station and of those even fewer with whom he is encouraged to make friends. He paints, either curled up in the window-seat in the drawing room, if he is allowed in there, or else on the floor of the schoolroom, the glass tumbler fascinating him with its swirling colours each time that he dips in his brush. Everyone says how 'artistic' he is; but for many of the army officers, tea-planters, missionaries and civil servants, that word carries a certain taint. Such people are not merely touched but also embarrassed when he gives them one of his paintings of purple trains, with white and brown people waving out of them, or of lurid sunsets over a lake that has the flatness and hardness of one of those disks with which he plays tiddlywinks with his grandmother, Clare and Helen. He is happy in being spoiled intermittently by his family and constantly by the servants. The latter call him *chotah sahib* or Little Master, they bring him saffron-coloured cakes or emerald-green sweets from the bazaar, which his mother takes away from him in case they should be dirty, they carry out his peremptory commands and they listen in wonder as he sings in his thin, clear, slightly eerie treble. In remote villages, further up in the hills or down in the plains, they have children of their own; but they love this alien child more than they love them, just as a monk or nun loves God more than kith and kin. Angry with the syce, he lashes out at him with the crop he carries for his pony; but the syce only laughs and later tells the other servants with pride of the incident.

He is a loving child, if capricious in his loving. When his mother has one of her bridge parties, he will be allowed into the drawing room when the servants are bringing in the tea. 'Come and talk to me,' one of the more elegant of the guests will cajole him, her face heavily powdered under her hat. But he will deliberately go to some plain, unimportant guest, not because he feels sorry for her with a wart on her chin and straggling grey hair which peeps out from under a plaid tam-o'-shanter, but because he wishes to show the others that he will never belong to any one person, however beautiful, charming or generous, for more than a few minutes at a stretch. The women coax him with bits of cake from their plates or slabs of chocolate and bags of sweets from their handbags. Politely, he either takes what they offer or, more often, refuses.

He loves Clare, who is Eurasian, whose father is a ticket collector for the BB and CI Railway, and who, here up in the hills, is so far from her family and friends. Even more he loves Helen. Secretly, he has been making her a bead bookmarker under the instruction of his grandmother. His grandmother, who has little to do in a household not her own, is always making bead-fringed doyleys as covers for bowls, jugs and glasses. In a paper bag he has all the multi-coloured beads, which he and his grandmother bought in the bazaar. Carefully he threads them, screwing up his eyes, at the table by the schoolroom window. 'Oh, you are a clever boy!', his grandmother exclaims in genuine admiration for a skill which neither of her daughters, much less Toby, possessed when they were children. Peter has come to want the bookmarker for himself as it grows, millimetre by millimetre, under his fingers, but that wanting makes it all the more valuable as an offering for Helen. The fact that Helen does not kiss him, does not hug him, does not give him presents or exclaim how sweet, attractive and intelligent he is, in the manner of the other women, makes him wish all the more to do something for her. He so much longs to attain what has so far been teasingly unattainable.

Helen says that he is a terrible tale-bearer and he knows, with shame, that she is right. It was he who told his father and mother of how the young soldier, in the uniform permeated with a not disagreeable guava-like smell of sweat, stopped him and Clare when she was taking him to the German refugee dentist and talked so long to her that he was late for his appointment and had to wait until the patient who should have been after him had had a tooth removed. Clare later said, defensively indignant, that the soldier was a cousin of hers, but no one believed her.

Clare sensed that lack of belief. 'Anyway, even if he isn't a cousin, why shouldn't I speak to him?' she demanded.

Isabel's reply was chilly. 'What you do in your free time is no concern of ours. But when you're with Peter . . .'

After he and Clare had gone into their bedroom, she cried out, 'Oh, you little beast!' and raised a hand to strike him. But, miraculously, the long, prehensile fingers, their nails painted scarlet ('You should speak to her about those nails,' Peter once overheard his mother tell his father) stopped a fraction of an inch from his cheek.

He let out a bellow from the shock of it. 'You're not allowed to do that! I'll tell Mummy and Daddy!'

'Tell them what you like!'

She sat down at the dressing-table and for a long time stared at the reflection of her pouting, dissatisfied face with a rapt intensity, as though she were seeing it for the first time. Peter was transfixed by remorse and, never felt before for her, also by pity. He sidled up and put an arm round her shoulder, his cheek to hers. But she pushed him away, not brutally but with an irritable absent-mindedness. 'Oh, leave off, do!'

At that, she opened one of the dressing-table drawers and took out first a packet of De Reske Minors and then the long cigarette holder, the ivory of which was streaked with nicotine. She was not supposed to smoke in their bedroom; indeed, Isabel did not like her to smoke at all – 'filthy habit' she would say. But, for once, Peter did not betray one of Clare's many infringements of the rules laid down for her.

Peter also tells tales about the servants. There is, for example, the one that, originating with him, has come to be repeated, with more and more embellishments and exaggerations by the grown-ups, to illustrate that, however long and however hard you try, you can never turn an Indian servant into an English one. The cook, Ahmed Ali, was with Toby and his first wife, Eithne, Helen's mother, before the First World War, coming to them, a skinny, pock-marked boy, from a remote Rajputana village to assist their then cook. The first wife and the second both, in turn, taught him their skills, so that 'You won't eat better at Government House' is something which some missionary or planter, who has never had more than a drink at Government House, often tells a newcomer. Since so much of the lives of Ahmed Ali, Muhammed and the other servants remains a secret to him, Peter, fascinated, is constantly spying on them. Though forbidden to do so, he is always wandering about their quarters behind the house, peering, with a mixture of excitement and apprehension, into the dimly lit, shed-like buildings. Standing on tiptoe, chin on ledge, he also watches what goes on in the kitchen and scullery.

It was while spying on the kitchen, shortly before Sunday supper, that he discovered Ahmed Ali carving what was left of a cold leg of lamb in a manner of which his parents would have hardly approved. The cook was seated crosslegged on the flagged floor, the carving knife in his right hand and the carving fork in his left, while the joint, also on the floor, was held between his left big toe and the toe next to it. Slice after slice of meat fell to the floor, to be picked up and nonchalantly tossed on to the silver platter beside him. That Sunday evening the family had supper, not off that cold joint, but off chunks of ham hacked clumsily thick by Isabel, who, Toby being away on business, had taken over from Ahmed Ali as a less expert but more fastidious carver.

Not for the first time Isabel told Ahmed Ali that he would have to pack up and go, she had had enough, this was really the last straw; and not for the first time he went through an elaborate charade, curiously satisfying to both of them, of pleading with her on his knees and in tears. 'Well, I'll have to talk to the sahib about it, we'll see,' she eventually relented. And there the matter ended.

Peter also spies on the *mali* or gardener and the gardener's 'boy'. The latter's coughing, like the raw squawking of a fledgling bird, often makes the family speculate as to whether he has tuberculosis or not, though none of them has any inclination to do anything further about the possibility.

This summer has been an unusually warm one in the hills and the *mali*, a hillman, goes about his duties, weeding and planting on his hunkers or swaying perilously as he transports

23

buckets of water down the narrow path from the well above the tennis court to the rose garden below it, in nothing but a *dhoti*. His legs are streaked with mud and mud is also caked between his strong, bare toes, on his hands and even on his hair; but as in the case of the huge, garish dahlias blossoming all the way down the *cud* between the verandah and the Collector's chalet-style bungalow hundreds of feet below it, the soil from which he seems first to have sprung and now to derive all his sustenance, has produced in him a beauty so surprising that more than once Peter has caught Clare gazing out of the window of their bedroom or the schoolroom, dreamily fascinated, as he carries out his tasks. Peter also watches him, thrilling precociously to the sheen of his flesh between the daubs of mud and to the muscles, so hard and solid that they might have been carved from mahogany, of his straight back, chest, legs, arms, hands. 'Let him get on with his work, don't be a nuisance to him,' Isabel calls out from her writing-desk by the open window of the drawing room when, with a stirring of unease, she sees the boy, in his open-necked, short-sleeved shirt, grey flannel shorts, fastened with a snake-belt, and his sandals, trailing behind the gardener as he moves back and forth between the well and the rose garden.

The gardener's 'boy' is so tiny that, seen from a distance, people assume him to be a child; but a close view of the delicate, sad, huge-eyed face, as of an ailing marmoset, shows him to be of an age even greater than the gardener's. He does not interest Peter, any more than he interests anyone else, except when he coughs.

Above the well, bowered by the overhanging branches of a deodar, there is a shed, narrow and whitewashed, which the child has been forbidden ever to enter. He has asked repeatedly what it is and has first been told nothing, only a godown, and then at last, his mother by now exasperated, that it is a servants' outdoor lavatory, rarely used now that a new one has been built for them by their quarters. It is dirty, Isabel says, adding: 'I don't want you going in there and picking up germs.'

24

But that prohibition merely encourages him to creep inside when no one can observe him. The interior of the shed is almost as dark as the locked cellars to which he never descends except with his father on an expedition to bring up wine and it has the same chilly clamminess, despite the heat of the afternoon, and the same odour of mustiness and decay. This is because of the bushes crowding around it, the layers of deodar, green on darker green, going up and up above it, and the absence of any window other than a narrow, unglazed rectangular aperture high up in a wall. Peter feels apprehensive, yet excited. At the far end, there is a concrete platform, covered by a wooden slat with a hole in it. At first, he wills himself not to look down into that hole for fear of what he might find. Then he has to look, he cannot contain himself.

Dark objects lurk beneath a viscous slime, with an iridescent sheen, as of oil, on top. He stoops, peers. He opens his mouth and then closes it, swallowing the saliva with which it has filled. He is horrified, yet he cannot look away. Beside the concrete platform there stands a huge *lota* or pot, full of stagnant water. When at last he tears himself away from the hole and looks into the pot, he sees that this water has the same rainbow sheen on it as the water in the hole. He has no idea that the servants, on their rare visits here, use this water, not paper, to cleanse themselves. He shudders, suddenly cold, and stares up at the narrow, rectangular aperture above him, noticing, for the first time, that a huge spider's web all but fills it. The spider is motionless near the centre, a large, black scab. He puts out a hand and, on an impulse, rocks the pot to and fro. Then, lowering it, slowly so that it should not break, he tips it on its side and watches as the water gushes out from it between his legs, splashing his bare ankles.

Giggling to himself, he then rushes out. No one sees him and no one mentions what he has done.

After that, he often creeps back into the whitewashed shed, though he never again tips over the pot. Once Clare sees him from the tennis court, where she is playing a lethargic game of pat ball with Helen, and she shouts up at him, her coarse black hair pulled back from her face in a pale blue bow so that her features look unnaturally taut: 'Peter! What are you doing? Come out of there – at once!'

Helen laughs: 'Oh, leave him!'

But Clare persists: 'Come out! Do you hear me? You could pick up anything in there. We don't want you down with enteric.'

The child comes out; but he returns both that same day, after the game of pat ball is over and the girls have gone back into the house, and on other days. So it is that, one afternoon, when his mother is asleep, his grandmother is down in the bazaar shopping for wool, and Clare, Helen and his father are seated out on the verandah aimlessly talking, he stealthily creeps up the narrow path, through the bushes and into the shed.

It is not empty. Two people are in there. They start apart from each other, their faces in shadow but their naked bodies gleaming in the light filtering down from the narrow, rectangular aperture above them. There is something about those bodies, slowly recognized as those of the gardener and his 'boy', which the child finds monstrous and terrifying. Yet he is also obscurely thrilled. The gardener snatches up his *dhoti* from the floor and rapidly winds it about his loins. The 'boy', eyes wide with shock in his marmoset face, seems to be paralysed, as a glue-like fluid trembles on a thigh and drips from a hand. Then the gardener shouts something, his usual sleepy expression transformed into one of extraordinary ferocity. The child runs out of the shed and races down the path and across the tennis court. Breathless, he arrives on the verandah. The adults stare at him.

'What is it, Peter?' His father raises a hand to shade his eyes from the sun behind the boy.

Peter tries to tell him; but there are no words to describe what he has witnessed. He stammers, his voice becomes tearful, he falls silent. But Toby knows from the jaggedly broken phrases what he is struggling to express. A large man, already in his fifties, with reddish eyebrows, scant reddish

26

hair and a reddish tint to his skin, he jumps up and, with a barked 'Keep him here!' to the girls, marches along the verandah and vanishes from sight.

The two girls gaze at each other, as though neither is sure how the other will take all this. Both have paled and there is sweat, not from their game, in small beads on the down above Clare's wide, heavily lipsticked mouth. Helen is the first to speak: 'Disgusting.' She grimaces.

Clare gives a high-pitched laugh. 'Well, they're different from us. What do you expect? And, anyway, what does it matter?'

They talk as if the child were not there.

'Father thinks it matters. Perhaps he'll kick them out.'

'I doubt it. You don't find another gardener as good as that in a hole like this.'

Now Helen also laughs, throwing back her head so that a thread of spittle between her teeth glitters in the sunlight. 'You'd no business to be there in the first place,' she tells Peter. 'None at all.'

'Sneak!' Clare puts in, out of the rancour of the many tales which he has repeated about herself. 'Why do you always have to tattle?'

Peter feels an irresistible urge to throw himself into the lap of one or other of the girls in an easy luxuriance of repentance and self-humiliation. But, head erect and arms held stiffly to his sides as though he were a toy soldier at attention, he merely blinks ahead of him.

'They won't like you at school back in England if you play the sneak,' Helen says.

He hates to be reminded that one day, in two or three years, he too, like Helen in the past, will have to make the long journey away from India and his mother and father to a country of which he knows only what he has read in those magazines which arrive, weeks late, in the house on the hill above the violet eye of the lake. People always speak as if, when he has reached there, some retribution will overtake him.

*

27

The summer passes, the violet eye of the lake fades to grey, the fallen leaves scrape across the tennis court at each gust of wind and pile up against the wire netting which surrounds it. The gardener no longer has to carry water, effortful pail by pail, down the steep, narrow track from the well. The petals of the roses are becoming friable and pale and when the child snaps off one of them, holding the small, tight bloom to his nose as he drinks in its scent, Isabel chides him: 'Oh, you've picked one of the last and best of the roses! Why did you have to do that?' Clare repeatedly says that she cannot wait to get back to the plains, she will see her family again, she will see all her friends. His grandmother wears one cardigan over another and a shawl over the cardigans. Helen sits close to the fire in the drawing room, now reading a book and now merely staring into the flames as they lick at the sizzling, aromatic pinewood. The baby – by now Peter has been told of its imminence – will first come and then they will all pack up and leave this house which has all at once grown inhospitable to them.

Even now Peter is happy, though the adults, he obscurely senses, are suffering a chilling and darkening of mood as the season chills and darkens. Each morning he still trots out on his pony, with the syce puffing along beside him, up one hill and down another. He has finished the bead bookmarker, with some help from his grandmother, and he has given it to Helen, who for once has hugged him. 'Oh, what a lovely present! It's just what I want!' But though she is always reading beside the fire, her face burnished by her closeness to it, he never again sees the bookmarker. What can have happened to it? He never likes to ask.

His grandmother cooks divinity fudge in the kitchen, telling him how one must look for the thread to know when it is ready. 'I can see it, I can see it!' he cries out, glimpsing the frail white filament dangling from the wooden spoon in her hand. Later, she gives him the saucepan and spoon and says 'You can scrape it out.' He loves to do that even if, later, he feels bilious and wonders if he might not perhaps be sick.

Clare teaches him the beginnings of geometry and says that in a year he will be able to start algebra. His father says that he is a clever little monkey and pinches his ear. The pinch is affectionate but it hurts him and brings tears to his eyes.

There is a children's fancy-dress party at Government House, in a larger hill-station some eleven miles away, so that it takes a long time to reach it in the dandies, Clare carried by four coolies and he by two, with two more pattering beside them as reliefs. He goes dressed as a pathan, with a velvet waistcoat embroidered in gold, white flared trousers, slippers which turn up at the toes, and a *pugree* on his head. He wins first prize. 'Oh, isn't he just adorable!' the Governor's wife exclaims to everyone around her.

On his birthday, his parents give him a fairy-bicycle and Helen, Clare and the bearer take it in turns to support him as he wobbles around the tennis court, the crisp leaves snapping into bronze shards beneath the wheels. He was hoping that his parents would give him another bull terrier but now he decides that a bicycle is better.

Suddenly, he learns to listen to music. He stands over his grandmother while she inexpertly plays the Barcarolle from *The Tales of Hoffman* or a Mozart Sonatina on the grand piano which, because of the dampness, always needs tuning. He cries out: 'Teach me! Teach me, please!' The old woman tells him to draw up a chair beside her and then makes him play a scale. 'Thumb under third finger, thumb under third finger!' she commands.

He is happy; but beneath his happiness there is always an undertow of dread. He thinks of Uncle Jack and of that *kukri* which the demented Gurkha soldier plunged again and again into the body against which, in the past, his own small, tremulous body has so often pressed itself. He even has nightmares about Uncle Jack, waking up screaming, so that Clare has to jump out of her own bed and put her arms around him, soothing him 'There, there! It's nothing! It's only a dream!' Often his mother, sleeping lightly in the room opposite to theirs, is also aroused and hurries in, her Chinese wrap swishing about her, to demand 'What is all this?'

Like someone who lives far inland but occasionally hears, so distant as almost to be inaudible, the rage of the ocean, and occasionally feels, so gentle as almost to be illusory, the tremor of the earth as wave after wave crashes down on it, so from time to time he senses that the same storm which has swept Uncle Jack away to extinction may also sweep away this house and everyone in it. This is a year of unrest and civil disobedience and, though he is not supposed to learn of such things any more than he was supposed to learn of the death of Uncle Jack, yet somehow, creeping around the verandah, standing outside the drawing room door or crouching on the stairs, he manages to do so.

The mission to which they once travelled for a jumble sale, so long ago that he can hardly remember the occasion, is burned to the ground. A receptionist at one of his father's hotels has suffered some terrible humiliation, he cannot discover what. Then there is the army officer, passing through from one posting to another, who tells the story of how, when he was driving out with his wife and two children in his ramshackle Morris Cowley, they were suddenly surrounded by an angry mob. 'I had no idea what to do. I thought that was it. Then I had a brainwave – and I don't often have those. I put my hand in my trouser pocket and I took out all the change I had there and I chucked it as far as I could all around us. Of course the brutes all began to scramble for it, they forgot us entirely, and so I put my foot down on the gas and we shot off at a speed of at least sixty miles an hour.'

Then, most terrifying of all, there is his father's illness. Every Saturday, Ahmed Ali, forgetting his hot-pot or his roast beef and Yorkshire pudding, prepares for them a curry. There are poppadums, chapattis, puris, mounds of fluffy rice, dahl bright with saffron and various kinds of chutneys and pickles. Of these pickles, only Toby ever eats the lime one, since the others all find it far too hot. On this occasion, Toby, a greedy man, behaves as he always does on Saturdays. Voraciously he wolfs the food piled up before him and then shouts for more. He helps himself liberally from the fluted glass bowl of lime pickle for his first helping, he empties it for his second.

Later, as Clare and Peter play a game of draughts in the schoolroom, they hear a terrible retching and groaning. 'Wait here!' Clare tells the child and gets up and goes out. Peter sits, numb, on the edge of his chair, listening. His mother gives a brief wail, he knows it to be hers, and there follows a hubbub of servants. Still Peter sits motionless. He hears Clare cry agitatedly: 'We must get Dr McGregor! We must get Dr McGregor!' and Helen, the only calm one among them, answering 'I'll ring him.' But the telephone is out of order, as so often, and so Helen rides off down the hill and round the lake in search of the drunken doctor.

Toby does not die; but for days he is strangely shrunken, like a balloon from which the air has suddenly escaped, and around his mouth there are small blebs, each so scarlet that it seems as though they must be gorged with blood. At first, it is thought that he must have had food poisoning; but then, when Ahmed Ali comes with the news that the kitchen-boy has vanished, no trace of him, his room in the servants' quarters empty, all his possessions taken, a darker suspicion is aroused; and when, on investigation by the police, his references are revealed to have been forged and the address which he has given in a distant village not to exist, that suspicion is intensified. But the drunken doctor, suspecting nothing, has allowed the fluted glass pickle bowl to be washed, and so no one will ever know for sure.

One day – there has been a brief flare-up of the summer which everyone supposed to have died – they all go on a picnic into the hills higher up above the lake. Isabel is carried in a dandy by four sweating and grunting coolies; Toby and Helen ride; Peter either walks with his grandmother and Clare or, when he feels tired, sits up in front of Helen on the gelding. Peter would be on his own pony, if it had not gone lame. The servants trail behind with their impedimenta of folding tables and chairs, wicker hampers and bottles clinking in pails of ice.

It is when Peter is sitting in front of Helen on the horse, her left hand pressed against his diaphragm while her right holds the reins, that he suddenly points up into a tree. 'Look, oh, look!' There is a huge snake, grey mottled with green, uncoiling itself sleepily from a branch. Its eyes glitter at him. His grandmother, leaning on her stick, glances up from under the rim of her grey Henry Heath hat and then lets out a squeak. Helen's hand suddenly presses so tight against his diaphragm that he can hardly breathe. The servants set up the shrill chatter of monkeys. 'Isn't he beautiful?' Peter says. He looks up at Helen and sees her rapt expression, the lips parted and the eyes wide open. 'Beautiful,' she agrees. The child cries: 'Let me down, let me down!' He wants to approach this supple, shimmering, immensely powerful creature; he wants to touch it. But Helen grips him tighter. 'Don't be silly! It's poisonous. It could kill you.' The snake suddenly slithers from one branch to another and then disappears into a hole in the trunk of the tree. They all continue to stare at the empty space where once it was. Then, summoned by Toby, who has halted ahead of them, they at last move on.

'Yes, it was beautiful,' Helen says. 'Extraordinary.' As he now leans back against her, Peter is aware of the thudding of her heart against the vertebrae of his spine.

Dead. Death. He knows those words. He knows them, understands them. The bull terrier staggers forward, sits down with a surprised expression on her face, topples. His father vomits uncontrollably on the floor, writhing in agony, while the white-faced women stare down at him in horrified disbelief. A *kukri* slashes and plunges. A snake uncoils, swells, shimmers.

HELEN

'Are you sure you don't want any help?' Isabel asks, standing in the doorway and giving an involuntary shudder as, firm shoulders hunched, she wraps her arms around herself.

'Quite sure, thank you.' Helen's voice is formally polite.

'The room *has* been aired,' Isabel says, the emphasis seeming to contradict an unspoken accusation. 'But, oh dear, it does seem damp. Everything seems damp up here in the hills, once it starts to rain.'

'It doesn't matter.' That Helen does not deny that the room is damp irritates Isabel, who first says curtly, turning away, 'I had the ayah put a bottle in your bed,' and then 'Well, if there's nothing else I can do . . .'

'Nothing, thank you.'

Helen stoops over the cabin-trunk, which, covered in scuffed labels of luxury hotels, once belonged to her mother, takes up a bundle of crepe de chine and begins carefully to unwrap it. She lets the crepe de chine, a petticoat, fall to the carpet and holds in her hands the silver photograph frame with the blurred photograph in it of a woman standing at an open window with a child in her arms. There is a white blur above the child where the wind blew out the muslin curtain at the precise moment in the Bordighera hotel bedroom when the invisible photographer, Toby, clicked the shutter of the outsize Kodak. There used to be another print of the same photograph on the grand piano in the drawing room but Helen has already noticed that it is no longer there. She imagines it lying, face downwards and forgotten, in some drawer or even suitcase. She places the photograph on the warped dressing-table of fumed oak and stares at it with an appraising intentness.

Then she crosses to the window and tries to force it open. But, since no one has slept in this room under one of the two gables for a long time, the catch is rusty and will not shift. Later, she will ask the bearer for a hammer. A hand to the faded cretonne of the curtain and a shoulder pressing to the wall, she looks out. Below her is the verandah, with geraniums in pots, and below that is the *cud*, where the land falls away in dahlias and rhododendrons and an occasional deodar clinging to an untidy outcrop of rock, and below that again is the violet eye of the lake, with the road which encircles it and, at its farthest end, the bazaar, the bus station and a squat, square, red-brick building, which is an army convalescent home.

There are no roads for cars or carriages up here in the hills. After they had abandoned the Rolls-Royce Henley Tourer in the garage close to the convalescent home, she was carried up to the house in a dandy, and her father rode. There are one or two sailing-boats on the lake, incising its tranquil surface with their swift, erratic wakes. The hills are an intense green at this time of year, the sky an intense blue, with an accumulation of fluffy clouds, as though white and grey feathers had been swept up into a heap, low down in the west, where two of the hills divide and the road serpentines, through innumerable nauseating hairpin bends, down to the plains.

She lets the cretonne of the curtain fall, straightens herself and returns to her unpacking. But soon she wearies of that, as she never wearied of the incessant shaking and swaying on and on through a day and a night in the train, of being driven up and up in the huge, lurching car, or of being carried in that kind of palanquin by four gasping and sweating little men with bandy legs and sloping shoulders. So she lies out on the damp bed, the back of one hand against her cheek, and stares up at the ceiling, where a diagonal crack runs from one corner almost to the rose of the light in its stiff parchment shade. She sighs deeply, the small breasts under the cashmere jersey rising and falling.

She does not want to be here, though through all the years in England she wanted, oh so forlornly and oh so desperately, to be with her father. She wished to go on to university, to become a doctor, and all the mistresses encouraged this awkward, hard-working, reserved girl in that wish. But her father would have none of it: 'We're far too impatient to have you back with us,' he wrote flatteringly in one of his brief, rapidly scrawled letters, which took at least two weeks to reach her by sea to Marseilles and then overland.

Her mother's unmarried sister, Aunt Sophie, thinks it a shame. Many years before the War, when only a girl of sixteen, Aunt Sophie herself had travelled out to India to stay with her sister and the penniless young man, invalided out of the Army because of a leg shattered in a fall at polo, whose marriage to an heiress, conspicuously older than himself, started him on his career as hotel proprietor, land owner and financier. On the ship, a raffish, over-painted, middle-aged woman, divorced and travelling out to be companion to a maharanee, said that she supposed that Aunt Sophie was 'one of the fishing fleet'. Aunt Sophie did not understand the expression and, when it was explained to her, felt angered and humiliated by the assumption that she was making this voyage in the hope of netting a husband. Whatever else she did in India, that was something which she was resolved not to do. She stayed briefly with her sister and brother-in-law and then, much to their disapproval, left them to become a nurse in a native hospital in the slums of Calcutta. 'Sophie has never been quite all there,' Toby would explain to those who asked what had happened to her. He made a joke of what he felt as a shame – as he so often did. He purposely avoided any subsequent visits to Calcutta, since, once there, he would have to call on this eccentric sister-in-law in the hostel in which she lived with her fellow nurses, many of them Eurasian or Indian, and might even have to agree to being shown around the hospital, with its patients crammed higgledly-piggledy into dank, evil-smelling wards. All his life, despite his heartiness and robustness, he has been squeamish about such things as blood, vomit, excrement, illness and death.

Helen thinks now of Aunt Sophie, since, her mother dead, she is the one person in the world, apart from her father, for whom she feels any real love. This does not mean that she has not been often embarrassed by her, in the way that the young are embarrassed by eccentricity or even singularity in those to whom they are related or with whom they associate. Aunt Sophie wears the kind of clothes, shapeless and rumpled, and above all the kinds of headgear, checked jockey-caps, towering shakos or garden-party straws with chenille flowers in pastel shades pinned above their dipping brims, which excite derision at bus stops or on underground station platforms. She leaves one of a newly bought pair of gloves in a taxi, mislays the books which she borrows from Mudie's, and is forever locking herself out of the room which she rents in a lodging-house in Earls Court. Much of the capital which she inherited from her baronet, businessman father she has squandered on seemingly good causes and seemingly good people, both of which have, in time, proved to be worthless. She has retained all the impulsiveness, the faith and the simplicity of a child. She is silly, in the original meaning of the word, wholly a fool and a holy fool.

Staying with her in that long, narrow room, bereft of all but essential possessions – what became of the silver, the pictures, the furniture inherited, with her sister, from their father? – Helen senses something exceptional, if exasperating, in her. She works for nothing in a settlement in the East End, among girls who, in many cases, openly deride her, cadge off her and respond to her many kindnesses with insolence. Part of Helen is angry with Aunt Sophie when she talks of these same girls as 'such dears'; part of her is moved. Once she went with Aunt Sophie and the girls on an expedition by charabanc to Brighton. She hated the inane chatter, convulsive giggling and, above all, feral stink. But she hated herself for that hate; she wished that she were capable of Aunt Sophie's love.

Now Aunt Sophie is far away, heating up baked beans on her gas ring, visiting in hospital someone who does not want her visit, puzzling over Ouspensky, writing a letter of protest to the old MG (as she calls the *Manchester Guardian*), selling flags at some gusty street corner, or meticulously recording in her diary one of more of these activities, and she, Helen, is here. Helen has known this house before, when her mother was alive, but it now seems so much smaller, darker and danker than she remembered it back at school in Oxford. Didn't the lake expand far wider and weren't those hills once mountains? Was the surface of the hard tennis court always covered in that green rash? And the *cud* – what has become of that sheer precipice tumbling away vertiginously from the edge of the verandah? It now seems so tame.

'Don't be too long, dear. We'll have some tea,' her grandmother, old Mrs Thompson, calls from the other side of the door.

Helen does not want to go down. But she must go down.

The half-brother whom she has never seen is painting under the grand piano in the drawing room, while her stepmother is seated in a high-backed chair, just as her mother used to be seated, before the silver tea service passed down through generations of her family. This alien woman, once the keeper of the house and now its mistress, has no business to be seated there, as though the dead woman's chair, tea service and position were all hers by right. Isabel smiles nervously at Helen, as though she guesses these thoughts of hers.

'Unpacked?' Helen's grandmother asks.

'Partly.'

'I've told Muhammed to put one of the kerosene stoves in your room,' Isabel says.

'Oh, I hate the smell of kerosene.'

'There's no other way to heat it. If one uses an electric fire in this house, it causes a fuse. You probably remember that.'

Helen remembers a late afternoon when a thunderstorm fused all the lights as they sat in the drawing room, she, her father, her ailing mother and the robust woman who had come to be their housekeeper, with a lamp flickering on the grand piano and the sky a lurid orange darkening to purple above the rain-shrouded hills. Her mother said to the other woman: 'You pour out for me. I haven't the strength to do it.'

As Isabel poured out, the lightning zigzagged from the crest of one hill to the next, to be followed by a hollow boom of thunder. Isabel let out a scream and, doing so, involuntarily tipped the silver teapot forward so that steaming liquid cascaded to the carpet. She put down the teapot and then raised shaking hands to her ears. 'Oh, oh, oh, oh!' Toby crossed over to her and put a hand on her shoulder. 'It's nothing. It's too far away to strike us. There's no need to be frightened. No need at all. Isabel, I promise you.' She looked up at him, strangely calmed. He said nothing more, he removed the hand. Helen's mother reached out for the Benares brass bell on the table beside her to summon the bearer to wipe the carpet. Helen stared across at her father.

Peter crawls out from under the piano, the dripping paintbrush in his hand, and sidles over to his mother, at the same time gazing at this tall, thin girl whom he has been told is his half-sister.

Isabel throws an arm round him and draws him close to her knee: 'This is your half-brother, Peter, Pete, Peterkin.' She puts her cheek down to the child's, as though deliberately to draw Helen's attention to the likeness between mother and son, despite her robustness and his delicacy. The child turns his face away from the newcomer, burying it into the side of his mother's neck. Then, coquettishly, he peeps round.

Toby comes into the room: 'Tea! Tea!' he all but sings, rubbing his hands together. He has changed out of his pinstripe suit into baggy flannels and hacking jacket, and there are slippers on his large feet. Then he asks: 'Where's Clare?'

Isabel's face momentarily darkens. 'Is she ever on time for a meal?' She gives Peter a little push: 'Go and tell Clare the tea is getting cold.'

'Must I?' He pouts.

'Do what Mummy tells you,' Mrs Thompson puts in, risking Isabel's frequent reprimand: 'Oh, please don't interfere! It only makes things more difficult with him.'

Peter goes, but slowly, trailing one reluctant foot after the other.

'Lazy little blighter!' his father exclaims, taking up two cucumber sandwiches and stuffing them into his mouth and then taking up a third. Isabel hands Helen a cup of tea. The cup belongs to the Crown Derby tea service, now sadly depleted, which was also an inheritance of Helen's mother, Eithne.

'Clare, I don't think you and my daughter have ever met,' Toby says. 'Helen – this is Peter's governess, Clare.'

The girls stare at each other; then shake hands with awkward formality. Helen thinks that Clare uses too much make-up, not yet realizing that the Eurasian dabs on all that rouge and powder to conceal the darkness of her complexion. Helen also thinks that she is overdressed, with that dangling amber necklace, all those bangles and rings, and those extremely high heels beneath shoes covered in an impractical, shimmering pale green silk. Clare thinks that Helen cannot have changed after her journey, so grubby does her blouse seem above her tweed skirt. She also thinks that the newcomer is plain, terribly plain.

The child pushes between them, one hand thrust out masterfully to remove Clare from his path, and approaches the tea table.

'Peter!' Clare cries out in her sing-song chichi accent. 'Manners, please! Don't push me like that!'

Peter pays no attention.

Helen stares at him as he picks up a buttered scone and, with some of the voracity of his father, bites into it.

Helen would like to be alone with Toby; but her grand-mother, her stepmother, her half-brother and the governess are constantly obtruding and obstructing presences. In any case, since Toby is a man whose greed for food and women is equalled by his greed for money and success, he is often away on business; and if he is not away, then he is in his office, the low, two-storied building at one end of the house, into which none of them must enter. He employs a babu, Mr Ram, who went to a Christian school in Lahore and then took an External Degree in Economics at London University, and a Eurasian woman, Hilda, who has sparse grey hair and bloodshot eyes magnified by thick, horn-rimmed glasses, which keep slipping down her nose.

'Everything all right?' Toby asks Helen absently, when chance brings them face to face, and she then answers: 'Oh, yes, thank you, father, fine, fine.' She sometimes wonders whether he would react at all if, instead, she replied: 'No, everything is hell.'

It was so different when he met her in Bombay. 'Darling!' he had called out and, racing across the deck to where he was standing, a white panama hat in one hand and his rubber-ferruled stick in the other, she had flung herself into his embrace. He had kissed her over and over, as though she were someone whom he had imagined that he would never see again. That night, at dinner in the Taj Mahal Hotel, he insisted: 'We must have a bottle of the Widow to celebrate.' The Widow? She did not know what he could mean. But when the turbaned waiter brought the bottle of champagne in its bucket of ice, she cried out, her cheeks flushed: 'Oh, father! Champagne! Champagne! I haven't drunk champagne for, oh, years and years.' (The last time when she had, in fact, drunk champagne had been at the wedding of her father to her stepmother, but she did not want to think of that.)

'To the happiness of my girl.' He held up his glass and slowly raised it to his lips.

'To . . . to happiness.' She blushed. She could not say 'To

our happiness,' as she had first intended to do. It sounded too proprietorial; it might imply, as many of the other diners assumed, that they were lovers.

He was wonderfully thoughtful and kind to her on the long journey, a day and then a night, in the private coach put at his disposal by a railway director for whom he had once done an unobtrusive but all-important favour. There were two narrow bedrooms and a drawing room with chairs covered in red plush, lamps of burnished brass and a highly polished, round mahogany table. There was a lavatory, a kitchen, with kerosene stoves and an ice-chest, and servants' quarters from which came a constant murmur of voices as Muhammed and the cook hired for the journey talked to each other. 'Oh, this is fun!' she cried out more than once, thinking that she wanted nothing more than to travel on like this, for immeasurable mile on mile, across plains and beneath hills and over dusky winding rivers, with this man who was both a stranger and her father.

After the train journey, they climbed into the Rolls-Royce, the two of them in the back, while the chauffeur, perpetually grinning to himself in the mirror, drove recklessly up and up the hairpin bends. The servants, with the luggage, followed in a truck. Toby put a hand over his daughter's. 'It's lovely to have you back,' he said, not for the first time. 'It's lovely to be back,' she answered, thinking that, for all her previous reluctance, she was now glad that she had come. She peered out through the window beside her at the lush slopes rising up, broad sweep on sweep, above the dusty road. 'Oh, how wonderfully everything has been arranged! How lucky I am!'

'Yes, I like to think that my little set-up works efficiently. Not many things work efficiently in this blasted country.'

Now that closeness has gone. It is as though a love affair flared up briefly between them and then burned itself out. But she still loves him. She will always love him. She knows that for sure.

Isabel is not the wicked stepmother of a fairy story but she is not a mother either. Isabel remembers that Helen must remember that once, many years ago, there was another mistress of this household, who, ailing, needed a housekeeper. Helen remembers that Isabel must remember that, when that other mistress had been dead for only five months and Toby and Isabel came to tell the eight-year-old child that now she was to get another mother, she had screamed: 'No, no! You can't! You mustn't!' and had begun, in hysterical frenzy, the tears pouring down her cheeks, to punch her father in the chest, until, grasping both her arms in his hands, he had at last managed to control her. Isabel is now always coolly polite to Helen and Helen, in turn, is now always coolly polite to Isabel. The two women are scrupulous about passing things to each other at table, at greeting each other, at each waiting for the other to enter or leave a room first. But there is a constant awkwardness between them, as between two people who have each done the other some injury which neither will now ever mention.

There are few young men in this remote hill-station sprawled around the lake who would be suitable companions for Helen. Toby says that she must wait until they have returned to the plains. Then there will be plenty of young men, dances, parties, gymkhanas, tennis tournaments, she won't have a moment to herself. On the other side of the range of hills, there is the other, bigger lake, with many more English people – half the Government of the province in retreat from the hot weather now scorching the distant plains. But it is a long and tedious journey and, though Helen at first receives many invitations, she rarely can be bothered to accept them. Clare is envious of her: 'If I were asked to that dance, I'd go like a shot.' No one asks Clare out, except that 'cousin' of hers, the soldier convalescing from malaria in the Army rest-home.

Clare and Helen have little in common. The Eurasian girl is bright but indolent, often spending her free time lying on her bed, a De Reske Minor cigarette burning itself in an ivory cigarette holder as she looks up, with a squinting gaze of her almond-shaped eyes, to watch its smoke wreathe away to extinction. When she reads, it is what Isabel contemptuously calls, even to her face, housemaid's trash. She does not ride and on the first occasion when Helen persuaded her to go for a walk with her along one of the rocky paths through the woods above the house, she appeared in a dress, hat and pair of high-heeled shoes all of an identical pale blue colour, as though for a garden party. Clare is vain about her appearance, spending many patient minutes retouching her face whenever she finds herself alone before a mirror. But sometimes she wonders what is the point of all this attention to lips, cheeks, eyes, to frock, stockings, scarf, when there is no one, except silly old Toby, to notice. Clare likes to be noticed.

Helen is slow and painstaking. She has an immensely strong inner obstinacy, of which most people are unaware. Her progress through a book is so leisurely that sometimes Toby says to her in amazement: 'You're not still reading that, are you?' The books which she reads, classics of Victorian fiction, belonged to her mother. The damp has foxed the pages and silverfish have fretted them. No one has opened any of them since her mother died. She hates idleness and so she secretly exasperates Isabel by insisting on taking over a number of household duties from her. She also becomes a leader of the local Brownie troop; but in India, for obvious reasons, they are called not Brownies but Bluebells. In her uniform of sepia-coloured twill ('You'd have thought they could have come up with something a little less unchic,' is Clare's disparaging comment), fastened at the waist with a leather belt, her brown cotton stockings, her brogues with their flapping tongues and the jaunty hat under which she tucks away her hair, she has the awkward wiriness of an adolescent boy. The troop, some thirty in all, under the winsome, scatty leadership of the drunken Scottish doctor's wife, is composed both of white girls of any class and of Indian girls from what the Scotswoman calls 'the better type of family'.

One weekend they travel higher up into the Himalayas, the two adults on horses and the excited children in dandies or on ponies, to a small lake, embedded like a dark blue glittering bead in a setting of snow-capped mountains. The air is clean and sharp and except for a few scattered farms, owned by English people, a few low-roofed dwellings, owned by Indians, and, high up on the first slopes of a mountain, partly cantilevered over a steep face of rock, a long, low white building, with wooden huts untidily grouped around it, there is no sign of the domestication of a once-wild terrain as in the hill-station from which they have journeyed for all but a day. In a field belonging to one of the farms, the servants – it would be inconceivable to travel without them – set up the tents. They are expert at it, from years of accompanying their masters on tour or *shikari*. There are even folding tables, chairs and beds, enamel washbasins on folding stands, and three thunder-boxes, each in a tent of its own, which a local sweeper had been engaged to empty, since the servants are all of a caste too superior to do so.

As they pass through a narrow defile, first ascending a rocky road, with the children in the dandies delightedly shrieking and clutching at the sides with every roll and bump, and then descending towards a golden haze, the afternoon sun a misty bubble low in the west before them, Helen suffers that bewildering, disconcerting sense 'I have been here before.' Before they emerge into the valley, she already knows how it will look; and when, craning her neck, she sees that long, low white building, with its many balconies cantilevered over the rock face, a shiver runs through her even though, here in the shelter of the surrounding mountains, out of the wind, it has become suddenly warm. Yes, everything is mysteriously familiar and blotted with a sombre aura of dread, even though the sun is glittering on the lake and on the high mountain-tops and even though the girls, under the leadership of the Scotswoman, have begun to sing 'This old man, he played one . . .' The girls squawk like a flock of starlings at approach of evening; but the adult contralto beneath them is strong and true. Helen tries to join in the singing; but her mouth is parched, the sounds refuse to come.

Later, when the girls have been refreshed with a tea of doughnuts and thick, mahogany-coloured tea in which the condensed milk, poured from the tin, swirls in yellow eddies, the Scotswoman, Mrs McGregor, asks if Helen would be an angel and go to the farm over there – she points – to arrange for some milk to be sent for breakfast. 'This condensed milk is so sticky and sweet, though the kids love it.' The farm which has lent them the field does not have cows; the other does. Helen sets off with one of the Indian girls, the daughter of a Christian civil servant, who insists on clutching her hand tightly in hers, as though, so far from her home and her numerous siblings, she feels somehow endangered. Helen is still overcome by the strangeness of the familiarity of this remote place in which she now finds herself. It is as though she were living a dream and were not sure if that dream were a nightmare or not. She puts out the hand which the child is not clutching, snatches at an overhanging branch and snaps it off. The smell, as she crushes some of its leaves in her palm – mint, eucalyptus, rosemary, it is all of these things and none of them – insists: 'Yes, yes, you have experienced all this before.'

Helen's face is drawn and wan when at last, having passed through a field of grazing cows (the child, terrified now, grips her hand with an extraordinary ferocity), climbed a stile and made their way through the straggling, overgrown rose-bushes of what looks like an English cottage garden, they approach an old woman, in a faded pinafore and bedroom slippers, who is rocking herself, eyes closed, on the porch, a black-and-white mongrel with a long, sweeping tail out-stretched beside her. The dog looks up with a beseeching look in his rheumy eyes and then sidles towards them on his stomach as though to placate them before, suddenly raising himself on all four legs, he instead decides to start a low, insistent growl. The Indian child squeals and runs behind Helen, clutching her about the waist. The old woman opens her eyes with no alarm or surprise; and it is then that it all becomes clear to Helen.

The old woman had a kindly, simple face, with heavy lines

45

from the sides of her nose to her mouth and pale blue eyes, as washed out as her pale blue pinafore. On the sagging dewlap of her throat there is an angry purple stain, an ineradicable birthmark. Strange. Helen remembers that birthmark better than the lake or the surrounding mountains or the long, low white building cantilevered out over a void. When she lived in this farmhouse, a frightened and bewildered child, with her father and the woman who was soon to become her step-mother, occupying the whole of the upper floor, while the old woman, her husband and a brood of children and grand-children somehow squeezed themselves into the lower floor, a ramshackle caravan, two tents and what looked like a cowshed, that birthmark always made her shudder, so that she could hardly bear it when the old woman, then not so old, would put her face down to hers to ask: 'Now, what would my little angel like? Scrambled egg or fried egg?'

They were staying down here in the farmhouse in the valley because they could not stay up there, with Mother, in the sanatorium, and there were no hotels. Toby would go to the sanatorium each day, the path so steep that, a large hand to each plump thigh, he would seem to lift now one leg and now the other, at each step he took.

'Do let me come too!' Helen, only seven, would plead.

'No, sweetie. You stay down here with Isabel. She'll take you for a walk round the lake.' Or she'll play Bézique with you. Or she'll give you an arithmetic lesson. Or she'll help you with your sewing.

He would limp back from the sanatorium strangely grey and remote, as though he had made an arduous journey from some foreign country far, far away. It was only after he had devoured the food piled before him (chunks of stringy beef, glutinous dumplings, boiled carrots, turnips and potatoes, a gravy thick with cornflour) that the colour would return to his cheeks and the joviality to his manner.

'How is she?' Isabel, fiddling with the stopper of the vinegar bottle on the silver cruet stand, would lean forward to whisper. Helen, seated opposite, could hear the whisper; so why not speak in an ordinary tone of voice?

'Making progress, making progess.'

Helen knew that her mother was ill; but she did not know that she had had yet another recurrence of pulmonary tuberculosis. For that reason she could not understand why, when her father trudged up that stony path, with the huge, grey-green ferns, as stiff as cardboard cutouts, on either side of it, she could not accompany him. 'I don't see why I'm not allowed to visit her too. I don't see it!'

'Germs. This thing of hers is infectious. We don't want you to pick it up.'

'But what about you? You go to see her. Every day.'

'At a certain age one acquires a certain immunity,' he drawled, as he scraped the sides of the hive-shaped honeypot and then put the spoon in his mouth.

Isabel laughed delightedly: 'You look like a child doing that. Exactly like a child.'

He smiled across at her with a flash of complicity like the lightning which, in this remote valley among the mountains, would suddenly leap from one peak to another or snake across the lake. Helen was excluded; she might not have been there.

That same morning, after Toby had started to limp doggedly up the narrow, steep path to the sanatorium – there was also a drive but that swerved back and forth in enormous loops – Helen told Isabel that she was going out to play with the other children. The other children meant the grand-children, raw-boned and freckled, with thick, matted blond hair, of the woman with the birthmark. Helen, in fact, seldom played with them, since she was afraid of their good-humoured teasing and even more afraid of their rough, dangerous exploits – climbing trees or rowing out into the centre of the lake in a boat far too small to contain them all with safety, or savagely wrestling, even girls with boys. Isabel did not really care what Helen did provided she did not do anything dangerous or amiss for which she, Isabel, might later be held responsible and so she looked up from her embroidery and nodded: 'All right. But see you don't get dirty. And don't tear that new frock.'

Helen made furtively for the gate at the corner of a field in which some goats were tethered. She was made to drink goat's milk, instead of cow's milk, while staying on the farm; and each time the thick, strong-tasting warm liquid, produced from an earthen crock, would make her gorge rise. No one told her that goat's milk was healthier than cow's milk, since it was free of the dreaded tubercle, and in consequence she regarded it as a peculiarly cruel caprice of her father and Isabel not to allow her the cow's milk which everyone else drank and which she so much preferred. She began to walk pensively up the hill, careful to remain so far behind her father that, if he should happen to glance round, he would not see her.

It was a sultry day, with an overcast sky and mist, metallic in its leaden sheen, sealing over the centre of the lake. Huge flies settled on her lips, her nostrils and the corners of her eyes, so that she was obliged repeatedly to brush at them. An Indian woman in a white sari approached, a load of wood on her head, but they did not look at each other. Perhaps the woman had been stealing the wood, since she at once quickened her pace as soon as she had passed. From somewhere, presumably a clearing, Helen heard distant voices, a man and a woman talking in English. But, no, it was not her father and mother.

Eventually, the path joined the drive and she was treading on gravel instead of on rough stones and slabs of rock. Brilliant rhododendrons arched high on either side and beyond them, glimpsed through gaps, were wide lawns and rosebeds, with white-painted garden furniture set out here and there. The whole place seemed to be deserted, until suddenly, glancing up to the building, she saw, to her amazement, that on each of the balconies, both those facing the gardens and those cantilevered over the abyss, there were people lying out on day-beds or seated, wrapped in scarves and blankets, on chairs. They were all staring at her, she was sure of that; and the conviction that they were doing so all but paralysed her legs.

Carefully, she walked around the building, passing an open window from which came other voices, this time in Hindustani, and a sweet-sour stench, as of something rotting. There was a mound of garbage, buzzing with flies, in a clearing under some straggly trees, and behind it a rusty metal wheelbarrow, lying on its side. A diminutive male Indian was pinning dishcloths to a clothesline, standing on tiptoe and reaching up, the pegs between his teeth. She sank into despair. Everything here was so vast and so complex, lawn beyond lawn, room beyond room, balcony beyond balcony. What chance did she have of ever finding her mother? She moved on. A white man in a grubby white coat passed her at one moment, making her draw back into the shelter of a doorway; but he seemed totally unconcerned about her presence as, with lowered head, pursed lips and a deep frown, he marched on.

Then all at once, miraculously, she heard her mother's voice. 'Oh, but I get so tired of being here! I'm all right now, as right as I'll ever be.'

'They say you need at least another –'

'They say! Of course they say! Think of all the money they're making. It was the same in Davos. Don't you remember? If they'd had their way, I'd be there still.'

Then, there before her, was her father pushing a wheelchair in which her mother, in wide-brimmed felt hat, tweed overcoat and scarf, was sitting with a plaid rug tucked so tightly over her lap that it seemed intended to imprison her.

Helen raced forward, both arms outstretched. She tripped, all but fell, recovered. She threw herself on her mother: 'Mummy! Mummy!'

'Helen!' That was her mother, delighted and amazed.

'What the hell are you doing here?' That was her father, angry.

But strangely, disconcertingly, even as Helen pressed herself against her mother, she became conscious that, instead of holding her, her mother was pushing her away from her. 'Helen. Helen! No! No, darling!'

'But why can't I –'

'I've told you. We have to be careful. Of germs.' Toby had taken her hand in his. His pale green eyes had in them an expression of humiliated sadness. 'You shouldn't have come up here. This isn't a place for you.'

'It's only a hospital. I've visited hospitals. Aunt Sophie worked in a hospital once. Didn't she?'

'It's different for grown-ups. They don't – catch things so easily.'

'I had to see Mummy. Had to, had to!' She was on the verge of tears.

'Of course, darling.' Her mother put out a hand, then quickly withdrew it. 'Of course. And I often feel, marooned on my own up here, that I have to see you. But it'll only be a short time now. A week or two. All this mountain air and cosseting and feeding-up have done wonders for me. I'm a totally new person.'

Helen gazed at her mother and, yes, her eyes looked unusually bright and her cheeks unusually red.

'I've missed you.'

'Darling! And I've missed you too. But you mustn't come here again. Ever. Promise?'

Helen hung her head.

'Promise?'

Helen nodded. Her lower lip trembled, she felt an unshed burden of tears beneath her eyes.

Suddenly, as though dead leaves were being trampled underfoot, there came the dry, friable sound of her mother coughing, with a terrible, long-drawn-out insistence and patience, on and on, while Toby asked: 'Are you all right?' and all Eithne could do was to nod her head as yet another paroxysm shook her. Involuntarily, Helen put her hands to her ears. She did not know how she knew, but she knew that she was listening to the sounds of death.

At last the coughing ceased. Her mother withdrew her crocodile leather handbag from underneath the rug, in hands from which, Helen now noticed, the rings were hanging loosely, clicked it open, and took out a small bottle of a wonderful shade of blue. Helen thought, as her mother carefully unscrewed the top, that she was about to drink some medicine; but instead, lowering her head and turning away, she spat into it. Then she screwed the top back on again and replaced the bottle in her bag.

'You see, Helen? Excitement is bad for your mother.' The quiet accusation bewildered and affronted her.

'Oh, it's nothing to do with her, poor little mite. From time to time I still get these attacks – wherever I am, whatever I'm doing. But they come less and less often now.' She smiled at Helen. 'And how are *you*, darling?'

'Oh, fine, fine.'

'You get my letters?'

'Yes, Mummy, of course. Daddy's a wonderful postman. It's just that – oh, I miss you so much and I so much wanted to *see* you.'

Again her mother put out her hand impulsively and then at once withdrew it. 'And I've missed you so much and I so much wanted to see *you*. But . . .' She shrugged and gave a little shiver.

'You're getting cold.' Far off, thunder growled. 'And it sounds as if a storm's on the way. I'd better wheel you into the conservatory or at least to the verandah . . . Helen, be a good girl, go home now the way you came.'

'Oh, can't I stay with Mummy a little longer – with both of you? Can't I? Please!'

'Helen!' It was like a slap on the cheek, imposing a reluctant discipline.

'Go, darling!' Eithne's voice was tremulous.

'Did you tell Isabel that you were coming up here? Did you?' Helen hung her head. 'Well, that's another reason for going back at once. She'll be frantic with worry when she finds you've disappeared.'

'Dear Isabel. Yes, go back for her sake too. We're so lucky to have her. Helen, sweetie . . . please. Do what we ask you. Really, truly, it's for your own good . . .'

51

Her mother blew her a kiss and she blew one back, her eyes filling with tears as she did so. Then she turned reluctantly and, with quickening steps, went back past the clothesline, the rubbish tip and the open kitchen window and down the drive with the garish rhododendrons towering on either side. She put a finger to her damp cheek and then placed the finger between her lips, tasting her tears. Somehow their salt appeased her.

. . . Now, as the Indian girl stoops and nervously pats the dog, Helen reminds the old woman with the birthmark how, ten, eleven years before, she, her father and the woman who was then looking after her and is now her father's second wife occupied the top floor of the farmhouse.

'Did you, dear?' the old woman says vaguely, in the north-country accent which she has never lost, despite her sixty and more years in this alien country. 'We get many of the sanatorium people here. Convalescents, relatives. It's a miracle, I always say, that none of my lot has ever caught TB. One of the doctors up there, an Indian chap, told me once that they must have developed an immunity. Well, thank God for that!'

'I used to play with your grandchildren,' Helen says.

'Did you now?' The old woman sighs. 'Well, some are still about the place and some have married and moved on. And one of the boys is in an office in England,' she adds proudly. 'An accountant. Jim. He was always the bright one.' She shows no inclination to summon those still about the place; and Helen's memories of them are now so faint that she cannot even recall who Jim might have been.

'You used to give us honey from your bees for breakfast. My father always made a pig of himself over it.'

'Yes, we still have our bees.' The old woman, though friendly, is again not really interested.

Eventually, having given the order for the milk, Helen and the Indian child make their way back home the way they came. The dog patters along behind them until, in a surprisingly strong, harsh voice, the old woman calls him back.

'May we come and see the dog again?' the child asks Helen.
'Oh, I don't think so. I don't think we'll come again.'

Later that evening, as the sun suddenly dips behind the
mountain to the west and her skin contracts at the chill of its
abrupt departure, Helen leaves the party and makes her way
up the path to the sanatorium. As when she first returned to
the house on the hill above the lake, she is amazed by how
small and constricted everything seems now when measured
against her recollections. Can this sparse wood really be that
forest? Can this gentle incline really be that steep path? Can
that building above, with its dozen or so balconies, really be
that huge edifice from which innumerable eyes seemed to
glitter down at the apparition of a slender little girl in a new
cotton frock, cardigan and sandals? She takes a few more
strides; then, on an impulse, decides to give up.

Hurrying back down the path, the jagged stones from time
to time biting into her shoes, she thinks, momentarily, that
she hears a sound, as of dead leaves being trodden under foot,
of an insistent, patient coughing. But of course, she tells
herself, that is only an illusion.

Helen and Mrs McGregor share a tent, with camp beds side
by side, kerosene lamps by which they undress, and a tin
chamber-pot discreetly placed behind the larger of the two
folding chairs. 'This is rather fun,' Mrs McGregor says,
meaning it. Helen is not sure. Later, when the lamp has been
put out, Mrs McGregor says: 'You probably won't remember, but your mother was one of my dearest friends. I loved
her, really loved her. She was, oh, such fun and so kind and so
generous.

Helen can say nothing.'

'That strange sister of hers,' Mrs McGregor murmurs and,
soon after that, she falls asleep.

Helen lies awake, a yellow bar of moonlight falling through
the tent-flap on to the right side of her upturned face.

Her mother came down from the sanatorium and they all

53

returned home. Helen went riding with her and they played a kind of tennis together, taking it in turns to hit the ball against the wall which shored up the hill above the tennis court. Her mother taught her English and French, while Isabel continued to teach her all other subjects. Her mother often rested and, when she was not doing so, Toby was always reminding her of the need to take things easily. Toby did not like the rides, however gentle, or the tennis, however desultory. 'You must remember you're still a sick woman,' he would tell Eithne. Isabel was more silent and more still than when her mistress had been in the sanatorium.

A few months later, Toby had to go to Simla to see what was happening in one of his hotels and, though he protested, Eithne decided to accompany him. 'I need *un petit changement de décor*, I need some excitement.' Toby still protested but could not move her – what harm could a journey so short and easy do?

Eithne never came back. In later years, Helen pieced together the story of what happened. On the train she ate something which upset her; and the strain of vomiting brought on a heart attack. In some dusty little town, they carried her from the train to the consulting room of a flustered Indian doctor. He had injected her with what he said was camphor; but soon after the injection, with a little moan and a sigh, she died. Toby often wondered if the doctor had not made some mistake – he had become abject with terror when his patient had not responded. But seeing that he was a humble Indian and Toby an important Englishman, that terror was natural enough.

. . . Mrs McGregor is snoring, her mouth wide open. Her false teeth, which she has unashamedly placed in a container on the floor beside her, gleam in the moonlight. On the chair which she has decided is hers, her stays and brassière are spread out like items of armour. Helen gazes at her, then she looks away. Somewhere, some of the girls are whispering and giggling. But Helen cannot be bothered to get up and tell them to be quiet.

It is odd, she thinks now, that it took her so long to remember when she had been in this place before. After all, she was a child of eight when her mother died and memories of that time should be easily recoverable. She has never forgotten the sound of her mother coughing and she has never forgotten that blue bottle, such a beautiful colour, into which her mother spat. But the calm of the lake and mountains, the apprehension of that climb up the path through the wood, the shock of her mother inexorably pushing her away from her: how strange that all those things should have become as faint in her memory as in a photograph so inadequately fixed that its faces are now blank and its background a blur.

CLARE

Clare leans across the balustrade of the verandah, cigarette holder between fingers, and stares morosely down over the dark green of the deodars, the yellow-green of the already withering lilacs and the yellow of the grass, waist-high in the *cud*, to the lake far below. She shudders in her pink shantung frock, with its inset, at the neck, of some Chinese embroidery bought from the same pedlar from whom Isabel bought her wrap – how 'unsuitably' the poor girl dresses is a constant comment at the bridge table – but, consumed by the restlessness which nowadays so often afflicts her like some unappeasable hunger, she has no desire to go into the drawing room where Isabel and Toby face each other, each with a copy, weeks old, of *The Times*, and Helen, Peter and dreary old Mrs Thompson are playing pelmanism. She herself cannot be bothered with the news and her mind is too easily apt to wander off for her to be successful at a card game which Peter almost always wins.

She wishes that the calm lake were a mighty river, like the river by her home, sweeping on, brown, broad and muscular, through half a continent. She would like that river to carry her, as it carries its ships, logs, sewage, dead animals and even dead humans, out from this constricted hollow among the hills into the plains and perhaps even to the sea. She yearns for the sense of distance to be restored to her. At evening, from the outskirts of the city in which she was born and brought up, she could see, on one side, the plains stretching away

56

illimitably to the desert and the desert then stretching away illimitably to a far, pearly haze, and, on the other side, the whole vast, complex structure of houses, roads and parks laid out before her, each roof, spire, dome, terrace, tree so distinct that it seemed only necessary to put out a hand to touch it. She dreams of sailing out on that river, as her great-grandfather, the pilot who came from a famine-stricken Ireland to live with an Indian woman, would sail out on it, and then of embarking on one of those liners which she has never seen except in pictures and voyaging on and on over seas now rough and now calm until she reaches – well, Australia, New Zealand, America. She does not dream of reaching England, since she guesses that there too the people will comment on the darkness of her fingernails, the thickness and blackness of her hair and that accent which, more than anything else, betrays her. She fancies Australia most of all.

Yet again she wonders why she ever took on this job. Madness. Oh, yes, she is paid well; and there is nothing on which to spend her wages except on the clothes which she orders from the *durzi*, so that she can both save for herself and send money home to help to pay for the youngest of her brothers to go to a good boarding school and so – who knows? his teachers are optimistic – to win a scholarship to some college or university in England. But she regrets now that she gave up her job at the reception desk of the hotel owned by Toby, even if the peremptory commands, the irrational complaints and above all the condescending pleasantries of the customers had long since become all but unbearable to her. 'May I have my bill, please?' 'Yes, sir, of course, sir, one moment, sir.' 'There seems to be something wrong here. Why does this hotel always manage to get something wrong? Every time I stay here, every bleeding time.' Or else: 'The last time I was here, some old dragon gave me my bill. Not nearly as attractive as you are. A welcome change.' Or else: 'How much longer do I have to stand about here, waiting? Isn't there any service in this place? I want my bill – *now*, pronto, double-quick!'

On the jolting tram, which none of the hotel customers would ever have dreamed of taking – the apocryphal story is that the trams were all bought second-hand from Bournemouth, after a switch there to trolley-buses – she would make her way home as the fag end of the once-scorching day smouldered away to a grey, powdery ash. Then, with so many alien identities crowding in on her, she felt her own identity first dissipate and then coalesce into the indifferent mass. Where was she? Who was she? What had happened to her? As she stepped off the tram, often having to push her way through the people clinging to its outside like so many bluebottles clustered thick on a hunk of putrefying meat, she had a habit of touching her clothes, hat, hair, lips, even lobes of the ears, with those long, prehensile fingers, their nails red-laquered ('I don't think the customers really like painted nails,' the dragon remarked more than once), as though to reassure herself that, yes, she was all of a piece, she did really exist, a nineteen-year-old, attractive, convent-educated Eurasian girl.

Her home is a red-brick villa, with a steep gable, a tufty front lawn and a crazy-paving path which leads up from a gate which, for months, has been hanging askew on a single rusty hinge, to a front door with a gnome knocker on its chipped red paint. If one of her innumerable relatives is visiting, there is a camp bed, sometimes folded but usually open, at the far end of the hall. If the camp bed is open, then it is usually unmade, with clothes flung across it and over the chair beside it. The family lives in a comfortable, crowded squalor of meals eaten anywhere and at any time, often separately; of clothes, money and intimate secrets shared; of dogs, cats and a mynah bird enjoying all the privileges of their owners.

Clare hates that life, because she hates mess. Everything she has ever known has always been a mess, such a bloody mess. Her genes, part Irish and part Indian, are a mess, and the family home is a mess, and the family itself is a mess. Her mother and father are not legally married because somewhere, she does not even know where, her mother still has an English sergeant husband. It would not be impossible to find him and arrange a divorce, if indeed he is still alive – the War Office could surely tell her his whereabouts or his fate; but Clare's mother, like all the rest of the family, does not want to emerge from the mess, she takes no action despite Clare's urgings. Clare's father has made a mess of one business after another – his grocery store failed when an Indian opened one, much cheaper and more efficient, next door to it, he was cheated over his dry-cleaning business, the equipment all in need of replacement or repair, no one bought the Japanese kitchen gadgets for which, briefly, he became exclusive agent – and so he now sells tickets for the railway on which one of his five sons is a guard, one a fireman and one an engine-driver. 'We're really a railway family,' he boasts, 'always have been.' It is all part of the mess that that boast is not even true.

In the whole house, only Clare's room – now full of the mess of two visiting cousins – was ever clean and tidy. She would frequently scrub the woodwork, sweep the floor or shake the bedclothes out of the window with a violent malevolence, as though she were ordering each of them in turn 'Be clean, damn you, be clean!' She would never trust a plate taken down from the crowded kitchen dresser or off the no less crowded kitchen table but would always rinse and dry it before allowing her mother to put food on it for her. 'Not so much, not so much!' she would then cry out, her appetite as dainty as her clothes.

Bored, she would sometimes fling aside one of the women's magazines (*Home Chat, Britannia and Eve, The Lady*) or one of the romantic novels (Ethel M. Dell, Ruby M. Ayres, Countess Barcynska) which she would read for hours on end not in the communal living room but upstairs on her own bed, and would agree, with morose reluctance, to accompany her brothers to one of the railway socials. Though far too attractive to be a wallflower, she would place herself on one of the straight-backed chairs ranged round the dance floor, among a number of plain, lumpish girls, each achingly, humiliatingly longing, unlike her, to be asked to dance. Many men, friends or colleagues of her brothers, would come up and make a formal bow to her and then either she would wordlessly first shake her head and then turn it away or else she would rise with a little sigh of resignation, smoothing down her frock and raising hands to pat her hair, before condescending to let a partner take her. In fact, she loved to dance and danced well, spending many hours practising alone to her wind-up gramophone with a chart open on her bed; but she hated proximity to these awkward, often sweaty youths, their fingernails engrained, for all their scrubbing, with engine-oil and their hair stuck down, in stiff, lifeless prongs, by the glue-like Anzora hair cream which they lavished on it. Sometimes one would press indecently close to her, a mouth to her ear, as he muttered some inanity. (Terrific . . . You're terrific . . . Do you know, I could fall for you? . . . A corker . . .) She thought of Fred and Ginger, he romantically dapper in tails and top-hat, she romantically elegant in lace, flounces and furs. Somehow, somewhere, she would find that world. She would leave all this mess of frothy beer, stewed tea, thick sandwiches and garish cakes set out on trestle tables, of wild, good-natured horseplay and clumsy sexuality.

Toby came on one of his visits to his hotel and the manager, Signor Volpi, an Italian with wary, care-worn eyes and an inability to smile, accompanied him as he wandered round the crowded kitchens or into empty bedrooms. 'Everything all right?' Toby would say to this or that member of the staff and never wait for the routine 'Yes, thank you, sir.' It was usually Isabel's task to examine such things as the state of the linen, the curtains, the carpets and the furniture but, now that she was pregnant, she had decided, in view of her many miscarriages, not to accompany her husband. Toby was relieved.

Toby always came last to the accounts department of the hotel, housed in a room so dark – there was only a single, high barred window, looking out on a well – that, in order to see to work, it was necessary to keep the lights on all the day. 'Do you need that light at this hour?' Toby would ask, always eager for some economy, however small; and the Italian manager would then go 'Tsk, tsk!' in reproof to the staff and walk over and turn it off. But as soon as Toby had left, someone would turn it on again.

'Everything all right?' Toby asked Clare; and though that morning everything had been far from all right – the dragon had dumped on her desk the bills normally the responsibility of a girl who had only to have one of her periods to go off sick at once – Clare nodded and replied, 'Yes, thank you, sir.'

'You're new, aren't you?' Toby asked, never having seen her before.

'I've been here three months, sir.'

'Well, new to me. Do you like the job?'

'Oh, yes, sir.' She might have added: It's better than idling around at home. At least, there's no mess here.

'Good.'

She had already noticed the glistening of Toby's stiff collar, the perfect knot of his tie, the carefulness with which the half-moons of his fingernails had been pushed back and the pink gloss to which the nails themselves were burnished, the crispness of his thinning, reddish hair and the clear skin beneath it, the neatness of his moustache in a face obviously shaved that morning (her father and her brothers often deferred shaving until their return from work), the gleam of his brogues, the gleam of his teeth. He smelled of a perfume which later, creeping into his bathroom in the house on the hill above the lake, she learned to be Caron Pour Un Homme.

Toby kept returning to the sombre room behind the reception desk on what, it soon became apparent to her, were the flimsiest of pretexts. On the first occasion, remembering that 'Do you need that light at this hour?' she had jumped up from her seat before her abacus as she saw him approaching, and had hurriedly switched it off. But to her surprise, he himself, having peered around him through the gloom, turned it on again.

'I wanted to have another glance at that new specimen bill for business conferences, Miss er – er – ' Surprisingly, the manager was not with him. He gave her a smile from under the reddish, severely clipped moustache. 'I never remember names. I've forgotten yours already.' In fact, no one had ever told it to him.

'O'Connor,' she said.

'Miss O'Connor.'

She brought out the specimen bill from a drawer in her desk – Toby, restlessly acquisitive, was always changing the methods of accounting at his companies – and was about to hand it to him when he leaned over her desk. She could feel his breath on the back of her neck, she could smell that acrid perfume. The dragon paused for a moment in her typing, looked over her glasses, touched the jaunty chiffon bow at her neck and then resumed. It was none of her business, she always told herself; but after each such incident involving the boss and one of the girls, she would later talk in the staff rest room or dining room.

'I think it'll work rather well. Don't you, Miss – er, O'Connor?'

'Oh, yes, sir. Very well.'

He straightened. 'Yes, I'm really rather pleased with that.' He smiled down at her and then sauntered out. The dragon began to whistle as she typed:

> She wore a little jacket of blue
> She wore a little jacket of blue
> And all the sailors knew . . .

Those days one heard the tune everywhere, as much at a *thé dansant* in the Manhattan Room of the hotel as at an evening social at the Railway Institute.

Toby came back again and yet again, sometimes with the Italian manager, who would give Clare a sardonic, appraising look when he thought that Toby would not intercept it, and sometimes, as on that first occasion, alone. Clare noticed that each day he wore not merely a different, clean shirt but also a different suit and a different pair of shoes. She was always aware of such things.

One evening, as she was waiting for her tram, the still, humid air soft and cool on the skin of her bare arms, forehead and the back of her neck, and the cracked pavement hard and hot beneath her low-heeled, calf-skin shoes, she was conscious of a large car – Bentley, Rolls, Daimler? unlike her brothers, she knew nothing of makes – drawing up beside her, to the astonishment of all the people apathetically waiting with her for their buses. A door opened.

'Let me take you wherever you wish to go, Miss O'Connor.' It was Toby, his head tilted to one side as he smiled up at her from the driver's seat.

She hesitated.

'Please!'

Slowly she approached the car and then eased herself into the seat beside him. He leant across her and pulled the door shut.

She had no idea where she wished to go; she certainly did not wish to go to her home with him, since she would then feel obliged, out of politeness, to ask him in and he would see all that mess.

'Well, I wanted to do some shopping before going home. Victoria Place.' As soon as she had spoken, she wondered if he knew that she was lying. If she had been going to Victoria Place, she would have been waiting at the bus stop on the other side of the road.

'Victoria Place it is.'

She stared ahead of her, saying nothing. She had travelled from time to time in ramshackle taxis, their leather seats cracked and spewing horsehair and their side-screens yellowed and flapping noisily; but she had never been in a limousine such as this.

'It's hotting up,' he said. 'Next week or the week after we'll make for the hills.'

'Oh, really?'

People like her family did not go to the hills. At night, they lay sleepless and naked, the fans above them churning the sluggish air. During the day, their clothes became saturated, their hair limp, their faces glistening.

'One day I want to put air-conditioning into the hotel. I have it in my office. The latest thing. But it costs so bloody much – to instal, to maintain. The Americans insist on it. Which is why, in the hot weather, they prefer the Royal to us.'

He slowed as he threaded his way, through dense, erratic pedestrians, into Victoria Place. 'Where exactly?' he asked.

She saw the haberdashery at which she sometimes shopped. 'Over there. Jones's.'

'My wife buys her gloves there.'

'I have to buy some gloves.' It was true. When the summer came, she always wore white cotton gloves out of doors and sometimes even in the office.

'Right.' He parked the car, got out of it and held open the door for her with a mock bow. 'There you are, my lady.'

'Thank you so much.' She smiled at him; then, not sure if this was the right thing to do, she held out her hand. 'Thank you,' she repeated.

'Oh, I'll come in with you. Somehow I've got to get through the next hour before meeting some friends at the club.'

She was disconcerted and became even more so when he began to take part in the selection of the gloves. 'No, not those. No. They look cheap. Flimsy.'

'But I want cheap gloves. I can't afford others.'

'And those look cheap too. Yes.' He examined them. 'Yes, I thought so. Made in Japan. Now these – these are perfect.'

'But they must cost a fortune.'

'Nottingham lace,' the Indian assistant told them.

'Would that be your size? Try it on. Go on, try it on.' He dangled the glove before her, between forefinger and middle-finger.

She eased it on to a slightly trembling hand. He peered down. 'Perfect. Have those.'

'But how much are they? I must know what they cost.'

'Why? Why must you know?' He turned to the assistant.

64

'Memsahib will take those.' He drew a crocodile-skin wallet out of the inner pocket of his grey pinstripe suit and went over to where a large woman, a vermilion caste-mark in the centre of her forehead, sat slumped despondently before a cash-register. He began to pay.

'Oh but . . . please . . .' Clare was partly appalled and partly delighted. When he continued to put down one crisp note after another, paying no attention to her, she touched his sleeve: 'Please! Please, Mr Thompson! You mustn't! It isn't right!'

Still he paid no attention.

She felt, as they left the shop, that some secret bargain had been struck; but the nature of that bargain remained worryingly obscure to her.

No less irresistible in his quiet insistence, Toby took her to the races, where she lost some of his money, to the cinema, where they sat in armchair-like seats in a private box at the rear, to a dance at the Royal, not at his own hotel, and to innumerable meals in restaurants, during which she picked daintily at a single course and he stuffed himself until the sweat poured down his face and, dripping off it, made his stiff collar limp. He did not offer to take her to the club and she would not allow him to take her to her home.

'What's going on?' her amiable, lazy mother eventually asked, not in disapproval. 'Got a boyfriend?'

Clare shook her head, carefully dipping the brush into the bottle of red nail varnish before her and then beginning to apply it with meditative strokes.

'Then?'

'Then nothing.'

Her mother was satisfied. She had seen the gloves in their pale blue tissue paper in a box inscribed 'Jones's' in elaborate copperplate. She had also seen a string of cultured pearls, a pair of sheer silk stockings, and a rolled-gold Waterman fountain-pen. Sooner or later the girl would tell her. 'Well, provided you're happy.'

But Clare did not know if she were happy or not. She liked the huge, silent car, like a luxurious sofa on wheels, the crisp, white napkins in restaurants, those armchair-like seats in boxes at the backs of cinemas, the hushed, expensive shops and their obsequious assistants. But she did not like the hands, large, square and with reddish hair on them, which seemed forever to be touching her, on the shoulder, at the back of the neck, on the cheek, even on the knee. Once, when they were saying goodbye, Toby even leant forward and sideways in the seat beside her in the car and attempted to place his mouth against hers; but she quickly turned her head aside, so that his lips merely brushed a cheek.

'Oh, you are a tease!'

'I don't really . . . don't really like that kind of thing.'

'What kind of thing?'

She did not answer; but what she meant was mess – the mess of entangled bodies and entangled lives, of conspiracies and secrets, of possible pregnancies, diseases, scandals. She wanted her existence to be as clean and crisp as his collars and handkerchiefs.

At dinner in a restaurant the following night – it was the first time she had ever eaten smoked salmon and she hated it – he told her that, on the morrow, he would be returning to the other, even bigger city in which he had his home and that a week after that he would be taking his family up into the hills. The news genuinely saddened her. She bit her lower lip, stared down at the pink, nauseatingly salt slivers of fish before her, and thought, with surprise, that she might be going to cry.

'You're sorry I'm going?' His voice was joyful; he could see that she was sorry.

Head still lowered, she nodded.

He put a hand across the table to cover the one which was restlessly fingering a knife. 'Clare, you could come to the hills too.'

She looked up now, startled.

'Our little boy's nurse is about to leave. She's fallen ill. Nanny Rose. She nursed my daughter too. A stroke. He's old

66

enough and bright enough to need a governess now – not a
nurse. You told me you'd passed matric. That the nuns
thought you'd have been able to get into teaching-training
college if the money had been forthcoming.'

'A governess . . .' She said the word in a tone of such numb
stupefaction that it moved him more than anything he had
ever heard her say before.

'Why not? Far better than your work in the hotel. You'll
have much more free time. Time to read, time to study, time'
– he grinned at her – 'to improve yourself in every way.'

'And you really think I could do it?'

'A boy of barely five? Why not?' Again he grinned. 'Simple
– no problem. Oh, Clare, it's a terrific idea!'

'Well . . .'

. . . Clare bites on the cigarette holder and then draws
smoke deep into her lungs. She exhales it with a cough. She is
not used to this damp and cold, it'll be the death of her. No
wonder that TB finished off that first wife of Toby's. She
would rather be sweltering in the plains, even though each
letter from her mother – she is the only one of the family who
can be bothered to write, the brother to whom she sends the
money never does so – tells her how much they all envy her,
up there in the hills.

An Indian woman strides confidently, bare feet wide apart
as they go slap-slap-slap, along the steep path which zigzags
down the *cud*. There is a bundle of what looks like washing on
her head – perhaps she is the *dhobi*'s wife and joins him in his
constant petty pilfering of the clothes sent to him? So noiseless
is everything at this hour that Clare can hear two brass
bangles on the woman's wrist tinkling against each other.
Momentarily she wonders about the woman's life – where is
she going? What is she thinking? Is she happy? – as she often
finds herself wondering momentarily about the lives of others.
But an innate lethargy makes her flag; the effort to reach out
and encompass something so alien is too much.

In a similar manner, when she was playing catch with Peter
this afternoon and the ball, misdirected by him, soared over

the verandah and bounced down the *cud*, she at first genuinely wished to retrieve it. 'I can see it!' Peter cried, as the two of them leaned over the railing. He pointed excitedly: 'There! By that bush!' Peter behind her, she began to descend. But it was all too much trouble, there might be snakes in the undergrowth, it was an easy enough walk down but it would be a tiring haul back, her shoes would get ruined. She turned, she gave up.

'Aren't you going for it?'

'No point. It's not worth it. It's miles and miles down.'

'But I want my ball!' he whimpered.

'I'll get you another.'

'I don't want another! I want that one!'

'Oh, don't be silly.'

As she began to climb back on to the verandah, he grabbed her hand. 'Clare! Please!'

'Oh, let go, do!' She snatched her hand away. 'And stop that whimpering! You know how I hate it! When you whimper like that, I feel like choking the life out of you!'

She glanced up at the face of the house, hoping that no one had heard her say that. Only the day before, when she had supposed that she and Peter were out of earshot in the garden and she had scolded him, Isabel had put her head out of the open drawing-room window and cried out: 'Clare! Clare! You mustn't speak to him so roughly. There's no need.' How could one hope to teach the brat discipline and good manners if his mother always took his side?

. . . The sun is low. It seems, throughout this fag end of summer, so terribly distant. Looking at it, she feels a crazy impulse to stretch out her fragile arms and cry: 'Come closer, closer, closer!' She gives a little shiver and again bites on the ivory of the cigarette holder with her small, white, slightly prominent teeth. Everything here is much as she imagined it would be and yet the happiness which she also imagined as flooding into her has somehow proved elusive. There are the eleven indoor and outdoor servants, each with his scrupulously defined tasks, whereas, back in the red-brick villa by the

68

railway depot, one ancient woman, with wild, greasy hair, and a boy with the prematurely withered arms and legs of someone who has all his life been hungry, lackadaisically attend to the innumerable chores which Clare's mother does not have the time or energy to finish or, often, even to start. Each day here, the indoor servants dust the furniture and sweep the floors, and the sweepers, having emptied the commodes in each of the bathrooms and lavatories, then scour out the enamelled containers, rubbing sand into them with their bare hands, before repeatedly rinsing them in a strong, opaque solution of Jeyes.

She likes this sense of constant renewal. Even the clicking sound of the gardener and his 'boy' cutting deadheads from the roses or pruning back the creepers which, if left to themselves, would soon smother the house, gives her a tranquil satisfaction. Nothing is allowed to get dirty or shabby or out of hand. Nothing gets into a mess.

But that tranquil satisfaction is always being disturbed by a restless dissatisfaction. What does she want? She does not know but she knows that she does not have it.

'I hope Clare is happy,' Isabel said last evening, as she smeared cream over her face before her dressing-table mirror.

'Isn't she?' Toby replied from his narrow dressing room, in which, since Isabel's pregnancy, he now always sleeps.

'I didn't say she isn't. I said I hoped she was.' Isabel now raised her chin and began to pat the flesh beneath it with the back of a hand – a nightly exercise. 'Strange girl,' she added.

'Strange? How?' He stood in the doorway between the two rooms, taking the studs from his evening shirt. Usually, he left that task to Muhammed.

'I never know what's going on inside her.'

'Perhaps she doesn't know herself.' Toby can be as shrewd about people as about money, though in general he values the latter more.

. . . Clare's bedroom is far larger than any room in the red-brick villa by the railway depot; but she has to share it with Peter and she does not care for that any more than she cared for sharing a bedroom with two of her brothers until she was fifteen. Not that she's not fond of the little beggar – in as far as she can be fond of any child. His fragility touches her, as does his dependence on her and his eagerness that she should love him. He is capricious and spoiled, oh, dreadfully spoiled, and he has often made trouble between her and Isabel by repeating something, in a garbled or exaggerated version, which she has told him, or reporting something – with or without malicious intention? she can never be sure – which she has done. Curiously she feels fondest of him when he is frightened. Like his mother in the past, he is frightened of thunder and, woken by it, he always screams: 'Clare, Clare, Clare!' Muffled in blankets and in vague, comforting dreams of once again being a child back in the house by the railway depot or in the convent, she sits up, pushing her dark hair away from her forehead with a hand pricking with pins-and-needles. 'Don't be silly, it's nothing, it's far away.' The lightning flashes again, he screams again. Then, if his screaming has not summoned Isabel, he whimpers that he wants to get into her bed with her. Eventually she gives in. 'Oh, all right then! All right!' He cuddles up to her, his arms around her. She feels a palpitating quickening of the senses; the blood suddenly seems to be coursing through her veins with a speed of which she has not before been conscious. She has a sense both of vertiginous excitement and of discomfort and dread. Last night she had to tell him: 'No, don't do that! Don't do that!' His small hand was clawing at her breast.

'Nanny Rose never minded.'

'I daresay not. I do! Go on, leave me alone, you little beast!' But she was laughing and then he too began to laugh, a high-pitched crowing.

. . . Clare knows that the ayah, moving soundlessly about the room as she tidies it, hates her. The fragile, uncertain Eurasian girl, with her silks, her heavy perfumes and her boxes of paints and powders, has come between the strong proud Indian woman and her *baba*. The ayah has long since decided that Clare is no good.

70

Shall she go down into the town this evening or shall she stay here? The soldier, Pat, whom, improvising a lie, she claimed to be her cousin, will be waiting for her at the Gardens Hotel. But does she want to see him? Pat is Irish and she feels a vague, ancestral kinship with him. He is 'rather sweet', she has written to her mother. Clare is touched by his yellow faintly lined, youthful face, with its suggestion of some anxiety that he can never wholly put out of his mind. Already he is better, soon he will be leaving the convalescent home, to return to the plains. He is too young to have fought in the war but he has been shot at on the North West Frontier, his arm grazed – he has shown Clare the milky scar, above the elbow, just as he has shown it to many other women – by the bullet of a Pathan insurgent whom he still wants to kill. Like Clare, he is one of many children and, like her again, he has always had a craving for tidiness and discipline. It was that craving which brought him from a village in County Down to a battalion in India.

When, only the day before, Clare and Helen were on a walk together round the lake, they accidentally ran into him with a group of other soldiers from the home. He was embarrassed that Clare had a companion with her and even more so that he was surrounded by companions of his own. But he halted awkwardly, a tall, handsome boy, still yellow and thin from the ravages of malaria. 'Hello, there!' he called. The other men stood behind and some distance from him, appraising the girls.

'Hello, Pat.'

'How are things then?'

'How are things? Oh, as they always are. How are things with you?'

'The doc saw me this morning. He thinks maybe in another week I'll be on my way back.' He shifted his weight from foot to foot. One of his companions caught Helen's eye but, when he winked at her, a sunburned hand stroking his moustache, she quickly looked away.

'Well, that's fine.'

'I'll be seeing you this evening. As arranged.'

71

Clare did not answer. Would she be seeing him? She did not know then, any more than she knows now.

He has taken her rowing on the lake, his khaki shirt darkening under the armpits, even though the 'doc' has told him to go easy on the exercise until he has finished with the quinine. He has walked her around the lake, an arm about her narrow waist, with his nicotine-stained fingers – the 'doc' has also told him to go easy on the cigarettes – from time to time pressing against her ribcage. She likes his sense of humour ('Did I ever tell you the one about the priest, his housekeeper and the parrot?'), the transparency of his nature, so different from the opacity of her own, and his dogged perseverance in attempting to woo her, even though she gives him no encouragement. In the fleapit, when they are watching a Chaplin film, he keeps glancing at her to see if she is laughing; then he puts out a hand, its palm hot and sweaty, and takes her hand in his. She leaves her hand there, as though it were some inanimate possession of hers, a book or pen, which she is happy enough for him to borrow. When he presses it, she does not press back.

Because of his upbringing – one of his many brothers is a priest, his mother is profoundly devout, if not profoundly religious – he is tormented by his carnal thoughts about her; and because of that upbringing, he shrinks from turning those thoughts to action. Often, as he walks round the lake with her, he is obliged, deeply ashamed, to put the hand not round her waist into his trouser pocket to contain his erection; and later, having said goodnight to her, he succumbs, again deeply ashamed, to the temptation of masturbating into the thunder-box which, next morning, the sweeper will empty. Clare allows him a chaste kiss on her cheek or on her forehead – the taste of strands of her hair on his lips fills him first with an intoxicated exaltation and then with a draining despair – but it is only rarely that she does not turn her head away when he tries to meet her lips. 'No, no,' she murmurs.

'When we're engaged?' He admires her for the strength of her abstinence.

'*If* we're engaged. Ever.'

It is her way of telling him 'Never' but he is too simple to see that. He has had many Indian women in flimsy, dusty rooms buzzing with flies and shaking with the exertions of his fellow soldiers. That he cannot have this woman convinces him that she is the only one he wants for his wife.

'He's handsome,' Helen said with a faint note of interrogation in her voice, on that afternoon when they ran into him and his companions by the lake.

'Yes,' Clare agreed. Yes, he was handsome, even when he looked so yellow and emaciated.

'Do you like him?'

'I like him.'

'Love him?'

'Oh, love, love!' Clare laughed, throwing back her head, and Helen laughed with her, the noise making some teal clatter up out of the undergrowth by the margin of the lake and take off into the sunset with a dazzle of wings and water.

'What's it like to be in love?' Helen asked. 'I don't think I know.'

'I'm not sure I know either.'

'Oh, you must!'

'Must I? Why? Do I look so experienced?'

'No. But someone . . . someone like you . . . so attractive . . . I bet you've had lots and lots of men after you.'

'Oh, yes, I've had those.' She did not mention that Helen's father was one of them. 'But men will go after anything.'

Not me, not me, Helen wanted to say; but she did not do so. Instead, she put an arm around Clare's waist, exactly (though of course she does not know this) as Pat does when walking with his 'sweetheart' – as he terms Clare to his pals – around the margin of the lake.

. . . 'What are you doing here, all by yourself?'

Clare now starts at the voice. It is Helen, holding a book, with a forefinger between its pages, to mark her place.

'I'm supposed to be keeping an eye on Peter. But the gardener can do that.'

'He's fascinated by that gardener and his boy. Weird!'

'You don't really like him, do you?'

Helen is disconcerted. Clare, who is usually too lack-adaisical and self-centred to notice the reactions of others to anyone but herself, has for once been observant. 'He's such a spoiled brat,' Helen says.

'He's fond of you, you know. Very fond. He worked so hard at that bead bookmarker and now you never use it. Look at you – you have your finger in your book.'

'I put it away somewhere. I can't remember where. It kept slipping out when I tried to use it. Oh, yes, that was nice of him, I must buy him a present when next we're in the bazaar.'

'It must be odd to have a stepmother.'

Helen nods. The tawny disk of the sun has just begun to slot itself into the divide between two hills in the west. 'When I was a child, I had this idea that, but for Isabel, my mother would never have . . . ' She cannot say the word 'died'. Suddenly she thinks of that glass bottle, such a beautiful shade of blue, into which her mother coughed away her life.

'But what could she have had to do with your mother's death?'

'Witchcraft?' Helen laughs with the same surprise as Clare – as though, now that she has expressed it, she finds the idea no less odd. 'I thought of her as a witch. Who first put a spell on my father and then put a spell on my mother. We think witchcraft impossible, we're so civilized, aren't we? But he' – she points to the gardener who, no longer stripped to his loin-cloth but wearing trousers and a woollen jacket, has come round a corner of the verandah, with Peter behind him – '*he* would find it a perfectly acceptable notion, I'm sure.'

'It's a pity she spoils Peter so.'

'Well, he's the only thing she's got,' Helen replies.

'She's got your father.'

'Has she?' Helen's voice, previously so gentle, takes on an edge. She turns away and wanders off down the verandah.

Clare stares after her. Surely she cannot know?

TOBY

Toby lies on his side on the narrow dressing-room bed, one hand beneath a cheek, while his *chotah hazri*, brought into him by Muhammed a long time ago, lies untouched. He heard Peter enter Isabel's room, his voice high and clear, and, propping himself on an elbow, then saw him, in dressing-gown and slippers, through the door left carelessly half-open by the bearer, as he sat perched on the edge of his mother's high brass bedstead. He has often told Isabel that, at five, the child is too old for such intimacies, but she has merely laughed, shaken her head and asked what harm they can do to him – 'He's an innocent, a complete innocent.' An innocent? Is he? Toby finds it hard to remember a time when he himself was innocent.

There was the nursemaid – or was it nurse? – in the bleak Lincolnshire vicarage, who, when she bathed him, would each time insist on easing back his prepuce ('You must always be clean down there'), even though it hurt him so much that he would wriggle and the tears would prick his eyes. Lying here on the bed, the tea gathering a pale film of milk and the butter congealing on the fingers of toast, he can see her hand in all its strong, implacable, chapped, marvellous beauty. Later, with her or with some other nurse or nursemaid (he frowns now, as he struggles to define the memory), he got into some argument over a game – demon-grab was it? – and as, half in play and half in earnest, he snatched away her cards, they suddenly began to wrestle. They rolled over and over

75

each other on the floor, her skirt rode higher and higher and all at once, on some wild, terrifying impulse, he pushed a hand up to where he could glimpse the pink of a suspender against shuddering marbled flesh. 'Ooh, you little devil! How dare you!' Then his mother, old Mrs Thompson came in, stared down at them and demanded: 'What on earth are you doing? Get up from there at once!' He knew from the tone of her voice that he had done something wicked but in the weeks ahead, until the nurse or nursemaid was sacked for some misdemeanour never clear to him ('I'd never have believed it of her,' he heard his mother tell an aunt), he longed for some opportunity to do it again.

Innocent! Were children ever really innocent? Was it all not a myth?

Toby ought to get up, if only to relieve the pain of the erection throbbing beneath his bedclothes. Can there be something wrong with his prostate? Drunken old McGregor, making a joke to relieve the embarrassment ('I bet you've never allowed anyone to do *this* to you before, I could be clapped into jug if I didn't happen to be your doctor'), was reassuring. 'No, no sign of anything, nothing at all. Just a little spongy.' Perhaps he wakes each morning like this because Isabel is no longer willing to fuck, and here, up in this little hill-station, it is difficult to find anyone else to do so, other than some Indian bint. He will never forget the shame of that time when, after a hurried visit to a woman in the bazaar (Muhammed arranged the assignation), he suffered, urinating a few mornings later, that sensation of pissing red-hot needles – as they used to put it in the Army. The cure took a long time and, clumsily administered by a venerealogist at the Army convalescent home, had been hideously embarrassing, uncomfortable and even painful. ('This works on the same principle as the umbrella, it's not nearly as bad as it looks.') He had tried not to tell Isabel, but of course she had discovered, how could she fail to, with that sleepless curiosity of hers? It was from that discovery that he dates the failure of their sexual life together. Once she even mused: 'All those miscarriages. I sometimes wonder ... .'

'Wonder what?'

'Well . . .'

'This is the first time I've ever had anything like this. The first bloody time!'

She stared up at him, her head and shoulders propped on a mound of pillows. Then she gave that small, derisory smile which always maddened him. 'Oh, I never believe a word you tell me. Not now. I've long since learned my lesson.'

. . . Well, it's true enough – now he reaches out for the lukewarm cup of tea, his muscular, freckled arm bare as the loose sleeve of the pyjama jacket falls away from it – oh, yes, it's true enough, he's never been wholly straight with her. But what the eye doesn't see and the ear doesn't hear . . . He sips and pulls a face at the bitterness of the tannin. It might be the aloes which that other nurse ('Give you a kiss? What an idea! You're far too old for kisses') would put on his fingernails to prevent him from gnawing them. But, for all that, he's always been a good husband and it's not as though he were cheating her out of anything she really wanted. For God's sake, after those first months, when poor little Eithne was dying and he must have someone, anyone to clutch to him in his terror and desolation, she had never even made a pretence of enjoying sex with him. Odd that. It was as though her rivalry with the dying woman had been an aphrodisiac and then, when the unequal battle was over, all that wild, clamouring frenzy of desire was over too. 'Don't you ever think of anything else?' she was in the habit of asking when he eased himself into the bed beside her at night or, as they were dressing for some dinner party, inserted a hand into her wrap and attempted to rouse her by touching one of her nipples.

'Oh, I think of many things! But of this most of all.'

It was true, though neither she nor his male intimates believed it. In the city where Clare had her home, he had got into the habit of borrowing from an ageing bachelor, one of his senior employees, his frowsty, untidy flat. 'What, again! Of course you can have it, dear chap – only too willing to oblige –

but, gosh, I'd be a wreck if I kept at it, day and night, as you do. How on earth do you manage to run all those businesses of yours? I'm at an age when once a week is all I can manage – if that!' There was both admiration and the disapproval of envy in the voice with its oddly strangulated vowels.

Toby would bring up from his car his own bottles of Scotch and gin and even, if his partner was someone whom he was particularly eager to impress, champagne. 'You left half a bottle of champers behind you, so I finished it off,' his host would say. 'I didn't imagine you'd want it kept for you.' In the guest room, Toby would leave two or three notes tucked under the base of the bedside lamp. It was a tacit agreement between the two men, to pay for the cost of having the bed linen laundered and the room cleaned. The narrow, high room, with its amateurish woodcuts of Lincoln and Ely cathedrals facing each other across the bed, always accentu-ated Toby's mood of self-disgust and depression when, his partner gone, he went back into it to pick up the twists of Bromo scattered on the floor, to remove the sheets and pillowcases and neatly fold them for the *dhobi*, and to make sure that he and his partner had left behind them nothing other than the smears and smells of their congress.

. . . Sometimes, as now, lying on this bed of his, while from the verandah he can hear Clare's low voice and Peter's shrill one in some protracted argument ('Won't!' 'Oh, yes, you will!' 'No, no, no!' 'Now Peter, that's enough!'), he thinks with longing of that dim, dingy room, with its frayed Persian rug (Good God, the man can't be that badly off, why doesn't he replace it?), its cracked enamel basin, jug and slop pail on their rickety stand, and its Victorian bedside table, far too high for the bed, with a flowered chamberpot in the cupboard at its base. But there are other times when, in memory, that same room seems to him like some place of torture.

There was that Italian violinist from the girls' orchestra engaged to play at the hotel, a child she seemed despite all her experience, who showed first shock and then a wondering delight when, having shot his sperm (her purple-lidded eyes screwed tight, her mouth twisted as though in agony), he performed the difficult feat, the opening of the bladder being contracted on such occasions, of pissing inside her. The urine steamed out of her cunt and began to drench the bed. Oh, Christ, Christ, Christ . . . What would the owner of the flat, so finicky and conventional, think?

. . . Or there was that married woman, grass widow of a civil servant absent on tour, who, during a game of bridge at the club, had made it clear to him, by the intermittent pressure of her knee against his own, that she would be as reckless in undertaking an affair in the future as in now overbidding her hand. How bored she had been, both during an interminable sequence of rubbers and then, perpetually yawning and glancing about her, during dinner alone with him; and how frantic she had become in the room in the flat, kneeling down on the floor and tearing at his flies, even while he was unknotting his tie and unbuttoning his shirt. There was a despairing greed in her lovemaking, as of one long famished. When she left him ('Oh God, I hope no one sees me, one of my closest friends has the flat two floors up'), her face was ashen, her hands trembling.

. . . Or that Indian girl, so silent and solemn, a waitress in the Viennese patisserie, who, for some reason never confessed to him, needed money so badly that, though it was clear that her hairless cunt had never had anything larger than a finger up it, endured with silent stoicism, an extended hand gripping one of the brass bars of the bedstead, as he first put his mouth down and sucked, sucked on those marine juices and then savagely mounted her, thrusting deeper and deeper. Through her clenched teeth, he could hear her 'Oh – oh – ah!' She would not answer him when he spoke to her afterwards, averting her face as she clambered off the bed and then standing with her back to him as she frantically pulled on her clothes. She took the notes which he held out and, without counting them, tucked them into her scuffed leather handbag. 'Shall I see you again?' Once more no answer. When he went into the bathroom to wash – she had shaken her head when he had suggested that she might want to do so – he found blood on him and there was more blood on the counterpane, which he soaked in cold water. Two days later, he returned to the Viennese Patisserie, but there was no sign of her. He asked one of the other girls, pallid and wary in her black dress with a white frilly apron, whether her colleague were not on duty and, her tray balanced on a corner of his table, she replied: 'She went away. Last Thursday. She said someone in her family was sick and went away.' It was on the Wednesday that he had had her. 'Where did she go?' The girl shrugged her narrow, bony shoulders. No one in the café knew. He was overcome by a terrible sense of mystery and a no less terrible remorse.

. . . Still he lies here and the pornography of memory and the memory of pornography (in his locked desk in his office he keeps the books, magazines, photographs, drawings) become confused as in a dream so that he cannot always remember if certain things really happened to him – the girl in nothing but her riding boots, a switch in her hands, the two enormous women, their tongues intertwined, on a balcony overlooking the sea, the girl strapped to the iron bedstead in the cavernous, weirdly creaking brothel, ripe haunches, silky hair, darkly aureoled nipples, sights of pleasure, sights of pain – or if he merely read of them or saw them depicted.

Again, from the verandah, he hears Clare's voice. He lumbers up and crosses, in bare feet and pyjamas, to the open window. Through her tennis dress, he can see the outline of her small rounded breasts. He even persuades himself that he can make out the dark triangle lower down, though that is impossible. She lifts an arm, her hand patting her hair into place, and he notices, not for the first time, that unlike most other women whom he has ever known, she does not shave. He watches her as she bends forward to examine one of Peter's drawings. Then he becomes aware that his mother, Isabel and Helen, seated out on the lawn, are in turn watching him. He must be careful, oh so careful, but he does not know for how long he has the strength to be so. He is afraid and he guesses that Clare is afraid, as she so persistently avoids being alone with him or even near to him. She must fancy him, he is sure that she must. He has that kind of vanity, since, even if he were not so rich, he would be attractive to women. Oh Clare, Clare . . .

At last he starts to dress, with the debilitated feeling of someone who is either sickening for a fever or just recovering from one. This afternoon he must start on a long journey, first on horseback, then by car and then by rail, to Simla, where he has a meeting with the Viceroy. There are rumours that he is to be asked to join the Viceroy's Executive Council. There are people who do not like him, thinking him devious, unscrupulous, ruthless and ambitious; and there are those who like him but who know too much about his private life to regard him as suitable for office – suppose some scandal blew up? The Viceroy is a pious High Anglican, and his innocence has the high and unyielding burnish of steel.

Toby goes round to the stables to mount the horse which the syce has been grooming for him, and there is Helen, in jodhpurs and an aertex shirt, just returned from her usual morning ride. Sometimes they ride together but usually it is he who is too early for her. As he looks up and she looks down, he thinks how like her mother she has become, and that gives him a pang, as though, somewhere deep inside him, some long-borne weight had suddenly slid first to one side and then to the other. People all supposed that he married Eithne, an invalid eleven years his senior, for the money which she had already inherited from her mother and would eventually inherit from her father. But, though it was true that it was her fortune which became the strong foundation of his, he had really loved her, even if he had also hated her for being host to the bacilli which, frantically multiplying like the population of this bloody country, had eventually done for her. She had appeared so ethereal, with her shifting, dark-ringed eyes, her temples so delicate that one could see the veins throbbing within them, and her husky, often barely audible voice; but what extraordinary hours of lovemaking they had had

81

together, their bodies involuntarily coalescing in a frenzy even as they were in process of doing something or saying something wholly mundane. Toby would be leaning over her as the two of them examined the household accounts kept in her small, neat handwriting, or they would brush against each other as one entered a room at the same moment as the other left it; and then, all at once, there they would be clinging to each other, as though some tidal wave were about to sweep through the house and sweep them away with it, or some earthquake were about to shake it until the roof collapsed over them, hammering them down into the rubble.

. . . 'Did you have a good ride?'

'Oh, yes, Daddy.' She swings herself down from the gelding. 'First I thought you must have gone out ahead of me and then I waited a while. But mama said you were lying in this morning.'

'I didn't mean to lie in. But, I don't know why, I felt terribly tired. It's not as though I'd done anything particularly exhausting or been to bed particularly late. Odd.'

'You do too much.'

'That's the only kind of life I enjoy.'

'And I do nothing. Nothing!'

He senses dissatisfaction, even though she is smiling as though she has said this in joke.

'What do you want to do?'

'You know what I wanted to do.'

'Well, it's not too late . . . After a year or two.'

'You won't succeed in marrying me off, you know.'

'Won't I? An attractive girl like you . . .'

'Bosh!'

She walks away towards the house and he thinks that that lithe, erect body, the hands and feet a little too large and the legs and arms a little too thin, is oddly sexless, despite its health and youth. Perhaps she is right, perhaps he will not succeed in marrying her off. For that is what he and even more Isabel are bent on doing. Women do not have careers unless, like those countless shopgirls, waitresses and typists, unless

like Clare, frowning before her abacus as her hands push
along the beads, they have to have them; and in any case to be
a doctor is no career for a woman – it was bad enough that
Sophie, dotty old dear that she is, should have insisted on
working in that hospital. He does not like to think of hospitals
but, as he now rides out of the stableyard and the grey begins
to pick its high-stepping way up the hill towards the woods, he
cannot put out of his mind that horrible sanatorium on the
foothills of the Himalayas.

Each morning he would have to steel himself to say
goodbye to Isabel and Helen, to trudge up the zigzag path,
and to enter that wide, airy, linoleum-covered vestibule,
stinking of formaldehyde. Eithne too stank of it, as he bent
down to kiss her cheek and quickly she warned him: 'Don't
come too close, darling. They say I'm still teeming with
horrid germs.' He feared and loathed the other patients to
whom she introduced him, because he feared and loathed
their illness: the elderly Begum, so rich that she had taken
over a whole floor for the use of herself, her private doctor and
her servants; the pallid boy with a stutter, who wrote weak,
wet poems to Eithne, not knowing that, later, she and Toby
would laugh over them in the privacy of her bedroom; the
irascible old man, an impoveris. ~d tea-planter, his estates
mortgaged to one of Toby's comp.~nies, who was always
shouting out for attention in both English and Hindustani
and to whom no one paid any heed. It was a relief to go out
into the gardens and so escape from both that horrible
chemical smell and all those horrible human reminders of
mortality.

. . . In a clearing in the woods, two women in saris, their
faces half veiled, are cutting grass with bill-hooks and then
stuffing it into burlap sacks. He wonders, idly, what they will
do with it – use it or sell it for goats, bullocks, rabbits? – as he
reins in his horse a little above them and looks back. He notes
appreciatively the firm, glabrous smoothness of their arms,
ankles and bare feet; the round of a buttock upturned to him;
a breast pressing against the coarse fold of a sari. The women

know that he is watching them and he knows that they know. The knowledge only serves to excite him the more. One woman mutters something to the other and they then pause for a moment in their slashing at the soft, moist grass and glance up at him from under lowered lids. One of them giggles. He feels his erection harden yet further against the hardness of the saddle. Enough. He kicks with his heels at the belly of the horse and, with a grunt, it resumes its ascent.

He will ride past the Anderson house in the hope that, as he looks down from the road above it, he will catch a glimpse of young Mrs Anderson, working in the garden or playing tennis or sitting out on the verandah of a house so much smaller and darker than that of the Thompsons, her envied neighbours. If she is somewhere outside, he will shout a greeting; but he will not go down, because there has already been gossip, in the form of innuendoes and jokes among the men at the club and of suspicions and surmises among the women at their bridge parties, and he does not want, and even more she does not want, that it should spread any further. They have never, in fact, slept together but in the past he was in the habit of riding down, tethering his horse to one of the posts of the tennis court, and then joining her for a mid-morning cup of coffee, while her husband was at his office. She is a pretty, insipid little thing, who longs for the children which, either through her fault or that of her husband, she has never been able to have.

Toby could give her those children, he had no doubt of that; and as he trots on – she is nowhere to be seen – Toby now begins to brood darkly on that girl whom, when he was a cadet at Sandhurst years and years ago, he seduced when he was her widowed mother's lodger. The girl became pregnant; and, after days of hysterical pleading on her part and quiet obduracy on his, he eventually took her to a young, contemptuous doctor, recommended by a fellow cadet, with a practice in Kentish Town.

'You realize this will cost you a packet?'

'Yes, I realize.'

The girl was shivering in her cheap, light overcoat, though the day was a warm one, with flies buzzing noisily against the surgery window.

'I don't put my head on the block for nothing,' the doctor went on, so callous and cool that Toby had an all but irresistible urge to punch him in his sallow, prematurely lined face.

But you do not punch someone from whom you want something which no one else will give you and so Toby merely said: 'Of course not. What's the tab?'

The doctor shrugged and then drawled: 'Well, let's settle for fifty.'

Toby barely had that money in the bank, he would be skint.

'Cash,' the doctor added.

'Of course. Cash.'

The girl began to whimper, drawing the lapels of the coat over her breasts.

'Have you got it with you?'

'No.'

'Well, you'd better get it. No cash, no deal.'

Toby got it.

Once the whole crude, horrible business was over, the girl, who had previously been so panicky, showed an amazing stoicism. Her mother never guessed or, if she did, pretended, with no less stoicism, not to have done so . . . What became of the girl? Only now, as he canters under the trees, a stout, muscular, ageing man on a grey horse, is he troubled that he has no idea, no idea at all. Perhaps she is happily married, perhaps she is an embittered and lonely spinster, perhaps she is dead. He who is usually full of complacent self-love now feels abrasive self-hatred.

It is odd, he thinks, that Isabel, who often boasts 'Oh, I'm never ill', who is so serene and so strong, should have never been able to carry any child other than Peter beyond her fifth month. It is as though her body deliberately expelled, with the least fuss and the least mess, any possible rival to her cherished darling. Or perhaps – the weirdness of the idea makes him smile to himself – it is the child himself who somehow, by some magic, ensures that he will never have that rival. Peter, after all, does not welcome even other people's children for long in the house, finding occasion to quarrel with them on the frail pretexts that they have broken or appropriated toys of his, have ganged up against him or have made disparaging remarks about the family. Toby wonders if this child which Isabel has miraculously carried into the seventh month will, for once, survive. Somehow he doubts it. He will come home from Simla or Bombay or Calcutta and Isabel will tell him, with no grief, shock or even surprise, 'I'm afraid I lost the baby while you were away.' Lost – it is the word she always uses. Strange word, as though she had gone out and then somehow mislaid it like a glove or a handkerchief.

In the office, Mr Ram – he is always Mr Ram to Toby and Toby is always Sir to him – has again made a muddle of something. 'Don't you realize, you bloody fool, that *that* account is separate from *that* one?' Toby stabs with a forefinger first at one sheet of paper and then at another. 'Are you completely moronic?' Hilda types away as though nothing of this was happening, her myopic eyes swimming back and forth, like creatures from ocean depths, behind those thick glasses which always irritate Toby with their reminder of a weakness. 'Have you sent off that letter to Millett's?' Toby now demands, though he knows that Mr Ram cannot have done so, since he only mentioned it to him the last thing the previous evening. Mr Ram shakes his head with a drooping, yielding sorrow and Toby yells: 'Jesus Christ!' Toby always knows when he is behaving badly, as now; but he cannot stop himself. He longs for Mr Ram to hurl something hard and sharp back at him – 'You bloody bully!' 'Who the hell do you think you're talking to?' 'Fuck off!', that kind of thing. But Mr Ram has to think of his wife and his wife's mother and the four – or is it five? – children all crowded into three rooms. So Toby goes on: 'I don't know why I employ you. I don't know what use you are to me – or what use you'd be to anyone else. I sometimes even wonder if you ever got that degree. I just can't believe it. BA in *what*, for God's sake!'

Mr Ram looks up at Toby and Toby recoils. The eyes under the arched, silken eyebrows are, yes, murderous. There is no other word for it. Toby has never seen them like that before, usually they are so soft, so gentle, so pleading, just as Mr Ram's voice is usually so soft, so gentle, so pleading with its Sorry, sir, yes, sir, I'll try to do better, sir, please forgive me, sir, I was up all night with my youngest, my youngest is sick, sir. Now Mr Ram says none of these would-be-placating, exasperating things. He merely looks at Toby. Silent. Toby goes off to his own office, throws himself down into his chair and, tilting it back, puts his hands, the reddish hair thick on their backs, one to either cheek. He's gone too far, that's torn it. Oh Christ!

He tries to work but the words of the company report before him – extraordinary credit of rupees 35,000, acquisition of 15% holding of, wholly owned United States subsidiary, interim dividend – flicker and fade, flicker and fade. His heart is thumping. He remembers that terrible burning sensation behind the sternum, that overmastering thirst, the hallway darkening, his falling, falling, falling, and then the vomit jerking out of him in uncontrollable spasm on spasm, as though he were having some endless, agonizing orgasm. Someone poisoned him. Perhaps it was the assistant cook, who fled with all his belongings and was never traced. Perhaps it was someone like Mr Ram, who has that murderous look in eyes once so meek. He has always known that his employees do not like him, one does not expect to be liked if one insists on a decent day's work for a half-decent day's pay in this godforsaken country. But now, for the first time, he realizes that they hate him. It is an unpleasant realization.

But why should he be surprised? Last week, urged by Isabel, he rode over the hills to the mission-station, to condole with the two absurd women, sisters from Huddersfield, who run it between them. The sisters belong to some obscure low-church sect, which pays them the most meagre of pittances to interfere in the lives and beliefs of people who are too courteous to tell them, as Mr Ram is too courteous to tell him, to fuck off. One of them, a former hospital nurse, hands out medicaments, usually aspirins and laxatives; and the other, whom Toby suspects of never having read anything but the Bible and English language textbooks, gives classes. 'Oh, dear, we ought to have them over,' Toby often sighs; but they rarely do so. 'They are so terribly *not* handkerchief drawer,' Isabel also often says, using an idiom, common in both senses, of that time and place. But now Toby obeyed Isabel's urgings to ride over to see the poor old things.

The square, whitewashed building, with its hideous roof of corrugated iron scabbed with rust, had become only a blackened, jagged shell. Like some huge, decaying molar: that was the image which came to Toby as he rode up. The tiny chapel lay in pieces on the ground, as though some fractious child had pushed over a rickety meccano construction in a tantrum. The servants' quarters were still standing and, in front of them, two tents had been erected. The tents were not of the kind to which Toby is used, with soaring poles and rooms ample enough for sofas, chairs and tables to be set out on rugs. These were the sort of tents in which, back home, boy scouts crowd to sleep when camping. The two women, in the shapeless cotton dresses and plimsoles which they always seem to wear, were seated out in front of them, one in a deckchair and one in a chair of plaited cane. They were doing nothing.

Toby dismounted from his horse and handed it to the dishevelled servant, his turban askew and his mouth full of food, who had hurried out from the servants' quarters. The women had meanwhile sprung up to greet him with a wild, startled eagerness. 'Mr Thompson!' one of them cried out, clapping her hands together. 'We never thought to see you!'

As he approached, the other sister grabbed at his arm. 'How kind of you to come! And you so busy! And such a long road!'

'Well, I felt . . . All of us were so distressed to hear . . .' In fact, he was now embarrassed, rather than distressed.

'How kind everyone has been. How wonderfully kind. Mrs Anderson was over here yesterday and she said they'd be happy to put us up in their lovely home for just as long as we wanted. And the Governor's ADC . . .'

They prattled on, calling to the servant first to bring a third chair and then to make some tea, yes, Toby must have some tea. They would like to offer him a drink but, as he knew, their religion . . . Yes, Toby knew.

The tea was black and bitter, with an overlay of nauseating sweetness from the condensed milk already poured into the cups before the servant brought them out on a tin tray decorated with blowsy purple roses.

Toby was gazing about him. Then he said bleakly: 'You must have lost everything.'

'Well, almost everything,' the older sister confirmed, far from bleakly. 'But we still have our friends. And we still have our faith.'

There was a terrible pathos in that last remark to Toby, since he himself has no faith at all. Did they mean faith in their arid, rigid form of Christianity? Or faith in the people whom they had for so many years tried to serve and who had now repaid them in this fashion? Probably both, he decided.

'The vicar has been wonderful,' the younger sister said; and the older took up: 'Yes, Mr Andrews has been wonderful, considering we're not of his flock. In fact' – she laughed, putting a hand to her mouth, as though to reveal its interior were indelicate – 'one would never guess that he's one of the opposition, as it were! He's getting up a collection for us. He's already collected hundreds, literally hundreds, of rupees.'

Toby stirred his tea in its thick, hospital-style cup. He sighed. 'Well, of course, I'll be contributing,' he said. He felt tongue-tied, he did not know why.

'Oh, Mr Thompson, how good you are! What a good, good man!' The younger sister, who must once have been pretty, again grasped his arm. Her nails were far from clean and she smelled, he suddenly noticed as she leaned closer to him, of charred wood.

'Who could have done such a thing?'

'Who? Yes, who indeed?' The sisters looked at each other, as the older spoke. 'It's a mystery to us. We cannot imagine, we just cannot imagine.'

'Well, although I've spent most of my adult life in this country, I still don't understand them.'

'But they're no different from us, Mr Thompson! No different at all!' The younger sister again leaned forward and again that smell of charred wood filled his nostrils.

Toby shrugged. How could one contradict them?

When he rode away, having told them that Isabel had made up some parcels for them, which two of the servants would be bringing over later, Toby experienced a sudden coldness and dread. What harm had these poor, silly, trusting, loving women ever done to anyone? And again he asked, silently now, as the horse picked its way round boulders and over hillocks: Who could have done such a thing? Who? Who?

Then this countryside, gentle hills gathered round a tranquil lake, seemed to him to hold a sudden menace, akin to that which had led to Jack's murder on the verandah of the bungalow which he had shared with two other bachelor officers. A hand hovered, then rested on a grey rubber sheet. 'I don't want to see him. Don't. Please.' There was panic in Toby's voice. 'I want to remember him – remember him as he was.' The young English police officer was embarrassed. It was Isabel who had insisted that they wished to be shown the corpse. The police officer looked over to her. She nodded. Toby lurched away. The hand folded back the sheet, clammy and cold on healthy palm. Isabel gazed down at her twin for seconds on end. What did he look like? Had they patched him up? Toby never dared to ask her, either then or later.

Toby heard the swish of the sheet being once more drawn up. He turned, sought Isabel's face. It was frozen, as though she had been lying with her twin in his bed of dry ice.

She emitted a tremulous, long-drawn sigh.

. . . Toby often now thinks of Jack, though he tries not to do so, just as someone who has resolved to put a decaying tooth out of mind is reminded of it by intermittent twinges. He is leaning across the billiard table in the club, he is pouring out a glass of whisky for some guest after dinner or, brows knitted and hands dangling between bare knees, he is straining at the thunder-box; and then, all at once, the *kukri* is flashing down, stabbing and ripping at the flesh beneath it. It perplexes Toby that, now that he is dead, Jack should so often squirm and slither into his mind unsummoned, whereas, when he was alive on the other side of the subcontinent, he would forget all about him for days and days on end. He was a bit of an ass, Toby had decided as soon as he had met him, with that braying laugh of his, that love of practical jokes and that reckless passion for gambling, which would often drive him to borrow money openly from his brother-in-law or, more often, secretly from his sister. Despite their undemonstrativeness with one another, the closeness of the twins to each other was at once clear to Toby, simultaneously baffling him and filling him with resentment. So, too, he was both baffled and resentful when he saw Peter squirming and giggling in delighted abandonment under Jack's exploring, nicotine-stained fingers. Why couldn't the fool leave the boy alone, instead of over-exciting him like that? It was a relief when Isabel intervened with her 'Oh, for God's sake, Jack!' or 'Do let him be!'

. . . Toby and the women are sitting out on the lawn in the warm, slanting light of evening, while Peter plays near them with a huge doll, almost his own size, the present of a maharanee who has, she declares, 'fallen madly in love with him'. Peter first shamed Toby by saying a doll when the maharanee asked him what he would like for a present; now he shames him by playing with it in front of visitors and servants. Mysteriously, the child has christened the doll Alfred but refers to it as 'she'.

Helen, who has returned from a meeting of the Bluebells, is

still in her sepia uniform, her cocked hat on the ground beside her deckchair. Peter approaches, drops the doll and then picks up the hat and places it on his head. It comes down over his eyes, resting on the upturned tip of his nose. 'Look, Mummy, look! Clare! Helen! Granny!' Only the old woman laughs. He pulls off the hat and chucks it down beside the doll.

He approaches still nearer to Helen, slowly, furtively, on tiptoe, as though in a game of grandmother's footsteps. She is aware of his approach but ignores it as, hands clasped, she gazes down to the lake. Then he asks, forefinger tapping: 'What's that thing on your belt?'

'My scout knife,' she says. Now the forefinger is tracing the stitching on the sheath. 'Oh, leave it alone!'

'Can I see it?'

'No.'

He grasps the sheath. 'Please!'

'You'll only cut yourself on it. It's sharp.'

'Show it to him, Helen,' Isabel looks up from her sewing to say. 'But don't let him touch it.'

Reluctantly, Helen pulls the knife out of its sheath. Its edge, cruelly sharp, glints in the sunlight. Fascinated, fingers of one hand pressed to his lower lip, the child stares at it. They are all staring at it, even Helen.

Toby sees the *kukri* flashing downwards and the blood spurting in a high, scarlet arc. He sees the brown, muscular fist, the brown, muscular forearm above it. He hears a yell.

He looks away, a hand to his eyes. 'Put it away,' he grunts.

Helen returns the knife to its sheath. Peter, who has already lost interest in it, has picked up the doll and is wandering off.

Toby's eyeballs feel sore, as though that glint of sunlight on honed metal had seared them. Normally so energetic, he has a sensation, increasingly common in recent weeks, of life suddenly ebbing from him. It will flood back, he knows that from experience. Of course it will flood back. But suppose, suppose – the thought suddenly terrifies him – that that outgoing tide, ebbing away to leave inert, wrinkled mud-flats behind it, were, by some mysterious caprice, to refuse to renew itself.

He thrusts the thought from him, with an effort, as though it were something heavy and slack which had fallen across his body. Then he stretches out his arms, the sleeves of his shirt rolled up to reveal his freckled forearms, out to the sun, a red ball above the hills to the east of the lake. 'What a day! What a wonderful day!' Already he can feel the tide returning.

As he says this, he smiles across at Clare. But, her right leg swinging restlessly as it is balanced on the knee of her left, she refuses to look at him.

Suddenly, as though that flash of knife had been a zigzag of lightning striking first Toby and now, much later, her, Isabel puts down her sewing on her lap and says, quietly pensive: 'I often wonder . . . How could anyone have brought himself to do what that man did to Jack? How, how?'

'It's better not to think about it,' old Mrs Thompson says. Over the years she has acquired a technique of wiping from her mind whatever might eventually prove gritty or corrosive.

But Isabel goes on: 'That's the only reason why I should like to have gone to his trial. To see what kind of man he could possibly be.'

'I expect he looked like any other Indian,' Toby says, using the past tense, since the man has already been hanged. 'He certainly did in the newspaper photographs.'

'And yet he was a monster,' Isabel insists. 'Or possessed. To kill someone for so trivial a reason – and to kill him in that way. Unthinkable.'

'Unthinkable only to us,' Toby says. 'To an Indian . . .' He sighs. 'Strange people. All these years and I still don't understand them, not one bit. So quiet, gentle, kindly, good-natured. And then suddenly . . .' Again he sees that flash of steel, that high, scarlet arc.

Mrs Thompson laughs nervously. 'When you talk like that, you frighten me,' she says.

'Things like that can happen anywhere in the world. The

Indians are no different from us – or at least they're no more wicked.' Helen gets up, goes to the wooden palisade above the *cud*, and leans over it.

Again Toby looks over to Clare and again she refuses to meet his gaze.

ISABEL

In dressing-gown and feathered mules, her hair in a net and her sturdy legs, their blueish marble finely streaked with the darker blue of veins, supporting her out-thrust belly, Isabel stirs the fudge in the saucepan before her on the primus stove. Her mother-in-law began to make it but then, overcome by standing and the heat, had what she called 'one of my little turns'. Soon, the thread will appear; and soon, no doubt, lured by the smell of chocolate and vanilla, Peter, Pete, Peterkin will also appear from the schoolroom, where Clare, suffering from one of her migraines, has left him to do some sums. So precocious in all his other lessons, he has a hatred of arithmetic. He will never be able to take over the business, Toby has often said, half in benevolent joke and half in acrid criticism. 'Everything that I have ever achieved rests on the foundation of knowing that two and two make four.' Toby, so clumsy with words, is brilliant at juggling with figures. At a glance, he can appraise a balance sheet or point out a mistake in a bill.

The unborn child shifts within her. Stirring, stirring, stirring with a rhythmic movement of the firm white arm from which the sleeve of her Chinese silk wrap falls away, she smiles to herself. It is a habit of hers, that small, secret smile, which irritates Toby, since it excludes him. 'What's the joke?' he asks; and to that she either murmurs 'Nothing' or else shakes her head. She smiles because she is happy, whereas Toby rarely is. She is happy in stirring this fudge by the

95

kitchen window while, outside, drops of water glitter, small, transparent glass beads, on the blue of the hydrangeas which, many years ago now, the gardener planted, with her standing, sturdy legs apart and arms akimbo, to give him her brisk commands. She is happy in thoughts of the long, cloudless day ahead of her, of the pheasant which Toby shot on his visit to Simla and which they will eat for tiffin, and of Peter at any moment coming through the door, crying out: 'Mummy, Mummy, Mummy! Let me scrape the saucepan!' Above all, she is happy in the thought of this child inside her, even though, two hours earlier, she was retching over the chill enamel bowl of the thunder-box. The child is, secretly, a present neither for Toby nor for herself but for Peter; and because it is that, she is calmly certain that she will not lose it. 'You will have to be careful, dear lady,' Dr McGregor told her, the whisky raw on his morning breath. 'With your history, extremely careful.' Crankily unorthodox, he then listed all the things which she must avoid. 'Undue indulgence in alcohol' came first, the mention of it from this man whose face is covered with the broken veins of a heavy drinker, making her give that small, secret smile of hers. Smoking, of course; riding and lifting; late nights; too many spices and too much fat; strong tea, strong coffee . . . 'Most of the illnesses I have to treat are dietary in origin.' She can believe that. Where there are so many servants and where everyone vies with everyone else in entertaining, meals are both too heavy and too frequent.

She decided to give Peter, Pete, Peterkin this present when, on their previous stay in the hills, she and he were upstairs on one of those daily visits which, however much he protests, she forces him to make to his grandmother's room. He was staring out of the high window, watching a kite being flown by someone invisible to him – could it be one of the many children of the rich, obsequious Parsee, Mr Mukerjee, from whom they rent this house each year? – far, far down the hill. The kite soared, lunged dangerously and, jerked by that anonymous hand, soared again. Beautiful. Its tail streamed behind it, now rigid and now lashing from side to side, as though it were some snake high up there in the sky.

'Granny is asking you a question.'

'Oh, don't bother him,' the old woman muttered, shifting irritably in the armchair in which she now spends so much of her time, when not in bed or lying out on a deckchair on the verandah. 'It's of no consequence.'

'Peter!' Isabel's sharp voice at last jerked him round, as that invisible hand had jerked the kite to its bidding. But, though his face was turned to them, his eyes still glanced sideways out of the window.

'Granny wants to know what you want for your birthday.'

The boy, then only four, shrugged.

'You must want something.'

'I don't know.' There were many things which he wanted; but since he had so often heard his mother and father say that poor old Granny had hardly any money, he now shrank from naming any of them.

His grandmother stared at him, her gaze clouded by the pearly cataracts which, in a few months, would have ripened enough for an opthalmic surgeon to remove them. Then she gave a snorting laugh: 'It must be difficult to decide what one wants for a present when one has everything.'

Isabel was about to protest when Peter, Pete, Peterkin said, eyes still skittering sideways to watch what was happening to the kite: 'Yes, I *have* got everything. There's only one thing I really want.'

'And what is that, dear?'

'A sister.'

The two women laughed. The boy did not like that. Stamping his foot, he cried out: 'I do, I do, I do! I don't want to be an only child. I want to have a sister.'

'Well, I'm afraid I can't oblige there,' his grandmother replied, crossing her hands, knobbly with arthritis, on her lap. 'But perhaps your mother can.' She has had four children herself – Toby, two daughters, both married back in England, another son, her beloved, long since rotted away in the mud of

Flanders – so that she has always shown a pitying contempt for Isabel, incapable of carrying a foetus to its term.

Peter now stared angrily at his mother. 'Why can't I have a sister?' he demanded.

Isabel laughed, though she felt humiliated and raw. 'Well, I'll have to see what I can do. Won't I? It's not all that easy, you know. The stork may be too busy to visit us.'

But it was at that moment that she decided. For him she could and would do it.

Toby was surprised, bewildered and shocked by her sudden ardour. He had already supposed that she knew about the affliction, like some ill-concealed illness, of his obsession with silly, pretty little Mrs Anderson down the hill. (Clare had not yet glided, insidiously potent, into his daily life and nightly dreams.) Was this a ploy to win him back from the intruder, just as Eithne, in those last frenetic, doomed days, had put forth all her ebbing strength and all her fading beauty to win him back from Isabel, implacable keeper first of her house and then of her husband? (In the railway carriage, their bodies swaying and jolting as they rushed into the night, she had suddenly struggled away from under him, a look of terror on her face and her right hand making tearing movements at her left breast, as though some invisible beast had fastened its fangs there. Later, to the cowering Indian doctor, he explained: 'I think she must have overstrained her heart through exertion. She had this vomiting attack – something she must have eaten.' That remained his story and so eventually became the story of others.) He was seated on the edge of the narrow bed in his dressing room, massaging the sole of the bare foot which lay across his knee. His boxer shorts cut into the muscular thighs covered with reddish down. His eyes were moony and sad. Somehow he knew that he would never make it with Lola Anderson. In her night-dress, a coarse plait over her shoulder, Isabel swished towards him, ran fingers through his close-cropped, thinning hair, nails scratching scalp in memory of what once would arouse him, and then stooped and grasped the hand with which he was massaging his foot. 'Come!' Reluctant and wondering, he allowed her to draw him up. 'Come, come.'

He pattered after her into the bedroom in which he had not slept for so long, stretched himself out beside her and, her nightdress now an opalescent pool on the moonlit floor, submitted to the arms which, a predator with her victim, she fiercely threw around him.

After a long-delayed, jerky, painful consummation – 'What's the matter with you? Old age? Or have you been back to that brothel?' – he tumbled off the bed and, with a sensation of physical nausea, picked up the nightdress as though it were something soiled and threw it over a chair.

Isabel lay back on the rumpled pillows, her breasts, still moist from his saliva, sticking up above the sheet now wrapped around her. She smiled that mysterious smile of hers, as though at some joke which she would never tell and he would never understand, even if she were to tell it.

He pulled on the boxer shorts, then thrust his arms into his vest.

Later, hearing him leaving the dressing room through the door to the corridor, she called out: 'Where are you going?'

'I've not yet locked up.'

Each night he observes a ritual of going from downstairs room to room, turning keys, pushing home bolts, fastening latches. Out there, in the windy darkness, there are people with knives, guns, bombs, stones, brands. He can safeguard this house, this family and the multiple businesses essential to their maintenance only if, by this nightly ceremony of exorcism, he keeps those dark, invisible demons at bay.

'I'm sure Muhammed has seen to everything.'

'One can never be sure.' He meant that one could never be sure not merely of Muhammed's efficiency but of his loyalty.

In his expensive cashmere dressing-gown, bought from Sulka when last in England, Toby stood for a long time by the landing window. Opposite his dressing room was the room in which Nanny Rose and Peter slept. Far down the hill – he stood on tiptoe to peer – was Lola's bedroom, with its wide balcony overlooking an irregularly shaped lawn. Her husband was away. As Toby had sweated and grunted over Isabel, he had imagined Lola asking herself, sleepless: 'Will he come tonight? Will he?' Preposterous! But the idea persisted. She was lying there in a nightdress so transparent that the dark aureoles of her nipples and the dark triangle of her sex were visible through it. She moaned, tossed her head from side to side, bit her lips, placed a hand between her legs . . .

Upstairs, someone moved with a creaking of floorboards. No doubt, since it was far too late for any servant to be in the house, his old mother had been making her way, hand outstretched, to the commode which stood in one corner of her room. She had been embarrassed to ask for it and Isabel had deliberately exacerbated that embarrassment by exclaiming with a mixture of surprise and disgust: 'You mean you want a commode in your room? But the bathroom is only next door.' Now, sleepless as so often, she would probably be adjusting her glasses, taking up a book, settling herself on a high mound of pillows . . .

He shook himself, as though to break all the invisible filaments that bound him there, a silent, yearning, self-disgusted presence above the bedroom separated from him by a tennis court, trees, walls and that lawn shaped with what seemed to be a deliberately perverse irregularity. Then slowly, one step, two steps, one step, his hands clutching the dressing-gown to him, he began to descend as though into an icy pool. He could see that all the drawing-room windows were closed but none the less he went up to each of them and tested their keys and bolts, resting fingers on the metal, a gesture of magic. He tried the front door, again resting fingers on the metal of keys, bolts, chain. He went on into the dining room, with its smell of the cigar which he had smoked, sitting on there alone, the bottle of port before him, while the frail old woman and the robust middle-aged one sipped, in a lassitudinous ennui, the coffee which had bubbled up through the glass funnel of the Cona percolator. 'Coffee, mother?' Isabel

would have asked, as she always did; and old Mrs Thompson
would have replied, as she too always did: 'Well, why not? I
won't sleep anyway.'

Eventually, the elaborate ritual done, he crept back up the
stairs. Isabel had shut the door between the main bedroom
and his dressing room and her light was off. Sometimes, after
his tour of the silent house, she would call out, her voice sharp
with irritation at being woken, or with incipient alarm at a
possible intruder: 'Is that you, Toby? Toby!' but on this night
she was silent. She slept like someone gorged to repletion.

Toby went out again from his dressing room, into the
bathroom. The bearer had left out the usual jug of hot water,
with a towel over it; but instead of using that, he splashed cold
water out of another, larger jug into the basin on the high,
mahogany washstand. Dipping in his sponge, he began to
wash off his body all traces both of the woman who was his
wife and of what he had just done with her. He worked with
the grave, patient absorption of someone washing a corpse,
his lips sucked inwards each time that the icy water trickled
down his flesh, to soak into the floorboards. He had not
thought to remove the bathmat from its rail and place it
beneath him.

Oh, Christ, I hope that doesn't happen again . . .

But it did, for many nights.

. . . Peter comes in as Isabel has expected. 'Oh, Mummy,
let me scrape out the saucepan!'

She hands it to him with a smile. 'Now don't scrape too
hard. If you scrape too hard, you scrape off the enamel, and I
read the other day in the newspaper that enamel can be bad
for you.' The article to which she refers attempted to establish
a link between the swallowing of enamel chips from cooking
utensils and cancer of the stomach.

He scrapes with the wooden spoon and then sucks it, a
cheek smeared.

'Is Clare still lying down?'

He nods, scrapes, sucks. The smear extends to his pointed,
girlish chin.

'I'd better see how she is. Here, give me that. There's nothing left in it. Give it to me!'

Reluctantly, he hands the saucepan to her, the spoon in it, and she fills it with cold water, to make it easier for the scullery-boy to wash. The fudge, thick and dark, lies out on two shallow dishes, which she now carries into the stone-tiled pantry, to cover with bead-fringed doyleys, the work of her mother-in-law. When it has set, she will carve it with a crisscross pattern, remove the pieces one by one and place them in the tin, once full of chocolate biscuits ordered from Calcutta, with the regal profile of Queen Mary imposed on the no less regal one of George V and 'Dieu et Mon Droit' inscribed in gold curlicues above them.

Peter follows her up the stairs; but instead of going with her into the room which he shares with Clare, he remains out on the landing. 'Oh, go away, do!' Clare exclaimed fretfully to him when, only a short while before, he put his head round the door and peered through the curtained gloom.

'How are you, Clare?' Isabel asks briskly.

'Oh, oh, oh!' Clare groans and then the groan becomes a bilious yawn, as she raises bare arms above the head propped up on a heap of pillows and stretches extravagantly. 'These migraines make me unfit for anything.'

'You should really have a word with Dr McGregor about them.'

'Oh, what does he know!'

'A lot,' Isabel replies sharply, though she has never believed it. 'He's a first-rate doctor, even if he does drink too much.'

'There's nothing anyone can do about a migraine. They come, they go. I always get them before my period.'

'If it's your period, then I can let you have some pills.' Though so healthy, Isabel has pills for everything. She can understand Helen wanting to be a doctor and Sophie having worked as a nurse; she is fascinated by illness as a stay-at-home is fascinated by tales of the distant, exotic countries he will never visit.

102

'The best pill is to lie in the dark and do nothing. Undisturbed,' Clare adds pointedly. 'Eventually a migraine passes. Oh!' Again she groans, a hand cupping her right eye.

Isabel purses her lips. Can the girl really be suffering as much as she makes out? Eurasians are notoriously lacking in guts, they give way to the smallest afflictions. After her last miscarriage, Isabel went out to a party on the same day. She cannot imagine any Eurasian woman doing that. 'Well, I'd better leave you. I'll see if Helen can take over.'

'She won't thank you for that.'

Isabel detects an insolence; but since she is habitually good-natured, she decides to make nothing of it. She slips out, shutting the door quietly behind her. Peter is still standing outside, waiting.

'We'll find Helen,' Isabel says.

'What did Clare say?' Peter asks, as he prepares to slide down the banisters.

'She's still got her migraine.'

'What *is* a migraine, Mummy?'

'A pain in the head.'

'When I went to see her, she told me to "Bugger off!" '

'What!' Isabel halts on the stair and looks up at the boy, who, straddling the banisters, has not yet launched himself on the exciting journey down. 'I'm sure she never said that.' But Isabel can well believe it. Once, when Clare accidentally spilled some tea into her lap while filling her cup, Isabel, who happened to be passing the open schoolroom door, had been amazed and angered to hear a loud 'Fuck!' Fortunately, on that occasion the child had not been with her.

'She did, she did! She said "Bugger off!" I promise you, Mummy.'

Isabel decides that, yet again, she will have to talk to Clare. If it had been anyone else, she would have asked Toby to do so, but in this case it will have to be herself. 'Nonsense!' she tells him. 'And I don't want you ever to use that word again. It's not . . . nice, Remember?'

'But what does it mean?' Peter persists.

'It means "Go away" – which she might well have said to you. But it's not a nice way to say "Go away", in fact it's a very rude way to say it. So, please, Peterkin, *please*, never let me hear it again from your lips.'

Peter, Pete, Peterkin slides down the banisters with a high-pitched 'Whoosh!'

Helen looks up, surprised, from her chair by the window in the drawing room when Isabel comes in. In the afternoon, her stepmother usually goes up to her room for a siesta.

Before she says anything, Isabel glances around her, taking in the disorder, of books on floor and papers scattered over table, which Helen has managed to create in a room so recently tidied by the servants. Why can't the girl use her own room, instead of treating this one as though it were her own?

Isabel's disapproving scrutiny annoys Helen, who asks sharply: 'Did you want me?'

'It's Clare. Another of her migraines.'

'Poor Clare.'

'And also poor Peter.' Isabel now smiles, revealing her large, white teeth above her slightly pendulous lower lip. She wants to be placatory to this odd, distant girl, who, when she calls her mama, always seems to be putting the word into ironic inverted commas. 'I wonder if you could possibly take over his lessons?'

'Oh lord!' Helen closes her volume of Trollope and throws it across to the table. Only two or three days ago, Isabel noticed some scratches on its surface, where Helen had pressed too hard on a sheet of paper while writing there.

'It's just a question of giving him something, anything to do. He loves it when you read to him.' Isabel decides to flatter her. 'He makes so much more progress with his reading when he follows you. You get the results which Clare often fails to get.'

Reluctantly Helen rises, pushing her left foot into one of the shoes which she must have kicked off when she settled herself in the chair. Isabel hates to see someone ruining a good shoe like that, using neither shoehorn nor even a finger, as Helen first treads down the heel and then wriggles her foot about.

Isabel, watching her, says 'The servants complain they can never get into your room to clean it.'

'Oh, I hate the idea of other people going over my things. You know how inquisitive they are. The ayah especially.'

'The room must be cleaned some time, dear.'

'Must it? Oh, all right. I'll let them in tomorrow.' Helen begins to assemble the sheets of paper strewn across the table. They look as if they have been torn out of an exercise book. Surely she cannot be using that kind of coarse, lined paper for her letters? Or does she keep a diary?

Isabel crosses her hands over her swollen belly. 'Clare looked so ... No make-up. A different person. Sallow, terribly sallow. And those eyelashes – they seemed so short without all that mascara. A surprising, sandy colour.'

Helen, head lowered, goes on stacking the sheets of paper.

'You're lucky to need no make-up. You have your mother's complexion. I envy you.'

What Isabel really means is that she used to envy Eithne. For Helen she has never felt any envy.

The two women leave the drawing room. 'What's happened to Peter? Peter!' Isabel calls. 'Where are you?'

Peter, seated on a step half-way up the staircase, is peering down at them through the banisters. At the sight of his half-sister, his face was briefly irradiated, as though someone had given him an unexpected present. It amuses him to see the women bewildered by his disappearance and to hear his mother calling, with increasing sharpness: 'Peter! *Peter!*' One of his games is to hide himself. But now he can no longer contain himself. 'Helen!' he cries out.

'Oh, there you are!' Isabel says. 'For a moment I thought something must have happened to you. Come down from there!'

'Hello, Peter. I'm going to teach you.' Helen's tone, though not unfriendly, has about it something cool and measured, which both disappoints the boy and irritates his mother. As he reaches the bottom of the stairs, she puts out a hand. 'Come!' The boy rushes forward and grabs the hand in his.

As Isabel sways on alone, thrusting her protuberant belly before her, first to the hall cupboard for some rubber boots, then into the drawing room and out, through the French windows, on to the verandah, where she picks up a pair of secateurs off the floor, her annoyance with Clare and her irritation with Helen both begin to dissipate. Once again she begins to feel happy. Happiness, she has long since decided in the course of a life blotched with poverty, disappointments and sudden deaths, is akin to health. One possesses it or one does not possess it, one loses it and one regains it. Outward circumstances are seldom relevant. Why should she be so happy on this ordinary morning of an ordinary day? Her husband wants to carry on, or is perhaps already carrying on, with that sallow, sleepy, groaning girl on the rumpled bed in that curtained room. The father whom she cannot remember has long since vanished, God knows where, perhaps he is dead. Her heroic mother, who taught at a primary school and took in lodgers in the high-gabled, damp Victorian house overlooking Clapham Common, is mouldering in an old people's home in Bognor, her fierce independence making her ungracious in the manner ·in which she accepts Toby's monthly cheques. The mutilated body of her only sibling, her twin, must by now have rotted away or been devoured by jackals on the edge of the Rajput desert; but even the thought of him – such fun, oh such fun, people always said – cannot take away this happiness which she draws into her and exhales, evenly and calmly, as though it were the clear, thin autumn air up here on the first foothills of the Himalayas.

As she snips at the deadheads of the roses, each dissolving on her palm as though into dust, a memory stirs. It is the faintly acrid odour of the roses, a ghost of an odour, which brings the memory back . . . Sister and brother, nine years old, were at the far end of the garden, where, instructed by their fretful mother, they were struggling to raise a pergola, a tangle of snapped wire, twisted supports and murderously trailing branches, swept down by a gale. Their mother was among her shrill, unruly pupils at the school down the road. The lodgers were all out. The clammy deadheads – no one in the house had either the time or the inclination to deal with them – had the same ghost of an odour as these deadheads now disintegrating, one by one, in her palm, before she empties their petals into the trug beside her. The day was one on which a thundery heat haze enveloped the Common.

The two struggled to raise the pergola, heaving, tugging and panting, but each time it fell back. Isabel kicked at it: 'Stupid old thing!' 'Bloody old thing!' Jack amended. Isabel kicked again and a dust rose and drifted over them. They both began to cough. Again they struggled and this time, somehow, Isabel managed to hold it upright while Jack wound wire first round and round its base and then round and round its concrete support. Completed, the job looked, like so many others performed in that fatherless household, flimsy, amateur and botched. Wiping his nose on the back of his hand, so that he left a greyish smear of dust and grime across its narrow bridge, Jack said: 'Chuck me that other bit of wire and the cutters. I'll do the same the other side . . . but try to hold it straight! Straight!'

The sturdy girl, who at day school jumped highest and farthest and ran fastest of the pupils of her age, heaved at the swaying half of the pergola and at last got it erect.

'Terrific! Now we'll have to see to the roses,' Jack said. He put out a hand: 'Secateurs!' He was always issuing peremptory commands to her and she was always docile in complying.

Later: 'Blast!' As she tugged at it, a branch scraped against her elbow. She peered round at the wound, then squeezed it and watched, with both wonder and satisfaction, as small beads of blood began to swell and coalesce with each other.

'You'd better wash that.'

'You'd better wash your nose.'

Satisfied that they had done all they could, they wandered

back towards the house. There was a cavernous downstairs cloakroom, by the back door, which was also used as a store for unwanted luggage belonging to the lodgers, piles of dusty newspapers bundled up with twine and preserved against some eventuality, who could say what, gumboots, ancient raincoats, and the bowls and lead used for a dog long since dead. In one section of this cloakroom, there was an old-fashioned, high-pedestaled washbasin, with spindly brass taps, a gas geyser above it. A door led on to the other section where, under a high window, there was a lavatory-basin, with a mahogany seat set up on a wooden platform to give it the appearance of a throne. The paper in the holder was abrasive and brown, the linoleum frayed.

Isabel raced into this second section. 'Gosh, I must have a pee!' She struggled with her knickers with one hand, while with the other she pushed the door half-shut. She heard the preliminary bark and then gargle and hiss of the geyser, as Jack began to run water into the washbasin. She seated herself, legs wide apart, and felt the intense pleasure of the long-retained urine streaming from her.

Suddenly the door creaked wider.

'Hey! Do you mind?' She put out a hand and pushed at the door; but Jack pushed too, so that for a while the door shifted an inch forward and an inch backward between them. Then, as he put his shoulder to it, it smashed open. 'What are you doing?' she demanded, scrabbling for her knickers.

'Let me have a look, let me see. I want to see what it looks like. Then you can see mine.'

Many years ago, they had shared their baths for reasons of economy, with their mother stooping over them, sponge or flannel in her hand. They had glanced occasionally down at each other but, so alike in every other way, they had not speculated on that trivial unlikeness.

'No! Certainly not!'

'Oh, come on!' He was undoing his flies with hands still damp from the washing he had given them. Then suddenly he leapt forward and hitched up her skirt, as she struggled to rise, her legs still fettered by the elastic of the knickers at which she was tugging. She saw the pink thing dangling out of the fly and suddenly a wondering curiosity stirred in her.

'Touch it,' he said. 'Go on, touch it.'

The pink thing began to harden in the hand which, with infinite caution, as though she had been told to touch a snake in the zoo, she had extended. His own hand went down. She turned her head aside, looking away and down at the coarse roll of paper in its holder, and he turned his head the other way, to gaze out of the window. His mouth opened, she heard his breathing, like that sound of the geyser coming to life, and the thing in her hand kept growing and stiffening, while she felt his finger exploring what she herself had never until then explored.

For a few months, whenever they had the house to themselves, they would continue what each of them regarded as no more than a game, even if a secret and vaguely shameful one. 'Let's explore,' one of them, usually Jack, would say – that being the way in which they had come to speak of it. The other would demur half-heartedly and then the two of them would go into the cloakroom or, more safely, into the potting shed, with its rusty, seldom used tools untidily stacked, caked with soil, against its cobwebbed walls, its pots trailing rank, etiolated growths like seaweed, and its deckchairs, their canvas frayed and faded, piled higgledy-piggledy in one corner, in expectation of the next unlikely heatwave. Always associated with those rapt moments, when neither their lips nor their eyes ever met, was, for Isabel, the faint odour of roses and dust. On the first occasion, when they had stood in the cloakroom, the curve of the lavatory-basin chill and hard against her bare legs and the edge of the door sharp against a shoulder, that odour was all about them, on their hands, in their tangled hair, impregnating their grubby clothes.

. . . Isabel clicks on with the secateurs, serene and happy, despite, or perhaps because of, these memories which have drifted back, an aromatic dust, unsummoned to her. Jack went away to a church boarding school, at fees drastically reduced because his grandfather, his mother's father, had been a clergyman. Their mother worked even harder now, dispensing with the services of the diminutive skivvy, little more than a child, who had once come in to make the lodgers' beds and clean their rooms. Isabel, disconsolate in her isolation, awaited Jack's return. When next she saw him, he had broadened; his thighs were strangely muscular and his knees strangely knobbly between stockings and shorts. He had also developed a habit of roughly teasing her. He never now said 'Let's explore' and she, though she wished so much to do so, never said it either. He no longer liked her to touch him, protesting 'Oh, don't be so soppy!' 'Get off, do!' 'Do you want to suffocate me?' if she put a hand on his arm, a cheek against his or, most daring of all, threw herself down near to him where he lay out on the tangled, overgrown lawn and then cautiously, deliberately rolled over and over until her body came to rest against his.

This physical diffidence between them never passed. It amused Toby, as it pained their mother, when the twins would meet after some long separation and Jack would say 'Hello, old girl! How are things?' and she would say 'Jack! How nice to see you again!' No kiss, not even a handshake. They might already have seen each other breakfast that same morning, Toby would remark. Their demonstrative mother would sigh: 'You seem so far from each other and you used to be so close.' But they were close, innumerable, inextricable filaments joining them to each other. On the night before the news of Jack's death, Isabel had woken out of a deep sleep, with the sensation of a hammer crashing down repeatedly on an anvil within her, so that her whole body shook and reeled beneath its onslaught, and had at once known, with all the cold, cheerless clarity of the dawn beginning to break over the eastern end of the lake, that he was somehow gone from her. When Toby, the telegram shaking in his hand despite all his efforts, had come up to the bedroom where, to compensate for that early, terrified waking, she was having a siesta, and said: 'Isabel, prepare yourself, darling, prepare yourself, I have some terrible news,' she knew the news already, she had no need to prepare. After the funeral, as Toby, embarrassed in his helplessness, held her stiff, desolate form in arms which ached as though they had been carrying some heavy burden and murmured: 'Don't cry, sweetie, don't cry,' she, who was not crying and who never cried over this bereavement until days later, whispered into his ear, her cheek strangely cold: 'Oh, Toby, he was half of me.'

. . . She picks up the trug laden with the shrivelled, disintegrating heads of the roses and then sets it down on the path. The gardener will see it there and will empty it for her, as the sweeper empties the thunder-box and the ayah picks the long strands of black hair from her hairbrush with the intentness of a monkey gathering fleas. She does not have to carry the trug round to the rear of the house, to the rubbish heap, unless she wants to do so. There is so little that she has to do unless she wants to. She stands, erect, her belly thrust out before her, and looks down to the lake. A single sailing boat moves in an unerring line across its surface and, above, a flock of small birds – starlings? she does not know – wheel, spray upwards and regather, as though at the caprice of every gust of wind. Beautiful, beautiful world. She is happy.

II
ACT

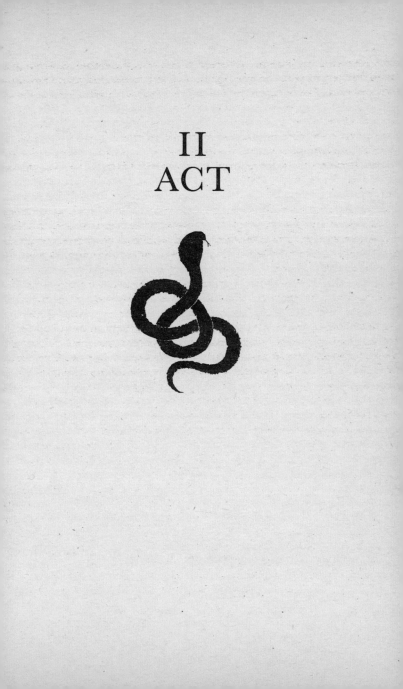

I

Now that deliverance from her pregnancy was so near, Isabel slept propped against a mound of pillows, hands crossed over belly as though to protect it and mouth slightly open. Each night, as she humped her ungainly body on to her creaking bed, it was with a sense of physical and emotional repleteness. She hardly had time to switch off the bedside lamp, put her head back and draw up the bedclothes before, no longer a creature of flesh and blood but a figure of marble, she plummeted down into a fathomless lake of oblivion. To draw her up from it again required a violent shake or some loud, persistent noise.

It was such a noise that Clare, her eyelids leaden, was making as she first knocked and then hammered with the palm of a hand on the door.

'Yes! Yes! What is it? What time is it?'

Clare turned the door-handle and entered the frowsty, curtained room, where her mistress now lay beached, a statue dragged up from icy depths, on the high, Victorian brass bedstead. She looked all around her. 'Isn't he here then?' she said.

'Isn't who here?' Isabel demanded, stretching up her arms and yawning.

'Peter.'

'Peter? But isn't he with you?'

Clare shook her head, her hands deep in the pockets of a wrap stained and scented from having so often been worn

115

while she was making up her face. Then she swallowed and said: 'I overslept. And when the ayah roused me – I couldn't find him.'

'Overslept! But you must have heard him getting up.'

'I took one of those pills you gave me. For my migraine. It must act like a sleeping pill. I don't usually sleep as heavily as that.'

'Well, he must be somewhere.' Isabel picked up the clock on the bedside table, held it in both hands up to the wedge of light slanting through the curtains, and squinted at it. Eight twenty-five. Muhammed must have knocked with her *chota hazri* at seven as usual, got no answer and either have been told by Toby to go away or else have decided to go away on his own initiative. 'Haven't you looked for him? You know how he loves to hide.'

'This was the first place I thought of.' If the child woke before she did, Clare would send him out of the room while she dressed; and on such occasions he would often wander across to his mother's room, clamber up on to the high, creaking bed and lie against her, one of her arms around his shoulder. If the bearer had already carried in the tray with the *chota hazri*, Isabel would from time to time feed him one of the narrow fingers of butter-saturated toast or hold her half-drunk cup of lukewarm tea to his greedily gulping mouth.

Isabel shrugged, swung her legs off the bed, groped for the wrap thrown across the bottom of it, and stood up. For a moment she tottered; then, barefoot, her hair in its thick, black plait hanging over a shoulder, she crossed to the door to the dressing room. 'He's unlikely to be in there with my husband. They'd have heard us talking.' Calling 'Toby! Toby!' she opened the door. The crossdraught made the cretonne curtain above Toby's narrow bed billow outwards and slap against the wall. The dressing room was empty.

'Where on earth can he be?' Clare said.

Usually it was Isabel who worried about Peter's disappearances and Clare who remained unperturbed. Isabel now sat down at her dressing-table and stared at her face. Pregnancy had made it too full, too matronly, she decided, with a sudden self-disgust, Clare stood behind her, also looking at Isabel's face over the shoulder on which the thick, black plait of hair lay stretched out like some sleeping animal. Isabel turned, exasperated. 'He's not here,' she said. Why did the girl still hang around? 'As you can see. What about upstairs? He might be with Helen. Or with my mother-in-law.'

Clare did not move. 'He never visits either. Not at this hour. They don't like visits in the early morning, he knows that.'

'Well, I'm sure I've no idea.' Isabel rose from the stool, hairbrush in hand. She began to unknot the ribbon round the plait on her shoulder. 'You'd better look in the garden,' she said. 'Do that. He's always trailing after the gardener and that boy of his.'

'Oh, I don't think . . .'

But as Isabel began to brush the hair now tumbling around her shoulders, Clare turned away and made slowly for the door.

II

Old Mrs Thompson, a worn flannelette dressing-gown over her petticoat, sat by the window alternately looking down to the lake and writing a letter to one of her daughters, Janet, in her large, straggling hand:

' . . .Toby is always good to me, on that score I have no complaints, and little Peter, though terribly spoiled by his mother, is a joy. Helen is a thoroughly nice girl, even if I sometimes feel she really has little time for her poor old grandmother. Isabel now seems to think I'm less of a burden than at first! The house is spacious and comfortable and of course it's bliss to have servants to attend to one's every want or whim. But I must confess that I'm often homesick and wonder if I did the right thing in coming out here. There's so much I miss. I suppose the real trouble is that everyone needs to be needed and I just feel that, though everyone is so kind to me, I no longer have any useful purpose.

'How depressing and worrying what we read from home! Though we have all this civil unrest, with that wretched Gandhi constantly stirring up trouble, we seem mercifully far from threats of war. Typical of . . .'

She stopped there, the thick-nibbed fountain-pen first jerking and then trailing downwards on the paper, as a violent knocking startled her.

'Isabel?' she quavered.

Clare had never been up to this room. Her hands deep in the pockets of her wrap, her shoulders hunched and her lips, which old Mrs Thompson had never seen before without lipstick on them, looking oddly blue, she ventured a few steps forward.

'Yes, dear?'

Mrs Thompson did not trust Clare. She was sure that she was after her Toby. He, poor lamb, had always been so susceptible, bringing home a whole series of girls, each more unsuitable than her predecessor, until, at long last, he had married that poor little thing who, but for her TB and her age, would have been just perfect.

'Has Peter been up here?'

'Peter? No, of course not. He never comes up here except when his mother drags him up on his daily visit. I'm afraid he finds an old woman's company rather of a bore. Not that I blame him,' she added, though secretly she did.

'He's vanished,' Clare said, taking her hands out of her dressing-gown pockets and spreading them out. Those nails! Like talons dipped in blood. Isabel or Toby ought to say something to her about them. Totally unsuitable for a so-called governess.

'Vanished?' Like Isabel, the old woman wondered why Clare should be so upset. 'Oh, I expect he's wandered off somewhere or other. He's such an independent little chap. Perhaps he's with Helen.'

Clare hesitated. 'I hadn't thought of that.'

The old woman reached out for her stick and, using it as a

fulcrum, painfully eased herself up from her chair. She limped, crab-wise, out on to the landing and then, raising the stick, rapped with it on Helen's door. 'Helen!' she called. 'Helen! Are you there?'

The door opened. In jodhpurs and aertex shirt, the vee of her neck sunburned and her shingled blond hair, with its deep diagonal wave, crisp on either side of cheeks radiant with health, Helen emerged on to the landing. 'Did you want something, Granny?'

'Is Peter with you?'

'Peter? No. Why?'

'He seems to have vanished.'

Clare had sunk down on to the straight-backed chair by the landing window. 'He's nowhere in the house,' she said. 'And the servants haven't seen him. I'd taken a pill your step-mother gave me and must have slept more deeply than usual. When I woke, his bed was empty. He's not with your stepmother.'

'He's probably somewhere in the garden. Or gone for an early ride with my father.' Helen was brisk. 'Let's go downstairs and have a look.' She put out a hand to draw Clare out of the chair in which she was crouching. 'I'm sure there's nothing to worry about.'

'It's such a responsibility, looking after a child like that.'

'If you don't like that kind of responsibility, then you shouldn't have become a governess,' the old woman said tartly over her shoulder, as she returned to her room. 'Come!'

Helen still held Clare's hand, as she guided her down the stairs.

III

The two girls, Clare's hair streaming backwards and her knees close together as her legs flew sideways in their absurdly high heels, ran between the rank-smelling hedges and over the small, brownish flowers which the wind had scattered from them. Toby was riding slowly towards the house, with Hilda walking beside him, her face upturned to his in conversation. The sun shone on the boots which, each morning, the bearer buffed with so much care, on his sparse, reddish hair and on the sweat on his naked forearms and his forehead. 'Father! Father!' Helen cried out, in a loud, clear voice; and behind her Clare panted: 'Oh, Mr Thompson, Mr Thompson!'

Toby did not quicken the pace of his horse, but his conversation with Hilda ceased. Eventually, beside them and above them, he looked down. 'What is it? What's the matter?' Then an anxiety darkened his face. 'Is the baby on the way?'

'No, no. It's Peter, Father. Peter.'

'Peter?'

'We thought he might have been out riding with you but then the syce ... ' Helen grasped a rein as the grey impatiently tossed his head from side to side and then let out a whinny. 'He's nowhere to be found. And no one has seen him.'

Hilda looked from her employer to the girls and then back again to him. Her thick spectacles flashed fire as they caught the sunlight.

'He must be somewhere,' Toby said.

'No, no. Nowhere!' Clare all but wailed.

'Christ!' Without saying another word, Toby kicked at the side of the horse so that, curvetting sideways, the animal jerked the rein from Helen's grasp. At that, Toby began first to trot and then to canter towards the stables.

The girls looked at each other and, turning, ran after him, Helen in the lead, graceful in her effortless athleticism, and Clare following with that ungainly throwing-out of her legs, her arms flailing, while she gulped, as though drowning, for air.

In the stableyard Toby jumped down and began to bellow for the syce. Abandoning his mug of thick, bitter tea, the man ran out in panic. Usually his master did not return home so soon. 'Hold the horse', Toby ordered him in Hindustani. 'But don't unsaddle him. I may need him.' The girls, who had taken a short cut along the perilously disintegrating path above the tennis court, joined him as he was striding into the house. Old Mrs Thompson was anxiously awaiting them in the hall, from time to time peering out from the doorway, her grey hair blowing untidily about her face.

'Someone must have stolen him,' Toby said. It was an odd word to use – as though he were talking of the bottles of drink, table linen, bed linen or small items of money which occasionally disappeared from the house. 'I'd better telephone down to the police station.'

'Oh, Toby, I'm sure there's no need to do that yet,' the old woman intervened. 'He's probably wandered off . . .'

Ignoring her, Toby turned to the girls: 'You've looked everywhere, haven't you? You've questioned the servants? The ayah? The bearer?'

'Oh, yes, yes.' Clare dabbed with a lace-fringed handkerchief, screwed into a sodden ball, first at her forehead and then at her cheeks and chin. 'We've been all over the garden and all over the servants' quarters and half-way down the *cud*.'

'God! This country!' In the drawing room, Toby banged with increasing impatience on the telephone cradle with forefinger and middle finger. 'Dead! The fucking thing would go dead at a moment like this.' Neither his mother nor the girls had ever heard him use that expletive before.

Helen pointed downwards. 'Someone has tugged out the wire from the socket,' she said calmly. 'Look.'

Toby stooped and, though it was immediately apparent that what she had said was true, he picked up the end of the wire and examined it carefully.

Again Helen pointed. 'And that window's unlatched. Or did you unlatch it when you came down?'

'No, I haven't been in here this morning.' Toby now went over to the French window, although, again, there could be no doubt about Helen's observation. He put his hand to the latch

121

and jerked it back and forth. 'I made sure it was secure last night. I always do. You know that.'

Old Mrs Thompson ventured: 'I suppose one of the servants might have . . .'

'The servants never do anything more than they have to do. And why unlatch the window unless to leave it open?' Toby stood by the window, legs wide apart and thick, reddish eyebrows drawn together, while the green eyes gazed, in bafflement, first at the old woman and then at the girls. 'Are you sure none of you . . . ?'

'None of us touched that latch,' Helen said, in a calm, steady voice, totally unlike Clare's agitated, breathless one.

'I'd better get down to the police station as quickly as possible. I'll take the horse. Singh is often there on Sundays. Otherwise I'll get them to call his house.'

'Couldn't you ring from the Andersons?' the old woman suggested. 'Or the Mukerjees? The Mukerjees are nearest.'

'Yes, I suppose I could do that. I suppose so. Anyway, there's no time to be lost. Go on with the search while I'm gone but don't – for God's sake don't – upset Isabel. A shock could so easily . . . It's so near her time. For the moment, say nothing more to her.'

He hurried out, leaving behind in the drawing room the acrid smell of his exertion and anxiety. The girls gazed at each other, the old woman gazed at them. Clare put a hand to her mouth and let out a whimper. Helen told her sharply: 'Stop that! Stop that at once!'

IV

Though the morning sun had no warmth in it, Mr Mukerjee was watering his garden in striped cotton pyjamas. Beneath the pyjamas he wore a woollen vest and woollen longjohns, their ribbing visible above his ankles. On his hair, which his elder daughter had just washed for him, he wore a fine net, its elastic making an indentation just above his eyebrows. His high-instepped feet sported a pair of unlaced patent-leather shoes, more suitable for a formal dinner party than for gardening. Although he owned so many of the houses occupied by the British, the house in which he himself lived was modest. He employed only two paid servants, though an elderly female relative might be regarded as an unpaid one.

Soon, when the hot weather had smouldered out in the plains, most of the British would begin their migration; and then, though his houses would lie empty and damp for another six months, and no money would come in, he would be happy. From time to time he would supervise repairs and redecorations in desultory fashion; but for most of the day he would remain, in pyjamas and dressing-gown, in his study, overheated by two paraffin stoves, with its glassed-in veran-dah overlooking the lake. He would read the newspapers, he would entertain his cronies, he would suck on the cigarettes which he himself rolled in their delicate, grey-tinted papers and would chew on the betel-nut which he himself enfolded in its coarse green leaves. Above all, he would drowse, as the flies drowsed against the panes of the verandah, pleasurably poised between consciousness and unconsciousness, reality and dream.

The clatter of hooves made his head jerk up; and there, hurtling precipitously down the path beyond his garden wall, Mr Thompson appeared on his grey. Horses, such strong and violent creatures, frightened Mr Mukerjee. He winced, the hose now lowered, so that its jet sprayed his shoes and bare ankles above them. Toby reined, the grey tossed his head from side to side, so that yellow froth spattered the bougain-villaea trailing over the retaining wall of the hillside. What could Mr Thompson want of him? Oh gosh! Had there been a fire, a burst pipe, a collapsed ceiling? Mr Mukerjee dreaded all such things and, dreading them, also dreaded any contact with his tenants.

'Mr Mukerjee! Mr Mukerjee!' At this distance, Toby's voice had the hortatory loudness of someone shouting at a football match.

'Yes, sir, yes.' Mr Mukerjee advanced in his unlaced patent-leather shoes, the hose still spitting water. Then he stopped and put down the hose against the base of a rosebush. 'What is it, sir?'

'Mr Mukerjee, have you seen my boy?'

'Your bearer, sir? Muhammed, sir?'

'No, no!' Toby's exasperation made Mr Mukerjee quail. 'My son, my Peter!'

'Well, no, sir, no. Was he planning to come on a visit here?' The possibility amazed Mr Mukerjee, who had long since realized that his white tenants did not want their capricious, domineering child to associate with his dogged, docile ones.

'Good God, no! No! He's lost, vanished! I'm afraid that someone – some gang – some dacoits – must have stolen him.' Again that odd word, with its suggestion of household filching.

'Stolen him, sir?'

'I'm on my way down to the police station. Whoever took the boy, also pulled out the telephone wires.'

'The telephone! You have no telephone! But if you wish, sir, you may use . . .'

Did Toby hear the suggestion? Later, when he was asked, Mr Mukerjee could never be sure. After all, as he well knew, his sing-song voice lacked power; and there was a strong wind blowing off the lake, sending rose petals whirling across the garden.

'Janoo! Janoo!' Mr Mukerjee called to his wife. 'Are you there, woman?'

He thought, momentarily, that perhaps he should himself telephone down to the Assistant Inspector, a remote relation of his. But then he decided against a course so presumptuous. The sahibs did not care for one to poke one's nose – Mr Mukerjee's English was painstakingly idiomatic – into their affairs.

V

Soon after her arrival, Helen had made her father and stepmother laugh when she had remarked of the ayah that she had 'an amazing dignity'. What *did* she mean, Isabel had demanded. Priceless! But old Mrs Thompson, nodding her head over the knitting which constantly grew from beneath her arthritic fingers, had not laughed but had nodded her head. 'She's so – so . . .' Helen went on. Then, embarrassed both by Toby's and Isabel's derision and by her inability to define that dignity, she, blushing, gave up.

The ayah, with her erect carriage, her long, narrow feet, bangles around the ankles, and her strong hands with their strangely yielding, pink palms, seemed ageless to the girl. There was a gold stud in one of her nostrils; her teeth, stained by betel-juice, were the colour of Clare's ivory cigarette holder. She never smiled, except at Peter; she rarely spoke unless some question was put to her. None of the family knew anything of her former life, except that she had worked for the family of a general, now back in England, before she had come to them with a highly laudatory reference; but then no one had attempted to get to know anything about it.

The ayah hated Clare, who gave her peremptory orders, the cigarette holder jutting up and outwards from between her full lips, who threw her soiled underclothes on to the floor for her to pick up, who scattered powder over the dressing-table for her to wipe away, and who, worst of all, had come between her *baba* and herself, stealing him from her. Clare's predecessor, Nanny Rose, who had also spent all her life in India but who, unlike her, was not a Eurasian, had been different; but Nanny Rose, suddenly collapsing on her knees on the bathmat like some felled animal, her mouth half-open and an eyelid flickering, while the two women had been bathing their darling (that was how Nanny Rose always referred to him, her darling) was now far away in a home for

125

old people near the daughter whom she had come to love so much less than her charge. The ayah had struggled to drag Nanny Rose up to her feet, while Peter looked over the side of his zinc tub, toy boat in hand, with a faint, unalarmed curiosity. Then, noticing the widening pool on the bathmat, she had cried out again and again: 'Memsahib! Memsahib!' Finally, Isabel had appeared, had asked crossly, seeming not to notice Nanny Rose, now slumped, head on chin, in an ancient wicker chair: 'What is it? What's all this noise?' had then taken in the situation and had at once snatched up the naked, dripping child in her firm arms, the water staining her evening dress, and had rushed him away. The ayah sometimes dreamed of visiting Nanny Rose, half-way across the subcontinent.

Now, when the bearer, whom she dreaded and disliked, told her that the *baba* was lost, she at once joined him in searching. The two of them went into the empty rooms into which the two girls had gone before them. They even disturbed the old woman, back alone now at the top of the house, a game of demon patience laid out before her. Querulously she told them in an English which neither of them could understand: 'Oh, but I've already said – he's not here – not here! Not with me! My son has gone to call the police. The *police!*' She spoke that last word with extreme emphasis, dividing its syllables. In growing panic, the ayah opened cupboards, looked under beds, and wandered, the bearer pattering behind her, between the sheeted furniture, tea chests, cabin-trunks and suitcases crammed into the loft which formed the spine of the humped, sprawling house. It was in the loft that the two girls, hearing movements overhead, came on them.

'We've looked here already, he's not here,' Helen said, in her fluent Hindustani, learned as a child. The ayah folded her hands before her and bowed, as though to ask forgiveness for some delinquency. She then asked: 'What about the memsahib's room?' Helen replied that he was not there, no one must disturb the memsahib.

Eventually the two girls went and sat out on the verandah, to wait for Toby's return with the police. They sat, the ayah noticed, as, alone now, she still went on with her search in the garden, far apart from each other, Helen lying back, her eyes closed, in a deckchair at one end of the verandah, and Clare leaning forward, one hand clasping the other at the wrist as though to take her own pulse, on an upright, wooden one at the other end. Clare was gripping the ivory cigarette holder between her clenched teeth but for once there was no cigarette in it. Far off, from the Victorian Gothic church invisible but for its spire sticking up like a needle through the dark green fabric of the branches knitted roughly together around the lake, there came a monotonous pealing. It was Sunday, the ayah realized. Now that Nanny Rose, the only church-goer in the family, was no longer there, Sundays went unremarked except for the leg of lamb or round of beef at luncheon.

The gardener padded towards her over the tennis court with his shrivelled 'boy' behind him. The boy seemed reluctant, even fearful. The gardener said, 'The *chota sahib* is lost?' The ayah nodded. The 'boy' stood a few feet away from them, picking his nose with a long, exploratory finger. The ayah said, a note of panic for the first time in her voice: 'What can have happened to him?' and then the bearer, who had abandoned the ayah to go about his usual morning tasks, came out to join them in his crisp white trousers and tunic. He combed his beard with his fingernails, a faintly supercilious expression on his face. They were Hindus, only he and the cook were Muslims. 'The *chota sahib* is lost?' he said on the same note of interrogation as the gardener. 'Lost,' the 'boy' repeated vacantly. He rubbed one bare leg, stork-like, against the other and some of the soil caked to the dark brown skin crumbled and scattered. 'What are we to do?' the gardener asked. He turned, not to the bearer, but to the ayah, sensing in her a quiet authority which the bearer, for all his overweening manner, lacked. The ayah spread out her hands, with those strangely pink, yielding palms. Then she looked distractedly around her, as though suddenly – from behind that privet hedge over there, from under that garden roller, from the shelter of a rosebush or the tangle of the tennis net rolled up by its post – radiant and laughing at them for all this needless fuss, her *baba*, the *chota sahib*, would emerge. She longed for that to happen, she half-believed that it would – just as, with a mingling of longing and half-belief, she repeatedly told herself that some day, somehow she would visit Nanny Rose, bearing her glutinous yellow sweets or a bunch of the wild flowers which she had taken such joy in pressing between the pages of her Bible.

Then something caught the ayah's eye, on the slope of the hill, over-arched by branches so dark that at this hour of the day they looked almost black, above the greenish rash of the tennis court which only the two girls now ever used. She pointed. 'Did you look there?'

The three men gazed in the direction of her finger. The gardener shook his head. The 'boy' backed away, as he did when Toby, in one of his brief, volcanic rages, shouted at him either for having done something amiss or for having failed to do something at all. The bearer shrugged his shoulders.

'We must look there then,' the ayah said, suddenly aware that the two white girls had left their chairs and were standing side by side, motionless and rigid, at a corner of the verandah from which they could watch the four servants. For a moment, the ayah gazed at them with an equal intensity. Then, raising the folds of her sari with one hand to make it easier for her to climb, she started up the zigzag path. The bearer stared down at the ground between his feet, twitched a shoulder, again ran fingernails through his luxuriant, greying beard. The 'boy' showed a similar disinclination to follow, going down on his hunkers and lethargically tugging at some weeds. Only the gardener went up after her.

Having ascended, spine erect and head thrown back, the ayah advanced along the path flickering ahead of her in rapid alternations of sunlight and shade. Her bare feet slapped down now on earth, now on rock, now on jagged stone, indifferent to the changes. The gardener, more circumspect, picked his way, head lowered. The ayah put out a hand, pushed at the creaking door of the little-used lavatory, hesitated on an indrawn breath, entered, stood motionless. In the gloom and stench, she looked about her. A shaft of light from the aperture high up in the wall made the side of the huge pottery urn glisten. A bird trilled, repeatedly, three falling notes. She turned head, right, left, right, all senses alert, as though she feared some ambush. The gardener stood in the doorway, picking at a frayed corner of his sweat-stained tunic. There were some dark blotches on the ground. There were similar dark blotches on the wooden slat with a hole in it, above the malodorous pit. The ayah peered at the slat, the wrinkles around her wary eyes deepening. She put down a hand, rubbed a palm on one of the blotches on the slat, raised it, examined the smear, sticky and near-black on pink flesh. Then she let out a brief wail, 'Ai-ee!' The gardener jerked back, the whites of his by now prominent eyes glistening like the sides of the urn in the light from the aperture above. Again the three bird notes fell through the silence.

Intrepid, the ayah stepped forward, the bangles jingling round her ankles. She peered down through the hole in the slat. Something silvery-grey glinted up out of the darkness of the pit. 'Ai-ee!' she wailed again. Then she turned to the gardener, motionless in the doorway, his head cocked on one side as though in an effort to hear those three falling notes of the invisible bird. 'It's as I thought, as I knew!'

There was a sound of feet outside the privy. Then Helen was there. 'What is it?' she asked in Hindustani. 'Have you found him?'

The ayah nodded. She pointed.

Helen went forward, she too peered down into the pit. 'Get a torch! Clare, get a torch!' Clare was standing outside, shoulders hunched and her fingers pressed to her lips. 'Clare!' There was no response. Helen ran out, pushing past the girl. 'Oh, never mind, I'll get it.'

The ayah looked over her shoulder. Then she bent forward, stretched out her arms, as she once used to do when she lifted this child, whom she thought of as her own, out of the zinc bath, and pushed them downwards into the fetid ordure. (Later, she was to be told: 'You should have waited for us to come, you should have left everything as it was.') She groaned, grunted, turned her head towards the gardener, silently beseeching his aid. But he merely stared in horror. She went down on her knees, feeling against them the harshness and dampness of the concrete floor. A fold of her sari, jerked out of place, now screened all her features but her nose, the gold stud glittering in it. Again her hands plunged, her face contracted in an anguish of effort. Dripping – how often had he dripped over her sari as she had lifted him, crowing and struggling, from the zinc bath, to wrap him in the towel warmed by the paraffin stove – she felt his body in her arms, the head falling back unnaturally and every part of him smeared and soiled. She held out the body of the child as though to pass it to the gardener, but he retreated from her, muttering something inaudible.

At that moment, breathless from having raced down the zigzag path and then up again, Helen appeared in the doorway of the privy, the torch, which always rested on the hall table in readiness for one of the frequent power failures, held in her hand. She pushed past the gardener, switched on the torch. In the dim, yellow circle of light – for weeks now Isabel had been telling Toby that the torch needed new batteries and Toby in turn had been telling Mr Ram and Hilda – the black gash under the child's throat, running from ear to ear, stood out against the pallor of the girlish chin above it.

Helen said: 'You've found him.' Her voice was steady.

She still held the torch on the corpse. The ayah looked down. Was that the filth from the pit or was it a bruise which darkened the whole area around the open mouth? The eyes stared up at her blearily, through lashes clotted with a grey-green sediment, which had also bunged up a nostril.

A suspicion, as cold and slimy as her dead darling's flesh on her flesh, slithered up, snake-like, within her.

VI

The Inspector of Police of the district was away in England on leave and it was therefore his assistant, Singh, whom Toby had ridden off in the hope of finding. Unlike Hunt, who was lazy, Singh, relentlessly ambitious, often worked on Sundays.

Singh, son of a wealthy Brahmin merchant, had been educated at a public school in England where, clever at work and a muff at games, he had been bullied by the other boys and patronized by the masters. His father had wished him to go to Oxford or Cambridge but, with a characteristic mixture of pliancy and stubborness, the boy had quietly resisted him.

Singh was in the habit of wearing pale grey suits, expensively tailored from the finest mohair or worsted in Delhi or even London, striped shirts with stiff collars and cuffs always showing crisp and clean an inch below each jacket sleeve, and wide, dark-hued ties held in place with a pearl or diamond pin. One of his eyeteeth was capped with gold and there was a gold signet ring, too bulky to be approved by the British, who thought it vulgar, on the curiously long little finger of his left hand. His melancholy, delicate face was of the same pale grey colour as his suits.

He had just seated himself at his desk in his office, having taken off his jacket with its narrow lapels and small ticket-pocket and hung it on the coat hanger presented to him by one of his *babus*, when Toby burst in, the freckles standing out on his white, sweaty face, to announce: 'Singh, something terrible has happened, my boy's been stolen. We must have a search party – at once!'

It maddened Toby that the tall Indian should uncoil himself so slowly from his chair and take so much time to slip first one arm and then the other into the jacket, lined with pale mauve silk, which he had removed from the coat hanger on the door. 'I don't understand,' he drawled in that parody of the British ruling class. 'Stolen?' The two men, so dissimilar, had always distrusted and despised each other. Singh, patiently well informed, knew about Toby's constant escapades with women and, with a queasy puritanism derived from his years in England, was shocked by them. Toby thought Singh a supercilious prig.

'Some dacoits must have taken him. Who knows? For God's sake get a move on! Do something, man!'

But Singh remained outwardly poised and deliberate, even if his usually pale face darkened with annoyance. Who was this fat, sweaty, blustering lecher to address him like a servant? He summoned some of his men and gave them instructions to comb both the area around the house and the native quarter. Then he picked up the telephone and began to ring round to his colleagues in the neighbouring towns and villages. It was not always easy to make the connections and, when they were made, the lines were not always clear. But while he watched Toby with wary, contemptuous eyes – restlessly, the Englishman flung himself down in a chair covered with creaking leather, jumped up, strode to the window and looked out, muttered under his breath, came and stood over the Indian, again strode to the window, again flung himself down in the chair, crossed his legs, recrossed them, bit on a knuckle – Singh never for a moment showed any impatience either with the operator or with the invisible people to whom he spoke. At the end he said: 'Well, that's that. Now we'd better go up to the house.'

Reluctantly, for all his impatience, Toby had been impressed.

'We've looked everywhere. There's no sign of him.'

Singh gave a small, superior smile. 'Children have a knack of disappearing and reappearing.'

Toby ignored that. 'How do you propose to travel?'

'I'll take the car to the end of the road. Then – well, I suppose I'll walk up.' Singh never mounted a horse unless he had to.

'Oh, all right. In that case, I'd better make my way back alone. But hurry, for God's sake! Who knows . . . ?'

132

Suddenly, the Indian felt sorry for this man, the stains of perspiration dark under the sleeves of his shirt, his small, green eyes peering from under the reddish eyebrows with a dazed intensity, and his voice jaggedly rasping.

'So many terrible things have happened in recent months. There was that attempt to poison me. Remember? I have enemies, a man like me has enemies.'

Again that small, superior smile as Singh stretched out a hand to the Englishman's shoulder and gave it a squeeze. He had learned how to patronize others from having so often been patronized himself. 'Yes, I know, I know,' he said, though he had never accepted that theory of poisoning. It was far more likely that some food had gone off. He himself, a bachelor, took meticulous care that his cook never kept leftovers for more than twenty-four hours in the icebox.

Toby galloped off in a cloud of dust, turning once to raise a hand to Singh, as though in warning, not goodbye.

Singh climbed into the police Austin beside his driver. Two uniformed men got in behind him. He drew a flat cigarette case, his initials inlaid in gold on its silver, from his breast pocket, clicked it open and removed a Sobranie Egyptian ('a woman's cigarette,' Toby would remark contemptuously of this preference to others). The driver produced a lighter with his left hand from the glove pocket. Singh leant his head forward, drew in, exhaled. The child would have wandered off somewhere, he would turn up. Stolen . . . He smiled at the word. Toby had always struck him as extremely maladroit in his use of language.

VII

The grey stumbled and all but fell as Toby urged him up a short cut so steep that he had to clutch with one hand at his mane and with the other at the saddle-bow to prevent himself from falling off. The hooves scrabbled, stones cascaded downwards. Then, with a heave and a lurch, the grey was back on the path.

Suddenly, far ahead of him, framed by overhanging branches, Toby saw them. They stood motionless, the three women, in the centre of the path, the sunlight, filtering through the greenery, making their faces come into focus and fade, come into focus and fade, as though with each pulse of the blood thudding at his temples. One of them, Helen, raised an arm and waved it, in slow semaphore, from side to side. Toby kicked at the horse with even more savagery than before, grunting: 'Damn you! Get on! Get *on*!'

The women did not move towards him. As he approached, the arm which Helen had been waving fell to her side. Her face was extraordinarily still and white against all the agitated greenery.

'Any news?'

Helen nodded calmly.

'Where was the little blighter? Where was he? Where was he?'

'Father . . . he's dead.' She stepped forward. She firmly took the head of the grey, as though afraid that, having received this news, Toby would gallop away.

All at once Mrs Thompson set up an eerie, uncontrollable keening.

VIII

The body lay out on a blanket woven in mills, hundreds and hundreds of miles away, belonging to Toby. The blanket had been spread on the dining-room table, the curtains drawn against the sunlight which flooded down, warm wave after wave, on old Mrs Thompson, outstretched, mute and motionless, on a deckchair in the garden, her usually hard, tight face, bound together by innumerable wrinkles, now seeming to deliquesce beneath it. It was Helen who had sent Clare for the blanket.

'Fetch a blanket!' she had shouted down to where the other

girl stood, as though in a trance, in the centre of the tennis court, her fingers once again pressed, in that gesture which suggested the choking back either of words or of sobs, against her mouth, while she stared, not up at the privy, but down the drive which had carried Toby headlong away on his horse.

Clare had merely raised her eyes up to Helen.

'A blanket! Get a blanket! Any blanket!'

Clare took a step, halted, then stared up again. 'Have you found him?'

'Yes. He's . . . Oh, get a move on!'

Still in that seeming trance, Clare began to move slowly towards the house. When she reappeared with a blanket off her bed, she trailed it behind her across the tennis court. Helen shouted to the gardener in Hindustani: 'Get it from her!' she shouted. The gardener went.

Helen held out the blanket (Nanny Rose held out the thick Turkish towel) and the ayah, with a deep, surrendering sigh, lifted the child towards her. 'Help me', Helen said. She spoke the words in English, not in Hindustani, but the ayah understood, going close to her and half-supporting the corpse about which Helen was wrapping the blanket to make a plaid cocoon. Stumbling and staggering, the girl and the woman, both strangely tranquil, carried their burden down the hillside, across the tennis court, past the Eurasian girl, once again motionless, those fingers pressed to her lips, towards the bearer who now stood, with Mr Ram and Hilda, both of whom he had summoned, by the French windows to the drawing room. Hilda's glasses, as thick as the bottoms of lemonade bottles, again flashed fire as she jerked her head away. Licking his lips, Mr Ram goggled. 'What could have happened?' he asked no one in particular. 'Who would want to do such a thing? My God!'

. . . Now Helen said: 'Don't go in, father. You don't want to go in. It'll only upset you.' But Toby pushed past her. Helen followed and then Hilda, an expression of determined eagerness on her face, as though this terrible confrontation between father and dead son was something which she could not possibly forego. Toby walked over to the table at which, with that relentless voracity of his, he had wolfed so many meals, put out a hand and jerked back the blanket. Hilda gasped, her open mouth, its corners downturned, giving her a fish-like appearance. The bruises round the mouth of the child made it appear, in the low wattage of the overhead light, as if some acid had burned away the flesh, leaving a gaping hole. A hand lay stiffly open, two slashes across the palm, each encrusted with beads of blood like tiny scabs. There was a slash in the pyjama jacket, puckered with the same scab-like beads. The smell was repellent.

Toby stared down for a long time, frowning as though in an attempt to solve one of those problems – should he or should he not buy into Cawnpore Textiles? Would it be wise or unwise to extend the hotel in Simla? – which daily beset him. But, for once, he seemed unable to come up with a solution. Then he turned: 'This bloody country! Christ, this bloody country!'

The old woman still lay outstretched on the verandah. Isabel was still in her bedroom. The servants and Mr Ram still stood in a silent group, crowded together, as though for safety, at the far end of the hallway. Clare was still alone on the tennis court, fingers pressed to lips. Only Helen and Hilda heard him.

'Father!' Helen stepped forward and tried to take him in her arms. But, an open hand to her shoulder, he pushed her away from him.

He stumbled across the hall, into the drawing room and out through the French windows, which he opened with a blind, blundering gesture of fingers refusing to do his bidding. Then he staggered over to an Albertine rose, a spume of white frothing over the red-brick wall beyond which the *cud* plunged downwards, made a sound as of clearing his throat, made it again and suddenly began to vomit. Tears filled his eyes.

'Father. Don't. Don't.' It was Helen.

He straightened himself, gasping.

Reaching up, she drew from the breast pocket of his

136

short-sleeved, sweat-darkened shirt an unused handkerchief, unfolded it and first wiped him around the mouth and then pressed it to his clammy forehead. 'Please. Don't, don't, don't.'

'Christ!' he muttered. 'Oh, Christ, Christ, Christ!'

At that moment the ayah appeared, holding a glass in a hand. She had never before, in all her years of service, poured out from a bottle of alcohol belonging to her masters. She extended the glass, her sari still blotched and stiff with blood and ordure, though she had washed her arms, hands and face.

'Drink it,' Helen said. 'Drink it. You'll feel better.'

'Is she trying to poison me?' Toby demanded with a brief, snorting laugh, almost a sob. But he put out his hand, took the glass and drained the whisky at a gulp. Then he asked: 'Has anyone told your stepmother?'

IX

Having returned to her bed, Isabel lay humped, left cheek to pillow and legs drawn up as though to ease some acute abdominal pain, in the darkened room. It was long past the hour when, so regular in all her habits, she would normally be up and about. It was impossible that she could have remained unaware of all the commotion in the house, with people hurrying around and above her in search of the missing child, Helen shouting orders to Clare, standing there in the middle of the tennis court, and first Toby galloping up the drive and then Singh and his two men hurrying up it on foot.

Toby, his red hair sticking up in dishevelled tufts, put out a hand. 'Isabel,' he whispered. Then louder: 'Isabel.'

She stirred, drew the sheet over her head. Then she groaned: 'Oh, go away, go away, leave me!'

'But Isabel . . . Isabel . . .' She did not move, made no further sound. The sheet cocooned her, as the blanket had cocooned the dead child. Toby strode to the window and tugged back the curtains with so much violence that, a brass ring at the end of one of them shooting off the rail, it sagged crazily downwards.

The light exploded into the room. 'Don't, don't!' she cried out in panic.

Toby threw himself down on the bed beside her. He attempted to pull back the sheet, as he insisted: 'Listen to me, listen to me' but, her fingers gripping it tightly, she would not release it. He put his lips to the sheet, his body shuddering heavily on hers, in a weird parody of the lovemaking which, for so many months now, ever since her pregnancy, she had refused to allow him. 'Isabel, darling . . . Darling . . . You must get up, you must listen to me. Listen! Listen!' He put his arms about her shrouded form. Then, all at once, he was sobbing, with terrible, heaving gulps, not unlike his retching by the Albertine rose. 'Something terrible has happened.'

He was amazed when, from under the sheet, he heard her despairing voice: 'I know. I know.'

X

Later, old Mrs Thompson knocked on the door. Isabel still lay on the bed but she was on her back, her arms to her side, her legs straight together, while her mountainous belly rose up under the bedclothes. Staring up at the ceiling, she did not turn her head when her mother-in-law sidled in crab-wise, the rubber ferrule of her stick lisping across the highly polished linoleum surrounding the Persian carpet.

'What is one to say?' Mrs Thompson asked, genuinely not knowing.

Isabel made no answer. The old woman cautiously approached the bed, sat down on the edge of it. She was breathing heavily both from the effort of climbing up the stairs and from the terror which kept squeezing her heart.

'Who would want to do such a thing? Who? To a child, a mere child. He never harmed anyone.' Mrs Thompson was convinced that 'a good cry' would do Isabel 'a world of good' – those were the words which she had used to Toby but, slumped in an armchair in the drawing room, while Singh, Dr

McGregor and Singh's men went about their tasks, he had not seemed to hear her.

Suddenly, Isabel sat bolt upright. She stared for a moment at the startled old woman as though she were a stranger, and then said in a thick, hoarse voice: 'Please give me my brush.'

'Your brush, dear? Yes, yes, of course.'

The old woman heaved herself off the end of the bed and tottered over to the dressing-table. She picked up the silver-backed hairbrush, once the property of Eithne, and, as she carried it over, absentmindedly removed from it a single, long, black, glossy hair. 'Shall I brush your hair for you?' she offered.

Isabel held out a hand, the sleeve of her nightdress falling away from her plump arm, without an answer. Mrs Thompson gave her the brush. Holding the brush in one hand and a hank of hair in the other, Isabel savagely lashed at it. The old woman stared, leaning on her stick.

Then Isabel paused in the rhythmical strokes. Above the life swollen within her, her breasts rose and fell. Suddenly, her previously impassive face trembled, widened, seemed to the old woman to shatter to pieces, as she had once seen the windscreen of Toby's Rolls-Royce shatter when a stone had flown up from the roadside and detonated against it. Isabel wailed and wailed again. It was a sound exactly like the ayah's 'Ai-ee!' when she had first realized that it was blood which blotched the floor and the slat of the servants' privy and when she had seen that shape in the slime. She hurled the hairbrush to the floor and then angrily demanded of the old woman quailing before her: 'Why? Why? Why?'

'I suppose it was God's will,' Mrs Thompson replied. Though she rarely went to church, she believed in God.

'Oh, fuck God! It was *someone's* will but let's leave God out of it, because God just isn't there.'

The old woman felt the imminence of tears. As in the case of the urine which now sometimes involuntarily trickled from her, she struggled to hold them. In a placating, importuning voice she said: 'Toby thinks that some of those men – those dacoits . . .'

'Oh, does he? Does he?' Isabel sank back among the pillows. Suddenly all the colour had once again ebbed from her face. 'How could that little bitch not have heard someone go into the bedroom and take him? How? How?'

The old woman shrugged. 'I don't know, dear. I just don't know.'

'Precisely.'

It was a relief to Mrs Thompson when, at that moment, Dr McGregor came into the room with Toby behind him.

'Well, now,' Dr McGregor said, his speech already slurred from the whisky to which he had helped himself from Toby's decanter. 'I came in to see how you were getting on, Isabel. I thought it might be a good idea if I were to give you a wee injection.'

'No,' Isabel said. She swung her firm, plump legs off the bed and stood up in her nightdress. 'No, I don't need anything. I must get dressed.'

'Isabel –,' Toby began.

'I must get dressed,' she repeated.

XI

Singh had decided that the pit in the privy must be emptied, but he could not order any of his men to empty it. He himself viewed caste as a preposterous anachronism – it seemed as if people, however humble, always needed others, even more humble than themselves, whom they could despise – but it was beyond his powers to defy its canons. So two of his men squatted on their hunkers outside the doorway of the shed, looking on, while the Thompsons' sweeper and another sweeper summoned from the police station used buckets and shovels to ladle out the ordure into oil-drums. With arms and legs so thin that they looked like constructions of wire and clay, they sighed, grunted and muttered, totally oblivious of a stench in which they passed their daily lives. One of the policemen held a blue-and-white checked handkerchief over

140

his mouth and nose. The other, more stoical, merely swallowed repeatedly, the adam's apple bouncing up and down in his scrawny neck.

Though so late in the year, it was a day of unusual heat. There was a greenish sheen, as of verdigris around the rim of the lake, as it glittered up, a brazen platter, beneath a sky of sulphurous orange. The policeman with the handkerchief remarked that there was likely to be a storm and his colleague, shifting uncomfortably in a uniform too tight for him, the fabric like a truss against his crotch as he squatted, nodded his agreement. The sweepers did not sweat.

What Singh had hoped to find was a knife, thrown into the pit with the dead child. What the sweepers found was first a blanket, similar to the one which Clare had fetched for Helen, and then, improbably and grotesquely, a brassière. Both were so much smeared and caked with filth that Singh, summoned by one of the two policemen, first had difficulty in deciding what they were. Later, the blanket was found not merely to be heavily stained with ordure but also to have blood on it.

In the gloom and stench of the privy, the flies, of which the sweepers had been totally oblivious, fretting him with their ceaseless buzzing and their settling on his face and bare arms, Singh felt a sudden, ineluctable weariness, such as often now overcame him in the course of his work. It was as though, all at once, a traveller paused in his lengthy journey and, deciding that he could not face yet another road, yet another railway station, yet another gangway to board yet another ship, had to resist the abject, insistent urge to turn and retrace his steps back to his by now far-off home.

XII

In a locked room at the police station, the small body now lay packed in dry ice. In Toby's long, low-ceilinged, empty office, Dr McGregor, biting on the stem of his pipe, frowned down at the sheet of paper before him, while with the nail of a forefinger he picked gently at a spot on the corner of his chin. Then he got up, shoulders hunched, and began to pull open the drawers of desks and filing cabinets and to open cupboards. 'Blast!' He said it aloud. Toby must have some booze somewhere, if only to offer to the bigwigs who came to see him on business. One cupboard, high in the wall above Toby's desk, would not yield to McGregor's persistent turning of the handle and tugging. Stingy bastard! Obviously he kept his booze under lock and key. He put a hand to the flask at his hip, as though momentarily hoping that, by some magic, it had refilled itself; but then, reality reasserting itself, he withdrew the hand. He thought of going out to look for the bearer or even for Toby. But when he had last asked for a refill, before he had come in here to write his preliminary report, Toby had gazed at him with the same fastidious distaste for his drinking which he himself felt for Toby's philandering.

McGregor again settled himself at the desk and the nicotine-stained forefinger again picked at the spot. Then he took up his broad-nibbed fountain-pen and, mouth dry and a slight feeling of pressure behind the eyes, he began to write: *. . . The blanket and pyjamas caked with excrement and blood – more of former than latter*. Excrement? Cross that out. *Night-soil. . . . Throat cut to bone by some sharp instrument, from left to right . . .* Right to left? No, no, left to right. He picked up the empty glass next to him, raised it to his lips, tipped it and his head back simultaneously. *Completely divided all membranes, blood-vessels, nerve-vessels, air-tubes*. Christ, what a filthy, fucking country! Toby was right. In eighteen months, thank God, he'd be out of it, back home, but Toby, with all his business interests, would have to stick it out. . . . *Afterwards found stab on body, evidently made by some broad, sharp, long, strong implement, as it penetrated through pyjamas passing below pericardium and diaphragm and severed cartilages of two ribs, extending three-fourths across chest*. He bit on the stem of the pipe, gazed at the green glass shade of the lamp, reaching out to him on its spindly brass arm, and then resumed. *Pericardium must have been pushed out of place by* *compression of side, or it would have passed through that. Could not have been a razor.* He rested his chin on his outstretched arm, thinking of his own cut-throat razors, kept in a mahogany case, one of which, each morning, his bearer would sharpen for him on a leather strap. *Must have been* – he paused, then made a faint question-mark above the 'must' – *a sharp-pointed, long, wide and strong knife.* Am I repeating myself? Check that later. *Wound not less than four inches deep. Also two small cuts on left hand but only vestigial appearance of blood on them.*

Time, time of killing? He got up, went to the door, the glass in his trembling hand, and then shambled back, with that humped stance of his, one shoulder higher than the other and an elbow uptilted, almost as though he were deformed. *Am of opinion that child* – no, no, cross that out – *that deceased had been dead at least eight or nine hours before I examined him at approximately eleven-thirty. Then quite cold and rigidity had set in. Guess that he was killed in early hours of morning.* Guess? Well, yes, it was a guess, he had performed a number of autopsies but he still abjectly distrusted his judgement. *Killed in early hours of morning.* Yes, in this country, that was the dangerous time, between dark and dawn, when, silently, thieves clambered through windows which seemed too small even for a child or, as nimble as monkeys, shinned up drainpipes. *Blackened appearance all round child's mouth most likely produced by violent thrusting of brassière into mouth to prevent screaming.* He paused again, the empty pipe clenched between small, yellow teeth. *Or could have been produced by hand thrusting downwards. My opinion death from suffocation preceded infliction of wounds. Otherwise, quantity of blood would have been much greater. Child of that size would have sent out with a gush, at one jet, quantity of blood not less than three pints, whereas I do not think there was more than* . . . Well, what? Estimate, estimate.

The door opened and Toby, changed now from his riding-breeches and short-sleeved silk shirt into dinner jacket, stood there, as though the office were not his. McGregor stared at him. Amazing thing, habit! Only that morning a patient of his, with no more than a few days to live, skin and bone, nothing more, had insisted that the Indian barber must be summoned because on the first and third Thursday of each month he always had his hair cut. And now here was Toby in a dinner jacket . . .

'How's it going?'

McGregor shrugged. 'Like to get my notes down when they're still fresh in my mind. Of course, so far I've done only a preliminary examination. . . . They'll have to do –'

'Yes, yes,' Toby cut him off, as though he could not bear to hear of it. He went over to the window and, hot forehead pressed to chill glass, stared down towards the lake, a silvery streak with lights glittering round it. 'Yes, yes,' he repeated mechanically. Then he muttered, as he had muttered before: 'What a bloody country!'

McGregor got up, went to him and, with extreme awkwardness, put an arm round his shoulder. 'What can one say?' It was what, in the future, many of the British were to ask Toby and Isabel. Their horror at the murder was as far beyond their ability to express as the Himalayas around them to climb.

Toby moved away, not caring to have this dishevelled little man, the combination of whisky and hunger sour on his breath, touch him so intimately.

'We're going to eat,' he said. 'Or try to eat. You'll join us, won't you?'

McGregor shook his head. 'Thanks. But I'll be finished in a jiffy and then I'll make for home. The wife's expecting me.' He could not bear the prospect of sitting with the bereaved family, all either silent or making effortful conversation, while they forced their cold Sunday supper down throats closing against every mouthful.

'Another drink then?'

'Well, that's mighty civil of you, mighty civil.' McGregor tried to show his gratitude, even though a truly civil man might have omitted that 'another'.

'Fine. I'll send Muhammed along. Whisky, isn't it?'

As though Toby did not know. But never mind, no sweat. At least he could polish off the rest of the preliminary report in a matter of minutes, once he had that drink down the hatch.

XIII

'Am I intruding?'

Toby pushed between the three men crowded round the French windows through which he had entered from the garden and approached Singh, who was perched, arms folded, on the edge of Isabel's desk.

'Not at all.' Singh rose. 'What can I do for you, Mr Thompson?' As always, he gave a slight, mocking emphasis to the 'Mr'. To Toby he himself was merely 'Singh'.

'How long is all this *tamasha* going on?'

'*Tamasha*?' Singh drew his sleek eyebrows together, as though puzzled by the Hindustani word, meaning confusion or to-do.

'It's damned inconvenient. And upsetting too – at a time like this. This is precisely the sort of time when one would hope to be left alone and in peace.' Yet Toby had kept a tally of those friends, acquaintances and business associates who had left them alone and in peace and those who had telephoned or written their letters of shock, outrage and condolence. He would not easily forgive the former.

'I can understand that, Mr Thompson. And truly I'm sorry. But we have our duty to do.'

'Yes. Of course. But I honestly can't see why you and your men have to continue to hang around the house.'

Singh gave a gentle, understanding smile. 'Well, at this precise moment we're fingerprinting this room. As you see. That has to be done. Then we'll match the fingerprints.'

'You mean, you'll want our fingerprints?'

Singh nodded. 'The family's. The servants'. A process of elimination. If we find a print not belonging to any of you, then we're on to something.' He explained as to a child, patient and reassuring.

'I see.' Toby sighed and picked up the copy of *The Times*,

four weeks old, for which he had originally come into the room. 'It all seems pointless to me.'

'Pointless?'

'Whoever killed my boy – the man, the men – must by now be miles and miles away. You never caught the people who set fire to the mission.'

Singh nodded. 'True.'

'These people might be those.'

'Yes.'

'You've not found the knife?'

Singh shook his head. 'A knife is an expensive thing – for a poor Indian. If it's needed for further use . . . ' He shrugged. 'No knife is missing from the house?'

'The cook and the bearer say not.'

'Yes, one of my men has already had a word with the servants about it. But I thought perhaps your wife . . . ?'

Toby compressed his lips. 'It's not something about which I'd like to ask her now. Not in her present state. In any case, I doubt if she keeps a tally. Knives get lost, broken.'

'This must have been a large knife. It would be difficult to lose.' Singh glanced at the two men dusting the windows and at the third merely supervising them. 'Mr Thompson, let's go into the garden. It'll be cooler and quieter there. No, not through those windows. We'd better go round.'

The two men walked in silence down the corridor, Toby's heavy footsteps dragging behind Singh's firm, sprightly ones. Singh held open the front door, inclining his head with the same mocking deference with which he used that 'Mr'. 'Please.' Toby all but tripped on the sill.

Singh stationed himself in the middle of the tennis court in the soft radiance of the late afternoon. He glanced all round him, as though afraid of eavesdroppers. Then he said: 'This case certainly has its puzzling aspects.'

'I'd have thought it perfectly simple. Well, yes, of course, it's puzzling in as much as we still don't know who precisely . . . ' Toby found that he was unable to continue 'killed my son'. His voice trailed away, to strengthen once

146

more: 'But the rest of it is clear. Surely? I have a number of enemies, no one can reach my sort of position without having enemies. Without intending to do so, one ruins a man. Or one sacks a man. You know about revenge in this country. My wife's brother . . . '

'Yes.' The voice was quiet. 'I know about your wife's brother.'

'And only a short while ago someone tried to poison me.'

Singh shrugged, turning down the corners of his mouth with a fleeting incredulity.

'If it's not an act of revenge against me personally, then it might well be an act against the Raj – through one of the most influential and richest of its representatives in this province.' He peered at Singh from under lowered brows. 'Mightn't it?'

'Of course.'

Toby sensed the underlying doubt in the assurance. 'Well, then, what are these puzzling aspects of which you talk?'

Singh brought the palms of his hands together, as though in the Hindu gesture of greeting. Toby stared at the gold signet ring, heavily embossed with its monogram, on the Indian's left little finger. Its ostentation had always irritated him, as it irritated others of the British. 'What I keep asking myself is – how did this man or men enter?'

'Through the window. The window was open.'

'Yes. But who opened the window? You've already told me that every night, last thing, you go round the whole house to make sure that every latch and bolt is fastened. Yes?'

Toby nodded.

'Well, then? You see my difficulty.'

Toby frowned down at the tennis court, like a small boy stumped by some elementary problem in mental arithmetic. 'Someone could have opened the window from inside,' he eventually said.

'Precisely.'

'A servant can't be ruled out. For example – your bearer lets himself and the other servants into the house each morning, with his key to the back door.'

'But Muhammed's totally loyal. Trustworthy. He's been with me for, oh, years and years.'

'His key might have been ... borrowed. Without his knowing. It might then have been duplicated. You've only got to go down to the bazaar to find stalls where keys can be duplicated in a matter of seconds. At those stalls you can also buy keys. A key will often fit a lock for which it was not intended.'

'Yes.' Toby nodded, biting on his lower lip. 'Yes, yes.'

'That's a possibility.'

Toby scuffed with his shoe at the gravel of the tennis court. 'I see no other.'

'Your governess?'

'Clare?' Toby's eyes widened, his face suddenly became congested.

'Her Christian name is Clare? Oh, yes, of course . . . She must be a heavy sleeper.'

Toby squinted angrily at the Indian. 'She'd taken a pill. A pill my wife gave her. For her migraines, she suffers from migraines. You know how silently a dacoit can move. The Elsworths – you must remember. They slept undisturbed while a man – men – ransacked their bedroom and went off with all her jewellery and furs.'

'Yes. I remember.' Singh was not at that moment interested in the story of the Elsworths' burglary. 'In the lavatory, the servants' lavatory up there, my men found a blanket. Well, we know what that was used for – the child, dead or alive, was wrapped in it. He was wrapped in it and then carried out through that window.' He pointed. 'We also found a brassière.'

'A brassière?' Toby screwed up his small, green eyes, as though trying to focus them on something in the distance.

Singh nodded. 'Apparently it belonged – belongs – to Miss O'Connor. Clare,' he added.

There was a silence. Then Toby asked: 'And what do you infer from that?' There was a sudden firmness, as of challenge, in his previously hoarse, tremulous voice.

'Well . . . ' Singh drawled the word and then hesitated, deliberating how much it would be politic to reveal to Toby and so, through him, to the household. Then he went on: 'It confirms Mr McGregor's supposition. Your son was suffocated, that was how he died. Later – the mutilation took place. He was suffocated by the brassière being pressed against his mouth.'

Toby gazed at him, his green eyes protuberant under lids puffy and reddened by sleeplessness and grief. 'I see.'

Singh began to walk slowly across the tennis court; Toby followed. The Indian plucked at a fern trailing out of the brick retaining-wall and squeezed it in his palm, as though it were a saturated sponge. Then he threw it away with a gesture of impatience. It had stained his palm green. 'Miss O'Connor – there's never been any trouble with her, has there?'

Toby licked his lips. 'Trouble? None at all. She's always been' – he swallowed – 'perfectly satisfactory.'

'Did she have a boyfriend?'

'A boyfriend?' There was a dazed look in the small, green eyes.

'An attractive girl. Young. It seems likely.'

'Well, yes . . . there was a soldier. She had a soldier friend. Perhaps still has him. I don't know his name. I know little about it, it's not something with which I'd concern myself. But my wife mentioned to me . . . ' Toby did not tell Singh of how Isabel had had to reprimand Clare for meeting the boy when she was out with Peter.

'He never visited her here?'

'Good God, no!'

'She was fond of your son?'

'Of course! Everyone was fond of him. He was . . . ' Toby's voice broke. 'One couldn't help being fond of him.' Again that strong, firm note, as of challenge. 'I can't, for the life of me, see the drift of these questions.'

Singh smiled. 'The life of a policeman is one of continual questions.'

149

XIV

A slow, expected death has a way of irresistibly sucking the members of a family together down its dark funnel. This death, as violent and unexpected as the explosion following the detonation of a bomb, had the opposite effect of blowing the members of the Thompson family in separate directions, however much they struggled to cling to each other. They were awkward and tonguetied in each other's presences. Each was afraid of seeming callous by talking too much or too loudly or too often of trivial things. Each felt under the scrutiny, not merely of the Indians in their midst, but of each other. Each felt an embarrassment as acute as their grief.

Isabel wandered about the house, her face grey and stern. 'You don't have to bother about all these things, forget about them,' Toby urged her. 'They don't matter. Mother can see to them. Or Helen or Clare.' But she would not be deflected. She insisted on resuming her daily routine of unlocking the store-cupboards and apportioning out to the cook everything that he would need for the next twenty-four hours. She supervised the cleaning of the house, imperiously ordering the servants in Hindustani 'There! There! No, *there*!' as she pointed to some piece of fluff still stuck to a rug or to some specks of dust still glittering in the sunlight on a table. At meals, she sat erect, her jaws chomping steadily, as though there were some heroic merit in forcing herself to eat food which plainly nauseated her. When, at night, Toby crept into her room from the dressing room to see if she were sleeping, she would close her eyes and draw deep breath on breath, in a simulation which he found profoundly moving.

He himself, haggard and wild-eyed, the skin of his face raw and nicked from his morning shave, his sandy hair sticking up in tufts, and his tie pulled into a tight, hard knot, would repeatedly massage his jaw with his hand, in the gesture of someone suffering from toothache, as he drew deep sigh on

150

sigh. Continually, he retreated into his office, conscious of Mr Ram and Hilda peeping at him with a voracious pity and a no less voracious curiosity, as he shut himself up behind the frosted glass door which, in the past, he closed only on some confidential interview. Behind that door, he would pull papers off his in-tray, study balance sheets, attempt to draft a letter; but his brain had suffered a paralysis, it would not function. Later, Hilda would find innumerable pieces of paper screwed up in his waste-paper basket, many of them with no more than a few disconnected words on them, some of them wholly blank. 'He's in a bad way,' she would confide to Mr Ram, and he would reply, shaking his head: 'Well, are you surprised?'

The old woman now spent hours on end in her room, even eating many of her meals up there off a tray. The knitting grew, almost without her realizing it, beneath her knobbly, arthritic fingers. A jumper for Peter: she appeared to have forgotten that. Sometimes she stared down at the lake from her seat by the window and then her mind would retravel, in reverse, each stage of the journey which had brought her here to something so terrible. She would be carried down the hill in a dandy, perilously swaying at each twist in the road or sudden incline, by four sweating coolies, and then she would get into a car and be driven, giddy from the innumerable hairpin bends, one coiling round beneath another, on and on, until she would step out at a cavernous railway station, echoing with high-pitched, alien voices, and board the special coach set aside for her on the train. Then the train would carry her to . . . But at that moment the chain of reverie, coiling backwards, would snap. Who would accompany her on the train? Toby had accompanied her from Bombay but would he accompany her back again? And if not Toby, then who? She shuddered and reached out again for her knitting.

Toby would put his head round the door. 'Everything all right?' he would ask in a flat, hollow voice.

'Yes, darling.' Then, more than once, she had cried out that question, by now so familiar to him from innumerable letters and telephone calls: 'Oh, Toby, what can I say?' But he would vanish without answering it, perhaps even without hearing it. He had never been a demonstrative child, she had never been a demonstrative mother. The habit of reticence was too strong for them.

Isabel never came to the old woman's room now that she did not have Peter to bring with her on his reluctant daily visits.

But Helen often came. When she crossed the landing from her own room to her grandmother's, she brought the relief of a cold compress applied to burning skin. She was as strong as Isabel but her strength, unlike Isabel's, seemed to have been achieved without any strain. Well, that was understandable, the old woman decided. Helen had lost a half-brother, Isabel an only son. Can I bring you anything? Shall I read to you? Would you like your chair closer to the light? Perhaps this book might interest you? 'Oh, Helen, what a dear girl you are!' Repeatedly the old woman cried it out. But though Helen was so solicitous, her visits were always brief. 'Stay with me, oh, do stay with me a little longer!' the old woman could not help exclaiming on one occasion; and Helen had then looked embarrassed as she assured her: 'Oh, I'll be back in a moment, Granny, truly I will. Promise.' But the promise had not been kept; and when Helen did at last return several hours later, it was only to ask yet again what she could do for her grandmother.

Visitors, curious, embarrassed and, in some cases, possessed by an almost erotic excitement, would call at the house. Isabel would insist on receiving them all, however little known or little liked, though Toby would urge her, as over the household chores: 'You don't have to, it's not necessary.' 'What can I say?' This or that visitor would again ask the familiar question and Isabel, sitting bolt upright in her chair, would slowly lower her head and gaze at the plump, white hands in her lap. The visitors would all agree that it would be better if this icy barrier of stoicism were to crack and dissolve; but it never did so. 'It's not human,' one of them would confide to another, as they walked through an alley of over-arching roses to where their coolies waited beside their dandies.

Isabel also replied to all the letters, even though most of them concluded: 'Please don't bother to answer this.' She would sit at her desk in the drawing room, if Singh and his men were not in occupation, and would pen answer after answer in her firm, generous hand. The recipients were amazed how she not only thanked them for their condolences, sympathies and kind thoughts but also asked for news of their ailments, their gardens, their servant problems, their children at home in England. They agreed that she was a remarkable woman.

XV

Singh gently, insidiously questioned each of them in turn.

He and the old woman got on best of all, since she alone felt no resentment at an Indian sitting opposite to her and putting question after question.

'Do you generally sleep well?'

She laughed. 'No, I'm afraid not. I've reached that age, you know.' Then she added skittishly: 'My husband used to say that you stop needing sleep at the same age that you stop needing sex.' So far from smiling, the Indian looked vaguely shocked. Oh, dear! She should not have said that.

'And on that particular night – how did you sleep?'

For a moment, she puzzled over that, her head on one side. Singh, watching her, thought: she must once have been extremely pretty. Then she said: 'Well, much as I always do.'

'You heard no unusual noise?'

'No, I don't think so.'

'The walls here are so thin. I've often noticed how you can hear voices from other rooms.'

'Yes, it's not a well-built house. Not at all. See that damp around the window-frame? And the crack in the ceiling over

153

there? My son says that many of the houses in India are badly built. *Kutcha* – isn't that the Hindustani word?'

Singh ignored the digression. 'Your grand-daughter. Can you hear her in her room from here?'

Again the old woman put her head on one side. 'Sometimes,' she said at last. 'If she's talking, I sometimes do hear. Or if she's moving about – slamming a drawer shut, that kind of thing.'

'Did you hear her move about on that night?'

The pale blue eyes shifted sideways as the old woman pondered. Then she nodded: 'I *think* I heard her going along the corridor to the bathroom we share. I think so.'

'You mean – after she had gone to bed?'

'Yes.'

'And have you any idea what time that might have been?'

The old woman sighed. 'None at all. I sleep a little, I lie awake a little, I sleep a little. That's how it is all night . . . She often goes along to the bathroom in the night. There's nothing odd about that.'

'No, I'm sure there isn't.'

He rose to his feet, pulling the cuffs of his shirt down so that each showed its half-inch below the sleeves of his pale grey jacket. 'You've been very kind to spare so much of your time and attention.'

She felt a sudden desolation now that he would leave her. He was the first person who had had a proper conversation with her since, well, since It had happened.

'What a terrible tragedy it's all been!' she said. 'My poor son! And my poor daughter-in-law!'

Singh did not answer, merely bowed slightly and nodded. Then he said: 'Thank you, Mrs Thompson.'

The useless knitting again began to grow under the stiffly moving fingers.

XVI

Clare herself precipitated Singh's second interview with her.

As he approached the house on the fourth day after the killing, she came towards him from the verandah, where clearly she had been awaiting his coming. Her knees close together, the legs flung outward while the arms flailed, she ran in that awkward, uncoordinated manner of hers, so different from all her other neat, graceful movements. Though a storm the previous night had caused the temperature to plunge, Singh noticed that the faint moustache above her upper lip and her wide, low forehead were both glistening with sweat.

'Inspector! Inspector!' she panted, as though appealing to him to intervene in some theft or assault.

'Yes, Miss O'Connor?' He halted, his expensive crocodile-leather briefcase dangling from a hand. The other hand went up to his dark glasses, removed them, deftly folded them against the cream silk of his shirt and then slipped them into his breast pocket. How suddenly plain she looked, her eyelashes sandy against her dark skin now that there was no mascara on them, her eyes lacklustre, and her cheeks fallen in on innumerable tiny wrinkles. He felt an easy contempt for her, marooned between one race and another, and also an uneasy pity.

'I want to ask you . . . Would you have an objection to my going home?'

'Home?' He spoke as if he had never conceived of her having any home other than this house above the lake.

She said the name of the city in which she had been born and had lived all her life except for the last few months. 'There seems nothing to keep me here now. I'm sure the Thompsons no longer need me. What's there for me to do?' Fastidiously he recoiled both from that sing-song chichi accent and from the sour breath, the result of lack of food and of sleep, which wafted under his nostrils as her distraught face approached close to his.

155

'Yes, of course, you may go.' At that she looked as if, in a miraculous instant, an intolerable pain within her had abated. Then: 'But I'd be grateful if you'd stay for another, well, two or three days. Until everything is tied up,' he added with a smile.

She glanced around her desperately, as though hoping that someone, anyone would appear to intervene. Then she asked, gripping her hands, the crimson varnish chipped from the nails, tightly before her: 'Is there anything you want to ask me which you haven't asked already?'

He hesitated. 'Well, yes, there are one or two things.' He pointed to a wooden seat by the tennis court. 'Let's sit down over there.'

Clare drew a handkerchief out of her pocket, spread it on one end of the seat, and then carefully placed herself upon it, crossing one leg high over the other. Singh was both surprised and touched by this care for her pale pink shantung suit on an occasion such as this.

'I've asked you about the pill you took that night. The blanket. The brassière.' It was as though all the details were already obscure in his mind and he was making an effort to recall them.

She nodded, the tip of her tongue passing over her top lip. Then she gave a little belch, put a hand over her chest and murmured, 'Excuse me.'

'Oh, yes,' he went on, stooping to pick off a burr which had stuck to his trouser leg. 'You've an army friend, haven't you?'

The already sallow face paled, the nostrils distended slightly. 'An army friend? Yes, yes. There's a boy I sometimes see. It's nothing serious.'

'When did you see him last?'

'Not for, oh, almost a week. Not since last Friday. He took me to a dance.'

'You didn't see him on Saturday night?'

'You mean the night of the . . . ?'

'The night the child was killed. Yes.'

She shook her head rapidly back and forth.

156

'Are you sure?'

'Of course. Yes. I'd have remembered such a thing. On that evening . . . '

'He never came to this house? On any occasion?'

'Never.' She deliberated, then she said: 'Oh, of course, he always walked me back. But he never came nearer to the house than here. This tennis court.'

'You won't mind giving me his name?' She stared at him, her mouth slightly open. 'He's at the army convalescent home, isn't he?'

'But he has nothing to . . . You can't imagine that . . . '

'Everything has to be checked. Routine. Routine, that's all.'

'His name is Patrick McNamara. Corporal.' Then she added: 'He rang me.'

'Rang you? When do you mean?'

'Yesterday. In the morning. When you had gone off somewhere. To lunch was it? He'd read in the paper about . . . what had happened.' At the last three words, her voice sank to a whisper. 'He wanted to know if I was all right, needed anything. He wanted to see me. I didn't want to see him.'

'And why was that?'

She turned towards him, startled.

'Why didn't you want to see him?'

'I was . . . not in the mood.' Suddenly her voice cracked, tears were imminent. 'I . . . I'm not really in the mood for anything.'

That uneasy pity, which he did not want to feel for her and yet could not help feeling for her, intensified. He put out a hand and placed it over the two hands which she was clasping before her as she leant forward, her elbows on her knees. 'I think you're taking all this too hardly, aren't you?'

Her eyes, dull pupils surrounded by yellow, fixed on him with a terrible desolation. 'I feel . . . responsible,' she said in a voice so low that he could hardly catch the words.

'Responsible?'

'I mean . . . If I hadn't taken that pill, hadn't slept so

soundly. He was in my charge and then someone slipped in like that and managed to steal him . . .' A strange word to use, steal; but it was even stranger that it should chime in Singh's memory with Mukerjee's account of how, thundering by on his horse, Toby had called out: 'My boy has been stolen!', and with his own recollection of Toby using the same word to to him.

'I don't think anyone can blame you for that. Dr McGregor has told me that those particular pills for migraine have bromide in them. If you'd taken two or three in the course of the day, the effect would have built up.'

'Then you've spoken to Dr McGregor about them already?' He smiled. 'Of course.'

Wearily, her head on one side, she said: '*She* thinks I'm to blame.'

'She? Who?'

'Mrs Thompson.'

'Has she said something then?'

'No. No, no. But I know. She has a way of letting me know – without any words.'

'I'm sure you're imagining that.'

Clare shook her head. 'That's really why I feel I must leave. As soon as it's possible.'

'As soon as it's possible, I'll tell you. It'll only be another three or four days.' He gave a sympathetic smile. 'Promise.'

Clare was about to get up. Then she sank back, as he continued: 'Oh, yes – one other thing. How did you – how did you get this job? Of nurse, governess.'

'Well, I . . .' She was clearly at a loss.

'I mean, did you answer an advertisement? Or did someone tell you about the job, recommend you?'

She shook her head.

'Well? How then?'

She turned her face to his, drawing back her lips in a curious grimace, which revealed not merely her teeth but also the gums. It was as if she were tasting something bitter. Then she said: 'Mr Thompson asked me if I'd like the job. I worked

158

for him in one of his hotels. The Plaza. I happened to mention to him that I . . . I wanted a change. And he . . . They happened to need someone to look after . . . It was just like that.'

'By chance?' He was gazing at her intently.

'Yes, by chance. At the time, I thought it was by luck.' Again that strange grimace, as though something intolerably bitter were resting on her tongue.

'What work was it that you did in the hotel?'

'What work? Clerk. In reception. Boring work. And the hot weather was just starting, so I wanted to get away to the hills.'

'Well, that's understandable. Perfectly understandable.' He rose and slowly she rose after him, stooping over the seat to pick up the handkerchief, which she then shook out before replacing it in her pocket. 'Thank you, Miss O'Connor.'

'There's nothing else you want to know?' Her voice quavered.

'Nothing else. For the moment.'

XVII

After a dinner during which those eating were as silent as the white-uniformed servants waiting on them, Isabel and Toby sat alone in the drawing room. Their chairs faced each other. Each body was awkwardly tilted away from the other and each face was shielded with a hand. Isabel read a women's magazine, Toby a copy of the *Statesman* in which there was a sensational account of the murder by an elderly journalist, known to him and disliked for his radical views, who usually wrote, not about crime, but about foreign affairs.

The case has its baffling aspects. The natural assumption is that this is yet another instance of the all too frequent acts of terrorism, some even against women or, as in this case, children, which have been taking place in this country in recent months. But a problem remains. A household is locked up for the night – its master has

even, as is his custom, gone from room to room to make sure that
every lock and bolt is securely fastened. All the members of the
family have retired. In the course of the night, at an hour estimated
as being between three and four, the child is removed from the room
in which he sleeps with his governess, either dead or still alive.
There is no indication that the house has been broken into, though a
window of the drawing room is found apparently unfastened from
within. Clearly the murderer was someone who could move without
disturbing the rest of the household; who knew how to handle a
child; who may even have been so familiar to this particular child as
to cause him no alarm; who knew how to unfasten the bolt and latch
of the drawing-room window without any noise and who also knew
the whereabouts of the servants' little-used outside privy, in which
the mutilated body was found . . .

Toby breathed deeply and yet more deeply; the innuendoes
were clear. Someone in the household, whether a member of
the family or a servant, was the killer and not a dacoit. He
glanced over the top of the newspaper at Isabel but, though
she had noticed the increasing heaviness of his breathing, as
though he had fallen into an after-dinner doze, she did not
look back at him. Her lips were pursed, one hand still shielded
her eyes. Toby crackled the sheets of the paper together and
then threw it to the ground. He laid his head back against the
chair and stared sideways at the window through which
Singh had decided that the murderer or murderers must have
carried the child. There was a sound as of a firecracker
exploding, followed by a reverberating boom. Earlier that
day, a storm had taken place, it had rained, the temperature
had fallen. Now it was clear that, as the curtained drawing
room grew more and more sultry, another storm was
coming.

'Strange,' Toby murmured.

Isabel looked up, frowning, as though she did not welcome
an interruption to her reading. 'What's strange?'

'When I first knew you, you were so terrified of lightning
and thunder. Remember? And now – you don't even notice
it.'

'There are many things of which I was once terrified.' Her

voice was hollow. 'One grows older, one grows more hardened.'

'Yes, yes, I suppose so.' Again he stared at the folds of the velvet over the window. *But a problem remains* . . .

All at once Isabel gave a snorting laugh. 'It's not true what they say about lightning, is it?'

'What do you mean?'

'About its never striking twice in the same place.' He stared at her, she stared back with narrowed eyes. 'Jack, Peter,' she said.

There was a knock at the door, so light that, as they continued to stare at each other, neither of them noticed it. The knock was repeated, more loudly.

'Yes!' Isabel called.

Clare's head appeared round the door. Toby gazed at her, as though beseeching her not to come in, to say nothing, to go away.

But: 'May I have word?' she asked composedly.

Neither Isabel nor Toby replied. Clare edged into the room. Then Toby half rose: 'Why don't you sit down?'

'Thank you, Mr Thompson.' Clare sat upright in the middle of the sofa, between their two chairs. A chiffon scarf was tied jauntily around her neck, left bare by the plunging vee, picked out in sequins, of her evening dress. She opened her purse, took out cigarette case, holder and lighter, and then looked first at Isabel and then at Toby: 'You don't mind?'

For two or three seconds, as though each of them was waiting on the other, there came no answer. Then Toby cleared his throat and said: 'No, go ahead. Please.' He picked up an ashtray from the table beside him and balanced it on an arm of the sofa.

Clare drew in on the cigarette, sucking the smoke deep into her lungs and expelling it through her nostrils. Suddenly, after her distracted air throughout the last days, she seemed to have achieved a surprising calm. When she spoke, it was in a firm, steady voice, totally unlike the tremulous, hesitant one

161

which she had been using whenever circumstances had obliged her to say anything, however brief, to any of them. 'I know you want me to go,' she said.

Again Isabel and Toby seemed to be waiting on each other for an answer. At last, Isabel laid her magazine down on one of her ample knees, a finger between its pages: 'It's not a question of wanting or not wanting. But there's nothing now for you to do here. Is there?'

'But of course there's no hurry,' Toby put in, embarrassed. 'And of course we'll pay your fare home and make sure that, well, that you're financially all right. That goes without saying.' He glanced over to Isabel, whose face had stiffened. 'You must stay just as long as you want to stay.'

'It's not a question of wanting or not wanting.' With extraordinary boldness, Clare now echoed Isabel's previous words to her. 'But for the moment I *have* to stay. That's really all I wanted to tell you when I came in here. Inspector Singh's told me I can't leave at once. I have to wait until he tells me.'

Toby stared at her, his mouth half-open to reveal his small, irregular teeth. 'He forbade you to go?'

'Well . . . yes.'

Toby stooped and picked up the copy of the *Statesman*. He began to tidy its sheets. 'I suppose that makes sense,' he said, head lowered. 'Until the inquest is over. Which, if I've understood him aright, won't take place for some time yet.'

Clare shrank. 'He said nothing to me about an inquest.'

Isabel gave a small, cruel smile. 'Well, there must be an inquest. There could hardly not be one. And you must presumably be a witness.'

'I?'

'Well, of course. How could you not be? You'll be asked to give your account of all the circumstances.' Isabel lowered lids over eyes suddenly feverish with resentment and hatred. 'After all, you were the last person to see my son alive.' She put the back of a hand to her mouth; for the first time for days she was about to break down. Then she added: 'Apart from his killer – or killers – of course.'

162

Toby stared at Isabel with a mixture of dread and shock. Then he turned to Clare, who had risen shakily to her feet, one hand to the frivolous chiffon scarf, while the other grasped the cigarette holder. The abrupt movement of her rising had sprayed ash in an arc across the arm of Toby's chair.

Clare cried out, with barely suppressed hysteria: 'You blame me, you blame me!'

Isabel shrugged.

Toby also now rose. 'No one blames anyone.'

'Your wife blames me!'

'No, no, no.' He held out both hands placatingly towards her, as though he expected her to take them.

But Clare swung away from him. 'You can be sure,' she said over her shoulder, a hand on the doorknob, 'that just as soon as this inquest is over, I'll be out of this house.' She slammed the door behind her.

Toby flopped back into his chair, put his hands over his eyes, drew them slowly down his cheeks. He gave a muffled groan.

Isabel raised her magazine, opened it, began to read.

XVIII

Helen had been out riding alone.

'Why don't you come riding with me?' she had suggested to her father but, slumped in a chair, hands deep in pockets and doing nothing, he had merely shaken his head, with a deep, shuddering sigh.

At first, she had walked the horse, the lethargic pace suiting her mood of lethargy; but then, when she had climbed up into the hills, beyond the last house or even mud hut or corrugated-iron shed, she felt a sudden upsurge of spirits. First she cantered, then recklessly she forced the horse to gallop despite the unevenness of the ground, with its jagged stones, exposed roots and sudden hillocks.

On and on she galloped, the tip of her tongue protruding

from between her half-open lips and her body straining forwards, when ominously, from the other side of the lake, she heard a clap of thunder. She had seen no lightning. Clouds began to amass, lurid bank on bank, with the swiftness with which, up here in this narrow valley, a day of gentle sunshine became one of raging storm. She jerked the horse round, kicked at his flanks with her heels. She was wearing nothing more protective than jodhpurs and an aertex shirt. Long before she reached home, with another, far noisier clap of thunder, the rain was streaming all about her; but as she felt it on her forehead and in her hair and then penetrating through her clothing to her skin, it only intensified her mood of sudden, inexplicable joy.

The syce, a hessian bag over his head like a hood, scuttled out into the yard and took the horse from her. He glanced involuntarily at the points of her nipples against her soaked shirt and then looked away. She smiled at him, though he did not see it, and ran round to the front door and so into the house.

In the morning room her father still sat slumped in the same chair as when she had left. Through the open door he gave her a stricken glance. 'Rain?' He seemed surprised that she should be soaked, even though he must have seen the storm through the window and heard the spatter of the raindrops which it hurled on to the glass.

'Yes, rain,' she confirmed and then, still feeling that unreasoning joy with which she had ridden at breakneck speed under that low, streaming sky, she let out a laugh. He turned his head away quickly, as though she had uttered some obscenity.

In twos and threes, she raced up the stairs, scattering water on banisters and carpet. She flung her bedroom door wide.

The startled ayah faced her, turning round from a drawer pulled open on an unaccustomed disorder of clothes. For a second the ayah appeared to be about to duck under her arm in order to flee. But instead she straightened, tucked her elbows into her sides and gave a little bow of acknowledgement.

'What on earth are you doing?'

The ayah pointed to the open drawer. 'I was tidying memsahib's things.'

'*Un*tidying them, by the looks of it.' Helen strode over to the chest-of-drawers, brushing so close to the ayah that her wet jodhpurs left a dark mark on the Indian woman's sari, and pushed the drawer back. She turned and glared at the ayah. The ayah did not flinch. 'Out.'

The ayah did not move.

Helen pointed at the door. 'Out.'

The ayah hesitated. Then, her spine rigid and her head high, as though she were carrying a pitcher of water in her village, she passed out through the door and began to descend the stairs.

Helen opened the drawer again and, with agitated fingers, began carefully to fold the underclothes which the ayah had disturbed. Then, all at once conscious of the icy feel of her shirt against her skin, she abandoned that task. She pulled off the shirt, unbuttoned her jodhpurs, kicked off her shoes. Though it was so sultry, she began to shudder uncontrollably as she reached over to the towel-horse for a towel.

XIX

'I think it might be a good idea if you were to pop over to take another dekko,' the Governor told his Inspector-General of Police. 'It's a damned nuisance that Hunt should be on leave. I'm not all that happy about the way Singh seems to be handling the case. There have been far too many rumours and innuendoes in the press. He must have been talking. That's always the trouble with Indians, even the most educated. Blab, blab, blab. Can't keep their mouths shut.'

The Inspector-General, Ross, had a high opinion of Singh, whom he thought a far abler officer than his white superior Hunt; but he had no intention of voicing any disagreement with the Governor, who could so easily become pettish and spiteful. 'I'll go over tomorrow,' he said. 'I've been in constant touch on the blower, of course – and Singh's been sending over his reports. But I've been meaning to take another look at things myself.'

The Governor drew in his lips and sucked on his bristly grey moustache. When his subordinates imitated him, it was always doing this. 'It's an important case, an extremely important case. I'd like to see the man – or men – caught as quickly as possible. Not only for the sake of the family but as a deterrent to any madman planning something similar in future.'

When he had left the Governor's office, Ross telephoned to Singh.

'Would you like to meet me up at the house?' Singh suggested.

'Good God, no. The case is yours. I don't want Thompson to think I'm involved in any way. No, I'll call at the station. About ten-thirty. I'll be riding over.'

Putting down the receiver, Singh experienced an all too familiar disgust with his English superiors. Why the hell shouldn't Thompson be allowed to think that the Inspector-General was involved? Presumably because it might make their next game of golf, bridge or billiards embarrassing.

On his arrival, Ross at once began to light his pipe, without asking Singh's permission. Singh loathed the smell of the shag, imported in huge tins from England. He could still detect it in his office days after Ross had gone. 'The Governor would like to see things brought to some conclusion.'

'So should I. But the conclusion has to be the right one. Hasn't it?'

'More than a week has passed.' Ross shifted his massive bulk in a leather armchair too narrow for it. 'What's holding up the inquest?'

'Inquiries,' Singh answered coolly.

'Frankly, I don't get it. You may or may not catch the brute or the brutes. The Governor very much hopes you will. I very much fear you won't. But why can't the inquest go ahead? Murder by person or persons unknown. That's the only verdict possible.'

'Is it?' Singh got up and went to the open window, to escape the pipe smoke billowing towards him. 'It seems to me increasingly likely that what we have here is an inside job.'

'One of the servants?'

'Possibly. Though I doubt it.' The Indian put a delicate hand over his mouth and coughed behind it. 'My almost immediate assumption was that the boy had been killed by the governess and her boyfriend.'

Ross raised his bushy eyebrows, biting on his pipe stem.

'Let's suppose that he was visiting her in secret. And let's suppose that the child woke up and began to scream. They had to silence him. One or other of them stuffed that brassière – the first thing to hand – over his mouth and suffocated him without meaning to do so. Then they had to make it look as if someone from outside – a dacoit, some old enemy of Thompson's paying off a score – had committed the crime. So they mutilated the child, left that window open and dumped him in the privy.' Singh walked back towards his chair. 'Unfortunately, however, that doesn't work. The boyfriend was in his ward at the convalescent home throughout the night. I have eleven witnesses.' He smiled: 'Though I suppose that eleven people could be lying. It's happened before.' He reseated himself and leant forward, elbows on desk and hands clasped before him. He stared at Ross. Then: 'The father?'

'Thompson!' Ross's square face, under close-cropped hair, grew congested with annoyance. 'No man kills his own child.'

'Doesn't he? Men *have* killed their own children. I don't have to tell you that. And perhaps he didn't mean to kill him. . . . I should guess that he and the governess are carrying on together.'

'Old women's gossip!'

Singh gave that small, supercilious smile which always irritated his English colleagues. 'Then there must be a lot of old women of both sexes around here at present. You know his reputation. Everyone says that he was carrying on with the present Mrs Thompson while the first Mrs Thompson was

dying on him. So he falls for Miss O'Connor, who used to
work as a clerk in one of his hotels. He offers her the job of
governess. They start an affair – after all, his wife is pregnant.
That night he goes to her, slipping out of his dressing room
without his wife hearing. Or if she does hear, she thinks
nothing of it. He's gone to the lavatory, she decides. Or he's
set off on his nightly round of checking all the windows and
doors. The child wakes, screams. There's a panic – which
results in one of them stuffing the brassière over or into his
mouth.'

Ross shook his head: 'I don't buy that one.'

'Isn't there a likelihood of Thompson being appointed to the
Viceroy's Council? Well, there you are! Another reason for
panic. If there were to be an open scandal on top of all the hints
and rumours . . . We all know what a prude the Viceroy is.'

'I still don't buy it. What *does* seem to me possible is that
some Indian, cuckolded by Thompson, may have decided on
revenge. Now what about that?'

'Well, yes, of course, that's something I've considered.'
Singh's eyes had begun to water from the smoke. He took out
a silk handkerchief from his breast pocket and began to dab at
them. 'I've considered everything. However unlikely.' The
arrogance of the claim annoyed Ross, even though he had to
accept that, yes, Singh was the kind of officer, patient and
pertinacious, who would examine every possibility before
reaching a decision. 'But now . . . there's one suspect I favour
above all others.' Singh paused, as though in a deliberate
attempt to prolong the suspense of the revelation to follow.

'Well?'

Singh turned his head sideways, to gaze out of the window,
as though to avoid Ross's gaze. 'The girl.'

'The governess?'

'No. The other girl.'

'The daughter?' Ross was astounded.

Singh nodded. 'Helen,' he murmured, savouring the name
on his tongue as though it were something exotically pungent.

'Why the hell should you pick on her?'

168

'Well, for one thing – motive.'

'Motive.'

Singh once more leaned across the desk, hands clasped before him. 'It wouldn't be true to say that she and her stepmother had open rows. But it does seem to be generally agreed in the station that they have little use or affection for each other.' Singh twisted the outsize signet ring on his little finger. 'A number of people have told me that Mrs Thompson was, well, not exactly enthusiastic about the prospect of her stepdaughter arriving in the household. And the stepdaughter, when she did get here, seemed to go out of her way to avoid Mrs Thompson.' He picked up a pen from the tray before him. 'Don't forget that the present Mrs Thompson had already entered Thompson's life as so-called housekeeper when the first Mrs Thompson was still living,' he said in a didactic tone, using the pen to emphasize each word. 'Helen would then have been – what? – eight or nine.'

Ross pulled a face, half closing his eyes and drawing down the corners of his mouth, the pipe jutting upwards. Clearly, he was not much impressed.

Singh continued patiently: 'The boy – Peter – was fond of his half-sister. There's no doubt of that. But was she fond of him? The ayah doesn't think so. Visitors to the house don't think so. She's a girl who's fond of children in general – a successful and popular leader of the Bluebells – but with this particular child everyone noticed how cold and even harsh she could be. A neighbour, Mrs Anderson, told me how, when she was playing bridge there one afternoon, the child tried to climb up into Helen's lap but she at once pushed him off. Mrs Anderson told me that some time ago – before the murder – but it stuck in my mind. Mrs Anderson said it was as if the girl could not bear him to be near her. I've heard the same thing from other people . . . The boy made a bead bookmarker for his half-sister – rather touching – but since then no one's seen it, she's not used it, not once. The ayah told me that.'

'Oh, the ayah!'

'There's another Bluebell leader of the same age – Colonel

Simpson's daughter. You know her, I'm sure.'

Ross nodded. 'Betty.'

'Well, Betty told me – when I was making what I hope were discreet inquiries – that Helen once spoke of her half-brother as a "beastly little brat".'

Ross shook his head, smiling indulgently. 'I've often referred to my own children as beastly little brats – or worse. But that doesn't mean I'd kill them. Though I may have wanted to do so on a number of occasions.'

'She's an odd girl.' Singh did not add that, from the start, this oddness had had an almost erotic fascination for him. 'A tragedy takes place, all the other members of the family, even the grandmother, are in a state of numb shock. But she goes on with her daily pursuits – her Bluebell meetings, her visits to the bazaar, her morning rides – as though nothing had taken place.'

'I'd have thought that to be a sign of innocence, not of guilt. If a young girl committed a murder as horrible as that, surely she'd go to pieces.'

'Not that young girl. She has an amazing strength.'

Helen reminded Singh of a deodar in his garden. A branch of the slim, graceful tree, with its pendant racemes, as though of pale green lace dripping from it, had begun to rub against his bedroom window. When the wind blew strong, as it often did up here, he would give way first to irritation and then to fury at an insistent scratch, scratch, scratch on the window-pane as he tried to go to sleep. One night he jumped out of bed, fetched a saw, opened the window, and leaning far out, attempted to sever the slender, elegant branch. But, so pliable and delicate in his hand, it resisted with an amazing persistence. He pushed the saw back and forth and then, when he looked to see what he had achieved, in the moonlight he could make out no more than a slight indentation, black on grey, where the bark had been fretted. Sweating and grunting and in constant danger of overbalancing, he had eventually managed to sever the branch. By the time that he had done so, he had conceived for the tree a murderous animosity, as for some living creature bent on thwarting his will.

Ross once again shifted his huge bulk – he had once been a Rugby football player and even now refereed games for the army. Then, massaging his broken nose with the tip of his forefinger as though in a vain attempt to coax it back into shape, he said: 'All right. There's a motive, let's accept that. But a motive is not enough by itself. Is it? We all have motives for committing a variety of crimes but the fact is that most of us do not commit them.' He stared challengingly at Singh. 'What evidence have you got, hard evidence?'

'Some. Admittedly not much.'

Singh began to relate what he had learned from the ayah.

One morning, when he had been climbing, with many pauses for breath, up the steep hillside path to the house – next time, he had decided, he must really come on horseback, much though he hated it – a white-robed figure had suddenly and silently emerged from behind some bushes. It was the ayah. She had bowed to him over hands pressed together, palm against palm, and had then said: 'Sahib, may I talk to you?'

'Here?'

Without replying, she had turned away from him and begun to walk off down a narrow footpath zigzagging into the woods. Singh, exasperated but curious, had followed her.

In a clearing, the folds of her cotton sari white against the pale grey boles of the trees, she had turned.

'Well?' His tone had been peremptory; but the ayah, used to people addressing her in that manner, had not flinched. 'I wish to tell you two things, sahib. But you must not tell anyone that I have told you.'

"You need not worry. What you tell me will be secret.'

The ayah had been satisfied. Calmly, in a low, measured voice, she had first told him about the nightdress. Helen had a nightdress, a pink chiffon nightdress, with embroidery here – the ayah had touched her wrinkled neck with a hand – beautiful embroidery. There was only one such nightdress. She had often folded it up when making Helen's bed, she had often laid it out when turning down the same bed. After the night when the child had been killed, the nightdress had vanished. She had laid it out but the following morning she had found another nightdress, a cream-coloured nightdress with no embroidery, in its place.

Then there was the knife. In the gloom of the trees, with a shrill cacophony of birds all around and above him, clamorously insistent, Singh had felt that quickening of the pulse, constriction of the temples and slight breathlessness familiar to him from all those occasions in the past when he had known, known with total certainty, that he was on to something. A knife? Deliberately he had suppressed any appearance of excitement. What knife did she mean? The girl had had a knife in a sheath, the ayah had answered. For her work with the Bluebells. A big knife, sharp, sharp. The ayah's eyes had widened. She always took it with her, on her belt, when she went down the hill to the Bluebell meetings. The knife was gone. Gone? Singh had again suppressed any appearance of excitement. The ayah had nodded vigorously. Gone! She had searched the room, not once, not twice, but three times. Usually the knife lay in the second drawer down of Helen's dressing-table, under a pile of underclothes. It was no longer there, no longer anywhere. Vanished.

'I see. Yes. Yes.' Singh had nodded, smiled, nodded again. He had not wished the ayah to know how important he had considered this information. 'Well, thank you. That may be useful to me. I don't know.'

Suddenly, under the fold of the sari over her head, there had been a dangerously glittering look in the ayah's eyes. 'I think she killed my *baba*,' she had hissed. 'I think so.'

Singh had stared at her for a moment and she had boldly stared back. Then he had begun to return along the woodland path, expecting her to follow him. But when, after two or three bends, he had glanced over his shoulder, she was nowhere to be seen. Was that the white of her sari between the tree trunks over there? He had peered, halting in his tracks. No, it was only a sheet of newspaper, probably used at some time by someone who had been obliged to come here, off the road, to defecate. He had hurried on, thankful when he had at last left the shrill gloom of the woods for the sunlit calm of the open road.

When he had arrived at the house, he had been amazed to see the ayah shaking a blanket out of an upstairs window. Clearly, she had taken some short cut. She had paused and, very still, had looked down at him, the blanket billowing outwards from the hands that had tethered it. Then she had given it a jerk, drawn back both it and her head, and vanished from sight.

. . . Ross shrugged. 'Well, yes, that's something. If not very much. I suppose you followed it up?'

'Naturally.' Did the fat slob, sucking away at his pipe like a baby at a teat, imagine that he had merely ignored a lead so important?

Once already Singh had interrogated Helen. No, she had heard nothing in the night. Yes, she had been along to the lavatory at about twelve-fifteen before switching off her light. Yes, before that, while she was reading in bed, she had heard her father going round the house, as he always did, to make sure that all the latches and bolts were fastened. Yes, she tended to sleep heavily. No, she had known nothing of Peter's disappearance until her grandmother had knocked on her bedroom door. Her manner had been possessed, her voice clear and steady. 'I wish I could think of something else to tell you that might be of help. But I can't.'

He had then gone over the whole story of the discovery of the body in the pit. Helen had remained composed, even matter-of-fact, as he had elicited one gruesome detail after another. 'I shouted to Clare to fetch the torch . . . We always keep it on a table in the hall – in case of a power failure . . . Unfortunately, the battery was all but worn out, so that it gave only this feeble glow . . . But I was able to make out . . .'

Now, after what the ayah had told him, Singh had asked to see Helen again.

One leg crossed over the other, her hands resting lightly on the arms of her chair, she had sat opposite him in the small downstairs room, used as an extra guest room, which Toby had suggested that the police should make into their office as long as their investigations continued at the house.

'I've one or two more questions,' Singh had begun.

She had inclined her shingled head, smiling. 'No objection.'

'Firstly, I want to ask you about a nightdress.'

'A nightdress? You mean, a nightdress of mine?' He had been watching her reaction closely; she had given no sign of shock or alarm.

'One nightdress had been put out for you by the ayah on the night of the killing. But it seems that that night you wore another one. Or, at least, the ayah found another one on your bed in the morning.'

She had thought for a moment, her chin on her palm. Then she had nodded: 'Yes, that's right.'

'You mean you didn't wear the nightdress laid out for you by the ayah?'

'No. I noticed it was soiled. So I put it in the basket for the dhobi and got myself another.'

'Soiled? How do you mean?' He had had to make an effort to keep the excitement out of his voice, just as he would do when, back in England, he came on a rare Kipling first edition priced at sixpence or a shilling.

'Well . . .' For the first time she had looked disconcerted; she had even begun to blush. Singh had thought: Now we're getting somewhere. His heart seemed to be hammering against his breastbone. 'In the way that women sometimes soil their clothes,' she had murmured. Then she had amplified, almost defiantly: 'I was beginning my period.'

Now it had been his turn to be disconcerted. 'I see. I'm sorry to have to ask these intrusive questions. But there's no way of avoiding them.'

'I understand that.'

'So the nightdress would have gone to the laundry?'

174

She had nodded. 'On Monday.'

'And when would it have come back?'

She had thought: 'Oh, I should imagine three or four days ago. The dhobi takes anything up to five days – if the weather isn't good. That's about normal, isn't it?'

'And has it come back?'

She had shaken her head. 'No.'

'No?'

'I was hoping that perhaps you were going to tell me what had happened to it. That's my favourite nightdress. Harvey Nichols. A present from my Aunt Sophie in England.'

'Why hasn't it come back?'

She had laughed. 'I only wish I knew. From time to time something gets "lost".' She had put the word into ironic inverted commas. 'I'm sure you must often have the same experience with your dhobi. And the odd thing is that it's always something new or attractive. Old handkerchiefs, for example, never fail to turn up.'

'You mean the dhobi stole your nightdress?'

'I don't know what to think. It appears on the list but the dhobi says that, when he unpacked the basket, it wasn't there. He often says that when something disappears.'

'And who made up the list?'

'I did.'

'You?'

'I often do it for my stepmother. On this occasion, it seemed obvious I must do it. She was – fit for nothing.'

'And you checked the laundry on its return?'

'Yes, I checked it. And told the dhobi that item was missing.'

'I see.'

'My father's terribly hard on the servants for the smallest dishonesty. He got into a rage the other day because a single banana had been taken from the fruit bowl. Booze, cigarettes, small change – it drives him up the wall. But it always amazes me they're as honest as they are. We pay them so little. Do you realize that nightdress probably cost three times the dhobi's

earnings for a month? If he pinched it and sold it in the bazaar
– as I suspect – well, I can't really be that angry.'

'I'll have a word with him.'

'Will you? But don't be too hard on him. No third degree, I
hope.' He had not been able to decide whether she was being
ingenuous or disingenuous. How could someone so intelligent
have failed to grasp the tenor of his questions?

'There's something else.'

'Yes?'

'Would I be right in thinking you're the possessor of a scout
knife?'

'Was.' Again he had been astounded that a question so
fraught with dangerous implications should have failed to
shake her. 'I lost it. We went to Biwali for a weekend camp not
so long ago and I must have left it or dropped it somewhere. I
need another but I've had no luck in finding one in a place as
small as this. I suppose I'll have to wait until we get back to
the plains.'

'Did you tell anyone about losing the knife?'

She had thought for a moment. 'No, I don't think so. Oh, I
may have mentioned it to Clare. In fact, I think I did. It
wasn't of much importance.'

He had looked closely at her. It was precisely because she
had remained so casual and relaxed that his suspicions had
been intensified. Any young girl in her position, obliged to
answer questions indicating that she was suspected of a
hideous crime, would, however, innocent, show some shock,
agitation, indignation. She had shown none. Her naturalness
was, in itself, unnatural.

. . . Now Singh tried to explain all this to Ross; but the
Englishman was irritably and irritatingly obtuse in taking his
point. Knocking out his pipe on the ashtray before him, with so
much vehemence that Singh feared that he would smash it,
Ross exclaimed: 'If she were the one, she'd have given herself
away! Bound to! At some moment or other. A hardened
criminal might succeed in . . . But not someone so young and
inexperienced.'

Singh shrugged. 'Anyway – I got nowhere with her.'

'Did you take up the question of the nightdress with the dhobi?'

'Of course.' Once again it exasperated Singh that the Englishman should feel obliged to check on something so obvious. 'As I expected, he said he'd never seen the garment. Told me that the girl had accused him of pinching it but was emphatic that he certainly hadn't done so. Mrs Thompson confirmed that at other times other items of laundry have gone missing – only two or three weeks ago the old lady lost a blouse. That time the dhobi said it must have been stolen off the line.'

'And the knife? Did you ask the governess about it?'

Singh picked up the ashtray between them and fastidiously emptied its charred debris into the waste-paper basket. He straightened, nodded.

He had knocked at Clare's bedroom door and she had called out: 'Yes? Who is it?'

'Inspector Singh.'

'Oh . . . Oh, all right. Come in.'

When he had entered, she was scrambling, barefoot, off her bed, her skirt unzipped and the top of her blouse open. With agitated fingers she had first pulled up the zip and then done up the buttons of the blouse. A hand had gone to her dishevelled hair, patting it into place. 'I was having a little nap. I've been sleeping terribly badly since . . . since . . . It would be even worse in *that* room but it's bad enough in here.' Her lower lip had trembled, distended itself. As she had stood facing him in her stockinged feet, her hands clasped tightly before her, she had looked so terribly thin, small and vulnerable that she had moved him to pity and then to anger with himself for feeling an emotion so alien to his nature. Almost roughly he had told her: 'Oh do sit.'

She had sunk down on to the edge of the bed and from there had looked up at him with a shrinking, beseeching look. Almost as though I were about to rape her, he had thought.

'I wanted to check something with you.'

Her tongue ran over her upper lip, like a child's exploring for traces of chocolate. 'Yes?'

'Did you know Miss Thompson owned a knife?'

'A knife?' The leaden-hued lids had blinked repeatedly over the terrified eyes. Then she had looked up at him and in a whisper had answered: 'Yes. Yes, a scout knife. She used to wear it on her belt when she went to the Bluebells.'

'And have you any idea of what's happened to it?'

She had peered all about her, like some hunted animal looking desperately for a hole or cranny through which to escape from its predator.

'Have you?' He had been disgusted to find that he actually enjoyed the spectacle and the smell (yes, he could smell it) of her terror of him.

At last she had gazed up at him. 'She told me she'd lost it. After that weekend they spent camping at Biwali. She came back and told me she'd lost it. Left it somewhere, dropped it somewhere. That's all I know.'

'You're sure of that?'

She had put her fingers to her lips, as she had done outside the privy when the body of the child had been found. It was a gesture similar to that which she used when she pressed a handkerchief, too ragged for any other purpose, to her lips to take off excessive lipstick. 'Yes, I'm sure.'

. . . 'Well, that confirms the girl's story,' Ross said, with obvious satisfaction. 'You haven't much to go on. Unless, of course, you think that the governess was her accomplice.'

Singh shook his head. 'No. I don't think that. But it's perfectly possible that Helen told Clare she'd lost the knife at Biwali merely in order to have a witness later. She then hid it until she needed it.'

'That argues premeditation over a period of – what? – two, three weeks.'

'Why not? The murder must have been premeditated – if she did it. She can hardly have decided on the spur of the moment to go down to the room, grab the child and kill him.'

'The trouble is – you just haven't got a case. Not one that

stands up. There are some suspicious circumstances –
nightdress, knife, both of them mislaid – but to a jury . . . No
one's going to convict on the strength of just them. *I* wouldn't.
You wouldn't.' Ross massaged his crotch with a large hand. 'If
you'd found the nightdress or the knife . . .'

'We've looked for both, of course – in and around the house,
everywhere. But in this sort of countryside – hilly, woody,
much of it uninhabited – it's hard enough to find a man, let
alone things as small as that. Under a rock, down a well, in
another privy. She goes for long rides, usually by herself. I'd
need a huge force of men to be sure every possible place had
been covered.'

'And even then they'd probably miss out.'

Singh picked up a pencil from the tray before him and
stabbed at the blotter. 'And yet . . . and yet I have this hunch.'

Ross shrugged and then flung out an impatient arm.
'Hunches are no good.'

XX

The inquest was over.

Singh walked away from it with that deadly weariness,
increasingly familiar to him, of a traveller who has lost all
heart and energy for continuing his journey. He was sure that
he was right: Helen had killed the child. But he was also sure
that he would never be able to prove that he was right. Helen,
coolly unshaken, had maintained her story. Clare had again
confirmed that Helen had told her of the loss of the knife.
When Singh had asked the other three members of the family
if any of them had also heard of its loss, Isabel and Mrs
Thompson had remained silent but Toby had stirred in his
chair and had then said that, yes, he seemed to remember that
he had done so. 'Seem?' Singh had taken up sharply, and
Toby had then replied with a fretful 'Yes, I did, I did.' When,
later, Singh had asked Isabel once again about the theft of the
nightdress, she had stared abstractedly into space as she sat at

her desk, yet another letter of reply to condolence half-written before her, and had then said, offhand: 'As I told you before, small things – and even big ones – are always going missing. We keep saying we must get rid of that dhobi, but all the others are just as bad – or worse.'

As Singh walked past the saluting men on guard outside the square, red-brick police station, the decision suddenly came to him: he would give it all up. Yes, the traveller would tear up his tickets and itinerary and head back for home. Why not? He did not need the money. He did not need this country, which had never, even in childhood, been really his. He would settle, briefly or forever – he did not yet know – in London or Paris or New York. He would dabble in picture dealing or take his piano playing more seriously or just do nothing at all. He would pick up a newspaper and read in it of the theft of some furs or jewellery, the burning down of a mission station or the murder of a child, and it would have nothing to do with him, nothing at all. He would fastidiously turn to the next page and read a review of a book, a concert or an exhibition.

One of his sergeants, catching a glimpse of him at the end of the corridor, hurried to join him in his office. Eagerly he said: 'We've got a new line on that mission station fire. Khan was in the bazaar and he heard . . .'

Singh waved a hand, as though brushing away a fly. 'Oh . . . Oh, tell me about it later! Not now!'

The sergeant backed out. Singh opened the drawer of his desk, took out a copy, six weeks old, of *The Times*, and began to do the crossword.

XXI

Clare was packing; but in the months during which she had been with the Thompsons she had bought so many clothes with her wages that she had no idea how she would manage to fit them all into the two cheap, battered suitcases which were the possessions neither of herself nor of any one member of the family but of the family as a whole. She pushed the overflowing contents of one of the suitcases downwards with both of her hands and then she perched herself on the lid, which creaked ominously beneath her weight, its thin, dry, scuffed leather in danger of splitting. She felt on the verge of tears with the frustration of it. From the top of the wardrobe, she took down three large paper bags. She would have to transfer some of her things into them.

There was a knock at the door. She stood perfectly still beside the suitcase, her hands rigid to her sides and her mouth half-open. Could Singh have come yet again to torment her? The knock was repeated, louder. She cried out: 'Yes, yes, who is it?'

'Me. Toby.'

She crossed to the door and pulled it open.

'Sorry if I'm disturbing you. I wanted to give you this.' He held out a khaki envelope.

She shook her head vigorously from side to side, her sleek, black hair swinging like a bell. 'No, no!'

'Please.' He thrust it at her. But she would not take it. 'Please!' Then he placed it on top of one of the inelegant, bulging suitcases. He stared at her in a terrible anguish. 'It all went wrong,' he said, from behind the hand which he had raised to his mouth. 'I'd . . . I'd planned something so different.'

'Please leave me. Please!' Her voice rose so shrilly on the second 'Please!' that he looked apprehensively over his shoulder for fear that someone on the other side of the closed door might have heard her.

'I'm sorry, Clare. It's something we must both forget – somehow, somehow.' He turned away. 'God knows how!'

She picked up the envelope, astonished by its weight. 'Take this,' she said brutally. 'I don't want it.'

But, shaking his head, he opened the door and slipped out through it, closing it quietly behind him.

Clare almost went after him. Then she stood motionless, balancing the envelope in her hand. She knew, without opening it, that an envelope so heavy must contain many, many notes. More, probably, than all her wages over these weeks. More than she had ever held at any one moment in her life. She raised the envelope to her mouth, as though she were going to tear it open with her teeth. Then she stooped over the suitcase, raised its lid and concealed the envelope under a pile of pink, frilly underclothes.

XXII

Isabel, seeing the stuffed paper bags in the hall – Toby had vanished – told Clare contemptuously: 'You can't possibly travel like that. I'll give you a holdall. I'll send the bearer for it.'

'How shall I get it back to you?'

'I said – I'll *give* it to you.'

'Oh, but . . .'

Isabel drew a deep sigh, her nostrils dilating, as she did when, exasperated with one of the servants, she checked herself from shouting to no purpose.

When the bearer returned with the holdall, Isabel herself transferred the clothes, heavy with scent, with an impatient efficiency, her mouth held taut in what was almost a grimace. At one point, when a blouse unrolled in her hands, she held it up before her, examining it with the wariness of some second-hand dealer, before she rolled it up again. Clare wanted to snatch it away from her but restrained herself. It was as though those large, plump, white hands were touching some intimate part of her body, in contemptuous appraisal.

'There!' Her task done, Isabel pulled across the zip of the holdall, locked it and handed Clare the key. 'Don't lose that,' she admonished. 'Put it somewhere safe.' Head on one side, she surveyed the holdall. 'Doesn't look too bad. It belonged to my predecessor.' Clare wondered if she were now regretting the gift.

Old Mrs Thompson was shuffling down the hall in dressing-gown and bedroom slippers. 'Clare, dear,' she said, with genuine warmth. 'I'm so sorry you're going. I've decided to spend the day in bed, I feel my age today. But I had to come down to say farewell and to wish you good luck.'

Isabel glanced at the watch pinned, on a gold chain, to the front of her dress. 'What's become of that brother of yours? If he doesn't arrive soon, you'll miss that bus, and if you miss that bus, then you'll miss that train.' She did not conclude: 'And if you miss that train, you'll be on our hands for another night.' But that was the implication.

'I can't think what's happened to him.' Clare wished that her youngest brother, whose school fees she had been partly paying, had not volunteered to come and fetch her back home. At the time, listening to his eager, indistinct voice on the telephone, as it approached, receded, approached on erratic waves of sound, she had been touched almost to tears. But she should have known that he would arrive late, might even arrive tomorrow, might never arrive at all. Typical. Again, as when she had tried to stuff too many things into the cheap, bulging suitcase, the frustration of it all made her want to burst into tears.

'He'll be here in a minute or two,' Mrs Thompson soothed. 'Probably he had difficulty in getting a horse or a dandy down at the depot. I'm sure that's it.'

'My brother doesn't ride. Can't.'

'Well, then, that explains it! Dandies are often scarce at this time in the morning. Don't worry, dear. It'll be annoying for you but lovely for us to have you here for another night.' She meant it.

Isabel looked at her mother-in-law derisively and then went over to the window and peered out.

'Oh, I all but forgot!' the old woman went on. 'Helen asked me to say goodbye to you from her. She was hoping to see you but apparently she woke up very early this morning and, since it was such a lovely day, decided to go out for a long ride. She popped into my room at about, oh, six-thirty to tell me – she must have heard me moving around. She just had her *chotah hazri* and left.'

'I was awake at six-thirty. I was up and about too.'

'Were you, dear? Well, she could hardly have known that – or expected that. Could she? You're not usually an early bird.'

'Far from it,' Isabel said with quiet ferocity, as she turned away from the window out of which she had been gazing.

Clare sank down on to a chest in the hall, all at once feeling giddy. Her hands grasped its side. She knew that Isabel was referring to the morning of Peter's death. Isabel would never forgive her.

There was a crunch of gravel outside the front door and then, all three women waiting in silence for it, the doorbell tinkled. None of them moved, though Clare all but did so. The bearer appeared, walked past them; his head held erect above his slight, sinuous body, and opened the door. An uncertain young man, in a cheap electric-blue suit and a dark blue tie with a silver thread in it, removed a straw hat such as no sahib in the hills at this time of year would ever have thought of wearing. The hat left a darker line across his dark forehead. He was handsome in his pliant, delicate-featured way.

'Clare,' he said. His voice was immature, as though it had only just broken.

'Robin.' They did not embrace, embarrassed to do so before the others.

The bearer stared at the visitor in impudent appraisal, then glided off.

'This is Mrs Thompson.' The boy's hand moved slightly at his side and then fell back, when Isabel did not move hers.

'Pleased to meet you, Mrs Thompson.'

Isabel nodded, silent.

'And this is Mr Thompson's mother.'

The old woman shuffled forward and put out her hand. 'You must forgive my dressing-gown and slippers.' She was not to know that the boy's and Clare's mother spent most of the hot weather dressed as though for bed.

Isabel had been consulting the watch on her outjutting

bosom, squinting down at it. 'You'd better step on it. You have precisely forty minutes to catch the bus.'

'Well, goodbye, Mrs Thompson,' Clare said to her.

'Goodbye, Clare.' Isabel gave the girl a long, steady look. She made no move towards her.

Clare turned to the old woman with a feeling of relief.

'Goodbye, my dear. Take care of yourself.' The old woman put up a skinny, blue-veined arm, placed it around Clare's shoulder and pressed her cheek to hers. Only recently she had described Clare to Toby as 'a rubbishy little thing'; now she felt sorry for her, as she had felt sorry, two days before, for the bird which had flown into her room and had broken its wing against the looking-glass in its frenzy to get out again. Toby had wrung its neck when she had summoned him. Clare breathed in a scent of lavender and, with it and less pleasant, one of old age, sour and musty. 'Forget everything that's happened here.' It was what the old woman had been repeatedly telling herself too – to no avail. 'Forget it all. That's my advice. Put it all out of your mind.' Though she whispered these words, as though in confidence, they were audible both to Isabel and to the boy, so close were they all standing to each other.

Clare grabbed the battered holdall and her brother then moved slowly forward, stooped his long back and began to heft the suitcases, one in either hand. The bearer appeared silently, as though he had been watching through some chink in the door leading to the dining room, and took the holdall from Clare. He would have taken one of the two suitcases from a sahib and summoned a fellow servant to take the other; but he was not prepared to do such a thing for this awkward, ill-dressed Eurasian. After further goodbyes, only the bearer followed brother and sister out to where the dandies, one belonging to the household and the other hired by the boy, stood out on the green rash of the tennis court. The bearer handed the holdall to a coolie. The boy, after an embarrassed moment of hesitation, handed the two suitcases to another. He put a hand to his breast-pocket, then inserted it in his

trouser pocket. He pulled out a few coins and slipped them to
the bearer, his dark face growing even darker as the blood
flooded it. The bearer took them impassively, his head erect,
with no word of thanks. Clare knew that they were far too
little, just as she also knew that she herself should have left at
least two or three notes from that buff envelope for the staff.
But it was too late now, everything was too late now, nothing
could be done. *Forget everything that's happened here. Forget it all.
That's my advice.* That, however impossible it now seemed, was
what she must do.

Clare seated herself gracefully in the dandy belonging to
the household. The boy scrambled into the other, clearly
unused to this form of transport. First her coolies and then his
let out a cry in unison, as they shouldered their loads. Then,
their bare feet pattering over the gravel of the tennis court,
they set off at a half-run. Clare looked back over her shoulder.
There was no one to whom to wave. Not one of them, even the
bearer or the old woman, stood out in the porch, though
everyone would have done so if she and her brother had been
guests leaving after a dinner party. Good riddance to bad
rubbish. She drew a handkerchief out of her bag and held it,
with the daintiness which had so much attracted Toby and
had so much got on Isabel's nerves, first to one delicate nostril
and then to the other. Despair surged through her and then
ebbed, leaving her feeling weak and nauseated.

Again she looked back, a final glance, before the coolies,
grunting and gasping under their swaying load, went out
through the gate and began to patter down the hill, past Mr
Mukerjee's modest bungalow and then the wooden villas of
the Andersons and the Collector, on exactly the same route
which Toby had followed on that terrible morning – only nine
days ago, was it? – shouting out 'My son has been stolen!'

The ample house, with its high, narrow gables pinching
pleats in its red-brick structure, its tidy lawns, flowerbeds and
rose trellises and its untidy servants' quarters, looked deserted at the far end of the tennis court which, in the
prevailing dampness, always had the appearance of a well-

worn billiard table. She would never see it again. *Forget everything that's happened here. Forget it all.* But how could she ever forget that bedroom which she had shared with the child?

Involuntarily, she glanced up to its window, one hand clutching the side of the dandy, while the other rested, fingers splayed, on her throat. As she did so, the net curtain billowed outwards. Toby stood there, motionless, looking down on the departing dandies. She had an impulse to take her hand from her throat, raise it, wave it in farewell. There was a terrible pathos in his round-shouldered, motionless stance, high up there, in the place where that unthinkable thing had not merely been thought but had also been executed.

It was too far for her to see, but she knew, with total certainty, that his burning, famished gaze was fixed on her death-cold, satiated one. Then the dandy descended, jolt by jolt, down the steps incised in the rock beyond the gate, and that final, flimsy thread of communication between them stretched, grew intolerably taut, snapped.

XXIII

Soon after that Helen and her grandmother also left the house, in their case for England.

'Do you really want to go?' Toby had more than once asked his mother, adding on one occasion: 'It only seems yesterday that you got here' and on another: 'I thought you were going to make your home with us.'

To that last reproach old Mrs Thompson answered: 'I meant to, I wanted to. But I feel homesick all of a sudden. I didn't think I would but I do, I'm afraid. I want to see England and I want to get away from India, and there are the two girls and the girls' children. Oh, Toby, don't be cross. Try to understand.'

He did not have to try. He understood already. He knew that she would go, whatever he said in his attempts to dissuade her, and he also knew that, despite all her promises, she would never return.

To Helen, the old woman was franker. 'I've come to hate this house, this place, this country. I know it's irrational of me, such a thing could have happened anywhere in the world. But it's ruined everything for me.' She peered into Helen's face with her watery blue eyes. 'As I think it's ruined everything for you – for a time at any rate. Oh, Helen, he was such a sweet little fellow. How could anyone have come to kill him? How, how, how?'

Helen shrugged. 'I don't know,' she answered stonily.

'I hate to leave your father. Perhaps I ought really to stay until the baby comes. But I don't think Isabel really wants me. I don't think she ever really wanted me.'

In that last judgement, the old woman was right. After Toby had once again tried to dissuade his mother from leaving, Isabel had hissed at him in the privacy of their bedroom: 'Don't go on urging her to stay. If she wants to go, well, let her go. We've done everything possible to make her feel at home. If that's not been good enough for her, that's the end of it. No one wants her to stick on here if she's had enough.'

When Helen announced that she wished to return to England with her grandmother, Toby's reaction was wholly different. He did not try to dissuade her, as he had his mother. Instead, he had answered curtly: 'All right. Fine. You must do what you want to do.' This was far from the attitude which he had adopted when Helen had declared that she wished to go from school, not to India, but to university. 'I'll make you an allowance, of course. And you have the money left to you by your mother. When you're twenty-one, it will cease to be in trust and you can do whatever you . . .'

'Oh, don't let's talk about money, it doesn't interest me.'

Toby felt as affronted as a clergyman told: 'Oh, don't let's talk about religion, it doesn't interest me.' He retorted peevishly: 'It would interest you if you didn't have any.'

That night, as Isabel sat before her looking-glass brushing the thick, black coils of her hair, she said: 'I think Helen's doing the right thing. For herself, for us.'

Toby, in his dressing-gown, the door open between them, was startled. 'For us?'

'It'll be easier to remake our lives – come to terms with everything that's happened – if she's not with us. Far, far away,' she added. 'On the other side of the world.'

Toby stood in the doorway, his black bow tie trailing from a hand. His bare feet were purple and swollen from having been squeezed into pumps too narrow for them. He looked overweight, apoplectic, dishevelled. 'Poor Helen.'

Isabel smiled bitterly at her reflection in the glass.

Toby raised an arm and brought it sharply down, cracking the tie as though it were a whip. 'Do you think we should wait up here until the baby arrives?'

Isabel shook her head. 'No. I want to leave this house as soon as possible. Like your mother. Like Helen. And I don't want ever to come back here. Next hot weather we'll have to find another hill-station and another house. Tell Mukerjee.'

'Do you think it's wise for you to travel?'

Again she gave that bitter smile, not to him, but to the reflection before her. 'I don't know whether it's wise or not. Probably it isn't. But I have to travel. I can't stay here any longer. We'll take Helen and the old girl down to the plains and I'll settle everything into the house while you can go on with them to Bombay. And then you'll be back with me before the baby comes.' She had decided it all. In the past, it had usually been he who made their decisions.

'But I'm afraid that with all the shock and strain you've had – and then with a long journey . . . I don't want you to have another miscarriage.'

'I'm not going to have another miscarriage. Anyway, it's my child, so leave me to decide.'

He was stunned by this odd claiming of the unborn child as entirely her own. But instead of arguing with her, he merely returned disconsolately to his dressing room, shutting the door between them.

On the day before they all departed, Toby went out for his

usual morning ride. The servants were busy packing the household goods in tea chests, which hired coolies would then lug down the hill to lorries at the depot. Isabel directed them, imperiously efficient. So far from needing Toby's help, she had cried out, when he had started to give the bearer some instructions about the disposal of his guns: 'Oh, do leave things to me! We'll only get ourselves and everyone else into a frightful mess if you start to interfere.'

Helen had brought little with her to India and she had packed most of it the night before. Now she was upstairs, helping her grandmother. The old woman was fretful and dithery, as at one moment she cried out 'Oh, throw that away!' and at the next demanded 'What on earth is that doing in the waste-paper basket? Did you put it there?' There was pathos in the way in which her scant clothes had been so carefully hung up in cupboards or set out in drawers, with lavender sachets and layers of tissue paper; and there was an equal pathos in the obstinacy with which she repeatedly edged Helen to one side in order herself to fold something – a darned cardigan, a worn petticoat – exactly right. 'Shoes at the bottom!' she instructed. 'But put in the trees. That's right. And books at the bottom too.' Around her innumerable medicine bottles she carefully wrapped handkerchiefs, which she then knotted firmly over their stoppers. That way, she explained, they would not leak; or, if they did, they would not make a mess.

Riding off, Toby concluded, with a terrible desolation, that he was nowhere needed or wanted. Clare had gone off on her journey, Helen and his mother were about to go off on theirs; and Isabel too seemed to be already embarked on a journey on which she would not allow him to accompany her. He was alone. He let the horse amble, reins slack, down the slithery path, and, as he did so, he thought of that headlong gallop of his, past the Mukerjee house and past the Anderson house and past the other houses – so many suburban villas and bungalows transported from Harrow or Surbiton or Ealing, to this lush, green bowl among the foothills of the Himalayas –

which belonged to all those people who had been so ready with their visits or letters of condolence and who now, whenever they congregated, sailing on the lake, or having picnics on the hill tops, or drinking or playing bridge at the club, whispered, whispered, whispered their insidious gossip.

'Yoo-hoo!'

It was small, silly, pretty Mrs Anderson, Lola, Lolly to her husband and closest friends, secretly Lollipop to Toby, who was shouting up to him, a pair of secateurs in one hand as she straightened herself, the other hand pressed to the small of her back, in an overgrown, yellowing herbaceous border.

He waved back, but only after a long pause, since he could not at first believe that the greeting was for him.

'Come and have a cup of coffee!' she called. 'I'm just about to have one myself.' She, too, had joined in that whisper, whisper, whisper of insidious gossip, which had suddenly given a dangerous attraction to a man whom she had previously regarded as 'just a teeny-weeny bit of a bore'.

Toby hesitated, the reins slack in his hands and his small eyes screwed up against the morning sunlight. Then he shouted back: 'All right, fine.'

Having tethered his horse in some long grass, where the Andersons' laundry flapped on a line – briefly, with a twist of the bowels, he thought of all that to-do about the missing nightdress – he accompanied Lola into the room which, an amateur painter, she called her studio. Her daubs of sunsets bleeding behind black trees or hills, of giant rhododendron bushes looking as if they had been constructed out of wire and garish paper, of fishing boats bobbing on the lake like toy boats in a bath and of still lifes of half-cut loaves of bread, half-eaten apples and misshapen cups, bowls and vases, hung from the walls, one above the other, or else were stacked against them. Toby peered around him. 'Rather jolly,' he said.

'I've been working like a black. I've this exhibition at the club next week. I hope you're going to come and buy. In aid of rebuilding the poor old mission.'

'Oh, we'll be gone by then, I'm afraid. What a shame!
We're setting off tomorrow. But' – he spoke on impulse – 'I'll
buy something now. How about that?'

'Will you? Will you really?'

At that moment, the kitmatgar came in, carrying the coffee
things on an elaborate electroplated tray. Lola pointed
imperiously to a table on which a glass jar full of brushes, a
half-eaten bar of chocolate and a spool of thread, a needle
stuck into it, already rested. Then she sat herself down on the
end of a wicker chaise longue and began to pour out. 'Do
make yourself comfortable.' She fidgeted with the lace-
fringed handkerchief which she had daintily wrapped around
the handle of the coffee pot, even though it was an inset of
wood in the metal. 'Anywhere.'

Toby sat; but he looked far from comfortable on the flimsy
wooden stool opposite to her.

'Tim and I wanted to have you both over to dinner before
your departure. But we didn't know if . . . at such a time . . .'
Her voice trailed away. 'We didn't want to appear to be
neglecting you and we didn't want to appear to be bothering
you needlessly. A problem.'

Toby did not answer, as he took the cup of coffee which she
was holding out to him, her head tilted slightly to one side and
her eyes shining. He noticed, with sudden pleasure, the small
blue veins – how blind he must have been in the past! – over
the collarbones exposed by the low neck of her simple cotton
frock.

'Isabel all right?' Isabel and Lola had never really hit it off.
'I mean' – she lowered her eyelids – 'considering.'

'Yes – considering. The lucky thing is that she didn't lose
the baby.' He surreptitiously touched the wood of the stool
between his legs, a gesture of propitiation to those dark gods
or demons who, during the past days, had seemed to him to be
constantly gazing in unwinking menace, uncoiling and
slithering, and preparing to strike again with their lethal
fangs. 'McGregor feared that. I only pray she'll be all right on
the journey down. I've urged her to wait, to have the baby

here, but you know how obstinate she can be.'

Bloody-minded, Lola thought, nodding her well-kempt head as she recalled arguments on the club entertainments committee.

'Tim away still?' Toby's voice, though he made a determined effort to steady it, carried a tremor of excitement.

She sipped, little finger curled as her hand raised her cup. Over its rim she nodded. 'H'm. He's gone to talk about another irrigation project – beyond Biwali. He has so many irrigation projects in hand that this province will soon be a marsh.' She laughed, then added: 'He's coming back tomorrow.'

'He's often away.'

Again she laughed. 'I sometimes think – not often enough! No, I don't really think that. But, oh, he's getting awfully crotchety. I suppose it was missing promotion to that job in Delhi.' All at once her small, pretty, pug-like face assumed a dissatisfied, even peevish expression. 'And he always seems to be too tired to want to go anywhere or to do anything. Last Sunday, the Noel-Smiths suggested a picnic to Mount Pleasant and he refused, refused just like that without consulting me. Not that he often consults me about anything.' She peered at Toby: 'You must be older than he is.'

'A good bit. Unfortunately.'

'But you've still got some life in you. A lot of life. By all accounts!' She peered at him again and then looked down into her cup, beginning to giggle.

'What gossip have you been hearing about me?'

'Oh. A lot.'

'Such as?' He felt his bowels now twist with excitement as they had previously twisted with apprehension at the sight of that washing line, with its reminder of the missing nightdress.

'Well . . . you're very much a lady's man, aren't you?'

'Oh, I don't know about that.'

'In the club the other day, someone called you an old lecher.'

'Charming! I wonder who it was.' But Toby was more

flattered than annoyed.

'Is it true that you sleep with native women?'

'That's something I'm certainly not going to answer.'

'Then it must be true.'

'I'm terribly uncomfortable on this stool.' He could feel his penis hardening. 'I'm going to come over and sit on that chaise longue beside you.'

'No. You can sit over there. On that deckchair.' She pointed. But already she had shifted herself further to the end of the chaise longue.

'I want to be close to you. Does that offend you?'

'Not at all. Why should it? But I think it might be . . . safer, if you were either to stay where you are or take the deck-chair.'

But he shambled over and placed himself, even more uncomfortably than on the stool, beside her on the wicker chaise longue. He was too far down it for the rest to support his back and, his body twisted askew in order to face her, something sharp and unyielding – a book? – was pressing into his left buttock.

'I hope you're not going to be naughty,' she said skittishly, pulling her skirt down lower over her knees.

'I feel naughty. Don't you ever feel naughty?'

'No. Just sad.'

'Sad?' He turned round and extracted the object digging into him. A writing pad. He held it in both his hands.

'Oh, I don't know. Tim's so often away – if not physically away, then away in his mind. And I haven't got any children. I wanted children. How odd it is, how cruel. Here are all these Indians, with too many children to feed, and here are Tim and I . . .'

'Perhaps you should try a change of partners. That often helps childless couples. So they say.'

'What an immoral suggestion!' But when he put an arm round her shoulder, swivelling round at an even more uncomfortable angle, she made no move or protest.

'I could give you a child. I'm sure I could.'

194

'I'm sure you could too.' She thought of the dead child, Peter, Pete, Peterkin, found in those horrible circumstances in the servants' bathroom (as she termed it); but, instead of that thought chilling her, it brought a flush to her face and a glitter to her usually moist, pale blue eyes.

'Then let me!'

She said nothing, turning her face away from him.

'Then let me, let me, let me.' He put a hand under her white, accordion-pleated crepe de chine skirt, feeling its incredible softness on the back of his hand at the same moment that he felt the incredible softness of the skin of her thigh under it. With the other hand round her shoulder, he now forced her face back, until they were squinting at each other, and then, with a groan, pressed his lips on hers. She gagged, squirmed, raised the leg that he was fondling. Then, all at once, she went strangely rigid and still.

'Christ, how smooth your flesh is!' He was babbling incoherently as his hand, venturing further, tugged at her knickers. 'Oh God, let me feel your cunt, let me feel it! Open your legs, open them, oh, please, please!'

She jerked her lips away from his. 'Careful. The servants . . .'

'Bugger the servants!'

He jumped to his feet, unbuttoned his fly and pulled out his penis and testicles. Involuntarily, she stared. The penis was enormous. He dropped down on his knees and, as she lay back, still strangely rigid, her pretty little pug-face pale and glistening, he began frantically to kiss first her thighs and then her cunt. He felt the moisture of the cunt on his tongue, its smell in his nostrils.

'No, no, no!' She spoke in the tones of a nanny admonishing a child. 'Stop that, will you! Stop that at once!'

Frantically licking her cunt, his tongue probing deeper and deeper, he slid both hands round her haunches and pulled her forward on the chaise longue, her knees by now pressing against his, until she was balanced precariously on its very edge. The wicker creaked, as though at any moment the whole structure would disintegrate under so much weight and movement. He guided his penis, swollen and purple-veined, towards her with a hand, but it was so stiff that he could not bend it sufficiently to get it up her. He thought of pulling her down on to the floor, among the stacks of canvases, or of himself mounting the chaise longue on top of her; but the challenge of their present uncomfortable position only excited him the more. He half raised himself on an elbow, leaned partly over her, the wicker of the rest pressing so hard against his forehead that it subsequently left a lattice of lines on the flesh, and raised one of her thighs with a hand. He put the penis in but at once it slipped out. She gave a little squeak. Somehow he got himself further forward, even though there was a danger that his forehead, pressing so hard against the wicker, might burst through it. He felt her clitoris, slid fingers backwards, then forward again. Her eyes shut, she neither helped him nor hindered him.

At last, by some miracle, he managed both to get his penis up her cunt and to keep it there. Oh, God, God, God! All at once, he thought of Clare: that fine down above her upper lip; the small breasts, unrestricted by a brassière because of the heat, which she had once inadvertently – inadvertently? he was not sure – revealed to him during one of their dinners together, as she had leaned forward to drink from the glass which he had just filled for her; her small white teeth biting on the cigarette holder, tanned with nicotine; the tendrils of coarse hair – like horsehair, Isabel had remarked contemptuously – above the tiny, lobeless ears. He thrust away, in, out, in, out, drops of sweat from his face falling on Lola's shoulder to stain the crepe de chine. In, out, in, out. 'What's the matter with me?' he thought; and then he said it aloud, 'What's the matter with me?' She was no longer gripping him, he felt his penis dwindle. 'Oh, Christ!' More and more frantically he shoved.

Then, suddenly, with a sound of splintering wood, the whole rickety edifice of the chaise longue disintegrated, depositing them on the floor.

196

Lola, Lolly, Lollipop put her hands to her flushed, sweating cheeks and burst into tears, rocking back and forth on her haunches, her knickers around her calves.

'Oh, how could you, could you, could you? What am I to tell Tim? He loved that chaise longue, loved it!'

III
DARKNESS

I

The other two aunts, Joan and Janet, in their tailor-made suits, their crisp blouses, their low-heeled shoes and their almost identical toques, wished that Sophie had not insisted on accompanying them to Tilbury. Sophie, without intending to do so, drew attention to herself. There was something comic about that rolling walk of hers, as of a sailor just off his ship, and something even more comic about the way in which, in time to the rolling, her breasts – was it possible that she did not wear, well, any support at all? – swayed from side to side. Then there were those hats: on this occasion, a grey felt one, like a schoolboy's sunhat, one side of which she had fastened to the crown with a large safety pin. And how she talked – so loud and with no sense that there were certain things which one did not instantly communicate to strangers on a train.

'Are you going to Tilbury to meet someone too?' she leaned forward to ask the little girl opposite to her.

The girl, who was busily smearing choc-ice over her mouth and chin, glanced up at her mother, her tongue, dark with chocolate, coiling round the ice, as though it were a snake.

The mother straightened and shook herself, arms crossed under her outjutting bosom, drew in her chin and said bleakly: 'That's right.'

'Isn't it exciting?' Sophie went on, looking first at the child and then at the mother. Neither answered. Joan pretended to be busy with her crossword puzzle in the *Daily Sketch* – quick crossword, they called it, but she had been intermittently working on it ever since breakfast. Jane looked out of the window, wishing that she had insisted, despite Sophie's objections, on travelling first class. The other passenger in the carriage, a supercilious young man in a charcoal-grey pinstripe suit, noticed that the stocking on Sophie's left leg had a ladder from instep to knee.

Irrepressibly, Sophie ran on. She and these two ladies – relatives in a sense of hers by marriage, no, not her marriage or their marriages but the marriage of their brother to her sister, her darling sister, now dead – were all going to meet their niece, Helen, on her return from India with her grandmother, the mother of these two ladies here. Helen had been through a ghastly experience – so ghastly that one could hardly bear to think about it, let alone talk about it. She had had the sweetest little half-brother you could ever imagine, like something made of china, and then, in a house which had seemed to be a perfectly safe house in what had seemed to be a perfectly safe hill-station in India, that half-brother, believe it or not, had been murdered . . .

By now the little girl had become so interested that, disregarded, the choc-ice was beginning to melt in her hand. The supercilious young man was also interested, though he pretended not to be, as, head on one side, he pinched the creases of his trousers between thumbs and forefingers. But the mother was plainly affronted, and the two sisters were no less plainly embarrassed.

'Who murdered him?' the little girl asked – as the young man had been wanting to do – only to be reprimanded by her mother: 'Now, Elsa, don't be nosey!'

Sophie smiled indulgently at girl and mother alike. Why shouldn't a child be nosey? How else was a child to learn? She leaned forward again: 'That's what makes it even more terrible. The man or men – Indian, of course – have never been caught. Never. Who would want to do such a thing? Who would want to cut the throat of an innocent, beautiful little boy? That's what I keep asking myself, day after day.

Somehow' – she rubbed at her forehead with the back of a hand, as though in a futile attempt at a physical erasure – 'somehow I just can't get it out of my mind, try though I may.'

Joan and Janet suddenly and simultaneously were stricken with guilt at the idea of poor Helen doomed to stay with someone so eccentric – or, as Joan later put it to Janet, someone so batty. In consequence, on the train back from Tilbury they felt obliged once again to ask her if she really and truly preferred living in London to living in the country with one or other of them. 'Cornwall has the better climate, of course, and the more attractive scenery,' Joan, who lived in Sussex, quickly added; and Janet, who lived in Cornwall, then took up: 'But of course it's much quicker and cheaper to get up to town from Sussex.' Each was relieved, though feigning disappointment, when Helen replied: 'No, it's very sweet of you both, but I think the best solution is for me to make my home with Aunt Sophie. If she's really prepared to have me, that is.'

'Really prepared to have you!' With that demonstrativeness of hers, as embarrassing to the two sisters as her extraordinary clothes and loud voice, Sophie clutched both of Helen's hands in hers. 'Oh, darling, I love the idea! You're going to transform my life!' She was being wholly sincere.

Mrs Thompson, who had been dozing in her corner seat during this conversation, with an occasional grunt or snore, now opened her eyes and said in a plaintive voice: 'I do hope that wretch of a porter got all our things into the van. He looked shifty to me – apart from being so slow.'

'Oh, don't fuss, Mother!' Janet told her, and then Joan took up: 'You're not in India now.'

'No, I'm not in India now,' the old woman answered with what, surprisingly, sounded like regret.

At Fenchurch Street they went their separate ways. Joan, who had five children and a vicar for a husband, opted for the underground to Victoria. She had to count the pennies – as she herself often put it with dry self-pity. Janet shoved, rather than supported, Mrs Thompson into the taxi which would take them to Paddington and their train to Cornwall; but, before that, the old woman had first to check her cabin-trunk, hatbox and suitcases for yet another time and then to embrace Helen.

'Goodbye, darling. Let's meet again soon. It made such a difference having you with me on that long, dreary voyage.' Her lips merely brushed Helen's cheek, because she had long since learned that Helen did not really like to be kissed. Then she gripped the tips of the fingers of Helen's right hand between the fingers of her own. 'Oh, you do deserve something nice to happen to you – after all that!'

'All that' was something which Helen had clearly not wished to discuss on the voyage, since, each time that the old woman had obsessively returned to it, wondering yet again who could want to do such a thing and how a supposedly good God could have permitted it, she would always become silent and distant, her eyes going out of focus in a face frozen into a sudden blank. Strange girl, the old woman would decide. She oughtn't to bottle things up like that inside her. A recipe for trouble later.

Sophie and Helen also took a taxi, the aunt insisting that the niece should get into it ahead of her, just as she had insisted on helping the porter and the taxi-driver with loading the luggage up in front. Standing by the open window, her squat legs astride, she had fumbled in her leather purse for a tip for the porter. Helen had known what would happen, since it had so often happened before. 'Oh! Oh lord! Oh, oh, oh!' Coins had rolled in all directions. Clearly Sophie had forgotten that the stitching had become unravelled at one corner of the purse. Passers-by had rushed to her assistance, proffering pennies, halfpennies and farthings, many of them laughing with the lofty indulgence shown by adults to a clumsy child.

Having first tipped the porter, so lavishly that he later remarked ungratefully to a colleague that the old girl must be barmy, and then heaved herself aboard the taxi, Sophie had put her hand over Helen's. 'Comfy, dear?'

'Oh, yes, Aunt Sophie. Thank you.'

Helen looked out of the window at the scarlet buses, the grimy buildings, the honking cars, the occasional horse-drawn carts and everywhere, like the termites which the gelding had once revealed, kicking open a nest beneath a tree in the woods above the lake, people, people, people. She said expressionlessly: 'When Daddy and Mama were over here last, we all stayed at Brown's Hotel. You probably remember? And Mama's mother came there too for a week. Mama, Mama's mother and I were always taking taxis, never buses or tubes, while Daddy was away on business. Mama and her mother always placed themselves on this seat, looking forward. And I was always left on one of those tip-up seats opposite. Of course it was Daddy's – or perhaps even Mummy's money – which paid for the taxis, as it paid for everything else. When we got out of the taxi, Mama would say to the driver: "Now let me see. That's seven and six, isn't it? And sixpence extra for the girl." I was always "the girl" and always the extra.'

Sophie looked troubled. 'Oh, I expect that was just a manner of speaking. Don't you, dear?'

'A manner of speaking can tell one a lot.'

'I think Isabel's really very fond of you. I think she looks on you as – as a daughter.'

Once again gazing out of the window, Helen did not answer.

'Or a sister,' Sophie amended.

II

In the lodging-house in Earls Court, aunt and niece shared a long, low-ceilinged room, with a wash-stand behind a barbola screen of cracked and yellowing arum lilies, two divan beds draped in counterpanes sent by Toby from his mills as one of the many Christmas presents over the years, and a gas ring, a kettle on it, which swung out on a swivel from beside the gas fire.

'You don't mind sharing with me for a day or two, do you dear?'

'No, of course not.'

'Signora Rossi promised me that you could have the first-floor back, oh, ages ago – when I first mentioned your coming to her. But then old Mr Lawrence, who was going to move to his daughter's, got this 'flu which everyone is having. Which reminds me – I must take him something tasty to eat. I wonder what would tempt him?'

When, many days later, grumpy, ungrateful old Mr Lawrence had recovered sufficiently to move out of the house without even a word of goodbye to Sophie ('I expect he was feeling too seedy and fussed to remember'), Helen showed no eagerness to transfer to his room upstairs. 'It's rather poky,' she commented when Sophie took her to inspect it. 'And it has such a funny smell. Don't you get it?'

It was the smell of old age; but Sophie, who had become used to far worse smells in the settlement in the East End, was puzzled. 'Smell, dear? Oh, it only needs the window open.' It was then that she noticed the look of anxiety, almost panic, on her niece's face. 'But you don't *have* to move up here. Not if you don't want to. I mean, if you'd rather share with me – if it's not too crowded and uncomfy for you . . .'

Helen gave herself a little shake, as though to dislodge herself from some imprisoning daydream. 'Yes, I think I'd really rather do that.'

Sophie was delighted. 'Lovely! Well, that settles that. I'll tell Signora Rossi. It'll be a little economy for us, won't it?'

Helen said softly: 'We don't have to think about economies, Aunt Sophie. Daddy's making me an enormous allowance. You know that.'

'Oh, but that's for *you* – that's your pocket money. So that you can buy some gorgeous frocks and go to theatres and concerts and parties and altogether have a lovely, lovely time.'

Sophie had a large income from the money which she and Helen's mother had inherited from their father; but, so generous with others, she was frugal with herself. Typically, when old Mr Lawrence had either forgotten or deliberately omitted to settle with her for the food which she had bought for him during the weeks of his illness, she never reminded him; and when, on the second day of Helen's stay, a one-armed ex-soldier in cloth cap and muffler had begun to play a barrel-organ in the centre of the square, she first had cried out in delighted recognition 'A wandering minstrel I!' and then, having plucked a pound note from her purse, had run out, leaving the front door open, to give it to him. People, as cruelly transformed by the smell of her innocence as animals by the smell of blood, would often overcharge her; but if Helen protested: 'Oh, Aunt Sophie, apples can't possibly cost as much as that!' or 'Four shillings for that tiny amount of gristly mince!' she would reply, shocked and hurt: 'Oh, but dear, they would never *dream* of cheating me! I've been going to them, week in, week out, for years and years.' Helen would then feel that it was she, not the shopkeeper concerned, who had fallen below expectations.

Though a heavy sleeper, Sophie would often be woken in the night by a sudden cry. She would prop herself up on an elbow, her hand to the switch of the bedside lamp between them, preparatory to putting it on, and would then stare through the near-darkness at the face of her niece. The face looked untroubled, the girl was clearly sleeping. Could she have dreamed that cry? But one morning, as she was returning from the bathroom, towel over an arm and sponge-bag in hand, she came face to face with the middle-aged secretary who lived in the room next door, and the secretary, having said good morning, asked: 'Is it you or your niece who has the nightmares?' 'The nightmares?' Sophie was discon-certed, but for a moment only. Then she smiled apologetical-ly: 'Oh, dear, am I disturbing you? I'm so sorry. I'm afraid I've had this silly habit of calling out in my sleep ever since I was a child. I'm never even aware that I've done it.' Pulling open the front door, the secretary said: 'Ah well, never mind. It can't be helped, I suppose.'

Helen rarely left the house alone. Indeed, she rarely left it at all. Seated in a deckchair by the French windows which opened out on to a grimy paved yard – at the bottom of it, there was a concrete shed in which Signora Rossi's son kept his motorbike and the tenants their dustbins – she could feel safe; but once she was out in the street, she felt that anything could befall her – a building might topple, a bus might veer off the road and pin her to a wall, a maniac might emerge from the crowd, an axe in his hand.

Sophie was at first reluctant to leave her to herself; but, if she stayed, Helen would show little inclination to talk. 'Would you like to come to the settlement with me? They're such a splendid lot – though their lives have been so awful. It might be an interest for you.' But Helen did not seem to want an interest. Or Aunt Sophie would coax her, as though she were a fractious child: 'Do come with me to my meeting. Ouspensky has made such a difference to my life. He's given me, oh, such perspectives. I was never religious in the conventional sense, as your mother was, but I always felt that there was a part of me – a spiritual part – waiting to be developed. This young man is quite remarkable. He gets impatient with me from time to time – I'm terribly slow and silly about understanding what he tells us – but, yes, yes, one does feel that he lives his life on a totally different plane from an earthling like myself.' The young man, though she did not tell Helen this, was another recipient of her money. 'Do come with me, dear!' But Helen shook her head, sighed and held up her library book: 'I think I'll get on with this.'

Letters arrived from Toby, occasionally for Sophie, regularly for Helen. Sophie would at once open hers, so excitedly that she would usually manage to tear the sheets inside as well as the envelopes. Then she would read passages out to Helen, with wondering interpolations of 'Fancy that!' or 'Would you believe it?' about the most ordinary of happenings. Helen, on the other hand, would place one letter, unopened, on the table by her bed; and then, a week later, she would place the next letter, also unopened, on top of it. The letters would accumulate. Sophie would tidy them from time to time, holding them in her hands and barely restraining herself from urging Helen to read them. Then, at last, she would burst out: 'Aren't you going to see what your father has to say?' 'Some time.' Finally, after a number of such verbal nudges and shoves, Helen would at last put down the library book of the moment with a sigh and begin systematically to read through four or five letters in sequence.

Before the letters, a telegram had arrived. It was addressed to Sophie, not to Helen, and it read: 'ISABEL HAS HAD GIRL STOP BOTH DOING WELL AFTER DIFFICULT DELIV-ERY STOP WRITING TOBY.'

'Isn't that lovely?' Sophie cried out. 'Old Mrs Thompson was so afraid she'd lose it. When we heard nothing, I began to think that no news was bad news. Do you think Toby has sent his mother a cable too? Or do you think I ought to put through a trunk call to Sussex? Oh, he must have told her!'

Helen did not answer. She picked up the cable between thumb and forefinger from the table where Sophie had laid it down, as though it were a handkerchief inadvertently drop-ped by one or other of them. Then she carried it over to the waste-paper basket, of the same barbola work as the screen – one of the girls at the settlement, a hunchback, so clever with her fingers, had made both, Sophie had once explained – paused a moment and then let it flutter down on top of a fuzz of grey combings from Sophie's hair, the peel of a tangerine and a circular about a new restaurant in Kensington High Street which Sophie and Helen would certainly never enter.

After the arrival of the telegram and many times subse-quently Sophie would urge, a puzzled frown drawing her brows together, so that she looked like an over-sized school-girl faced with an equation beyond her ability to solve: 'Oughtn't you to send your father a line? I've written to him, of course, but I'm sure he'd much rather hear from you. He's such a wonderful correspondent, though so busy. Through all

209

these years since your mother's death he's never failed to keep in touch with me – heaven knows why.' Usually, her gaze fixed on the page before her, Helen ignored all such promptings; but sometimes, with a wearily patient smile – 'Oh, all right then!' it seemed to say – she would rise, get down from the top of the wardrobe the crocodile-leather writing case which had once been her mother's, take out a pad, and write a brief, uninformative, undemonstrative note.

One day Helen did not get out of bed. Sophie was off to the settlement, where, that afternoon, they were going to hold a Rummage Sale. For several weeks, she had been badgering friends, neighbours and even the local shopkeepers to make their contributions, with the result that one corner of the room now contained a sour-smelling stack of worn, misshapen shoes, cardigans fretted by moth, rusty saucepans with blackened accretions inside them, cracked cups often without either handles or saucers, a dinner jacket bottle green with age, some stays trailing grubby laces. Dear Mr Kearney, a young bachelor who also worked voluntarily at the settlement, was going to transport all these objects in a van borrowed from a friend. Sophie had asked Helen if she would like to take a hand, telling her: 'Oh, it's going to be such fun! And it's in such a good cause! For a new handicrafts shed. Do come, dear! You've never met Mr Kearney, have you? Like you, he's a tremendous reader. Folklore's his thing. He knows everything there is to know about folklore. I'm sure you'd find lots and lots to talk about together.' But Helen had refused.

Now, as Sophie first vigorously sponged herself all over with cold water from the basin on the wash-stand – baths were extra – with no sense of shame and then began to dress, Helen, who usually got up before she did, lay on her side, watching her from her bed with wide, vacant eyes. Sophie felt vaguely troubled; something was not quite right.

'I'm afraid that Mr Kearney will have to come in here. I don't think I can carry all these things by myself.'

'That doesn't matter. I don't mind.'

Sophie wondered if Mr Kearney would mind. He was such

a proper young man, spending all his time on his folklore, the settlement or visits to the Roman Catholic Church in Farm Street, near where he lived. But that vague unease expanding within her, like some ill-digested meal, she said nothing more about Mr Kearney. 'You will have some breakfast when you feel like it, won't you?' Helen did not answer. She had refused even a cup of coffee when, in her dressing-gown, her hair still in curlers, Sophie had eaten her own breakfast seated on an edge of her bed, the 'old MG' open before her. Again Helen did not answer. Just as when the girls at the settlement mocked at her or teased her, Sophie now ran on, as though words, however foolish or unnecessary, would somehow make things all right again. 'There's plenty to choose from for your lunch. Baked beans. That cold gammon – I don't think it's gone off but make sure, dear, won't you? Cheese – some of that Derbyshire Sage you so much like, as well as some mousetrap. Oh, and tomatoes – I got them for almost nothing at a stall in the Mile End Road. Such a nice man, who last year spent months and months in prison for a burglary he never committed. And then, if you feel really ambitious, you could always do something with that chuck steak which I was too lazy to cook for us last night . . .'

She would have continued to enumerate possible items, if Helen had not said: 'Yes, Aunt Sophie, yes,' in a tone of extreme weariness and then turned away to the wall.

'My niece is feeling a little off-colour, so she's lying in this morning. You won't mind going into the room with her in bed, will you, Mr Kearney? I'm sure you'll understand.'

Mr Kearney, prudish and fastidious, did, in fact, mind; but fortunately, as he went back and forth, his pointed chin balanced on armful after armful of junk, all that he could see of Helen was the outline of what might merely have been a bolster under the bedclothes.

'Goodbye, Helen dear!' Sophie called when everything had been cleared. 'I'll try not to be too late home. But there'll be a lot of clearing up to do afterwards – there's bound to be.'

Mr Kearney stood out in the hall, shifting his weight from

one stork-like leg to another and thinking, as he often did at
the settlement: 'How can people live like his?' His pretty little
Mayfair house, inherited from a bachelor uncle, always made
him feel guilty. That was why he spent so much time at the
settlement or in the Farm Street Church.

When, yet again, Helen made no response, Sophie, who
was carrying her last load – a Pye wireless cabinet, a rising
sun fretted on it, empty of any wireless – edged towards the
bed. She peered round the cabinet, which she had refused to
allow Mr Kearney to take from her – 'No, it's terribly dusty.
You don't want to spoil that lovely pinstripe suit' – and
ventured: 'You *are* feeling all right, aren't you?'

'Oh, yes, thank you. Yes.'

'It's not your period, is it?'

Outside in the hall, Mr Kearney flinched. What a loud
voice that woman had! It was the one thing which, devoted to
her though he was, he simply could not take (as he put it to his
sister, who simply could not take anything about poor
Sophie). He did not hear Helen's answer, which was a low:
'Good heavens, no! That was last week.'

When Sophie returned that evening, her usually clear and
rosy complexion muddied by fatigue and her feet and calves
aching from so much standing, it seemed as if Helen had not
stirred since she had left her some ten hours previously. In all
that dealing with people looking for bargains where few
bargains existed, in pouring out innumerable cups of strong,
stewed Indian tea from an urn that constantly dripped on to
her shoes, in jovially stiffening Mr Kearney whenever, like a
plant bereft of a stake, he suddenly began to droop, in
separating two girls who, squabbling over a pair of downtrod-
den feather mules, had begun to bite and claw at each other,
and in sweeping up – all but one or two of her helpers
vanished – the debris afterwards, Sophie had forgotten her
unease; but now, as she peered down, her round face tilted, at
the humped form shrouded by bedclothes, it flooded back into
her, bitter and strong.

'Haven't you been up today?'

'No.'

'Aren't you feeling well?'

'I'm all right.'

'Had something to eat?'

Sophie sat down on her own bed, so close to Helen's that she had only to put out an arm to touch her, and began to unlace and tug off her shoes. She massaged her aching feet – they seemed at least one size larger than when she had set off or else the shoes had shrunk by a size – with a dreamy pleasure, screwing up her eyes.

Helen was silent. Then she murmured, long after Sophie had ceased to expect any answer: 'I didn't want anything.'

'Shall I give Dr Spencer a ring?'

'No. Why?'

'I thought you might be seedy.'

'I'm perfectly all right.'

'Good. Oh good.' Sophie rose briskly, in her stockinged feet, and, putting two hands behind her back, unfastened her brassière. She had been longing to do that all through the long, exhausting day. 'Well, let's have something to eat. What's it to be?'

'Nothing.'

'Oh, come along, dear! I'll make you some scrambled eggs as you always like them – in the double-boiler, runny, with some chives chopped up in them, those chives that Mr Kearney gave me from his pot. How about that?'

'I've no appetite.'

'Well, try to eat something for my sake.'

'The thought of food, just the thought, revolts me.'

'I hope you're not going down with jaundice. There's a lot of it about. That's exactly how I felt when I had it in Calcutta.'

'I'm not ill, Aunt Sophie.'

'Well, then make a little effort to get something down – just to please me. To make me happy. Will you?'

Helen wanted to make her aunt happy; and so, when the scrambled eggs had been ladled out from the double-burner on to the squares of buttered toast – they were curdled, not runny, since Sophie, rushing to stop the toast from burning, had left them unstirred – and the plate had been carried over to her on a small tray of Benares brass, also a present from Toby, she forced herself to swallow mouthful after mouthful.

'That's a good girl!' Sophie cried out. 'Now how about a piece of that fudge I brought back from the sale? Mr Kearney's sister made it, so it ought to be good.'

But by now Helen felt that she had done her duty.

III

Listlessly, Helen lay in her bed day after day. She would get up to wash herself perfunctorily at the wash-stand behind the barbola screen, finding a degraded pleasure in the odours of her own body. (It was usually Sophie, not she, who went along to the bathroom, enamel jug in hand, to fetch the water, and who later returned there with the brimming slop pail.) When she had to go to the lavatory, she would hurry down the corridor in dressing-gown and slippers, dreading an encounter with Signora Rossi, her son or one of the other tenants. 'You all right, love?' Signora Rossi asked in her Italian-Cockney accent, hurrying past, dustpan and brush in hand after a sweeping of the stairs. Her handsome, hulking teenage son, with his luxuriant, brilliantined hair falling to his collar and his large hands soiled with engine-grease, merely looked away when he and Helen came face to face at the lavatory door. 'Better, are we?' The secretary, already late for work, did not wait for an answer, as she slammed the front door behind her.

Helen no longer read, rarely talked. Sophie, going out, would switch on the wireless for her. 'There's something nice! Melodies from "Merrie England". Your grandfather knew Edward German – did you know that? They belonged to the same club, I think.' But as soon as Helen heard the front door close and the heavy feet thumping down the steps, she would extend an emaciated arm and switch off the set again.

'No, I don't want to see a doctor, I've told you, there's nothing wrong with me.'

'But, darling, it's not natural for a girl of your age to want to spend all her time in bed. Now is it? And Dr Spencer is such a kind, good woman. Impatient sometimes, but that's because she has so much to do. She'll give you something. You'll see. She'll put the stuffing back into you in no time at all.'

'I don't want to see Dr Spencer!' Helen's was the fretful tearfulness of a patient debilitated by a long and serious illness. 'I've told you and told you.'

'Very well, dear. As you think best.'

Helen felt a sudden love for this absurd, clumsy, saintly woman, and a sudden contrition. For her sake, she yearned to get out of bed, have a bath, put on her clothes, go out, do something; but it was the hopeless yearning of the victim of a paralysing stroke. She wanted; she couldn't.

'At any rate, will you allow me to get you a bottle of Metatone?'

'Of what?'

'Metatone. A tonic. It worked wonders for me last winter, when I had no energy. Or Sanatogen – that's a pick-me-up said to be awfully good.'

'All right, Aunt Sophie. If you wish, yes.'

'Which is it to be?'

'Which?'

'Metatone or Sanatogen?'

'Whichever you want.' It might, Sophie thought, be she herself who was going to take the tonic.

Sophie confided in Mr Kearney when next he drove her in his Armstrong Siddeley to the settlement.

'Sounds like some kind of nervous breakdown to me,' he murmured.

'Oh, she's quite right in her mind. I suppose it's the delayed shock of that terrible experience of hers in India. Did I ever tell you about it?'

'Yes.' Sophie had told him about it often.

'It could be that, couldn't it?'

'I'm sure it could.'

'If only she had some faith!'

'Faith in what?'

'Oh, anything, anything. I think faith is so important in life.'

'Faith in life is important,' Mr Kearney said sententiously.

Like a taper repeatedly applied to a sulky fire, it was Sophie's faith in life which eventually, after many weeks, reignited Helen's.

'Oh, the hail! The hail! Look, Helen, look! It's bouncing off the pavements! Beautiful!' The plain, rosy face, as of some old-fashioned nanny, was irradiated with pleasure, as Sophie stood, in knickers and stays, before the window on to the street. One hand raised the net curtain so that, opposite but unknown to her, a young, recently married couple, sitting at their breakfast, could giggle at the spectacle.

The one-armed ex-soldier with the barrel-organ returned and the square jangled with a waltz from *The Merry Widow*. Sophie, who had limped in, wan and dishevelled, from a day at the settlement, began to waltz, clutching a cushion to her bosom and singing in a surprisingly deep contralto: 'Vilia, O Vilia, the witch of the wood . . .'

'Ah, the muffin man!' It was winter now and the bell tinkled down the area steps of the house next door. 'Let's have some muffins. Let's make pigs of ourselves, Helen, let's have lots and lots of muffins, dripping with butter!'

Sophie held out a scarf, then drew it to her and stroked it with one hand as it lay over the palm of the other. 'Isn't it beautiful? Just beautiful. *Seta pura.*' She held up the scarf to show the label. 'That means pure silk. Mr Kearney brought it to me from Florence. Wasn't that good of him? So typical. Fancy remembering an old woman like me, when he must have lots and lots of girlfriends.' Helen was perspicacious enough to have realized that Mr Kearney had never had a girlfriend in his life; but after weeks and weeks of non-feeling, the old woman's rapture caused a painful, yet exhilarating

216

stirring within her, as of seeds beginning at last to germinate.

One morning, with no explanation, Helen got up. It was still dark, the hour only a few minutes after seven, with Aunt Sophie, exhausted from a visit the previous day to one of her girls in Holloway ('How can one blame people who have nothing for taking something?'), still lying, mouth open, on her back in bed. Helen pattered down to the bathroom, her sponge bag dangling by its strings from a wrist and a towel over forearm, placed sixpence in the rusty gas geyser and watched as the orange water coughed and spurted into the bath. Then, with voluptuous pleasure unknown to her for weeks and weeks, she climbed in, the water so hot that she almost screamed from the touch of it on her flesh, soaped herself over and over, immersed her head, shook out her streaming hair, splashed, splashed again.

When she finally emerged, the secretary was awaiting her turn outside the door. 'Well, you've been taking your time and no mistake!' But she said it without rancour. Then, through the drifts of steam, she saw that there was a pool of water by the side of the bath and another at its head. 'Oh!' she exclaimed, daintily recoiling. 'What a mess!'

'Sorry,' Helen mumbled.

While Sophie slept on, her mouth wide open like some baby bird's waiting for sustenance, Helen dried her still wet hair and put combs in it; took out a bottle of transparent varnish and carefully applied it to her nails; brushed her teeth up and down, back and forth behind the barbola screen. Then she went to the chest-of-drawers and got out some underclothes. Slipping into a vest, she thought: How thin I've become!

All at once, sitting up in bed, Sophie cried out: 'Oh, Helen, Helen! What a gorgeous birthday present!'

Helen had completely forgotten that it was Sophie's birthday. But she smiled over the dress which she was about to slip over her head and said: 'I decided I was going to take you out to lunch. A treat for you. And I couldn't take you out to lunch unless I looked my best.'

'Oh, Helen, how lovely! It's so long since anyone took me

out to lunch. But nothing too expensive. No extravagance. In fact, I'm going to pay my whack. Dutch treat.'

'Certainly not! I'm going to take you to the Green Cockatoo and you're not going to pay a penny.'

'No, not the Green Cockatoo, Helen. It's not my sort of place. Far too chic for me.' What she really meant was that it was far too expensive for Helen. 'But I tell you what. Take me to Derry and Toms Roof Garden. Oh, I love it there. The Spanish Cloister, the Old English Garden, the flamingoes and peacocks and ducks. I've not been there since Noel Coward was opening it for some theatrical charity or other. And then afterwards we can have a snack lunch in the Rainbow Room below. Oh, what a lovely day!'

Nine weeks after that, Helen became a medical student; and eighteen months after that the war broke out. Toby, Isabel and their daughter had been due to arrive in England on leave but they cancelled their passages. It was not that they were afraid of torpedoes or air-raids, Toby wrote to explain; but they did not think that they should needlessly endanger the life of their little girl, Angela, Angie, Angel. They would all just have to wait.

IV

The wait was a long one.

Helen eventually persuaded Sophie to move out of the bedsitting room into a basement flat near to the hospital at which she was studying. 'We'll be much safer there,' she said.

'But, darling, think of the expense!'

'I have money, Aunt Sophie — *money*, lots and lots of it. And the rent is nothing.' Everyone who could was fleeing London.

'Well, I must pay my share.'

'Certainly not!'

But, of course, Sophie insisted.

The entrance to the flat was down precipitous steps into an area filled with dustbins. Behind the peeling front door, there stretched a long, murky passage, at first containing the electricity and gas meters for the whole block and then leading to two square, low-ceilinged bedrooms, a bathroom, a sitting room and a miniscule kitchen.

'Oh, it's so cosy!' Sophie exclaimed, as she stood, sturdy legs wide apart, in the middle of the sitting room and looked all around her.

Helen crossed to a wall, unhitched a reproduction of Manet's *Au Bar des Folies Bergères* and placed it on the sagging sofa. 'That must go for one thing.'

'Oh, but dear, I love it. It's one of my favourite pictures.'

'Then you can have it in your bedroom.'

'May I?' Sophie was delighted. Again, she gazed around her, her mouth open on uneven teeth. 'A home of our own! Do you know, I haven't had a home – a real home – of my own since Daddy died. So many years ago now.'

There was a terrible pathos in her pleasure. Helen crossed to her and put her arms around her. She began to shake her gently: 'But you could have had, you could have had! If you didn't always spend your money on other people. That's what's so awful. You could have had.'

Embarrassed, Sophie gently extracted herself from Helen's embrace and wandered up the corridor. 'Which bedroom would you like me to have?'

'Whichever one you want.'

Sophie peered into the one bedroom and then into the other. 'You take the front one. It's bigger. You have so many more bits and pieces than I have.' Then she put out a hand: 'No, dear, I think I'll take the front one. If you don't mind. If it's not too selfish of me. It's so much brighter.'

Helen knew that Sophie had changed her mind because she had suddenly realized that there was less danger of blast in the room at the back. There followed a long argument, similar to their long argument as to whether they should rent this flat or a larger, better-furnished one; and now, as before, it was Sophie who, gently obdurate, emerged the victor.

*   *   *

Soon, the Blitz had squashed flat that area of Stepney which the settlement, founded by two pious, well-to-do Victorian spinsters, had been intended to serve. The settlement was closed.

'Why don't you move out of London?' Helen suggested. 'You've nothing now to keep you here.'

'I have you to keep me here,' Sophie answered with that simple candour which so often shocked or embarrassed people more complex and devious than herself. 'And – oh, I know it's terrible to say this – it's so exciting to be at the heart of things. I couldn't bear to be far away in the country.'

When, at the height of the Blitz, flock upon flock of planes, soaring, swooping, spraying outwards and regathering, had filled what would otherwise have been a tranquil summer evening with the roar and scream of engines, the thud of bombs, the stench of smoke, the wails of sirens and lurid colours welling up over the sky, Helen had come home from the hospital, running in panic from the bus stop, to find that Sophie was not at home. She went into the air-raid shelter, constructed in the other of the two basement flats, where she found an elderly man, three women and a child seated, in the damp and gloom, on canvas chairs set out in a row, as though at the seaside.

'I was looking for my aunt. I thought she might be here.' She had met the elderly man, a retired bank manager, before. The women and the child were strangers to her. She assumed that they were not residents of the block but there by his invitation.

One of the women first hauled the child on to her knee and then answered: 'When we came down in the lift, she was waiting to take it up. I asked her where she was going and she said up to the roof. I told her to do nothing so foolish but she wouldn't listen to me.' Clearly, even if Helen did not know any of the women, Sophie knew this one, if not the others.

Helen waited by the lift but it never came. The current must have been switched off. Eventually she ran up and up the stairs, past one silent flat after another. Silly old thing!

What did she think she was doing? This kind of anxiety was the last thing one wanted when one had spent the afternoon in the dissecting room. Her anger boiled up.

She flung open the door on to the flat roof. 'Aunt Sophie!' she called.

Sophie stood gazing alternately up into the sky, as the bombers droned over, and down towards the City, now spurting flames and billowing with smoke. Her hands pressed to her cheeks, there was a look of childish rapture on her face. 'Oh, Helen, Helen! Look! Just look! Have you ever seen anything so thrilling? Marvellous!'

Helen marched over and grabbed her by an arm. 'Come downstairs at once! Are you out of your mind? Come on!' She pulled Sophie behind her, first off the roof and then stumbling down the darkened stairs. 'What on earth did you think you were doing?'

Behind her, Sophie was gabbling: 'Oh, darling, don't be cross with me. I know it was naughty of me. I had no idea you'd be back so early. I didn't want to cause you any worry. Truly I didn't.'

Helen stopped, turned. Far off, there was a crump, followed by a strange, ominous rustle, like paper being screwed up in some giant fist. 'Whether I was worried is neither here nor there. But you're mad to risk your life like that.'

She began once again to hurry on down the stairs and Sophie stumbled and lurched behind her.

Once in the flat, Sophie panted, a hand pressed to her breastbone as though in an effort to stay the thudding of her heart: 'Yes, I'm afraid it *was* naughty of me. After all, one shouldn't regard as a spectacle something which is causing death, damage, suffering, oh, so much suffering. That wasn't just naughty, it was wicked. But, Helen, the colours! Beautiful! Extraordinary!'

'Damn the colours! It's *you* I mind about. You mustn't do these things.'

Sophie shook her head. She looked as if she were on the verge of tears. 'Wicked. Wicked of me, wicked of me.'

*   *   *

Instead of working at the settlement, Sophie now worked at a shelter, under one of the London bridges, for the vagrants whose number, instead of decreasing, had mysteriously increased with the war. Why did they stay in the danger of London, when they could escape to the safety of the country? No one knew the answer.

Helen, visiting the shelter, at once noticed how the other women working there had got into the habit of snubbing and patronizing Sophie. They unloaded on to her the dirtiest and most menial of their duties. They constantly ordered her about and found fault with her.

Even while Helen was talking to Sophie at the sink at which she was patiently washing up piles and piles of crockery and cutlery, the supervisor, Mrs Blake, a woman with a grey fringe over a bulging forehead and wide hips all but bursting her slacks, strode over with an admonishment: 'Four more spoons are missing. And a fifteen-pound bag of sugar. What happens to these things?' It was almost as though she were accusing Sophie of stealing them.

'Was that my fault?' Sophie asked with an abjectness that made Helen as angry with her as with the supervisor.

'Well, I don't know who else's it could have been.'

'Oh, dear!'

'You must keep an eye on them every single minute. They just cannot be trusted. You know that.'

But that was something which Sophie neither knew nor believed. 'I'll bring some spoons tomorrow. And I'll save up my own sugar ration.'

The supervisor gave a grim smile, not to Sophie, but to Helen, as though the two of them were in complicity against this dotty, inefficient old woman. 'It'll take you a long time to replace fifteen pounds of sugar. The war'll be over long before that.'

When not on duty at the shelter, Sophie was perpetually scuttling around on jobs and errands for others – friends, acquaintances, neighbours, strangers. Helen would protest that surely this or that person could find time, himself or herself, to return library books, buy stamps, collect a prescription, hand in a form, queue for cigarettes or cat meat. But invariably Sophie would find some excuse. Poor Mrs J had so much to do cooking for that demanding husband and all those children of hers; Miss T had such a terror of venturing out, ever since she had been trapped in that wrecked underground train; dear old Mr F from upstairs was in some kind of important hush-hush work that gave him few free hours. It was useless to try to dissuade her. And all the time she was tormented by the guilty fear that, at fifty-nine, she was not really doing enough. Perhaps she should volunteer as a nurse, even though she was so squeamish? Or Air Raid Warden? Become a bus conductress? Work in a factory?

'Oh, Helen, Helen, Helen, I hate to see you looking so pale and tired!' she would cry out when Helen returned home from the hospital, having worked for hours on end on casualties from the bombings. Sophie was never aware that she herself, having hurried up and down streets emptied by air-raids, having eaten almost nothing and having hardly slept for nights and nights on end, looked far paler and more tired.

Sophie would often tell Helen: 'I don't know how you can bear to deal with people in that condition. When I worked in that hospital in Calcutta, I was so easily upset. Blood terrified me. They had to take me out of the operating theatre. I couldn't work there. However much I tried, I always used to faint. You're so strong, Helen, so strong. That's what I admire about you, that's what I envy. Fancy being able to help with amputations and sewings-up and terrible things like that.'

At such times Helen would stiffen. Then she would say something like: 'Oh, one gets used to anything' or 'Well, one gets hardened.'

Once, after repeated invitations, Sophie and Helen went to spend a long weekend with Joan, her children and old Mrs Thompson in a village outside Chichester. Joan's husband, now an Army chaplain, was away in the Middle East. Joan was serving on innumerable committees – evacuees, civil defence, comforts for the troops – so that she was rarely at home and, when she was, had a tendency to be snappy and preoccupied. Mrs Thompson, far frailer than when Helen last had seen her, spent much of her time lying out on a sofa by the open sitting-room window or, if the weather was fine, on a deckchair on a lawn much of which had been given up to the growing of vegetables. Doing nothing, she kept peering up at the sky, as though fearful that, at any moment, aeroplanes would swoop down from it like giant birds of prey. Two of the five children were away at boarding school – one of the few advantages, Joan said, of being a clergyman's wife was that one could get one's children educated for nothing, or virtually nothing. The other three, all under eight, disturbed Sophie with their wildness and inarticulacy. They were supposed to go to a dame's school in the village but rarely seemed to be there. Clearly, they neither wanted nor needed regular meals – which Joan, distracted by her tasks, was too busy to enforce on them. Furtive and grubby, they wandered into the kitchen and then wandered out again, munching on doorsteps of bread spread thick with lard, sour cooking apples or eggs which they themselves hard-boiled, leaving the pan full of misty water in which strands of albumen, leaked from shells so thin that they had cracked, writhed like slender worms. From far beyond the towering hedge which shut in the garden, the three women – four, if Joan happened to be at home – would hear their voices ring out, stridently excited, after their mutterings, mumblings and silences at home.

Suddenly, Helen defected from the adults and became one of them. She taught them to play rounders in the field in which Joan and a woman neighbour kept the cow which each of them was always forgetting to milk. She took them, herself on a man's bicycle belonging to Joan's absent husband and they on rusty, rackety ones of their own, for day-long expeditions. She joined them in demon-grab, the four of them squatting on the carpet of the sitting room, with the labrador bitch beside them, as they shouted and pounced. In the evening, all of them perched on a stile while Helen extemporized a story. Joan, pausing in some task, would complain fretfully: 'It's far too late for those children to be out. What does the girl think she's up to?' and Sophie would then murmur: 'Bless her heart!'

On the train back to London, Sophie said: 'How wonderful you were with Joan's brood! I never knew you had that gift for children.'

Helen said nothing, as she traced her initials 'HT' in the grime of the window beside her. She had come to hate the grime of things left too long unattended and uncleaned. She was always remarking on it in the hospital – net curtains grey and greasy, window-sills encrusted with pigeon droppings, linoleum stained, scuffed and cracked – to be asked 'Don't you know there's a war on?'

'I've never been any good with children,' Sophie went on. 'Which is odd,' she added with a flash of percipience, 'because I sometimes think I'm still a child myself.' She turned to Helen in the crowded railway carriage, a dishevelled, dumpy woman in a dirndl skirt and embroidered peasant blouse, standing with a holdall between her legs, not caring who might hear her. 'Do you ever feel any older, Helen?'

'Older?' Helen spoke in a lowered voice, conscious of the eyes and ears around them. 'Of course I do. There are times when I feel, oh, ancient.'

'I don't feel I've aged at all. People look at me and they see a woman with grey hair and a lined face who must, obviously, be approaching sixty – if she's not past it. And yet to myself I seem no different from the little girl who was terrified the first time she ever travelled on a railway train.'

Helen was silent, hoping that Sophie would now be silent too.

But Sophie went on: 'You must have children, Helen.'

'I don't want children. I don't like children.' Again those eyes, those ears, all round them.

'You've such a gift for them. As I said.'

It was a relief to Helen when they had bundled themselves out of the overcrowded train at Victoria Station.

On the bus, where they once again had to stand, people pressing against them, Sophie suddenly said: 'I didn't offend you, did I?'

'Offend me? How?'

'With what I said about children – that you must have them.'

Helen shook her head. 'Of course not.' The elderly man next to her, his briefcase digging into her thigh, was clearly listening, his beak-like nose lowered to give him the appearance of a moulting bird hungry for a titbit.

'Oh, good! Because I thought you looked, well, cross with me for saying it.'

Helen did not answer.

Toby sent food parcels, which took weeks to reach them, if they ever arrived at all.

Sophie, now grown so thin that she had to pin together the necks of many of her blouses and frocks to make them, as she put it, 'half-way decent', would say to Helen something like: 'Do you want these dried eggs, dear?' and Helen would answer 'Why?' Then Aunt Sophie would explain that there was someone – the milkman, a colleague at the shelter, that poor little widow in the one-room flat above them – who was looking terribly pale and undernourished and for whom the dried eggs (or dried milk or dried fruit or sugar or tea) would do a world of good. Helen would sigh and acquiesce in a generosity which both touched her with its selflessness and irritated her with its gullibility.

Those were terrible meals that Sophie now prepared for Helen on her return from the hospital. Exhausted, she would want only to fall on to her bed and draw an eiderdown over her head, to shut out the world; but Sophie would come into the bedroom, a saucepan or frying pan in her hand, and, holding its contents out for inspection as though that would

226

tempt, instead of destroy, the appetite, would urge: 'Do look what I've prepared for you. Mr Bellamy let me have some whale meat and there was that rice left over from yesterday and I cut up some carrots. You need the carrots when you're walking home in the blackout. They say they help one to see in the dark.'

One evening, when the 'poor little widow' in the flat above had delivered to them one of Toby's parcels taken in by her in their absence, Sophie pounced on a slab of fruit-and-nut chocolate. 'Oh, I must take this across to Mrs Wadman. She's been laid up with shingles – I told you, didn't I, dear? – and I know it'll cheer her up. You don't mind, do you? You're not all that keen on chocolate, are you?'

Helen longed to bite into the slab, to devour it all in a single session; but she knew that, if she did so, it would be as cruel as if she had snatched it away from a hungry child. So she said quietly: 'Yes, do take it if you'd like to.' But she could not help adding: 'Isn't Mrs Wadman that disagreeable woman who made all that fuss because you had hung some washing in the area and she could see it from her bedroom window?'

Sophie looked pained. 'Oh, she's not really disagreeable, dear. She's really awfully nice. One has to make allowances – her husband leaving her for someone so much younger, her son in the Air Force, now this painful go of shingles.'

Helen watched Sophie as, blithe and sturdy, she marched down the corridor, the slab of chocolate clasped unwrapped in a hand, pulled open the front door and then slammed it behind her. Sophie seemed always to slam any door through which she had passed.

Mrs Wadman, who lived in the maisonette on the opposite side of the street, at once remarked, on taking the slab, that it was melting. 'You must have been carrying it in your hand and your hand must have been hot,' she scolded, as though Sophie were a child. She put the slab in a drawer and shut it decisively. 'Anyway, thank you,' she said. She did not invite Sophie to sit down but, instead, asked her, as so often, to do something for her. Her Tinkerbell had been out ever since breakfast, and that was so unlike him – usually he whisked out through his little door, did his business and at once came back in again – that she was getting anxious. If the doctor had not told her that she must on no account move around more than was absolutely necessary, she would have gone out long ago to look for him. But, as it was, would Sophie be an angel and . . . ?

Sophie agreed at once, she would be only too delighted. Then she asked: 'Where do you think he might have got to?'

'Well, he might be at number seven. Where that Frenchman lives, he often tries to lure him away with titbits. Or he might be in the garden of number twenty-two – it's so overgrown that it's like a jungle to him. I don't know, I just don't know.'

Sophie said cheerily: 'Now don't you worry yourself. You just sit down and listen to the six o'clock news and I'll wander round and look for him.' She turned as she was letting herself out of the front door: 'Oh, by the way, what do you call him?'

'Call him?' Mrs Wadman, who had once again seated herself and was drawing a rug up over her knees, was sharp. 'Tinkerbell, of course!'

'I mean what do you call him when you're calling him.'

'Oh.' Mrs Wadman gave that some thought. 'Tinkers,' she eventually said. 'Or Tinkles. Or Tinkertoes. It depends.' She did not specify on what it depended.

Sophie zigzagged down the street, in a wide skirt which she herself had run up on the machine from an Indian bedspread sent to her by Toby, sandals and a cartwheel straw hat, peering over walls and into areas while she called out: 'Tinkerbell! Tinkers! Tinkles! Tinkertoes! Where are you? Where are you?'

A group of children, returning from school, began to prance along behind her, chanting out in ragged unison: 'Tinkerbell! Tinkers! Tinkles! Tinkertoes! Where are you? Where are you?' At each 'are you', they raised their voices to a piercing falsetto shriek.

Sophie decided, as she always decided when people

behaved badly to her, that it would be better to take no notice. But then one of the children, a girl, with what looked like the scabs of impetigo encrusted around her mouth, touched her sleeve, with a hissing 'Miss, miss, miss!' Somehow no one, despite her age, ever called Sophie 'Missus'.

Sophie turned. A pretty little scamp, she decided, despite those nasty sores of hers. 'Yes, dear?'

The girl pointed. 'Is that what you're lookin' for?'

'Why, yes, I believe it is! Oh, thank you, dear!'

Number six had been hit by a bomb, which had sliced diagonally through it, to expose room after room empty of everything but scattered fragments of wood and glass. At the very top of the house, a tiny, black-and-white figure was marching up and down the edge of masonry which separated half of an unroofed room from the abyss into which the rest of it had tumbled.

'Can't you 'ear it?' the girl asked; and 'Must be bloody deaf', the boy beside her commented, so loud in his contempt that even someone deaf could have heard him. And yes, now that she strained, Sophie could hear Tinkerbell's piteous mews.

'Better get the firemen,' another boy suggested; but Sophie, thinking of all the far more important tasks which the Fire Service had to perform at a time like this, approached the house herself.

Rolls of rusty barbed wire, like giant balls of knitting wool, filled up the entrance; but she managed first to climb and then to squeeze past, with no more injury than a tear to her skirt and a slight scratch to her thigh beneath it. The staircase seemed to be intact; but it hung on one side from the still standing portion of the house, unsupported on the other. She supposed that it was safe. One could never be sure. Ah, well, in for a penny, in for a . . . Precariously, pressing as close to the wall as she could, with one hand moving up the damp, crumbling plaster as though for a hold that was not there, she began the ascent. Oh, how sad it all was, how sad! That lovely old William Morris paper, revealed now in patches where the paper overlaying it had shredded away! Her father's drawing

room in the country had had that same paper of giant
peacocks on a gold ground. She paused, stumpy fingers to
breastbone. She felt quite done in. That must be a lavatory;
but there was nothing there now but a cistern, hanging askew,
high up on the wall, and a lavatory-paper holder with some
grimy paper in it. On she climbed, and now she could hear
that frantic mewing, louder and louder. . . . A nursery, yes,
those pieces of wood, painted pale blue, one of them with a
fragment of a picture, yes, it was one of Mickey Mouse's ears
and some whiskers, yes, that must have been a cot. Oh, she
did hope some poor little mite had not been killed in it. And
then, all at once, she was thinking of that other poor little mite
out in India. But she musn't think of him, mustn't, mustn't
. . . A maid's room. Another maid's room. Would people ever
live in houses like this again? Or had that way of life, like the
house itself, gone for ever and ever?

Now, at last, panting, the sweat glistening on her forehead,
she entered the doorless attic and there, facing her, was
Tinkerbell. But, instead of welcoming her presence, he arched
his back, drew so near to the far edge of the floor with the
abyss beyond it that she let out an anguished, involuntary
'No, Tinkerbell, no!' and opened his mouth and spat at her.

You little devil, she thought; and for a moment, as he glared
at her, his tail twitching from side to side, she really thought of
him as some devil and felt an icy fear slither, snake-like, round
her heart.

Ridiculous! She knelt and then, putting her hands on the
dusty, gritty, splintered floorboards, went down on all fours,
her rump high, as though in an attempt to dupe the cat into
believing that, for all the disparity between their sizes, she
was of the same species as himself. In a clear, high-pitched
voice she called: 'Tinkerbell! Tinkers! Tinkles! Tinkertoes!'
She was unaware that, far below her, the children and the
passers-by who had now joined them were all turning up their
faces to gaze at the spectacle of a large, elderly woman
crouched ingratiatingly before a tiny and furious cat.

'Now, don't be silly, Tinkerbell!' She admonished him in

230

the same tone, at once severe and placatory, which she had previously used to girls at the settlement and now used to tramps at the shelter, when her patience had been tried beyond endurance. 'I've come to fetch you home. Come! Come, come! Good boy . . .' She began to crawl forward, the brim of her straw hat bobbing up and down and her skirt rapidly becoming stained with the grime off the floor.

'Tinkers!' She sang it out, as she extended a hand.

The cat withdrew to an even more perilous position, tiptoe, its back arched.

'It's only me, darling! I'm your mummy's friend! You know me!' Again she reached out and again the cat drew away. Devil, devil! She felt a sudden dread of him, far more intense than of the abyss above which he stood.

'Tinkertoes!'

Unless he descended into that abyss, the cat could go no further.

Sophie again put out her hand. The cat squawked, bared its teeth, shot out a barbed paw.

'Oh, you fiend! You little fiend!'

But Sophie had him, first by the scruff of his neck, as he impotently twisted his body and scrabbled with his paws, and then, all resistance having suddenly subsided, cradled in her arms. 'Good boy,' she crooned 'That's a good, good boy.' She began the slow descent.

'Your arm's bleeding,' the girl told her in a matter-of-fact voice, when she and the cat emerged into the street.

'You'd better put something on that,' one of the passers-by, a middle-aged woman with a number of shopping bags, advised.

'Oh, it's nothing.'

Mrs Wadman also thought that it was nothing. She thanked Sophie perfunctorily, without even asking her if she would like to sit down or wash her scratched arm, and then said that she must see to Tinkerbell's horsemeat. He must be hungry after an adventure like that. Tinkerbell had already jumped into the best armchair, where he had begun systematically to clean himself, a wary eye on Sophie, to whom he felt as little gratitude as his mistress.

'Well, I'd better be on my way,' Sophie said.

Mrs Wadman made no attempt to detain her.

'What *have* you been doing?' Helen was appalled. Sophie's straw hat was cocked over an ear, there were two moist, black patches on the Indian bedspread skirt, there was a smudge, like a bruise, under an eye, and she was covered in a greyish dust. Beads of dried blood encrusted an arm.

Laughing, Sophie explained: 'It was quite an adventure, dear. Particularly for me, since I've such a terrible head for heights, as you well know. If I'd let myself look down just once, then I'd certainly have fallen.'

'But why, why, why? Why do something so silly?'

'Why not? Fun.' She twisted her shapeless body round, to examine the scratch. 'The little devil did that to me.' Again she laughed. 'And the funny thing is – I just hate cats, don't I?'

'Perhaps he realized that.'

Helen washed the scratch and put iodine on it; but the next day it looked sullen and inflamed. Each day it worsened. Now it was Helen who urged Sophie to consult Dr Spencer and Sophie who resisted, instead of the other way about. 'Well, then, come to our casualty department. Or let me get you some M and B. Please!'

Finally, when the whole arm was so swollen that she could no longer use it, Sophie agreed reluctantly to accompany Helen to the casualty department of the hospital.

'I hate to worry them with something so trivial,' she said, not for the first time, as she and Helen walked through the devastated streets to the complex of grimy Victorian buildings and Nissen huts which made up the hospital. 'It seems selfish, when they've so many more important things to deal with. It's only a scratch that's gone septic. I'm sure that with a few more fomentations . . .'

'Fomentations are *no good*!' Helen's anxiety made her irritable, even angry; and it was because of that that Sophie added in contrition: 'And I hate to waste your time. You've so much to do as it is, poor dear.'

'You're not wasting my time! For God's sake!'

It was a long time before anyone examined Sophie's arm. Then she was told that she must enter the hospital for a course of sulphanomides.

Suddenly she was frightened; and that alarmed Helen, who had never once seen her frightened before. 'Oh, do you really think it's necessary for me to stay here, Helen? I've never been a hospital patient. Never in my life. Oh, Helen, please . . . I've such horrid memories of that hospital in Calcutta.'

But Helen was adamant. 'This hospital isn't in the least bit like that one. This is one of the best hospitals in the world, even if it does look so grotty. That arm needs careful treatment. And, frankly, I just haven't the time to look after it for you.'

At that, Sophie changed. 'Yes, dear, you're right. Of course you're right. I'd only be a burden to you at home. Yes, I'd better do what they tell me.' Although she was still frightened, she never again showed it.

Slowly she deteriorated, her skin yellowing, her voice growing faint and husky, the flesh melting from her. She smiled up at Helen, told her that she must not come to visit her so often, held her hand in the hand which was not swollen, said little else, other than that everyone was so good, so good to her.

One of the consultants, whose lectures Helen attended, asked her to go and see him. Fatigue made it seem as if he himself were terminally stricken. Lack of time made it seem as if he were in a state of constant irritation.

'Your aunt must have been ill for a long time.' It sounded like an accusation.

Helen was astonished. 'Oh, I don't think so.'

He stared intently at her across his desk. Then an eyelid flickered involuntarily and he looked down, embarrassed by a physical weakness over which he had no control. 'Didn't she run low-grade temperatures?'

'Not that I know of.'

'Complain of feeling tired?'

'Nothing ever tired her. Nothing.'

'Not want to eat?'

'She didn't eat much. But that was because she would give her rations away to others.'

He shrugged. 'There's little to be done for her. I'm afraid – she's on the way out.'

He began to explain, in technical detail which Helen was already qualified enough to follow, that Sophie was dying of a blood disease common enough among children but rare in people of her age.

'But how can she be? How can she be?'

Aunt Sophie dying.

'Don't stay with me, dear, I know you've such a lot to do . . . I was trying to remember that sonnet – by Meredith, wasn't it? – I learned for a recitation contest at school . . . Of course, I didn't win . . . But all these years it's stuck in my mind, don't ask me why . . . Each time I get to "He reached a middle height and at the stars. . ." and then, then I can't go on. My poor old brain seems to be even more addled than usual. . . . You've explained to them at the shelter, haven't you? I don't suppose they really miss me, I was always doing the wrong thing. . . . but I wouldn't want them to think I was letting them down. I ought to be out of here before Mrs Blake takes her holiday. Three weeks from now, four weeks? You see how my poor mind is going! If she's not there, there's no one but me to see to the . . . Oh, Helen, before you leave, you will go across and talk to that poor thing opposite, won't you? The Cypriot woman. No one ever comes to see her. Sometimes in the middle of the night I wake up and hear her moaning or sobbing and then someone shouts to her shut up. One can't blame them, of course, yes, it is a little disturbing, but she must feel so alone. . . . Oh, I must tell you, that reminds me, last night I had such a strange and vivid dream. It was of that time when Toby and Isabel were last here on leave. Well, as you know, Peter was not born then but somehow in my dream he was with them and it was as though I knew him, knew him well – as though he were close to me. He was in my lap and playing with my beads, you know those amber beads, well, you probably won't remember them, I always meant to have them re-threaded but, like so much else in my life, somehow I never got round to it. Well, the beads were intact and his little hand was holding them. And then he gave them a tug and the thread snapped and they were rolling, rolling, beads everywhere, many more than could possibly have been on a single string. . . .'

A sudden intensity kindled in the dull eyes under the heavy lids, as she squinted round at Helen: 'Who would want to do such a thing? Who? Who?'

All at once the voice was strong and anguished. She half sat up in the bed, clutching at Helen's arm with both her hands, the nails digging deep into the recoiling flesh beneath them. Helen all but cried out.

'Such a vivid dream . . .'

Helen stretched out, hopelessly empty through the hopelessly empty days, while Aunt Sophie sits beside her: 'Oh, Helen, one simply has to go on without asking why. . . . You have to find the strength in yourself, there's nowhere else to find it. . . . Sooner or later things always get better or, if they don't get better, one gets accustomed to them. . . . You must learn to look not backwards but forwards, not inwards but outwards. . . . Oh, Helen, I do believe what I'm saying to you, I do, I do. . . .'

Silly, sentimental clichés. But she had herself lived faithful to them and, in doing so, had somehow transmuted them.

Aunt Sophie dead.

She had left Helen her 'few bits and pieces' – as she herself referred to the worn clothes from Pontings and Marks and Spencer, the items of jewellery (ropes of glass beads, a gold christening brooch with a single pearl and her name 'Sophie' engraved on it, some coral earrings, an extravagantly carved

brass bracelet, a present from Toby) in their dented cardboard box, the gimcrack furniture, most of it of fumed oak,
and the ermine coat, once her mother's which, bundled up at
the back of her wardrobe, Helen had never seen her wear or
even known her to possess. All as squalid and sad as the
detritus left in an empty dock after an ocean-going liner has
moved out and passed below the horizon.

Everything else that she possessed went to the shelter. Mrs
Blake, though about to go off on a holiday to a daughter in
North Wales, none the less came to the cremation at Kensal
Green. 'We'd no idea she had so much money,' she whispered
to Helen as she seated herself behind her in the chapel. On the
telephone, Helen had already told her of Sophie's legacy.
'None at all. It'll make such a difference to our work. Oh,
what a dear she was and how we all miss her!'

After the plain coffin had slid away towards the devouring
flames, Mrs Blake said that, no, it was very kind of Helen, but
she would not be able to return to the flat with the others for a
drink, she had so much to do before her holiday, so much fell
on her. Then again she exclaimed, holding Helen's right hand
in both of her own: 'Oh, what a dear she was!' They stared
into each other's eyes, Mrs Blake's brimming with tears, and
Helen, remembering how peremptorily Mrs Blake would
speak to Aunt Sophie, in exactly the same tone which Isabel
would use to the Indian servants, wondered: Can she really
mean it? She felt the two long, cold hands pressing hers more
firmly. 'And I think she really loved working for us. Didn't
she? Of course some of our naughtier customers got up to all
sorts of tricks with her. She was so innocent, poor dear.
Gullible. But that was what really made us all so fond of her.
A child. She was always a child, right up to the end.'

Everyone at last left and Helen lay out on the sofa among
the empty glasses, the cut-glass fingerbowls greasy from the
potato crisps and nuts which 'the little man on the corner' (as
Sophie would refer to the Cypriot Greek owner of the store,
hardly more than a hole in the wall, in the Earls Court Road)
had unaccountably 'saved' for her under the counter, the

ashtrays overflowing with cigarettes thriftily smoked to their cork tips or the last scorched twist of paper around some fibres of tobacco, the copy of the *Daily Mail* that someone had forgotten. She stared out of the grimy window at the empty area, where a robin (each morning Aunt Sophie would sweep the crumbs from the breadboard on to the concrete paving for it to eat) hopped hither and thither, at once aimless and brisk. Would the winter ever end? Would the war ever end?

Suddenly she got up and walked into her bedroom, remembering how Aunt Sophie had insisted that she should have it, with no window except a length of frosted glass separating it from the meagre light of the hall, and not the other bedroom, which had the street above it and so was more vulnerable to blast. Perhaps now she would move. She felt totally fatalistic.

She opened one of the small drawers of the Victorian escritoire which Aunt Sophie had told the removers' men to place in her room – 'It's quite a pretty little piece, it belonged to your grandmother, I've no use for it' – and which was now crammed with her own and Aunt Sophie's things, and took out, from under a pile of Toby's letters, something sealed within a large buff envelope. She hesitated, then ran a nail under the flap and opened the envelope, to draw out an object wrapped in tissue paper.

She sat on the edge of her bed and, the tissue paper rustling under her hands, began to unwrap the past.

V

'You're a good doctor. But you'd be a better one if you didn't feel so much.'

'I?'

'Yes, you. Why do you think I'm such a good nurse? Because I feel nothing.'

'Nonsense.'

'Correction. I feel nothing personal. I hate the suffering

237

and the waste of it all, but for those individual suffering and wasted lives, no, Helen, no. And the children and the parents recognize that in me and, instead of being repelled by it, they feel reassured. No one child is more important to me than any other child. And if one has to go and die on me, well, there are hundreds more children I'm determined not to let die.'

Ilse and Helen sat facing each other in the flat, each with a mug of tea. Outside, the street was hushed and empty. It was V-Day and everyone, emerging into the sunlight from flats and houses in need of redecoration, was trekking westward towards the Palace. Though both girls were off duty from the children's hospital at which they had met, they had no desire to go along too.

Ilse irritated Helen with her constant desire to write out both of their personal equations. Yet Helen was sucked towards her by an undertow of emotion, like a swimmer towards some jagged, treacherously hidden reef. Ilse had come to England in 1938 with her Jewish grandfather, both of them the guests of a left-wing Roman Catholic peer and his wife far too busy to do anything for them but feed them and accommodate them in their huge, untidy country house, first with a horde of servants and then with two servants and a horde of evacuees, and, eventually, to convert Ilse to their faith. Both Ilse's parents had - as she herself would later put it, as though applying a cautery to a savage wound within her - 'been burned to a crisp in the gas ovens'. Her grandfather, lacking the incentive of a major talent to learn to write in English and so to continue with his work in this strange land where no one had heard of him, would busy himself with clumsily executed jobs of plumbing, joinery and wiring about the house, until suddenly, for no reason more focused than a general apathy and boredom, he had gone into one of the barns and hanged himself with the length of flex which he always carried round with him, in case of an emergency, in a bulging pocket of the worn, bottle-green Norfolk jacket handed down to him by his host. Ilse had disconcerted everyone by showing no grief or even shock.

A pale, angular figure, with protuberant eyes and almost no breasts, she passed, unobtrusive and friendless, through the expensive school to which her foster parents sent her as a day girl. She never won a prize but she never did badly. She took fastidious care of her appearance, darning her stockings with a web of stitches so fine that they were all but indiscernible, polishing her shoes tirelessly until their toecaps gleamed like black ice, and cutting her fingernails in a perfectly straight line above cuticles which she was always easing back with persistent fingers.

Ilse never laughed; but frequently she had a faint, sardonic smile on lips which, unlike the other nurses, she never touched up even on an afternoon off. It was that smile which first drew Helen's attention to her. There was no warmth or humour in it.

Admirable Ilse. She waited for confirmation of what she supposed to have been the fate of her parents with no apparent strain or dread. She offered to take over from other nurses whose boyfriends were on leave, she forwent cups of tea and even meals to sit on and on at the bedside of some ailing child, she never forgot anything or bungled anything or declared that anything was beyond her. Of all the nurses, she was the one whom the doctors respected most; but they never attempted to flirt with her or even to joke with her, as they did with her colleagues.

Soon after that V-Day session, Ilse mentioned to Helen, in the canteen, that she would have to quit the house in Clapham in which, for the past eighteen months, she had been a lodger. Her widowed landlady's son, whose room she had been occupying, never bothering to take down his rowing pennants, his photographs of rowing crews or even his pin-ups of film stars, had now been demobbed.

'Where will you go?'

Ilse shrugged.

'It's not easy to find lodgings in London now.'

'No. It's not easy. Perhaps I'll have to return to the hostel.'

Ilse had not enjoyed the nurses' hostel, where she had been

obliged to share a room with a silly, skittish girl, forever surreptitiously returning through the window after hours, after some meeting with a boyfriend.

Helen said: 'You could come and stay with me.'

'With you?' Ilse was cool. 'Would that be a good idea?'

'Wouldn't it? There are two bedrooms, after all. We could live our own lives.'

'Well, that's something. I don't think I'd want to lead anyone else's.' She gave that faint, sardonic smile. 'Least of all yours.'

Helen was not offended.

Ilse moved into the room which had once been Helen's, since Helen was now in the room which had once been Sophie's. On her first day, having unpacked her few belongings, Ilse came and stood in the doorway of Helen's room. She gave a little shiver. 'I'm glad I'm not in here. It feels – haunted.'

Helen looked at her in amazement. 'Haunted? Well, if my aunt *is* haunting it, her ghost can only be benevolent.'

'I didn't mean your aunt.'

Ilse loved classical music. She had a wind-up gramophone, to which she would listen, often lying sprawled out on the floor of her bedroom, her back against the divan bed, for hours on end. All her spare money she spent on records, which she kept ranged along a shelf on which Helen had once stacked her books. 'Do I disturb you?' she would often ask Helen, with a trace both of foreign accent and of foreign idiom, and Helen would reply: 'Oh no, of course not.' But as she heard Bach, Handel or Vivaldi faintly through the wall, she was disturbed, if not in the way in which Ilse meant. She had no feeling for music and it puzzled her that this strange, quiet, strong flat-mate of hers should give so much of her time to it.

Ilse was deeply, if undemonstratively, religious; and that Helen also found disturbing, since she herself had even less feeling for religion than for music, regarding it – as she once told Ilse – as 'silly superstition'. The German girl would eat no meat on Friday, so that if, in those difficult days, fish were unobtainable, she would restrict herself to eggs or cheese. She would get up long before Helen on Sunday mornings and take herself off to mass. Under her neat white blouses she always wore a crucifix. Once, blundering into her room to borrow a stamp, Helen had found her on her knees by her bed, her eyes closed and her hands clasped before her. Strangely she had not opened her eyes or turned her head at Helen's entrance. Helen tiptoed out.

Helen said: 'Music means a lot to you, doesn't it?'

'Yes.'

In each case the monosyllable gave away either everything or nothing. Helen was not sure.

Virtually silent for days on end, Ilse would all at once become garrulous. She would talk of her past: of a mansion, with many servants, in Munich; of her father's collection of Post-Impressionists, priceless, looted; of the house by the Bodensee to which her mother, a famous actress, had retreated when, because of her race, she was no longer offered parts; of the complicity of an uncle of hers in a plot to murder Hitler and of another uncle now working in Switzerland, Turkey, Sweden for Soviet Intelligence; of her descent, through her mother's family, from the Mendelssohns . . . Helen would listen, as enthralled as Joan's children when she herself would tell them a story; but afterwards doubts seeped in, a chilling tide. It was as though, during all the hours when she sat or lay out on the floor, listening to record after record, this girl, who had had her whole past ripped away from her, had been slowly, dreamily restitching another.

'Soon after the war started, this man – a friend of those people who gave me a home – made an approach to me. He asked me if I'd be willing to work for the organization – MI5, I suppose – of which he was a boss. I was to report on refugees, people like myself. . . . Of course, I refused.'

'Of course.'

Or: 'As soon as I can get back to Germany, my first task will be to try to trace all my father's pictures. Not for myself, of course. But to give them to the National Gallery, in return for all that England has given to me.'

'Of course.'

For Helen there was something both thrilling and degrading in drinking from the hallucinatory cup which Ilse proffered to her.

Ilse had no boyfriends, Helen had no boyfriends. They lived spiritually intimate but physically as strangers. Helen opened the bathroom door which Ilse, thinking her to be working late at the hospital, had failed to lock. 'Oh sorry!' Through the steam, Helen had made out, for a moment, the breasts almost as flat as a boy's and the dark tuft quivering like seaweed under the water. She retreated, appalled. Ilse, having returned from night duty, brought a cup of tea to Helen's room. She averted her eyes from the body sprawled out, nightdress rucked up above the knees, on the bed, with the bedclothes, on that sultry morning of summer, thrown back.

One day, as they ate a late Sunday breakfast in the kitchen, each of them in dressing-gowns, Ilse said, cradling her cup of coffee in both her palms as though it were something fragile, of great value: 'Was it you whose brother – half-brother – was murdered out in India?'

Helen went on deliberately spreading butter on a slice of toast. Then she looked up: 'Yes. But how do you know about it?'

Ilse shrugged. 'I think I read about it in the papers. It was such a horrific thing to have happened. It made such an impression on me.' She stared into space. 'Or did someone tell me? I don't know.'

Was it possible that Ilse had been going through her drawers? Helen's grip tightened on the knife in her hand, her knuckles went white.

Ilse gave that faint, sardonic smile of hers, raising thick eyebrows which all but met under her low forehead. 'Don't you like to talk about it?'

'It's something I prefer to forget.'

'Is that wise?'

(Aunt Sophie leaning solicitously above her: You must learn to look not backwards but forwards, not inwards but outwards.)

'I don't know.'

'Tell me. Tell me about it.'

'No. I don't think I want to.'

'Some time then?'

'Some time. Perhaps.'

'I've told you all my secrets.'

(You've told me all your lies.)

'I have no secrets. I just want to' – she hesitated – 'I just don't want to remind myself.'

'All right. Fine.'

Ilse's palm, warm from the coffee cup, covered the chill back of Helen's hand.

VI

Toby, Isabel and Angela at last came back to England.

As Sophie and the other two aunts had once travelled out to Tilbury by train to meet her, so Helen now made the same journey to meet her father, her stepmother and the half-sister whom she knew only from snapshots. Janet and Joan also went to Tilbury; but they made no effort to accompany Helen, since they had long since concluded, as Janet put it over a cup of coffee in a snackbar near Fenchurch Street Station: 'I'm afraid she's precious little use for any of us now.' It was a long time since Helen had paid a visit to either of them, though she had often been pressed to do so.

Old Mrs Thompson had stayed down in Cornwall, where she had now made her home with Janet. She had become all but bedridden, so that Janet and Joan were constantly debating whether the time had not come to put her in a home – for her own sake of course, they would say, she needed the constant nursing, one could hardly bear to think of not having her around.

Helen experienced an acute pang, like a stab of toothache, when she all at once realized that the small, elderly, stooped man tentatively making his descent down the gangway, one knobbly hand gripping the rail, could only be her father; and yes, that stately woman, grey hair wound round and round her head as though it were a toque, one arm clasping a frail, blonde child against her ample, outjutting bosom, could only be Isabel.

'He's aged terribly,' Joan muttered to Janet.

'Heavens! One would hardly recognize him.'

'And she's put on weight.'

'Quite grey.'

'Well, I suppose time hasn't dealt all that kindly with us either.'

The two of them laughed, not really believing it.

In Helen's embrace, her father smelled strongly of tobacco and not, as she remembered from the past, of that astringent French toilet water, Caron Pour Un Homme. One of his front teeth was missing; his collar was not clean and one of its points stuck out askew. 'Oh, Helen, Helen, Helen!' He rocked back and forth with her, in what seemed to be a paroxysm not so much of joy as of grief.

Isabel put a cold cheek to Helen's. Then she drew forward the little girl, in long white ribbed stockings and white strap-shoes, her hair tied in two powder-blue bows on either side of her unnaturally narrow head, who was hiding behind her, and said: 'This is my Angela, Angie, Angel.'

The child, amazingly, gave a little bobbing curtsey to each of the three women in turn.

Toby, once so imperiously efficient on such occasions, now left everything – passports, luggage, customs, transport – to his wife and two sisters. Whenever there was somewhere to sit or even perch, he would take it: on a bench, on the edge of the counter where the porters set out the luggage for the customs officers, even on a window-sill.

Helen tried to talk to him, with a growing sense of horror and sadness: 'Did you enjoy the voyage?'

'Not bad. Not bad.'

'I hope you got the letter I wrote to Marseilles?'

'Yes. Thank you.'

'And what are your plans now?'

'Well, first we'll go down to Cornwall to stay with Janet and Harry. I want to see your grandmother. Yes, that's the first item on our agenda.' He cleared his throat, in the fashion of old men choked up with phlegm. 'After that, well, we'll see, we'll see.'

'Aren't you going to stay in London at all?' She was almost beseeching.

'No. Straight to Cornwall. Can't abide hotels.' Again he cleared his throat, with that disgusting, loose rattle. 'Odd, since I made so much money from them.' He still did not look at her, his hands clasped over his protruding belly, thumbs twiddling restlessly. Then he said, as though in concession: 'But you'll visit us in Cornwall, won't you? I'm sure Janet would be delighted to have you. Large house, plenty of rooms.'

'Oh, yes, yes!' Then she cried out, as though in a last appeal: 'If only my flat were bigger!'

Isabel waddled over, head erect, Angela trailing from her hand like a toy dog on a lead. 'Have you got the key to the holdall?' As she spoke the words, Helen had an image of a ward-maid smartly slapping pillows or snatching up a bedpan.

'Let me see.' Toby began to fumble in his pockets until, impatient, Isabel herself inserted a hand into his left hand trouser one and came up with the keyring.

'How long are you here for?' Helen asked, when Isabel had gone.

'Here?' He looked bewildered, as though she were referring to the custom shed.

'In England.'

'Oh . . .' He hesitated, staring after Isabel and the child. Then he said: 'Forever, I think.'

'Forever? Oh, Daddy, how lovely!'

But she had the sensation of something black and leaden falling, falling, falling through her.

VII

Ilse deftly spun a letter across the room, so that it landed on the sofa beside Helen. 'From Papa,' she said. She took ironic pleasure in using such outmoded colloquialisms. By now she knew Toby's handwriting.

Helen went on reading *The Times*.

'Aren't you going to open it?' Ilse asked, as Sophie used to ask in the past.

'Eventually.'

'It seems so unfair. You get letters from your father and you never want to open them. If I could get a letter, just one letter, from my father . . .'

Ashamed, Helen picked up the envelope and inserted a finger under the flap.

Ilse sat down on the sofa beside her. 'What's gone wrong between the two of you?' she asked.

'Nothing. Nothing at all.'

'It's – what? – five weeks since he came back. And you've never been down to see him.'

'He's never been up to see me. Has he?'

'You said he'd aged. Become so frail.'

Helen began to read the letter. Like all Toby's, this one too had about it a curious, damp, crumbling deadness, as of mouldering wood. They were househunting, or, rather, Isabel was, since he could really not be bothered. They had found a local dame's school for Angela. Old Mrs Thompson was recovering from bronchitis. Then came the conclusion, like every other conclusion since his return: 'We do hope that you'll soon be able to come down and visit us. Janet says there'll be no trouble at all about a room.'

Ilse, her head tilted to one side and a slight crease between the pale, protuberant eyes under the eyebrows which all but joined each other, watched Helen closely, as her lips silently read the words.

Helen put down the letter in her lap.

'He's on at you again about going to see them.' A statement, not a question.

Helen nodded, all at once feeling suffocated by a personality, so controlled and yet so insistent, which constantly threatened to wrap itself round and round her own, its tendrils searching out the most secret recesses of her being.

'Why don't you want to go?'

'But I do.'

Ilse shook her head.

VIII

Nothing now interested Toby for more than a few minutes at a stretch.

He would limp slowly along the lawn in front of the square, red-brick neo-Georgian house, his hands in his pockets, and then, pausing as though in an effort to remember something, he would gaze down to the estuary. Sometimes the water would be so high that it seemed as if it would go on rising and rising until it had filled this bowl in the hills, submerging the garden and even the house above it. Sometimes the water would be no more than a distant shimmer beyond a vast, wrinkled expanse of mud. However things were, there would always be the same expression of morose desolation on his flushed, jowly countenance.

At her bedroom window, Helen would look down on him with a mixture of pity and dread.

He would shuffle between the rosebeds, occasionally stopping to cup a bloom in a hand and even raise it to his nostrils. Then he would break away, totter over to the white-painted garden shed, and emerge with some piece of the garden furniture of which Janet's stockbroker husband, Harry, was always so proud. He would set up the chair or chaise longue and would lower himself on to it. He would close his eyes. But soon, as though some voice, inaudible to

Helen high up at her bedroom window, had summoned him, he would hoist himself up and hurry indoors again.

Helen would descend the stairs. He was now seated in the hall, on a high-backed chair under the barometer which he was constantly tapping. He was holding the parish magazine which someone at some time had pushed through the letter box but he was not reading it. 'Helen,' he said, glancing quickly at her and then looking away. 'Helen.' No more. He put down the magazine on the Jacobean chest beside him, got up and wandered off. Whistling under his breath, he began to mount the stairs.

Harry, down for the weekend, was always organizing all of them in his jolly, slightly hectoring voice. He would summon Janet, Isabel, Angela, Helen and his other two guests, a colleague and his wife, to come and play croquet, to sail on the estuary or to make an excursion to some church or country house open to the public. But he never summoned Toby and clearly Toby neither expected nor wished to be summoned. 'All right, Toby?' he would ask briefly as they all moved off, Angela clutching Isabel's hand; and Toby, his jowls slightly quivering, would either nod or mutter 'Fine, fine.'

Angela rarely approached her father and then only with reluctance and even dread. When Isabel spoke of her to strangers as 'my child' or 'my daughter', she was merely stating a truth. Angela belonged exclusively to this tall, ample woman, at whom she was always grasping if the woman did not grasp her, whom she would seek through the house wailing on the same high-pitched note 'Mummy, Mummy, Mummy!' and in whose bed she always slept, even though there was a separate cot for her in the room which they shared.

Nor did Isabel show any closer attachment to Toby than did the child. Briefly, her life would brush against his, as she moved, gravely imposing, about her many tasks; then she was gone. A woman takes over a house and with it, reluctantly, she takes over the care of an ancient, ailing dog. She feeds it, she lets it out into the garden, she airs its basket, she gives it an occasional perfunctory, absentminded pat. It was like that.

Only old Mrs Thompson seemed to take genuine pleasure in Toby's company. Harry might perch himself on a garden bench beside his brother-in-law, pat his knee and ask: 'Well, how goes it, old chap?' Janet might comment chirpily over breakfast: 'Oh, Toby, I do like that tie of yours! Most dashing!' The two other guests might look out of the window and then turn to Toby and ask: 'Do you think it's safe to take a walk, Mr Thompson, or do you think it's going to rain?' But it was clear that, like many people who bore themselves, he had become fatally boring to others.

If she was well enough to totter down the stairs from her upstairs bedroom, her back now humped and wisps of fine grey hair making a cloud about her oval, high-cheeked face, Mrs Thompson would always seek out her son. So deaf now, despite her shell-pink hearing-aid, that she could hear only what was shouted at her, she rarely spoke to anyone and, if anyone spoke to her, would usually content herself with a violent nodding or shaking of the head or a sweet, vague smile by way of answer. To Toby she made no attempt to speak at all, just as he himself seldom addressed her except in greeting. But she would touch him on his shoulder with an arthritic hand as she approached him, and would then place herself as close as possible to him: beside him on the sofa, if that was where he was sitting, next to him at table, opposite to him in the garden. For seconds on end, she would stare at him with a wistful intensity, though he seemed to be unaware of it; then she would look down into her lap or outwards to the estuary, now draining itself to those lees of chocolate-brown mud and now renewing itself, an ever swelling bubble, and an expression of anguish would briefly convulse her face.

It was early on in the week that Helen realized that Toby felt acutely uncomfortable in her presence and was doing everything possible to avoid her. He would enter the panelled study, where she was reading a book alone, and would then stammer out: 'Oh, sorry, sorry, I was looking for Harry' and disappear again. Since Harry was then in London, it was an odd excuse to give. She would wander out into the garden, to where he stood, on its emerald lip, gazing out at the ebbing waters. But when he saw her, he would shiver, wrapping his arms about himself, and say: 'Turning parky. I think I'd better go in before I catch another of my colds.' Once, in the conservatory, she found herself pursuing him up and down the rows of waxen orchids in which Harry took even more pride than in the garden furniture. Sad, comic: an old man, his face congested and his hair dishevelled, shuffling faster and faster in his bedroom slippers to escape his own daughter, whom he pretends not to see or hear.

Finally, she got him to herself and, more difficult, kept him.

The others, since it was a clear, warm day of early summer, announced that they were all going on a picnic. Mrs Thompson was having what she called one of her bad days. At the last moment, Helen cunningly announced that she had a headache and would stay behind with her grandmother and father.

Helen took a lunch tray up to Mrs Thompson; then she and Toby sat down, facing each other, at either end of the long, highly polished mahogany table – now that there were no servants, only a daily cleaner, Harry himself would vigorously work at its surface with wax and a cloth – to eat the meal of scrambled eggs on toast, salad and fruit which she had prepared. There was half a bottle of Algerian wine but Toby, who had drunk so convivially, if rarely to excess, in India, now often refused even his bedtime glass of whisky, so that Helen was not surprised when he put a shaky hand over his glass when she attempted to fill it.

Toby cut into the toast on which his scrambled eggs rested and raised the portion to his mouth. He chewed, watery eyes gazing sideways out of the window at the estuary, in order not to look at Helen.

She sipped. 'Are you sure you won't have a drop of this? It's not at all bad.'

'Quite sure.' He masticated slowly, his jaw moving sideways, like some old, purblind bull chewing on the cud.

'When do you expect to move into the house?' Helen knew

the answer, since Isabel had told her, but she could think of nothing else to say to this man grown so distant and strange to her.

'I've no idea.' Again he masticated, slowly, relentlessly. 'I leave that kind of thing to Isabel now. Next month? Yes, I think she said next month.'

Yes, it was next month. The house lay in the neighbouring valley, shut in, like the hill-station in India, by a ring of low hills but, unlike the hill-station, without any lake. The house, red-brick and steeply gabled, with a hard tennis court before it, was like that other house. People decide to make new lives and then make them in the pattern of the old. 'Do you like the house?'

'I've not seen it.'

'Not seen it!'

'No. As I said. I leave that kind of thing to Isabel now.'

'And you really mean never to return to India?'

He swallowed, head lowered so that his chin quivered against the loose knot of the 'dashing' tie. 'I'll never go back. No reason to. Sold up everything.'

This was something which Helen did not know.

'But why? Why?' (And why has no one ever told me this before?)

'Life is finished for us out there.'

Did he mean for the family in particular or for the English in general? Helen did not know.

'How – finished?'

'They'll take over – next year, the year after. They'll nationalize what belongs to us. Or force us to sell. And then they'll forbid us to take out our money. I decided to get out while the going was good. Cut my losses.' He raised a tumbler of water to his lips with a trembling, swollen hand. 'And there were losses. Oh, yes, there were losses. But, all told, I got a good enough price not to have to worry about the future of Isabel and Angie.' No mention of Helen's future. But, of course, he knew that she had her mother's money, all of it now made over to her, since she had passed her majority two years ago.

'Won't you miss India?'

He stared out towards the estuary, his face averted from her so that she could see only his temple and the line of his jaw, with a tuft of bloodstained cottonwool stuck beneath an ear, where that morning he had nicked himself while shaving with his cut-throat razor.

'No.' The monosyllable glittered like a bead of ice between them.

Silence.

Then, involuntarily, not knowing how or why she came to do so, Helen said: 'I often wonder – what happened to Clare?'

'Clare? Clare?' He placed his swollen hands on either side of his plate, as though preparatory to pushing himself away and up from the table. There was a snarling panic in his repetition of the name, like that of some animal cornered by its predator. 'What made you think of Clare?'

'I often think of her.' Helen's face had all at once become extraordinarily pale, accentuating the brilliance of her eyes and the redness of a mouth which she had never had to touch up with lipstick. 'Often . . . Don't you?'

'I? No. Never.' Again that snarling panic.

'Don't you even know where she is?'

'No. There was some rumour. Australia, was it?'

Now the swollen hands quivering on either side of the half-eaten eggs, did push him away and up from the table. He swayed, as though from a momentary attack of giddiness, and muttered: 'I can't eat any more. No appetite. I'll toddle upstairs and see how your grandmother is getting on.'

When he had left her, Helen forced two or three more mouthfuls down her throat. Then she got up briskly, scraped the remaining contents of her plate on to the top of his, and began to pile a tray with everything from the table. Her heart was juddering wildly and she felt an excruciating pain, stab on stab, in her back, above each buttock.

Later, when she saw that Toby had come down from his mother's room and had wandered out into the garden, a tweed cap pulled down low over his forehead and a scarf wrapped round his chin as though to disguise himself, she herself ascended.

'Have you finished with your tray?'

'Oh, yes, dear, a long time ago. I was going to bring it down myself.'

'You mustn't attempt anything like that. I've told you that before. You might have a fall.'

'Well, I wouldn't want to break Janet's pretty crockery.'

'I wasn't thinking about the crockery. I was thinking about your bones.'

'I suppose they're almost as fragile!'

Helen began to stack the things securely, while Mrs Thompson, in nightdress, dressing-gown and slippers, watched her from her armchair.

'What's upset your father?'

'Has anything upset him?' Helen felt obliged to lower her head to the old woman and shout in order to be heard; but for once, she shrank from the proximity.

'Oh, yes, dear! I could see at once that something had. I know my poor old Toby. But of course he wouldn't tell me. Never does. He thinks I'm too old to be upset. But in fact' – she gave a bleak smile – 'as I get older and older, less and less seems to upset me.'

'Are you going to move with them?'

'To the other house, you mean? Oh, I don't know. I don't think so. Of course, I'd like to be with Toby – between ourselves, he's always been my favourite, as you may have guessed. But Isabel is fully occupied with little Angie, she's quite a handful, isn't she? It's only natural, after all that awful business, that she should want to take special care of the child. No, I don't think Isabel would want me to look after too. Though of course I'll visit them. And they'll visit me. After all, it's little more than ten miles between the two houses. No, I'd better live out my days here. Janet has been such a good daughter to me and Harry is a dear. I'd not want to hurt their feelings by moving in any case.'

There was an irony so sad in all this that Helen, stooping

over the old woman, would have put her arms round her, were she not so undemonstrative by nature. Only the previous evening, after Mrs Thompson had retired early to bed, Janet and Harry had been talking of the home, run by nuns, which they had recently inspected in a neighbouring village. 'If one could get the servants, it would be different,' Harry had said, helping himself to another glass of whisky from the decanter at his elbow. 'But all this carrying of trays on the days when she can't get down . . . Well, Janet may still look a slip of a girl but, frankly, it's getting beyond her.'

'And then there are our holidays,' Janet had taken up, frowning at her knitting. 'Now that the war is over, we want to get abroad again and see all the things we've been missing for so long. Of course we can always dump her on Joan, but Joan's hands are full enough already, what with that delinquent daughter of hers and all the work of the parish.'

Isabel had nodded in agreement; Toby had sat silent.

As Helen now began to carry the tray to the door, she heard behind her: 'Happy?'

She turned. 'What did you say?'

'I asked if you were happy.'

The old woman's eyes, strangely milky in her shrunken face, looked up at her with an expression which might have been of either pity or appeal.

'I don't know. Does one ever know? Until much later.'

'I think I'm happy.'

The declaration was defiant, not convincing.

Balancing the tray on a knee, as she used a hand to open the door, Helen went out.

IX

That evening, Isabel and Helen did the washing-up in the bright, roomy kitchen, while Janet, Harry and the two other guests settled to a rubber of bridge, with Toby watching them intermittently, a perplexed frown on his face, as though the game were strange to him.

'You can cut in later,' Harry had said; but Toby had shaken his head lugubriously: 'No, my bridge days are over.' Long ago, in India, he had been known both for his skill and his sudden anger or sarcasm when a quailing and apologetic partner had misread him.

Isabel, dipping her plump white arms up to the elbows in the soapy water, drew a deep sigh. 'There's only one thing I miss from India. The servants.'

'They were good, weren't they?'

'Good? They were terrible. Dishonest, disloyal, unreliable. But at least they were there.' She seemed to speak with as much contempt for Helen as for those far-off, former servants, now in the employment of people to whom she had recommended them.

Helen began to dry, with an agitated clumsiness. Then she said: 'Father tells me he's sold up everything in India. All his interests.'

'Of course. Didn't you know that?'

Helen shook her head. In all those formal, uncommunicative letters, so often stacked unopened for three or four weeks on end, there had been no mention of a decision so important. Odd. Chilling. 'No. I didn't know. No idea.'

'Didn't Joan or Janet tell you? Or the old woman?' Isabel often referred to Mrs Thompson as 'the old woman'.

Helen shook her head over the plate which she was turning round and round in her hands, as she applied the cloth. 'No. But then I saw so little of them, still see so little of them. There's so much to do at the hospital, I rarely get away.'

'It was best,' Isabel said. 'Best for him. Best for us.' By 'us' she clearly meant only Angela and herself.

'I can't imagine how he could bear to leave India. It was his whole life. He so often used to say that he hated the tameness of England.'

'Perhaps in the end India proved too wild for him.' Isabel spoke with cool sarcasm, as she handed Helen another plate.

'How do you mean?'

'How do I mean?' Suddenly the white skin of Isabel's neck began to redden; the colour mounted up into her cheeks. Mysteriously, alarmingly, she was angry. 'Do I have to tell you?'

Helen forced herself to continue the conversation, just as, long ago as a medical student, she had forced herself to swallow a snake-like tube, chill, slithery length by length, in order to carry out an analysis of the contents of her stomach. 'You mean – Peter's death?'

'That was the beginning of it. I daresay he'd have got over that. Eventually. It was all that followed.' Isabel violently shoved the next dripping plate at Helen, as though it were a weapon to be rammed into her chest.

'What followed?'

Water splashed up on to Isabel's apron and even her neck, flecking both with a greasy, iridescent foam, as she slid more plates into the sink with so much force that it was a miracle that none of them got chipped or broken. 'Gossip. How they gossiped.' She picked up a ball of wire wool and squinted down at a plate as she scoured some fragments of cabbage stuck to its rim. Janet would have been horrified to see her Wedgwood service treated in such a manner. 'Idle women. With nothing to do but dress themselves, paint themselves, play bridge, play tennis, have affairs and gossip, gossip, gossip. Then the men took it up. Innuendoes in the newpapers – rags all of them. The invitations stopped. No visitors. Oh, except those people too curious to be able to resist some contact . . .' Again she thrust a dripping plate at Helen. 'I didn't care. I didn't care a fuck. But for Toby. You know how sociable he was. Night after night in that ghastly club – drinking, playing bridge, playing billiards, gossiping with his cronies. And those affairs of his.' She had jerked the plug from the sink. Now, hands on hips, she stared down as fresh hot water spat out of the tap. Rapidly, she began to plunge one glass after another into the scalding water. Steam rose around her but she seemed to be impervious. 'Well, the affairs came to an end. Full stop.' As she withdrew one of the glasses, it cracked and disintegrated in her hand with a high ping. 'Damn!' She bent over to pick up the fragments and one pierced her finger. Angrily she sucked on it. 'Perhaps he no longer had the appetite. Perhaps. Or perhaps he'd learned his lesson. Perhaps. But more likely there just weren't any women who were prepared . . .'

Helen stood tugging the expensive Irish linen cloth be- tween both her hands. It was a long time since Isabel had handed her anything to dry or she had picked anything up off the draining board. 'But what – what was all this gossip?'

'You know! You know!' Her face and neck mottled and her hands dripping and scarlet from the water, Isabel whirled round on her. 'That girl – that, that, that Clare.' She fumbled for the name, as though, trivial and submerged in the distant past, it had slipped from her memory.

Helen stared at her; Isabel stared back.

'Well, of course, he was having an affair with her.'

'No, no! He wasn't! He wasn't!'

'What do you know about it? What do you know of the life of your precious father? Before he married your mother, when he was married to your mother, when he was married to me. A lady's man, that's what they used to call him at first. But then – after, after the murder – they had uglier words for it. Oh, yes!'

'But if they had accepted all his other . . . affairs, then if he and Clare . . . I don't see why that should have . . .'

'Christ! You really are a fool! Even more of a fool than I've ever imagined.' She wiped the back of her right hand, the mop in it dripping water down her dress, across first her forehead and then a burning cheek. 'Everyone decided that, between them, he and that, that slut had killed my Peter.'

Helen's mouth clicked open sideways, as though her jaw had suddenly been dislocated. Isabel glared at her, cruelly triumphant that she had been able to inflict a blow so unexpected and so lethal. Then she went on: 'It was all quite logical, what they decided must have happened.' She leaned, arms crossed, against the side of the sink. 'He'd gone into her

257

bedroom, because she obviously could not come to him in the dressing room, with its door on to the bedroom in which I might or might not be sleeping at the time. Perhaps they'd drugged the child – with one of those bromide pills I'd given her for her migraines. At the inquest, there was some doubt – remember? – about whether there were traces of bromide in his body or not. Obviously that old soak McGregor bungled the postmortem. Not enough dry ice, was that it? Something like that. Anyway, they'd started their fucking. And Peter woke. Saw. Was terrified. Was about to cry out. He or she grabbed the first thing to hand, that brassière, thrown across the bed or over a chair, and pressed it to Peter's mouth. Pressed too hard, too long. Then the rest ... the rest followed.'

Suddenly, her body, so tense before, relaxed, softened, crumpled. She gripped the side of the sink with both her hands, stooping over it, as though she were about to vomit.

'But you don't believe that?' Helen's voice was almost inaudible.

Isabel straightened herself and swung round violently. 'Of course I don't believe it! What do you imagine? Toby knew that I knew all about his countless goings-on. Better that slut than some diseased prostitute procured for him by Muhammed. Why should he kill his son, his only son, the son he loved so much, merely in order to hide from me that he . . . ?' Again she wiped flushed forehead and cheeks with the back of her hand. 'If Peter had gone on screaming, I'd have come in, as I often did when his nightmares woke me. I'd have told Toby to get back to the dressing room and the next morning I'd have sent the girl packing. I'd done it before. I'd have done it again. And I wouldn't have sent her packing because she was having it off with my husband. I'd have sent her packing because she wasn't a fit person to have the care of my child. But not one of all those so-called friends of ours, with their poisonous gossip, knew anything of that. To them I was the poor, pathetic, put-upon wife, who, faithful to hubbie, had kept her mouth shut and decided to make the best of things, even though I knew the whole truth. That was the role they created for me. Me!' She gave a strident laugh and once again began violently to scour a dish with the ball of wire wool.

'I never knew Father had been made to suffer like that.'

'No. Of course you didn't.' The tone was contemptuous. 'And Joan and Janet and the old woman never knew. He didn't want them to know, *I* didn't want them to know.' She picked up one of the glasses dried by Helen. 'This is all smeared. Do it again.' Helen took it. Then she went on: 'He's smashed. You've only to look at him to see that. Smashed. He's interested in nothing – not even in making money, not even in cunt. Certainly not in me, certainly not in Angie. Nothing, nothing. One day he'll kill himself. I'm waiting for that. It'll happen. You'll see.'

'Oh, no, no, no!' Helen cried it out in anguish.

Serene now, her grey hair sticking in matted strands to her forehead, Isabel nodded with a dreadful complacence.

At that moment, Janet put her head round the door. 'What are you both doing? Aren't you finished yet? I'm dummy. Perhaps I ought to lend a hand.'

'No, no, Janet. We're getting along fine. Thank you.'

'Sure? Well, then, I'll leave you to your natter.'

X

The awkward young man, with acne scars pitting his chin, cheeks and the back of his long, thin neck, gazed, troubled, at Helen. The child between them, afflicted with Addison's disease, might have been Indian, so dark was its colour. The young man was troubled not for the child, prematurely doomed in those days before the discovery of cortisone, but for his colleague. As they walked away from the bed, he asked her: 'Are you all right?'

'Yes, of course I'm all right. Why?'

'Oh, I don't know.' To other of the women doctors, however senior to him, he could have said something like:

You look worried, you look pale, you look as if your mind were hundreds of miles away. But there was something about this beautiful, straight, stiff, efficient girl, with her courtesy, her discretion and her willingness to take on any job at any time, which distanced and even chilled. If only, at some moment, she would exclaim like the other girls: 'I'm bloody well not going to do that! I've had enough!'; would agree to have a drink or to go to the cinema or to take a country walk; would laugh, tease, confide. One of the consultants, half in admiration and half in annoyance, would refer to her, never to her face, as 'The Ice Princess'. She was cold, everyone had decided; and she was superior, if not in her own estimation, then in the reluctant estimation of those with whom she worked.

Back at home, Helen stretched out on her bed. She never wanted to get off it. *Smashed*. A strange word to use. *He's smashed. You've only got to look at him to see that. Smashed.* It suggested some horrible accident, two cars in head-on collision with each other, a body tumbling out of a top-floor window, the explosion of a bomb in a crowded store.

She got off the bed, went to the secretaire and opened the small drawer. Once again she unwrapped the package concealed in it. Brown paper, tissue paper. Then she took the object in both her hands, stroking it with the balls of her thumbs, as she looked down at it. She climbed back on to the bed with a groan and held it to her mouth. She lay there like that for a long time as the light in the area dimmed, dimmed slowly as though a pool were filling up with chilly, cloudily brackish water.

Ilse came in. 'Hi!' she called. She knew that Helen must be back because her cashmere overcoat was hanging in the hall, her umbrella propped beside it. Ilse, always tidy, carried the umbrella over to the stand and dropped it in. 'Helen!' Still Helen did not answer. Ilse removed her cloak, to reveal her sister's uniform, and hung it up beside Helen's overcoat. She should have felt tired, after so many hours of work; but she never did, even though lack of sleep had ringed her eyes with bruise-like shadows and her face was even more sallow than usual.

She hesitated before Helen's door, then entered.

'Aren't you well?'

It might have been Aunt Sophie.

'Yes. Yes, I'm well. All right.'

'Then why are you lying like this in the dark? And why didn't you answer when I called?'

Smashed. He's interested in nothing – not even in making money, not even in cunt.

'Oh, leave me, Ilse.'

'But look, my dear –'

'Leave me.'

Ilse left her. She went into her own room and put on a 78 rpm record of the second movement of Mozart's Dissonance Quartet. She stood over the wind-up gramophone, watching the shiny disc revolve, until that constant circling, not the music of the andante with its febrile throbbing, induced in her a hypnotic state of calm. When the gramophone began to run down, the pitch of the dialogue between first violin and cello falling inexorably, she let it do so, arms crossed over her white, starched hospital apron and her eyes sombre. Then she knelt down beside her bed and, chin cupped on hands, formulated a silent, repeated prayer. Oh God, in your mercy, goodness and omnipotence, pluck away from her heart whatever is festering in it, as you would pluck a splinter from under a finger nail or a thorn from a heel . . .

As she squeezed her eyes tighter and tighter, oblivious of the floorboards pressing up, hard and cold, against her knees, she apprehended, rather than heard, a rustle and rushing, as of a vast flock of birds, which wheeled, swept down, crowded round her. The whole room and her whole being were clamorous with them. Invisible beaks rained down their blows, pecking and tearing; but she welcomed an agony which was also a joy. Oh God, in your mercy, goodness and omnipotence . . .

But God did not pluck away from Helen's heart whatever

was festering in it. Her face grey, rigid and scaly in texture, she travelled to hospital, performed her hours of duty, travelled back. Then she would retreat into that bedroom looking out on the area, with the traffic booming above it, and, the curtains open and the lamp unlit, would lie out on her bed, holding against her chest, her mouth or her stomach the clumsily made bookmarker with its pendent strings of multi-coloured beads. The bookmarker felt dry and friable; the beads were hard and chill.

Ilse would come in and stare down, usually without a word, the light from the street lamp above the area glinting on one of her protuberant eyeballs as her head tilted. Then she would go out and return with bread soaked in milk, a cup of soup, a bowl of porridge. Pap. She saw Helen as a terrified, distracted child. 'Eat,' she would say sternly. 'Come on.' And Helen would sit up, supporting herself on an elbow, and take one mouthful and then another, before, tears coming to her eyes, she would say, 'I can't, can't. No more.' The bookmarker lay under the bedclothes, where Ilse could not see it.

After some days, Ilse did not walk out of the room, as she usually did, once Helen had eaten, but remained there, by the bed, looking down, with those stern, passionless eyes, the half-empty bowl of chicken soup held, like some libation, in both her hands.

Helen stared back with famished gaze. Her tongue moved slowly over lips cracked with dryness.

Ilse said: 'Tell me. Tell me about it.' She sat down on the side of the bed, her body as taut as an athlete's braced for a final effort, and then she put out a hand, drew back the bedclothes and removed Helen's hands from over her breasts. The hands were holding the bookmarker. Ilse prised apart the fingers, one by one, as Helen, silent, beseeching, gazed up at her.

'What's this?'

Helen shook her head frantically from side to side.

'The boy. It's something to do with that boy.' Last night, as those invisible wings first rustled and then rushed all around

262

her and the invisible beaks had torn at her, she had come to it.
'That boy. The dead boy. Tell me.'

Helen suddenly put out her arms, placed them around
Ilse's shoulders, drew her down towards her. Her mouth was
against Ilse's ear, its breath sour. She shuddered convulsive-
ly. Then she said: 'Oh, Ilse, Ilse, Ilse, I killed him, I killed
him, I killed him.'

Ilse said: 'I know, darling. I know.'

XI

*From the summing-up of Mr Justice S – at the trial of Helen Thompson
at the Old Bailey*:

. . . You have heard the accused describe in detail how she
alleges that she committed the crime. She knew that the
governess, Miss Clare O'Connor – whom, unfortunately, it
has been impossible to trace in India, in this country or in any
other country – had taken a soporific, bromide, for a migraine
headache. She had in her possession a boy-scout knife, which
you have been able to examine. This, she explained, she used
in connection with her work as leader of a troup of Brownies –
or Bluebells, as they are called in India. On the night of the
murder, which she has told us was long premeditated, she
undressed herself and, after following her custom of going into
her grandmother's bedroom on the same floor to see if the old
lady wanted anything, she went to bed. She lay awake until
she was sure that all members of the household were asleep.
Soon after midnight she left her bedroom and went downstairs. She entered the drawing room and opened one of the
three French windows on to the tennis court. She left the knife
on its ledge, together with a pair of rubber boots. It was
always her intention to make it appear that the killing had
been the work of an Indian or Indians, as an act of revenge
against Mr Thompson, her father, in particular or of
terrorism against the British in general.

She then went up to the room in which the governess and

263

child were sleeping, approached the child's bed and lifted him out. He awoke and, though he recognized her and knew her well and had every reason to trust her, he appeared to be about to cry out. She therefore snatched up the first thing to hand, the brassière which the governess had thrown over a chair by his bed, and pressed it against his mouth. She continued to press it against his mouth as she carried him downstairs and through the drawing room. When she got to the drawing room window and was about to put on the boots, she realized that he was dead. She carried the corpse and the knife up the path above the tennis court, through the trees and into the privy. It was there that she inflicted on him the terrible wound that all but severed his head from his body. She has told you that she deliberately used this ferocity, in order to give credence to the theory that some Indian or Indians had been the culprits, rather than someone within the household. She has also told you, in particularly macabre detail, that she thought that, after the cutting of the throat, the blood would never come and has given that as the reason why she both sliced the child's hand and wounded it in the chest. In fact, as you have heard from the medical evidence both of Dr McGregor and of Dr Cathcart, if the child were already dead, then the blood could not be expected to spurt, as it would have done if he had been still alive. She threw the corpse into the privy. She has no memory of also throwing the brassière there and presumes that she must have let it fall, without being aware of it.

She returned to the house, taking off the boots before she entered it. She left the window open, in accordance with her plan that an intruder should be suspected. She went upstairs and into the bathroom, where she washed herself, the boots, her nightdress and the knife. Her grandmother heard her moving around but thought nothing of it. She replaced the knife in its sheath and hid it under some underclothes. She hung up the nightdress, which she had washed, to dry by the open window. She put on a clean nightdress.

The next morning, she noticed not only that the nightdress

was still damp but that there were still some residual stains on it. She wrapped the knife, still in its sheath, in the damp nightdress and concealed both in the laundry basket in the bathroom next to her room. Unfortunately, as you have heard from ex-Inspector Singh, the view at first taken by the police was the one that she hoped that they would take. They assumed that an intruder or intruders had murdered the boy and no immediate search was made of the bedrooms of the occupants of the house, though a thorough one was at once made of the servants' quarters. This, according to the account of the accused – I must stress yet again that it is her account that I am now summarizing for you – enabled her to take both knife and nightdress, hidden under her raincoat, out with her when she went for a ride on the afternoon following the night of the murder. She rode to a lonely bluff above the lake and from there hurled the bundle into the water, weighted with a stone and tied round with string. As far as she knows, no one saw her, though she says that there were some Indians fishing in that vicinity.

. . . I cannot too strongly impress on you that the utmost caution must be exercised in accepting a confession unsupported by evidence. But in this case, the knife was retrieved from the same area of the lake into which she declared that she had thrown it. You have also seen the affidavit of the ayah on the subject of the nightdress. She was all along suspicious of the accused and she voiced these suspicions to ex-Inspector Singh. Ex-Inspector Singh had a hunch, as he himself put it to you, that the accused was the killer; but without her confession and without the discovery of the murder weapon, and in view of the plausible explanations that she gave to him of everything which seemed to him suspicious in her conduct, he felt, as did his superiors, that no case lay against her.

. . . You may well ask yourselves: What possible motive could induce a young girl of reputable family and previous good conduct, with up to then no history of mental illness, to commit so horrible a crime? She has herself said that she bore no ill-will to the victim and that she killed him as an act of revenge against her stepmother. There is absolutely no evidence that her stepmother ever maltreated her or behaved to her in an unfitting manner. But it would be only human if she preferred her own child to her stepdaughter and if, however unwittingly, she made this preference clear. The accused plainly had — and still has — a close attachment to both her father and the memory of her deceased mother. You may think that jealousy may well have aggravated trivial slights and humiliations into wrongs to be avenged.

. . . You may also well ask yourselves: What, after so long a period of years, drove her to make this confession? She has spoken of her remorse. Indeed, as you have heard from her flat-mate, Miss Ilse Rothstein, who was in part instrumental in persuading her to seek out the police, that remorse, combined with pity for her father, suspected with cruel injustice by former friends and associates of having killed his own son, resulted in her having what was, in effect, a nervous breakdown. She almost entirely ceased to eat, she rarely spoke to anyone and, when not at her work, she spent all her time in the dark in her bedroom, usually on her bed. She herself has said in this court: 'It is a tremendous relief to lay down this terrible burden.'

You have heard both Dr McGregor and ex-Inspector Singh declare that, at the time of the murder, she evinced absolutely no symptoms of mental instability, much less insanity. She was, admittedly, not then examined professionally by Dr McGregor, who is not, in any case, a specialist in the field of psychology. You have also heard the evidence of Dr Aidan, eminent in this field, that, after extensive conversations with her, he is of the opinion that at present — naturally he cannot speculate about her mental condition at the time of the murder — she is entirely sane.

. . . Altogether, a more horrible story has never been presented to a jury in my whole experience. Here, if we believe her, we have had a description, given by a woman of twenty-four, of the way in which, at the age of eighteen, she murdered her little stepbrother for no motives other than

266

those of the most trivial nature. Can some sort of diabolic possession have driven this intelligent, educated, otherwise kindly and well-behaved girl to execute this premeditated atrocity? If we lived in another age, we might be tempted to believe so. . .

XII

Toby stumbled into the small, square, whitewashed room, with its surround of chipped lincrusta, his hair sticking up in tufts around his flushed, sweating face. He had recently had an eye-tooth removed, so that there was a gap at one corner of his mouth, which obliged him perpetually to suck in saliva as he was talking. In his once-expensive suit, now creased and worn, his striped shirt frayed at cuffs and collar and his light brown brogues, cracked over their insteps, he had the air, by turns farouche and ingratiating, of some old conman down on his luck. He held out his shaking, swollen hands but Helen did not take them.

'Oh, Helen, Helen, why, why, why? After all these years. Why?' He had put the question repeatedly to her before the trial.

Her answer was unaltered: 'I had to, Father.' In the past, she had always addressed him as 'Daddy'. He felt a strange disorientation that she no longer did so now.

'But it was all so pointless. Useless. You can't bring him back.'

'No. I can't do that.' Her voice was tranquil. 'I can't bring anything back.'

Soon he had left her, emerging from the cell as though from a deathbed, his face contorted, a hand to his forehead.

XIII

Ilse came.

'You'll get parole eventually. It won't be long. It's a light sentence anyway.' Under the overhead bulb in its inverted glass cone, her eyes looked even more protuberant. She fingered the chain of the crucifix which lay beneath her blouse.

Helen stared at her.

'I'll visit you whenever they allow me. And I'll pray for you, Helen.'

Helen smiled. 'Yes, visit me. But the other – no. Pointless.'

'I will, I will!' Ilse twisted the chain as though she wished to snap it.

Again Helen smiled. 'The judge spoke of demonic possession. Do you think that such a thing is possible?'

Ilse took the question seriously. Only later she decided that Helen had been intending a sardonic joke. She thought for a while. Then: 'Who can be certain?'

Ilse knew about demons. Both her parents had, as she had often put it, been 'fried to a crisp in the gas ovens'.

It was not impossible.

IV
INTERLUDE

From an unpublished, private memoir by Dame Pamela — , one-time Governor of — Women's Prison:

... On the first occasion when I met him, at (of all places) a royal garden party, he confided in me, a total stranger, that even now, as a Bishop, he never felt wholly at ease with the Church. He bit into a cucumber sandwich and then, having masticated for a moment, added: 'But the important thing is that I feel at ease with God.' I restrained myself from asking whether he thought that God also felt at ease with him.

It was because of that encounter that, a few weeks later, I found myself showing him round the prison. 'Prisons and prisoners have always been an absorbing interest of my life,' he had remarked on the decorous Palace lawn, on learning who I was. Later his male secretary had rung me to arrange the visit, gushing 'Oh, the Bish *will* be chuffed!', when we had fixed on a date.

As we wandered about the infirmary, I noticed how closely he peered at every woman worker under thirty. Clearly he had read in the newspapers that it was in the infirmary that Helen Thompson worked. Eventually, not to my surprise, he had come to the conclusion that one girl, with a provocatively flouncing walk and an air of sulky defiance, must be her.

He lowered his voice, bending his silvery head close to mine. 'Would I be right in thinking that that, er, girl would be Helen Thompson?'

'Which?' But I already knew which one he meant.

'The dark one with the tray over there.'

'Good heavens, no! She's not a murderess. She's back in here for burglary.'

'Burglary! Really? She hardly seems the type . . .'

'Over there. With the syringe.'

'*That* one!' He was astounded. 'But she doesn't look as if she'd ever have been capable . . .' He had difficulty in not continuing to stare at her. 'So insignificant, so – so apparently inoffensive.'

Not for the first time I thought that for Helen to efface herself so completely argued, paradoxically, a tremendous strength of will.

'Unfortunately, people don't always look what they are,' I told him drily. 'If they did, more criminals would be caught. And some prison officers would never be appointed.'

'Yes, I suppose so, I suppose so.' Furtively glancing at Helen once again, under those extraordinarily long lashes of his, each so distinct that they might have been stiffened and darkened with mascara, he had hardly taken in what I had said to him. That was probably just as well since, even then, I had realized that, if he had a sense of humour, it was one totally different from mine. He turned, with all the elegant, easy authority not so much of his position as of some actor-manager, a Beerbohm Tree or a Forbes-Robertson, of the past, to say, in a voice which a faint, not unattractive impediment made emerge as though he were constantly sucking on a cachou: 'Then she's allowed to, er, practise while she's in here.'

'As a doctor? No. But she's allowed to help our medical staff.' I thought it more prudent not to reveal that, due to our chronic shortage of staff, she was performing many of the duties of a doctor.

'That seems rather hard. After all, even in the concentration camps the doctors were allowed to follow their profession.'

'And in some cases performed experiments on their patients,' I reminded him.

He gave a queasy smile.

At that, I conducted him over to the bed of a dying patient, having explained her condition. Long, bony, beautifully manicured hands clasped before him, he looked down at her with what struck me – perhaps I was misjudging him, in my dislike of him – as a purely professional compassion, so that once again I was reminded of one of those great actor-managers of the past, to whose performances my grand-mother, a former Gaiety Girl, would take me as a child. The wretched woman, now reduced to no more than a rag and a bone and hank of hair, stared up at his apparition, in pale grey suit, silk shirt and lavender tie, with disbelieving awe. He began to talk to her about God's infinite mercy and love.

When we walked out of the infirmary, he gently took my arm, just above the elbow, between thumb and forefinger – I have always hated to be touched even by members of my family – and asked: 'What precisely is the attitude of the other women to the presence of a child-murderer among them?'

Managing to disengage myself on the pretext of picking up a used bus ticket and a paper bag littering our path, I explained how, when Helen had first been admitted, I had asked if she wished, at least in her initial weeks, to be kept in solitary confinement under Rule 14; but in a calm, clear voice, head erect, she had replied: 'No, thank you. I don't think that's necessary.' There had been a single incident two or three days later, when some scalding tea had been 'accidentally' tipped over her by one of the women – it was never clearly established which – in charge of the trolley. Then, amazingly, her fellow prisoners seemed to have accepted her, if not as one of themselves, then at least as a human being and not as a monster.

'How do you account for that?' By now we had returned to my office and he was sipping daintily at a glass of sherry.

'It's a mystery.'

I went on to tell him how even women who had done nothing more atrocious than batter their babies at some moment of inadequacy, frustration or rage, were either constantly assaulted or relentlessly cold-shouldered. It might be that Helen, for all her apparent docility, had a personality so strong that she could mesmerize the other women into an unwilling respect for her. It might be – and here I hesitated, since the possibility had already begun to disturb me – that they sensed that she was innocent.

'Innocent!' He pounced, as I had expected him to do.

I shrugged. 'So many women who come in here constantly proclaim their innocence. But no one believes them. It would be ironic if the women should have come to believe that Thompson is innocent, even though, so far from ever having made that claim, she has always proclaimed her guilt.'

'I remember the trial. There was something . . . The judge's summing-up was scrupulous in its fairness, her confession was fully confirmed by evidence – above all, by the finding of that nightdress and the knife. And yet . . . yet . . .'

As he once again sipped his sherry, lowering his head of thick, grey hair, the waves so deeply and regularly indented that they hardly seemed natural, I almost told him that I, too, had had the same instinct when reading of the trial and that that instinct had been strengthened each time that I had seen Helen, blank-faced and rigid-backed, moving efficiently and silently about her tasks in the infirmary.

That was the beginning of the Bishop's crusade, one of many similar ones over a period of years on behalf of prisoners usually far less plausible, to procure either her pardon or, if not her pardon, at least her early release on parole. He would have long sessions with her, from which he would emerge in a strange condition, both baffled and exalted. He wrote letters and gave interviews to the press. Once he confided in me: 'I was having dinner at No 10 the evening before last and I managed to say a word to the PM about our Helen.' He was certain, he declared, that she had confessed solely in order to shield someone else. It was clear that by this 'someone else' he meant her father; but since, though mortally ill, Thompson was still living, this was something which he could hardly make explicit. At one moment of hyperbole, in a letter to *The*

Guardian, the Bishop had even described Helen as 'saint-like'.

After this had been going on for several weeks, Helen asked to see me.

She was brought in by a wardress so plain, angular and spinsterly that it had always been a source of wonder to me that she had not merely married but had mothered three children. Her years in the service had bred in her a profound, weary cynicism, so that nothing surprised her about the women in her charge except some act of decency. She was one of a small minority of the staff in whom Helen aroused not merely disgust and suspicion but ill-concealed hatred. With her unerring gift for a cliché, delivered in a mournfully nasal voice with the trace of a West Country accent, she would say of her: 'Oh, she's as clever as a cart-load of monkeys' or 'That one could twist anyone around her little finger, given the time and opportunity.' In that 'anyone', she clearly included the Bishop and myself.

She remained standing behind Helen, until I said: 'Thank you, Lucy.' She hesitated and then, with a toss of her small, close-cropped head, went out.

I told Helen to sit in the chair on the other side of the desk from me and then, leaning across it, asked: 'What's the trouble?'

'I don't want to have any more visits from the Bishop.' Calm and firm, her voice was entirely different from the agitated, obsequious, sullen, distressed or defiant ones which I was used to hearing at such interviews.

'You don't have to have visits from him, if you don't want to. It's entirely up to you.'

'I want him to drop my case.'

'If he doesn't want to drop it, then neither you nor I can force him to do so.'

I knew the passion of the Bishop's advocacy and I also knew the vanity, elaborately concealed, which fuelled that passion. The wardress, Lucy, had shown an unexpected perspicacity when she had once remarked derisively: 'He's only interested in Thompson for snobbish reasons.' Misunderstanding, I had countered with a laugh: 'Her family's not all that grand, you know.' Lucy had corrected me: 'Thompson belongs to the aristocracy of crime.' She had brought out the phrase as though she had borrowed it from someone else – perhaps her schoolmaster husband. 'He wouldn't concern himself with anyone so common and low as, say, a conwoman or a shoplifter.'

Now I once again leant across the desk towards Helen, noticing both the extraordinary freshness of her complexion and the care with which she kept her hands and her hair. 'What made you decide this?'

She looked directly back at me, in a way in which few of the other women, their gazes slowly veering up or around to mine, as though to a light too bright for them, ever did. 'I don't want any pardon or remission. I want to make it clear that I am never, at any time in the future, going to apply to the parole board.'

She was the first prisoner in my experience to voice such a decision.

'Do you so much like your life here that you don't want it shortened?'

I had intended the question to be one of those dry sardonic jokes for which I know that I had a reputation among both the prisoners and my staff; but it was with complete seriousness that she answered: 'No, I hate it. But . . . it's something I have to go through.'

'I see.' I was both fascinated and repelled – as I was often to be in the future – by the strength of her self-sufficiency. It was that fascination which now made me prolong our interview, instead of concluding it, as I should certainly have done if she had been one of the other women at that moment waiting to see me. 'But if there's a chance of getting out of here sooner than you expected, then why not be sensible and grab it?'

'Sensible.' She repeated the word, not in interrogation, but as though she were tasting it on her tongue. Clearly, she did not like the taste, finding it synthetic. At once, cheeks burning, I felt that I had said something inept. She shook her head, smiling: 'I have something to do. I have to do it.'

'See it through to the end?'

She considered, head on one side. Again, I had the embarrassing sense that she had established some kind of superiority over me.

'Is that it?' I prompted.

Slowly she nodded. 'Whatever the Bishop may think or pretend to think, I'm guilty. I confessed, I've never withdrawn my confession. I've no wish and no reason to withdraw it now. I killed my half-brother exactly as I described it in court and I killed him for precisely the reasons which I then gave. Finis.' At that last word, she carefully placed her right hand on top of her left in her lap.

'I don't have to tell you – since you're a highly intelligent woman and a doctor as well – that, in a state of hysteria, people can convince themselves they did things they never did.'

She nodded, smiling. 'That's one of the dear Bishop's theories. The other, of course, is that I'm nobly taking the blame for a crime committed by my father. Neither is correct. I'm not an hysteric. And though I'd do many things for my father – whom, yes, I love and for whom I feel terribly sorry – I'd never do that.'

I stared at her and she stared back. 'You puzzle me,' I said at last.

She turned her head sideways, to gaze out of the window. 'I puzzle myself.' Her eyes again met mine, as she asked: 'Don't you ever puzzle yourself?'

It is unusual for a prisoner to put a personal question to the governor; and if any other of my women had put that particular question to me, I'd have given her short shrift. Instead, I laughed. 'Oh, yes. Often.' In fact, though I did not say so to her, I was puzzling myself at that very moment. Why was I spending so much time on this one woman, when there were so many others waiting to see me that morning?

'The Bishop will be – disappointed.' I could not keep the irony out of my voice; I was not sorry that he would be disappointed, not at all. 'He tells me he thinks you're finding your way to God.' Again, I could not keep the irony out of my voice, as I repeated the phrase which he himself had used.

She flushed. It was the first time that I had ever seen her other than completely in control of herself and her circumstances. 'That has nothing to do with him,' she snapped.

I leant forward across the desk, glad to have pierced her defences, however momentarily. 'Do you mean that, in finding your way to God, you've no need of his help? Or that, if you're finding your way to God, that's no concern of his?'

She stared at me, rigid and silent.

'You don't want to answer?'

Still she stared, with a terrifying penetration. Then she said drily: 'I see no reason to answer. All this is none of your business really.'

I rose. She also rose. At such moments, although I am a small, frail woman, I usually had the sense of being bigger than the women confronting me. I did not have it then.

'I'll tell the Bishop.'

'Thank you.'

I pressed the bell on my desk and Lucy came in. She looked from the girl to me and then back to the girl again, her elbows and chin jutting out sharply and her mouth pursed. Clearly, she thought it odd that our conversation had gone on so long.

When next the Bisop called, I told him of his protegée's decision.

His consternation gave me a secret, unworthy pleasure. 'But this is ridiculous! When things have gone so far – and so well. Only a week ago I had a confidential talk with the Home Secretary – when I was seeing him about something totally different. That was one of the things I wished to tell her today. You see, so far from her persistence in her confession of guilt and her determination to atone for it militating against an early probation, it makes it far more likely. I don't have to tell you, Pamela' – by now, he had started to address me by my Christian name, though I could never bring myself, however much he insisted, to reciprocate – 'that if a prisoner shows genuine remorse for her crime and the wish to atone, then that is, well, more than half the battle.'

'Her remorse is certainly genuine. And so is her wish to atone.'

'Well, then!'

'But she seems to feel that the best way to atone is to serve out her sentence in full.'

'That's an arid kind of atonement. A woman of her gifts and training could do far more to atone by making herself useful in the outside world.'

'Clearly, that's not her own view.'

He bit on his lower lip. 'In any case, I still have grave doubts – despite all she says – that she *did* do that thing.' I had already noticed how he always preferred the phrase 'that thing' to 'murder' or 'crime'.

Once again he repeated his theory, shared by many others then and even more now, that she had confessed either out of a desire to remove from her dying father the terrible burden of suspicion or else in a state of hysteria in which she had persuaded herself that she was indeed the culprit. He reminded me that the head of our medical staff was inclined to this second theory. He gave me examples of other women who had clamorously insisted, despite all the evidence to the contrary, that they had killed parents, husbands, children.

'It saddens me that she refuses to see me again. I thought we'd established a fruitful and understanding relationship. But I'll continue with the battle, I certainly won't abandon it, oh, no.' He rested his elbows on the arms of his chair and then, fingers interlaced to make a steeple, went on: 'Tell her that, please. Please!'

I nodded.

'You see, Pamela, I'm still utterly convinced that there's been a terrible miscarriage of justice. I'm still utterly convinced that, on some spiritual odyssey, she is acting out a strange lie of guilt.' The miniature steeple still erect before him, he now closed his eyes, the lashes making dark fringes on his high cheekbones. As though in some attempt at self-hypnosis, he continued: 'That odyssey hasn't been in vain, since it's brought her – I'm sure it's brought her – closer to the Kingdom of Love.' The voice had now acquired the thrilling plangency of the old-time actor-manager whom he so much resembled in appearance. 'She's approached that Kingdom by so selflessly taking on herself the atonement of another's guilt. Through this hideous self-annihilation, in a place which can only be hell to a woman of her sensibilities, she's attained a spiritual rebirth. Yes, I think one can say that – a spiritual rebirth.'

Nauseated by the stale, sickly odour of past sermons, speeches in the House of Lords, letters to the newspapers, interviews, gossip–column items and our own conversations, I wanted to shout at him: 'Oh, stop, for God's sake stop!' But, of course, I restrained myself.

Helen remained an obsession with him, though he never again saw her. He continued to crusade on her behalf; and each time that we met each other, whether in the prison or elsewhere, he would always ask me about her. 'A tragic case, a tragic case,' he would mutter, shaking his head.

For other people, too, Helen became an obsession. Prisoners – some educated, terrified, depressed, others brutal, ignorant, inarticulate – were visibly sucked towards her, like boats towards a weir, however disastrous the consequences. Their self-immolation was both joyful and desperate. Lucy and other of the prison officers would talk of 'something unhealthy'.

Attachments of this kind are of course common in prison, even among women who, in the outside world, are contented wives and mothers. But I had never previously observed one woman exerting so intense an attraction on so many other women, of so many different types. Helen was not, after all, strikingly beautiful; and she never seemed consciously to have set about her conquests.

One of the education staff was an untidy, disorganized,

happy Irish girl, who gave lessons in art. Helen became one of her pupils; and before long I realized that, between them, an intimacy was developing. The girl, Maeve, had already conceived the idea of a giant mosaic, representing Christ in His Glory, for the mean Victorian prison chapel. Helen, who showed a natural aptitude for the work, became her chief assistant. When I saw their heads, one so glossy and tidy and the other so dull and dishevelled, bent over their work together, I used to feel an angry qualm, which I concealed as I asked: 'Well, how's it going?'

Then it was reported to me that Maeve had smuggled into Helen some small luxuries and comforts and I had to reprimand her.

'Yeah,' she said, 'yeah,' lounging in the chair before me in her tight, threadbare jeans and a blouse torn under one plump arm. 'I'm sorry. I shouldn't have done it.' But she was not sorry; and I knew that she would do it again, if she had a chance not to be observed.

'I don't think they're a good influence on each other,' Lucy told me. I longed to reply: 'Then keep them apart.' But instead I smiled, shook my head indulgently and said: 'When that mosaic's completed, it really will be something.'

By now I had come to fear my own feelings for Helen. Days passed between one opportunity to see her and another, and I shrank from creating the opportunities, leaving them, fatalistically, to create themselves. I found that, when I was near her, she would scrutinize me with gentle, wary curiosity, as though trying, unsuccessfully, to puzzle something out. I would be determined not to scrutinize her in return. I knew only too well how, in that sultry, suffocating confinement, every woman, whether prisoner or prison officer, would notice any sign between us, as though it were a flash of lightning.

Slowly the mosaic grew, fragment by fragment; and in despair I kept imagining the two women, heads close and lips moving in conversations inaudible to others, putting together, fragment by fragment, a relationship which would eventually achieve a similar wholeness. 'It's beautiful,' I would say, as suddenly Christ's halo or one of his hands, raised in benediction, emerged; but really it was all hideous to me.

Helen had few visitors. Her father would come, stooped and yellow-complexioned, his hands terribly swollen. One or other of his sisters, Helen's aunts, would accompany him but never his wife. Then he went into hospital, then he died. Helen showed no grief when I told her of the bereavement, merely saying in a tone of quiet resignation: 'Well, it had to happen, sooner or later. Better sooner. He was so ill.'

'Does his death make any difference to your attitude to parole?'

'No. Why should it?' For the first time in all the months that we had known each other, she sounded hostile to me.

Helen's most constant visitor was her former flat-mate, a taut, brisk, emaciated little woman, with the protuberant eyeballs so often indicative of thyrotoxicosis. I often wondered what had been the relationship between the two and what they now talked about. I remembered that the friend had played some part, perhaps even a decisive part, in Helen's confession of guilt.

One day – it was my fifty-sixth birthday, I remember, even though I did not celebrate it – I reached a decision. Life had become insupportable and I must do something, however brutal to Helen, to myself or to others, to make it supportable again. I felt the relief of someone who, after weeks of dread, decides to undergo an increasingly urgent operation.

After I had completed the arrangements, I had Helen brought in to my study, seated her in the chair opposite to mine at the desk and then broke it to her: she was to be transferred to an open prison, where, I felt sure, she would be far happier.

She made no demur. 'I see,' she said calmly; and then no less calmly, placing right hand over left in her lap, in a gesture which I had come to know so well, she added, with a smile: 'I understand.'

282

I felt sure that she did understand: the strain of wanting to look for her and at her and yet not looking; the sleepless dawns, when my Siamese cat purred under my fingers as I tugged at her coat; the late-night walks along the canal, when I almost wished that someone, man or woman or demon, would suddenly emerge from the shadows and inflict some hideous act of violence on me; the longing, shame, guilt.

The next day Maeve erupted into my room.

'What's all this about Helen Thompson being transferred to an open prison?' she demanded, her round face congested.

I nodded calmly, as though in no way surprised either by her intrusion or by the peremptoriness of the question. 'Her conduct here has been excellent. It was time to give her a break.'

'But the mosaic! The mosaic!' She cried it out in anguish, as though she were a mother faced with the imminent loss of her child.

'I'm sorry, Maeve. But surely you have a lot of other people also working on it. Jenkins, Talbot, Cowell, that school-teacher – the one who came in last week. Thompson can't be indispensable. After all, she might even have been released – if the Bishop and those others had been successful.'

She stared at me with an unsparing, steely coldness. She too, like Helen, might have said: 'I see . . . I understand.' But she merely turned, her hands thrust into the pockets of her jeans, flung open the door and rushed out, without closing it behind her.

I got up and pushed the door shut. Then I returned to my desk, opened the drawer and drew out Helen's file.

I was about to close that file once and for all and, with that closing, also to close what had been one of the strangest and most painful episodes of my life.

V
ILLUMINATIONS

Many Australians assume that she is one of themselves. She has a parting low on the side of her head and from it the crisp, close-cropped hair springs away in streaks alternately dark-brown and tawny. In England, people would assume that variation of colour to be the result of skilful dyeing, but here they know it to have been caused by the sun. There are deep lines around the eyes, too often screwed up against the glare, and her forehead, cheekbones, bare arms and the backs of her strong capable hands are spattered with freckles. Some Australians might even guess that that small, white, scimitar-shaped scar on a temple is where she had to have a skin cancer removed. She dresses in elegant, slightly mannish trouser-suits, even for cocktail parties, dinner parties and visits to the opera arranged for the delegates. She is wearing one now, of an oatmeal-coloured raw silk, with a brown silk blouse beneath it. Her only jewellery is a plain gold ring on her wedding finger. A woman who is introduced as 'Doctor' may be married or unmarried; they assume, because of the ring, that she is or has been married. 'Have you any children?' hostesses, unqualified to discuss tropical medicine, ask her, and they wonder why she laughs in that way, as though they had said something ludicrous to her. 'No, I'm afraid not.'

Today her hostess, whose husband is part-owner and director of a fashionable clinic, is showing her her garden. The house is a long, low one, with cool rooms, full of pictures by living or recently dead Australian artists, opening out, one

287

off another, in luxurious perspectives. It stands on the ridge of a hill, one of a number of similar houses, each with a garden which falls away, in a series of terraces linked by steps and winding paths, to the sea far below. This suburb is a rich one. 'I'd really like to live in King's Cross,' the hostess says. 'That's where one finds some lovely old houses.' But she does not really mean it. Her daughter and son-in-law live there and, though she thinks their house 'charming' and 'quaint', she feels, each time that she enters it, that those narrow rooms, one above the other beside the narrow staircase, will close in and suffocate her.

There is an oriental gardener – Japanese, Vietnamese, Chinese? The visitor cannot guess for certain – working, back bowed and straw hat on his head, in one of the flowerbeds. 'Everything all right?' the hostess asks as they stroll past him, and he answers, surprisingly with an American accent, 'Yes, thank you, mam.' Out of his hearing, the hostess explains to the visitor that they have to pay him a fortune, no one wants to be a gardener these days, people think they're too grand for that kind of menial job. 'It's the same in England now, isn't it?' The visitor does not reveal that it is many years since she visited England. She merely replies, 'Yes, I suppose it is.'

The hostess, pausing for a moment, hand to forehead to shield her eyes as she gazes seaward, asks the visitor: 'Have you ever heard of funnel-web spiders?'

The visitor shakes her head. She has, in fact, heard of them but she cannot remember in what connection.

'Mr Otani – the gardener – found one yesterday. He killed it, of course. It was lucky it didn't sting him before he found it, as otherwise he might now be dead instead of weeding that border for us. I often wonder how God – if there is a God – can have come to create things as murderous as that.' She turns. 'This is, as you see, a dangerous, as well as a beautiful, country.'

The visitor does not reveal that she has come from a country far more dangerous and beautiful. She does not reveal that her companion of many years died, within a few hours, of a mysterious, undiagnosed fever. She does not talk of the marauders with their machetes and stolen revolvers nor of the troops, feared even more, with their machine-guns. She is immured in a flinty reticence. It is this reticence which has led her hostess to describe the visitor to her husband as 'rather heavy going'.

The hostess continues, as they now descend to the shore: 'I have a buddy who has this extraordinary phobia about funnel-web spiders. You may have met her. She's one of the guests tonight. Husband in oil. Rosie Freeman. She won't have a garden, she won't even go into anyone else's garden, not this garden, not any garden. She's terrified of the countryside. Isn't that strange? To allow one's whole life to be dominated by a single irrational fear.'

'I knew someone once who had that same kind of phobia about rabies,' the visitor says quietly, thinking of her dead companion, who was otherwise so fearless.

'My husband says it's not really a fear of funnel-web spiders, it's really a fear of death. The spider's bite and death are equally irreversible. Like rabies too, of course.'

'Irreversible,' the visitor repeats, in a way which strikes her hostess as odd. It is as though she were meditating on it and might even say, at the end of the meditation: 'But are they irreversible?'

The two of them, the plump, round-faced Australian, with her slightly bandy legs swelling above low court shoes, and her English guest, with her sinewy figure and back held so straight that she might almost be wearing an invisible brace, now make their slow way back up the paths and the steps to the house.

'Would it be painful to die of the bite of a funnel-web spider?' the visitor suddenly asks.

Her hostess, panting a little now from the heat of the December afternoon, pauses, one hand pressing a scented handkerchief to her upper lip. 'I imagine it would.' She laughs: 'It would certainly be quick. There are worse ways to die.'

The visitor, remembering the death of her companion,

thinks that she may be right.

Can it have been for this hard chip of knowledge, about the funnel-web spider and the instantaneous death following its sting, that she has been mysteriously impelled to make this journey from the country which sometimes seems to be the only one she knows to one which she knows not at all? After the death of her friend had precipitated within her a kind of infinitesimally slow dying of her own, she felt herself to be like one of those leaves which, looking up into the cloudless sky from the deckchair in which she would be lying out, a drink in her hand, at the end of a day of sweaty endeavour, she would see whirling round and round aimlessly, close to the giant sycamore from which it had detached itself. The leaf and she both spun on and on and on, in a frantic, unwilled spiral. But just as, on some rare occasion, a sudden wind would snatch away the leaf, so a sudden impulse snatched her away when the shabby, unshaved Greek who ran the local store and post office handed to her the Australian invitation in a bundle of letters tied up with string. She has come here for a purpose, she has no doubt of that; but, unless the purpose is to learn about funnel-web spiders, she does not yet know what that purpose is. Soon she will know.

The voices in the house seem louder to the visitor than when she and her hostess left it; but that may be because the garden was so quiet. 'Well, there you are!' The host greets them both. 'I was wondering what had become of the two of you.'

'I was showing Dr – er – the garden.' The hostess is bad at names.

The host turns to the visitor. 'Beautiful, isn't it? But it needs so much doing to it. Gardeners cost so much these days that we can only afford ours for three afternoons a week.' He fills a glass for his guest. 'Vodka and tonic, wasn't it?' It was, in fact, whisky and soda; but she politely takes what she is given. 'Did the wife tell you about the funnel-web spider?'

'Yes. I never knew of their existence before I came to Australia.'

'Sh!' He put a finger to his lips. 'We mustn't talk too loudly about them. One of our other guests has a phobia about them. The mere mention . . .'

Like others, he finds it difficult to talk to this woman about anything except medicine. Conversation with her is like a game of tennis with someone who has not grasped that it is not enough merely to stop the ball, one must also return it. He wanders off on a pretext and she finds herself alone. But that does not worry her. She is used to being alone, with people all around her. She feels none of the awkwardness or embarrassment which others usually suffer in such circumstances. She sips at her vodka and tonic, wishing that it were a whisky and soda, and examines the pictures. There is one of a naked young man, seated on a bent-wood chair, one shoulder sagging as though from an invisible burden, and his legs wide apart, revealing penis and testicles. There is a chilly abstract, bearing the title *Dream Chamber*, which might be by Ben Nicolson but which is signed indecipherably by someone else. There is a picture, clearly from another time, of a long, narrrow, pink cloud nervously fluttering, like a chiffon scarf, above a totally still, deep lake, surrounded by what are not so much trees as wispy, evanescent trails of lightest blue, the ghosts of trees long since fallen to the axe. This last fills her with unease, she does not know why.

A voice behind her asks: 'Do you know Ivor Fieldhouse?' For a moment she thinks that someone is trying to introduce her to someone else, but then she realizes that the man who has addressed her – she has met him, wasn't it he who told her that he had lived for many years in Papua New Guinea? – is speaking of the artist who painted the picture at which she has been gazing.

'No.'

'One of our best. He was originally English, trained at the Slade, but no Englishman has ever heard of him. Bet you never have!'

'No. But then I know so little about pictures. In Africa . . .' She shrugs. In the remote house, now empty but for its servants, there are some magnificent examples of primitive

African art, collected by her companion over a period of years.

The man who has addressed her looks terribly ill. As a doctor she knows that look. Probably the poison of the funnel-web spider is already at work in him. But she likes the pliancy, softness and grace of that boyish physique, the eager vibrancy of the voice, that sense of teasing irony.

'Tell me about him,' she says, going towards a sofa.

'Well . . .' She sits and he sits down beside her, carefully tweaking each of his trouser-legs at the knee so that it should not stretch. He left England – Southampton – on a cargo-boat at the age of nineteen. Went to Ceylon, Burma, the Seychelles, India. Painted part of the time, worked at innumerable odd jobs for part of the time. Part of the time did nothing, enjoyed himself. Few of his pictures from that period now exist – or, if they do exist, the people who own them have no idea of their value, since they never come on the market and are never exhibited. Then he landed up here. Married a rich woman, much older than himself. Inherited her money. And that enabled him to build Drumlanrig Castle.'

'Drumlanrig Castle?'

'You've never heard of it?'

She shakes her head. 'Well, not in Australia.'

'He called it after Drumlanrig Castle in Scotland. Apparently his mother was cook, maid, I can't remember, to the Buccleuchs. It's not really a castle, though it might be part of one. And there he lived happily ever after, with his numerous women and his even more numerous children and the pictures – like that one over there – which he painted in such profusion.' He leans his head forward, to say in an undertone: 'Our hostess was briefly one of the women – though you might not believe it now. That's how she got that picture and several others. Yes, in her day, she was really quite some girl!'

At that moment their hostess comes over. Her husband always tells her that she must not drink too much at one of their parties but somehow she always does so. She has done so now. 'Your glass is empty, my dear!' She calls the boyish middle-aged man 'My dear' not because she knows him well but because she knows him so little that she has forgotten his name. 'Do go and get yourself a refill.'

The visitor examines her surreptitiously as she stands before them, her glass in her right hand and her left hand, her arm crossing under her breasts, supporting her right elbow. It is still just possible to conceive of her as young, pretty and unconventional, the mistress of a painter who had other mistresses.

'This is fine.' The man gets up from the sofa and the visitor then also gets up. He points with his empty glass at the landscape of the long, narrow, pink cloud above the still river. 'Our friend here was admiring your Fieldhouse.'

'Everyone does. I think it one of his best.' When he first gave it to her, she pushed it, unframed, under the bed of the lodging-house room in which she was living. Now the Sydney Museum of Modern Art had offered to buy it from her for a large sum. But she does not need the money.

'I was telling her about Drumlanrig Castle.'

'Oh, Drumlanrig!' Her sigh manages to express both derision and a romantic nostalgia. 'Drumlanrig!'

'She ought to go there.'

'Yes, yes, you must! You're staying on for a few days after the conference?'

'For the weekend.'

'Well, then! It's only a drive of an hour and a half. Let's make up a party and go. A picnic – we'll have a picnic.'

'Do people still live there?' the visitor asks.

'Do people still live there? Of course they do! All the flotsam and jetsam of his life – the women and the children and the children's children and the friends and the friends of the friends. It's called an artists' colony. But the only real artist was Ivor. Those who are left weave or make jewellery or mess around with pottery or batik or woodcarving. You'll see.'

'Anyway, it's a beautiful spot,' the man says. 'Well worth a visit.'

The visitor has been wondering how she will spend the weekend before she flies back to Africa and that house, deep in the bush, from which someone may or may not have stolen the Benin bronzes and the other treasures about which she no longer cares.

There are five cars, because the party has grown; and the picnic has now become a dinner, so that Italian caterers have gone on ahead, with a van containing food, wine, crockery and cutlery. The hostess, who is called Babs Alexander, and who has arranged the whole evening, tells everyone that Alfredo is producing his *pièce de resistance*, his *vitello tonnato*. 'In this kind of weather no one wants hot food,' she says not once but many times, as though, if anyone did want hot food, the repetition might eventually persuade them otherwise.

Helen is in the Mercedes belonging to the man, now known to her only as Hank, who first told her about this English-born painter so famous out here and totally unknown in his country of origin. Babs is with them and a shy, charming couple, so recently married that they are interested neither in the scenery nor in their fellow-travellers but only in their proximity to each other, thigh against thigh, arm against arm and sometimes even cheek against cheek, in the back of the car. Babs, who is also in the back, thinks that, really, they're going a little too far. Surely they can wait until they get to bed? She is growing slightly deaf and she feels left out, since for much of the time she cannot hear what Hank and Helen are saying to each other above the hum of the engine and the purr of the air-conditioner.

Hank is trying to flirt with Helen, but she does not respond. He has told her that he is divorced, that his children are in Tasmania, that he is bored with his bachelor existence. Does she have any children? She replies truthfully no.

The countryside through which they are driving is beautiful in its wide, empty aridity. The soil, though brown when close at hand, seems to lighten to ochre in the distance; and, above it, everything seems to be tinged with the faintest blue, as though smoke were clinging to its outlines. The road is straight and shiny, rippling slightly in the late evening glow. It might be a canal flowing sluggishly from the base of the mountains to the plain.

'They really are blue,' Helen says in wonder.

'What are? My eyes?'

'No, the mountains. Though your eyes are blue too.'

'Not such an attractive blue,' says Babs from behind, since she has heard this exchange.

Helen looks back over her shoulder, The shy young man is nibbling his shy young wife's ear-lobe, like a rabbit nibbling at a lettuce. He stops when he sees that Helen can see him. But it is not at him that she is looking back but at the other cars, one, two, three, four, strung out behind them. Sunlight flashes from a hood. She shuts her eyes and there is a brilliant, jagged scar branded on their lids. She opens them.

They climb and, as they do so, the long day begins at last to burn itself out. A cool breeze passes across Helen's face, through her hair, over her arm resting along the open window.

. . . She and Ilse sat out before the dusty circle of buildings, their bungalow its hub, and then, as a faint breeze quickened from beyond the hills to rustle the canopies over their chairs, Ilse sighed deeply with contentment. The moment for which I wait each day, she said. For your whisky? No, for this cool. For the moment there were no more ulcers to be probed or lanced, no more needles to be jabbed into quailing flesh, no more skeletal bodies to be examined for their tumours or parasites. Ilse said: How far we have come. Helen knew that she did not mean geographically.

They pass houses, in an extraordinary variety of architectural styles – chalets, English seaside bungalows, Spanish villas, Japanese teahouses – set far back from the road. Then they are in the open country once again. Since his car is air-conditioned, it irritates Hank that Helen should have opened the window beside her. It means that so much dust will come in. But, looking sideways at her, as the onrush of their passage draws taut the skin of her face and blows her crisp, close-cut hair backwards, he decides to say nothing. Let her enjoy herself, let her do what she wants. Why not?

They turn through massive wrought-iron gates, each supported on a stone column surmounted by a stone eagle perched on a ball of stone. But there is no reason for gates so elaborate or indeed for gates at all, since there is no wall, no fencing, no hedges, no wire. The grass sticks up in tufts, on what must have once been a smooth gravel drive. There are huge trees with silvery boles, dead branches trailing from them, in the deserted parkland. Helen sees something move in the distance. A horse? A dog? Or would a kangaroo be found up here?

'Oh, how sad, sad,' Babs murmurs from the back. 'Each time I come here it's just a little sadder than the time before. Why can't they do something about keeping things in order.'

'Because most of them spend their lives high on pot,' Hank answers.

'Oh, nonsense!'

'Surely Ivor was never above a little sniffing?'

'What do you mean?' Babs is indignant. 'Cocaine? Utter nonsense. The only drug Ivor ever used was booze.'

'And sex,' Hank adds wickedly, with a glance of complicity to Helen.

Babs flushes and is silent.

. . . Ilse drew up the sleeve of her white jacket and twisted the rubber tighter. Ilse, should you? Helen pleaded, rather than asked. Why not? Ilse answered. I've done it for years. I'm not addicted. But when I'm deathly tired, as I am now, and when I'm deathly depressed, as I am now, well, I want a little nirvanah. Oh, don't, Ilse. But Ilse was always in control of everything: of the hospital staff, of Helen, above all of herself.

The 'Castle' is so extraordinary, with its four angle turrets covered by ogee caps, its bell-tower, its apsidal projection over a chapel set at an angle to it and its lancet windows, many of which have been sealed with corrugated iron, plywood or cardboard, that Helen begins to laugh. This puzzles Babs, who asks, 'What's the joke?' 'Oh, nothing, nothing,' Helen answers. Where parts of the structure have already collapsed, there are piles of rubble which no one has ever bothered to clear away. Once there must have been a formal garden; but the hedges, now black rather than green in the ebbing light, have grown so tall that they all but meet overhead. On the hillside which slopes up behind, there are a number of cottages, shacks and prefabricated bungalows dotted here and there, with no fencing to demarcate the land of one from that of its neighbours, no gardens, other than a few plants in pots set out in the occasional courtyard or on the bare earth, and no sign of any human being, other than two tiny children, a boy and a girl, who wander over, completely naked, their sunburnt bodies luminous with dust, to stare at the newcomers.

They all get out of their cars, with exclamations of amazement and pleasure. Babs points. In front of the 'Castle', a glossy van has been parked. 'Alfredo' – the gold letters glitter in extravagant flourishes as the dying sun catches them. 'Well, we can be sure of a good dinner. Alfredo's *pièce de resistance. Vitello tonnato*. I thought that in this kind of weather everyone would prefer cold food to hot.'

A tall, beautiful woman – fifty-five? sixty? – comes out through the arched doorway and walks, head slightly inclined to one side, towards the party. She is wearing sandals on her straight, narrow feet, no stockings, a loose, white dress. There is a blue ribbon holding back hair silver-gold in colour.

'Laurel!' Babs rushes forward.

Hank whispers to Helen in explanation: 'She was the last of them. She's now the guardian of the flame. The house-mother.'

Laurel and Babs kiss; but whereas Babs is eager, throwing her arms around the other woman and hugging her to her, Laurel is clearly determined to maintain a distance. Babs still holds Laurel by a hand as she turns to everyone and says: 'If you don't know her already, this is Laurel.'

But most people do know Laurel.

Bab's husband asks Laurel: 'Are they getting on OK with the dinner?'

Laurel replies in a bored, vague voice: 'Oh, yes, I think so.'

'You're having dinner with us?' Babs says anxiously.

'Am I?'

'That was understood.'

Laurel comes over to Helen. Though so many people mistake Helen for an Australian, Laurel does not do so. 'You're the English visitor.'

'That's right.'

'Dr Eliot.'

'Yes.'

. . . Ilse told her, meeting her outside the prison: 'You're Helen Eliot.'

'What do you mean?'

'Wasn't that your mother's maiden name?'

'Well, yes.'

'Then you're Helen Eliot.'

Later in the car, Ilse said: 'You've managed to escape the press.'

'Yes. Thank God.'

'Don't you want to make lots and lots of money?'

'I don't think so. No. Why?'

'Then you can go on escaping them.' Ilse stared ahead of her, silent, as the windscreen-wipers made a faint swish back and forth, back and forth. 'I could have made a lot of money,' she said.

Helen did not understand.

'By telling your story – or, rather, my part in your story. But, like you, I didn't want to make lots and lots of money.'

'That was decent of you, Ilse.'

'Not particularly. But it would have been indecent if I'd done the other thing.'

Now Laurel says: 'I once wanted to be a doctor myself. But I don't think I really care enough about people.'

298

'I'm not sure that I do either. But it's too late to think of that now.'

Imperceptibly, Laurel is leading Helen away from the rest of the party, along the side of the 'Castle' and then up the hillside.

'I thought you were running this wonderful hospital in Africa with another woman.'

'The other woman is dead. But, yes, we ran a hospital together and I suppose I'll go on running it. There's nothing better to do.'

Laurel asks: 'Do you know about this community?'

'I've heard something about it.'

'He left the money to me.' She says 'He' as though it would be impossible for Helen not to know at once whom she meant. 'On trust for the community. Not legally on trust, I could turn them all out tomorrow. But on that trust which we always had in each other. However' – she sighs – 'the capital is shrinking. Who knows how long we shall be able to go on? There's valuable land here and people think it's going to waste. One day, the "Castle" will vanish and there'll be a housing estate here – up, up, up.' She points ahead of her.

They pass a house. Through one window Helen can see a woman in a petticoat washing her long hair over an old-fashioned basin with high, brass taps. The woman looks up, bunching her dripping hair in a hand, and calls through the window: 'Hi, Laurel!' and Laurel waves a hand in salute, saying nothing.

'She's a sculptress,' Laurel tells Helen. 'He thought more of her than of her work, but I prefer the work.' Despite her age, her strides are powerful, as they continue to climb.

Out on a porch, before a hut which is really no more than a summerhouse, a young man, with his hair in a long plait down his naked back, ragged shorts and red, prominent nipples on his narrow chest, is hammering at some metal on a bench before him. He eyes the two women darkly but does not speak. There is a mongrel dog asleep by his bare feet. He has a blond, wispy beard, as silky and soft as the hair round a corn-cob.

Laurel is telling Helen about a retrospective of Fieldhouse's work to be held in Adelaide during the forthcoming Festival. 'When he was alive, people made fun of him. They thought he was just a dilettante rich enough to build this folly and mess around with women and paint. Now they say he's a genius and the messing around with women was a part of it. Women who never got nearer to him than a handshake now boast of having been his mistresses. Like Babs.'

'Oh, someone told me she really had . . .'

'Rubbish. She modelled for him, he felt sorry for her – working as a typist for some financier or other. She came to live out here for a while but she wasn't much good. Mooned around after him. But she wasn't his type. He hated fat women. She was fat even then.' Laurel has suddenly become vindictive. Helen wonders whether, out of retrospective jealousy, she is lying. Did Babs force her husband to buy those pictures for her? And if not, and if Laurel's story is true, why should Fieldhouse have given them to her?

The two women have now reached what was once a walled vegetable garden. In many places the wall has crumbled and, three or four cultivated patches apart, the ground is covered with giant thistles, clumps of brambles and cabbages grown to the size of bushes. 'They're all so lazy,' Laurel says. 'Lazy and getting old. I do what I can – I planted that asparagus bed over there – and there's a young Greek who keeps up his plot, even if most of it is taken up by hash. But the rest of them . . . Ivor would have kept them at it. He believed in discipline, for himself and for others. He had such relentless energy, all the time producing pictures, all the time producing children, getting the "Castle" built and all these houses built, and then running them and running the lives of everyone who lived here. It's all beyond me. Let them get on with it – or not get on with it. I have my flat, I deal with the visitors. *Basta*.'

They leave the walled garden, or what is left of it, and continue up the hill. Helen has begun to feel hot, even though the sun is sinking, a lurid orange beyond the misty, pale blue hills. She would like to sit down in some dark, dank corner of the 'Castle' and sip at a glass of lemonade or chilled white wine. She wonders why Laurel should have singled her out for this personal tour of the property and when it will end. But she is drawn to Laurel, with her athletic, bare, sunburned arms and legs, her unlined face, the lips tinted silver, and her air of cleanliness and crispness. That cleanliness and crispness she has noticed repeatedly in this country, since she has come from a country where so much is dirty and limp.

There is a corrugated-iron shack, so small, with a cobwebby window on either side of a front door hanging open under a steeply pointed roof, that one might mistake it for a gardener's shed or a place for battery fowl. Outside it, a woman is rocking, endlessly rocking, in an ancient wicker rocking-chair, her eyes closed and her hands resting, like little claws, on the arms on either side of her. She is wearing a loose, cotton dress, with a floral pattern on it, plimsoles and a large man's watch on an emaciated wrist. She is so dark and her skin is so wrinkled that she might be mistaken for some aboriginal crone.

Laurel passes her first, then Helen. Helen pauses in her stride, as though a frame of a film had suddenly been frozen, then lowers her foot, stares. Asleep or awake, the woman keeps her eyes closed. The dying sun glistens on her upturned forehead and cheekbones. On one of the claw-like hands there is a ring which flashes fire from a diamond. Helen feels an extraordinary terror and a no less extraordinary exhilaration, as though she were some warrior about to embark on a life-and-death struggle. Now she knows the purpose of her long journey. Laurel looks back. What is keeping the Englishwoman?

'Tired?'

Helen swallows the sweet-sour saliva which has welled up on to her tongue. 'Hot', she replies, so faintly that Laurel peers at her with concern and then returns down the slope, to stand beside her. 'Let's go back then. There's not much more to see. Only an overgrown rock garden and a gazebo that's falling into ruin. I expect everyone will be wondering what has happened to us.' She looks at the elegant gold watch suspended round her youthful-looking neck on a black velvet cord. 'They're probably wanting to eat. They'll certainly be drinking.'

They begin to walk away from the corrugated-iron shack. Helen at last says: 'Who was she?'

'Who was who?'

'That woman on the rocking-chair.'

'Oh, he brought her back with him from India, years and years ago. She had some of the worst years of his life, I had some of the best. He was terribly poor then, no one thought much of him as a painter. They had a little station somewhere in the outback. Then they ran a restaurant. Neither any good. Then he met the woman he married – the woman with the money, who started him making money. But she – she up there – remained a part of his life. He couldn't jettison things, you see. He clung to everything, to every single thing, even if he no longer had a use for it. The attics are full of theatre programmes and old Christmas cards and cheque-book stubs and bills long paid. The estate is full of people like that. They came, briefly they were cherished, then they outgrew their usefulness. But he hung on to them, as people hang on to memories, as the only weapon, however feeble, to use against time.'

'Does she do anything?'

'Nothing, absolutely nothing. She keeps a number of cats and some chickens. She has a plot of land but it's years since she went near it. If it's fine, she sits all day out on that rocking-chair and, fine or wet, she sits most of the night in front of her television set.'

'What's her name?'

'Her name?' The question surprises Laurel. 'Clare,' she says. 'Clare Thompson.'

'Thompson?' It is weird and Helen betrays that she finds it weird.

'Hm.' Laurel nods. Then she turns, puzzled: 'Do you know her?'

Helen shrugs. 'No. Oh no.' A shudder rattles her body briefly, despite the heat. 'There's just something . . . something about her . . . Perhaps – perhaps I saw her somewhere in Sydney.'

'In Sydney? You can't have done that – that's for sure. She hasn't been further than our nearest village for, oh, at least ten years.'

'Oh. I see. Then I must have been mistaken.'

'Where *have* you both been?' Babs demands under the barrel vaulting of the musty, panelled hall. In the gloom she seems to undulate towards them like some brightly-coloured carp through muddy water. There is a faint jealousy in her voice, as of someone who only comes to value a possession when someone else appropriates it.

'I was showing Dr Eliot around the community.'

'It's interesting, isn't it?' Babs says, in a tone which implies that really it's the most colossal bore.

'Yes,' Helen agrees. But 'interesting' hardly describes that experience of coming on the blackened, wrinkled woman rocking endlessly outside the shed of corrugated iron.

Bab's husband, being a physician, notices that Helen looks extraordinarily pale. Clearly, she is unused to this heat. He hurries over with a drink. 'Vodka and tonic, isn't it?' he says, and though, as at the previous party, Helen wants a whisky and soda, she takes it from him. 'See how clever I am,' he says. 'I remember your tipple.'

People begin to reminisce about Fieldhouse, whose paintings are hanging all around them. They all pretend to have known him better than they did and they all exaggerate the help which they gave him in his early struggles. No one mentions Clare. Helen sips at her drink, listens, sips, half-listens, sips, listens not at all.

. . . 'This is Peter's governess, Clare.' Toby spoke the words as though he were saying 'This is the Taj Mahal' or 'This is Fatipur Sikri'. Helen knew even then, as the girl advanced sinuously towards her, a cigarette holder jutting outwards and upwards from her clenched teeth, that her

303

father was in love with her. Clare seemed to move in a blaze of light, although the evening was late. The light dazzled Helen, making her feel nauseous and faint.

'Clare's not much older than you,' Toby said. 'She'll be a friend for you.'

Isabel looked contemptuously at him, her hands clasped over her swelling belly. She knew, she knew. Then, no less contemptuously, she looked first at the Eurasian girl and then at her stepdaughter.

In those first days, Helen hardly dared to speak to Clare, she even avoided her. Clare was a slow, finicky eater and the other four of them – five, if Peter were there for breakfast or luncheon – would seem deliberately to remain silent before their empty plates, as though to embarrass her as she went on cutting her food into miniscule pieces, raising each piece to her mouth, chewing, chewing. Helen felt both pity for her and a longing to say something to relieve the silence. But if anyone said anything, it was usually Peter. Toby would watch Clare with the same voracious eyes and the same salivating mouth with which he would watch the kitmatgar hand round a dish.

'Don't you ride?'

'No. I'm terrified of horses.'

'Pity. We could have gone out riding together.'

'We could go for a walk.'

'By the lake.'

'Yes.'

They took Peter for a walk. He ran ahead of them, playing one of those secret games of his in which he required no one else to join. They stopped and watched a fisherman, squatting far out on a rock on The Bluff, with a rod in his hand. He was so still against the still lake that he might have been asleep.

Clare sighed. 'How deadly it is here!' Helen had been thinking how beautiful it was, with the sun slanting diagonally across the water and the hills all around frothing with bougainvillaea and rhododendron blossoms. 'It was a mistake.'

'What was a mistake?'

'Accepting your father's offer. Oh, don't think I'm ungrateful, but I'm used to more – excitement. Here, nothing ever happens.'

'I thought you had a boyfriend.'

'Oh him, *him!*'

Helen almost said: 'I thought you had my father.' Perhaps to that, too, Clare would have replied: 'Oh, him, *him!*'

The life of the beautiful, dark-skinned, discontented girl was something which Helen felt, despairingly, she would never penetrate; but its impenetrability also excited her. Once, when she knew that Clare had taken Peter off to a children's party at Government House in the larger, neighbouring station, Toby was away on business, the old lady was up in her room and Isabel was playing bridge in the Andersons' house down the hill, she ventured into the bedroom, shared with the child, which smelled so strongly of the perfume of which Clare herself smelled so strongly. ('Really, that girl must douse herself in Evening in Paris,' Isabel had once remarked, as Clare had left the drawing room.) Helen had touched the perfumes, unguents, lotions and powders on the dressing-table with her fingertips. She had taken up a bottle, unscrewed its cap and held it to her nostrils, breathing the scent in deeply, as though breathing the troubling, intoxicating essence of Clare herself. She had opened drawers and looked down on neatly folded clothes. She had opened the cupboard, its doors warped from the damp, and run her hand over the dresses hanging there, their shoulders shrouded in tissue paper. So orderly, so clean! As she held against her own body the sequined dress, lime-green panels against chocolate, which Clare had worn the previous night to go out to a dance with that lumpish soldier from the convalescent home, she had felt a thrilling, shameful intimacy.

'Where's Clare?' Toby would often demand of Helen, as he wandered lugubriously, unlit cigar in mouth, from room to room. 'I wanted to ask her something,' he would sometimes add, never specifying what. Or: 'Clare seems to have vanished,' he would comment. Helen wanted to say the same things herself but she never did so. Her iron determination to reveal nothing would make Toby remark to her with melancholy regret: 'I wish you and Clare got on better together' or 'I thought Clare would be such a nice companion for you but it seems I was wrong.'

One day, when Clare and Helen were seated out on a bench in the garden while Peter wandered round after the gardener and his 'boy', Clare sighed and said: 'Oh, I can't wait to get back to the plains!'

'Well, it won't be long now.' Helen hesitated before putting the question which she had been wanting to put for a long time: 'Shall you be staying on with us?'

'Oh, I don't think so. I don't really like children – though Peter'd be all right if your stepmother hadn't spoiled him. But I prefer the life of a hotel. Things happen there, there's movement and change.'

Boldly Helen said: 'If you leave us, my father's going to miss you.'

'I daresay he will.' No one who answered so coldly and scornfully could be having an affair with the man about whom she was speaking – though she might have had one in the past. Helen felt all the elation of relief from some long-standing anxiety or pain. Then Clare asked, surprisingly: 'Do you think I'm his girlfriend?'

'I don't know.' Helen was disconcerted.

'Well, I'm not. Before I got the job, I used to go out with him – while I was working at his hotel. But there was nothing of – *that*. Of course he wanted but there wasn't.' Clare looked at Helen, tilting her head and turning it sideways. 'You don't believe me, do you?'

'Of course I believe you.'

'Because he keeps mooning around after me, your stepmother's managed to convince herself that we're having an affair. The servants probably think it too.'

'Oh, I'm sure –'

'Well, who cares!' With her court shoe, so unsuitable for the hilly terrain, she kicked out at the gravel. 'Who cares!' Once again she turned to Helen, with that tilting of her head sideways and upwards like some exotic bird listening for a sound of danger. 'And you – do you have a boyfriend back in England?'

Helen shook her head. 'Lord no!'

Clare laughed: 'One's better without them. Believe me. One's better without them.'

'You may be right.'

Clare intertwined her fingers in Helen's, she squeezed. 'Friends,' she said. 'We're friends.'

'Friends,' Helen echoed, feeling as though she were about to gag on something too large and hard for her to swallow.

Peter came running over with something wriggling between his fingers. 'Look, Clare! Look, Helen! Have you ever seen a worm so huge?'

Clare's face, wrinkling up in disgust, the mouth pursed, became suddenly ugly. 'Throw it away! How dare you pick up something like that! Dirty!' The child began to laugh, dangling the worm before her. She slapped out at the hand which held it. 'Throw it away! At once!'

Peter flung the worm in a wide arc away from him. He looked after it, shading his eyes, to see where it had fallen. Then he ran off, laughing delightedly to himself.

'Little beast!' Clare exclaimed. 'He needs a good hiding. But he'll never get it. My father would have taken the strap to any of my brothers – or to me – for doing such a thing. But that kid'll always have things just as he wants them. Silver spoon.'

Now Babs is taking Helen by the arm. 'Come and have some of Alfredo's delicious *vitello tonnato*. In this sort of weather, we decided we must have something cold. And there's an iced cucumber soup to start – oh, and a Pavlova to finish, since that's our national sweet.'

'I thought Peach Melba must be,' Helen jokes drily.

Babs takes her seriously. 'Oh, no, dear, that was something invented by some chef in Europe.'

'Perhaps one day they'll invent a Pear Sutherland,' Hank takes up.

There is no attempt to place the diners round the table. 'Just sit where you like,' Babs tells them. Helen notices that, in addition to Laurel and the people who have travelled out from Sydney, there are also, huddled together at the far end of the long oak table, a number of others, in many cases dishevelled and even ragged in appearance, who say little and that little only to each other and who seem to exude hostility, like some overpowering stench, towards the smartly dressed, gaily chattering visitors whose guests she assumes them to be. Helen looks for Clare but she is nowhere. She feels relief but also an acute sense of loss – emotions precisely similar to those which, on the day of Clare's departure from the house above the lake, she had experienced as she had trotted off into the hills at the first glimmer of dawn.

. . . On and on she rode, punishing the horse more and more brutally, as she forced him up and down slopes and through the woods at the farthest end of the valley. When the syce took the gelding, his sides heaving and his whole body flecked, Helen could see that he was angry with her; but of course he could never give voice to that anger, except by indirection, how could he?

'Memsahib has been far.'

'Yes. Far.'

In the morning room, which he had never been in the habit of using before the tragedy, leaving it to the women, Toby sat stiffly in an armchair by the window, his head pressed back and his mouth slightly open, as though he were bracing himself for the approach of a dentist with forceps.

'Hello, daddy.'

She must, at all costs, behave as though nothing had happened. Her father himself had said that. As though nothing had ever happened; as though things were exactly as they used to be; as though there were no change.

But there was a change. Peter was dead. Clare had left them.

He returned her gaze with an anguished reproach, so that she found herself, riding-crop in hand, recoiling towards the door.

'She's gone,' he said, his voice sounding as though he were writing the words with a blunt piece of chalk on a slate.

'Yes.'

'You never said goodbye to her.'

'I couldn't.'

His eyes glinted cruelly. 'I can understand that.' Then they grew heavy and dull, as though with a weight of unshed tears. 'I don't suppose we'll ever see her again.'

'No. I suppose not.'

'Poor Clare.'

It amazed her that he should say 'Poor Clare' and not 'Poor Peter' or even – why not? – 'Poor Helen'. It also made her angry. She wanted to hurt him; but, looking around for a weapon, she could find none. She turned and went out.

Bab's husband is calling up the table to her: 'Isn't this iced cucumber soup really something? Alfredo must be the best cook in the whole of this country.' The young man, with the beaky nose and the long, black hair falling wispily from under the towering, heavily starched chef's hat, smirks behind the table supporting both the next course and innumerable bottles of the white wine which Helen has found as clean, sharp and bracing as the country itself. There are also some bottles of vin rosé, standing separate, not in buckets of ice like the white. The young man whom Helen saw, almost naked, beating out some metal at a bench, now lurches to his bare feet, shirt open to his navel, pads across to the table, and stretches out a hand for a bottle in a bucket. But Alfredo says: 'Please, sir,' smiling but formidable, and hefts a bottle of the rosé. The young man, sulkily abashed, holds out his glass. Then: 'That's pink,' he says. 'I had white before.' He sounds like a querulous child, given a strawberry icecream instead of the vanilla one which he expected. Alfredo stares at him until, audible to everyone, he exclaims 'Oh, what the fuck!', allows his glass to be filled from the bottle of rosé and wanders back to his seat.

. . . Clare talked of her life with her family and at work in the hotel. At home there was never any privacy, there never had been any. 'I shared a bedroom with two of my brothers until I was fifteen, sixteen. Can you imagine? What I remember most now is the stink of them. Their shirts and singlets when they came back from the railway yards. Their socks. Even their shoes. I'd say, I'm not going to have those shoes in here, they stink, they're disgusting, put them in the hall.' She laughed: 'They'd do what I told them. They always did what I told them. Still do.'

Helen gazed at her. 'You're tough.'

'I've had to be tough. Fight, that's what I've always had to do, all through my life. You're lucky, you don't realize how lucky. You've got your Daddy with his millions to fight for you. You've got your Granny and those relatives back in England. You've never had to fight, never will have to.' When she spoke like that, she reminded Helen of some glittering-eyed, nimble, immensely cunning rodent, which could persistently and patiently gnaw its way through anything.

Clare admitted with a shrug – so what? It meant nothing – that she had 'strung along' (that was her phrase) other men than Toby. 'You get more by giving nothing,' she said with the famished wisdom of her upbringing. 'Girls who worked with me would go the whole way. And then they got the brush-off – and, with luck, a few rupees.' She stared out disconsolately at the lake, swinging a leg backwards and forwards as it rested over the knee of the other. Then she pulled that same face which she had pulled when Peter had run up with the worm dangling between thumb and forefinger. 'Awful creatures,' she said. 'Those sweaty hands. That taste of drink and tobacco in their mouths. Producing it from their trousers, all swollen and purple, as though the sight of it would be more than one could resist.' Helen had never heard anyone talk like this. She was appalled, fascinated, thrilled.

'Now tell me what you think of the *vitello tonnato*.' Babs, who has got up from her seat, is leaning over Helen. 'Try it. Try it. Go on, try it and tell me.'

Helen slices a piece and puts it in her mouth. 'Delicious,' she says. 'Marvellous.'

'What did I tell you?'

As the aromatic, creamy veal dissolves in her mouth, Ilse is saying: 'God, I'm sick of chewing, chewing, chewing on this leather. You know what I dream of, Helen? We're together, just the two of us, in the Jardin des Gourmets, just as we were for that birthday of mine, and we're eating – well, what are we eating? You choose. It's your turn to choose.'

'It's Alfredo's speciality,' Babs says proudly. 'That's why I chose it for today.'

. . . Clare was in Helen's room. They tried to make not a sound but at one moment, when Helen was on her knees by the bed and Clare lay across it, Clare gave a strange, choking moan and then old Mrs Thompson called out, alarmed: 'Was that you, Helen? Helen, are you all right?'

The two girls tensed. Clare put a hand over her mouth. Helen replied: 'I was just coughing. I have this tickle at the back of my throat. Sorry. Did I disturb you?'

'No, dear, no. It's just that I sleep so lightly. I thought . . .'

Clare giggled, her hand still over her mouth. Then she removed the hand, as Helen buried her face between her thighs, and whispered down to her: 'That was quick of you. And how well you lie!'

'One learns to lie and to lie quickly at a girls' boarding school,' Helen raised her head to say.

The Pavlova crumbles like stucco under the summer fruits and whipped cream piled on top of it. It is too sickly for Helen, suddenly she feels that she wants to vomit. But somehow she must eat, if not all, then at least some part of it. But she should have said what the woman opposite to her said, when the plates came round: 'No, I really mustn't, much though I long to. You see, I'm on this diet.' But would anyone believe that a woman as thin as Helen was on a diet? 'No, I really mustn't, much though I long to. You see, I'm a diabetic.' Better, much better. But too late.

. . . 'I'm frightened of coming up there to you. That's the second time the old girl has woken up.'

'Where else?'

Once they had gone to a cave, damp and malodorous, far off the footpath along which they had been walking high up in the hills. Once, when everyone was out at the cinema, they had lain, reckless of the servants, out on the flowered chintz of the drawing-room sofa. But both places, the one so alien and the other so domestic, had frightened Helen.

'You could come to me.'

'Peter?'

'I'll deal with him.'

'How?'

'I'll crunch up two or three of those pills your stepmother gave me and put them in his Ovaltine. He drinks his Ovaltine so sweet he'll never notice.'

'But you might make him ill.'

'Not with two or three.'

'All right.'

'Tonight?'

'All right.'

The man on Helen's right, who has, from time to time through the meal, attempted to talk to her – God, Babs was right, she certainly is heavy going – says: 'So you return to your African mission the day after tomorrow?'

'It's not a mission. Just a hospital.'

. . . There was a red-brick chapel, surmounted by a cast-iron spire which, in one of the violent storms so frequent in the region, had been hit by lightning and had shrivelled and blackened like a bean-haulm nipped by frost. 'Do you think that's a divine judgement?' Helen had asked. She had intended a joke but Ilse, who had no sense of humour, had taken her seriously. 'You mustn't say things like that.' They never replaced the spire. Helen did not enter the chapel unless in celebration of some wedding, birth or funeral among the Christian members of their staff, but Ilse often did so. She would emerge from it in a state either of morose depression or of feverish exaltation. The moods of morose depression became more and more frequent in the months before her death.

'It's not for me to convert anyone,' she would say. 'Not even you. I tried to convert you once and look how far I got. I leave that kind of thing to Father McCormick.' Once a month the Irish priest would arrive in his battered Land Rover to hear confessions and administer communion. An austere, finicky, sarcastic man, he had been deeply shocked and embarrassed when Helen had once entered his bedroom, assuming him to be in the chapel, and had found him outstretched, his naked, bony body covered in a fuzz of reddish hair, on top of his unmade bed.

'Everyone seems to be going out,' Helen's neighbour says, relieved that he need no longer make conversational forays always repulsed either by silence or a few non-committal words. Deliberately, he leaves Helen, having done her the courtesy of helping to draw back her chair, and joins a group of people with whom he works at his hospital.

'There are to be fireworks,' a young woman tells her. 'So I believe. Wasn't that a lovely idea of Bab's? She's so good at parties. On a night as hot as this one doesn't want to be indoors, does one?'

. . . Helen and Ilse walked arm in arm under a vast sky. Ilse had grown even more emaciated over the years and the obduracy of her purpose in running this hospital in a remote area of a hostile country had given her a tautness of expression that never seemed to relax even in sleep. Far off, from the choked jungle which perpetually encroached on the hospital compound, they heard a concerted baying. Then there was a sound like a single human scream. But they had lived there long enough to know that the scream was not a human one.

'Something has killed something else,' Helen said. 'Cruel, cruel.'

Ilse gave her humourless laugh. Was she laughing at the cruelty? Or at Helen's horror of it? Helen did not know. There was so much in Ilse's words and behaviour about which, baffled and fascinated, she could only guess.

Fortunately, everyone seems either to have forgotten the Englishwoman or to have decided that enough is enough, duty has been done, one can't be expected to spend a whole evening knocking one's head against a brick wall. People are now squatting or lying out on a grass slope, in groups of two, three or four. Some of the rockets and set-pieces are already in place. Bab's husband, assisted by the young metal-worker, wanders around to see that everything is in order. There is a naked electric light bulb in one of the two elaborate sconces on either side of the open postern but its light is so feeble that Bab's husband carries a torch. The young couple who were in the car with Helen are lying together in some thick grass above and beyond the rest. The girl giggles: 'I feel as if something were biting me.' 'I am,' her husband answers.

Helen perches herself on a crumbling wall, knees drawn up to chin. The poisonous sweetness of the Pavlova is still on her tongue, she can almost feel its brittle grains. A man who is no more than a shadow in the gloom in which she has placed herself has offered her a drink from a tray which he is carrying round; but she has shaken her head. The gesture has seemed to him unduly peremptory. After all, he is not a servant. Strange woman, he has thought, as others in the party have thought before him.

A rocket fizzes up into the huge, starry sky and then sprays outwards and plunges downwards in a cascade of lurid colours. Another follows it, this one a shower of silver coins, flung up and falling.

. . . Clare and Helen stood locked in each other's arms by the door. There was no sound but the heavy, regular breathing of the child in the bed by the window. Clare had been waiting, naked, lying out, one arm behind her head, her delicate ankles crossed. Helen was in her nightdress, her nipples hard against the softness of the picot-edged cotton. Their juices and their odours mingled, as Clare raised the nightdress, Helen extended a hand, their mouths sucked on each other.

A catherine wheel, bizarre memorial of the Alexandrian virgin whom the Emperor Maximus had strapped to a wheel like that of a chaff-cutter, whirls round and round, scarring the darkness with flame.

. . . The boy suddenly sat up, stared, opened his mouth.
Helen sees it open now, open eternally. Then Clare snatched
up the brassière from the chair beside her and, in a moment,
clapped it over the aperture, stuffing it in with frantic fingers.
Helen, torn between fleeing and helping her, hissed: 'Clare,
Clare, don't, *don't!*' The child's eyes skittered from side to side
in intensifying panic, he waved impotent arms, kicked
spasmodically. Then the eyes closed, the whole body gave a
single twitch, a leg kicked out feebly, kicked out again even
more feebly, was slowly retracted.

'What have you done?'

Clare hurriedly pulled on her wrap.

'What have you done?' Helen repeated. She stared down at
the child. She still did not believe that he could possibly be
dead. Grotesquely, protruding like ectoplasm in the moonlight, the brassière dangled from the mouth still open in its
silent, unending scream.

Clare sank down on to the bed, as though all strength was
draining from her, like blood from a severed artery. She said
nothing, her hands clasped between her knees. She stared up
at Helen. What are we to do? She asked the question without a
single word.

It was then that Helen felt something enter into her, as
once, on a picnic high up in the hills, she saw a shimmering,
speckled snake, startled by the approach of riders, walkers
and coolies laden with the elaborate impedimenta of food,
drink, cutlery, crockery and even folding tables and chairs,
deftly insinuate itself into the hollow trunk of the tree along
one branch of which it had previously been stretched in
drowsy satiety. What entered into her was not resource or
courage or cruelty or even a total insensibility. It was
something both stronger and more mysterious than any of
these things.

'Wait!' Without thinking, she had known – how had she
known? It was a question she was often to put to Ilse –
precisely what she must do and how she must do it. She had

315

first gone down into the hall, taking the steps with extreme caution, one by one, a hand gripping the banisters, and had felt along the shelf where her rubber boots stood among other boots and shoes, and had then gone into the drawing room, opened one of the French windows softly, softly, softly, and left the boots beside it. She had then gone up the stairs again, as quietly as she had come down them, past the half-open door behind which Clare lay out, shivering, her lips drawn back from her teeth in what was almost a rictus of death, on that same bed on which she had waited, naked and smiling, for the descent of her lover. Helen tiptoed down the corridor – pray God, her grandmother would think merely that she was going to the bathroom – and opened the door of her bedroom and crossed over to the rickety chest-of-drawers. The drawer creaked, the chest-of-drawers rocked. She extracted the knife in its sheath, then drew out the knife with a sudden ferocity, as though to rip the sheath apart. She descended. Strangely, she felt no fear, no doubt that she would succeed in doing what the Thing which had insinuated itself within her was telling her to do.

'Help me!'

But Clare only cowered, her red-nailed fingertips pressed to her mouth and her knees drawn up, as though she wished for nothing but to revert to being a foetus in the amniotic fluid of the womb.

'Clare!' That Thing within her now seemed to reach out, a tangible presence, to yank the girl to her feet. 'You must help me. I can't do this alone. He's too heavy for me.'

Helen put an arm under the chest of the child. What a weight he was! It was as though she were dragging up his corpse, bloated with water and entangled with weeds, out of the bed of a river in which it had been drowned. Again she said: 'You must help me!' Clare, whimpering, approached and took first one leg in a hand and then the other. 'And stop that noise!' Helen hissed. 'You'll wake everyone up.'

'What are you going to do?'

'Never mind. Come! Come *on*!'

316

One arm round the slumped body, she put a hand to the door-handle and gently turned it. Clare, one of the boy's legs in each of her hands and her face screwed up like a runner's making a last, superhuman effort, passed through. Then Helen followed. The two women, the child dangling between them, stood perfectly still, perfectly silent on the landing. They listened for some sound. There was nothing. They began their descent.

In the drawing room, the pair of them panting effortfully, the child still between them, Helen remembered that Clare's feet were bare. 'Go and get some boots from the cupboard.' 'What boots?' 'Some rubber boots. Any boots. Provided they fit you.' Helen took the full weight of the child in her arms. His skin against her skin, as he lay over her shoulder, was so warm that he might have been living. She waited. The Thing continued to tell her what she must do. She derived an extraordinary sense of power, such as she had never known before, from this clarity both of purpose and of the means to achieve it.

Clare returned in a pair of galoshes. 'They don't fit. They're too big,' she half whispered, half whimpered. 'What are you going to do?'

'Never mind. Come with me. Take his legs again.'

The galoshes were Isabel's. She wore them when she was gardening.

There was a large moon above the tennis court, which stretched, silver streaked with verdigris, before the dark house. A single lamp flickered from the servants' quarters. But no one would see them; Helen or that Thing inside her had decided that.

They toiled up the path to the privy, under trees juddering and rustling in the wind off the lake. At one moment, Clare, who was panting heavily, cried out: 'It's come off! It's come off!' She felt around with a foot, head bowed as she peered past the child's legs, and eventually retrieved the lost galosh. The moonlight glistened on the sweat on her upper lip, her forehead and bare arms.

Long before they reached the privy, Helen could smell its ammoniac stench. That stench revived her, as though someone had passed the dark green bottle of Yardley's smelling-salts, used long ago by her mother when she felt faint, back and forth beneath her nose.

'Not in there! No, I can't go in there! I can't!' Clare suddenly began to wail, uncaring whether she aroused anyone or not. It was as though she knew already what had to be done.

'Come on!'

'No!'

'All right. Wait here then. Wait here!'

Clare retreated to the shadow of some bushes, huddled up, her arms crossed over her breasts, hands over shoulders, and her hair falling across her face. Her eyes were closed tightly, as though in the conviction that, if she could not see these terrible things, then they would not be happening.

Helen went into the privy with the child over her shoulder, one hand clutching the back of his pyjama jacket to keep him in position, and the other the knife. Once, soon after her arrival, she had wandered in here, hoping that no one would see her, out of an ashamed curiosity, just as she had also passed and repassed the servants' quarters, in an attempt to discover the banal, pitiful secrets of their lives. The two nationalities, masters and servants, lived so close to each other, they even excreted so close to each other; and yet she knew nothing about them, nothing at all. On that previous occasion, she had stood, her heart beating rapidly, in the centre of the square, gloomy shed, with huge, lazy flies settling on her lips, eyelids and bare arms and buzzing all around her, and had breathed in that ammoniac stench as though it were some hallucinatory vapour which would, if endured long enough, grant some kind of vision. Then suddenly, there had been a swift patter of feet outside the door and Peter's head had appeared. 'What are you doing in there?' he demanded. 'Nothing,' she replied. Then she added: 'Looking.' 'You're not supposed to go in there. If Mummy knew, she'd be furious.' 'I can do what I like. Go away! Go away, you beastly little brat!'

The moonlight, filtering down through the cobwebs covering the oblong aperture high up on the wall, showed her the wooden slat with the hole in it. Countless servants must have perched themselves there, like famished birds, countless of times. Their naked feet, she had noticed on that previous visit, had worn the slat, a mat brown elsewhere, to a glossy tan. She rested the child's body on the slat, head tilted backwards through the circular hole above the noisome pit. She raised the knife, at the same time drawing back her body as far as she was able, so that the blood, which she imagined would spurt out, should not drench her. She cut violently and deeply, the muscles of hand, arm, shoulder rigid and straining. But the blood did not gush. The head, all but severed, fell back yet further, to reveal, black in the moonlight, the gash from ear to ear. Why was there so little blood? She was puzzled, as though by some scientific mystery for which her previous experience could provide no explanation. She took one of the small, perfectly formed hands and drew the blade of the knife across it twice. A few beads of blood oozed from the wounds. Then, jerking the body up by the front of the pyjama jacket, the blue-and-white-striped flannel taut beneath her hand, she drove the knife home beneath the ribs. *No need. Isabel. I promise.*

. . . There was a thunderstorm and Isabel cowered, white faced, her hands to her ears. 'Oh, oh, oh no!' she cried out, as lightning serpentined over the ridge of hills beyond the window. Toby went over to her, stood behind her chair, put a hand on either of her shoulders. Helen and her mother watched him. 'There's no need to be frightened. No need at all. Isabel, I promise you.'

She tried to push the body down through the hole, thrusting with both her hands, but it became grotesquely stuck, head and one arm dangling, the other arm pushed upwards, as though to ward off yet another blow. She threw the knife to the ground and put both arms round the waist of the child and dragged his body out again. Then, holding him under one arm, she raised the slat. The moonlight shone down on a silvery film over the liquid below her in the pit. She exerted all her force and flung the body downwards. There was a splash and she felt something moist flick across her cheek. Putting up a hand, she wiped it away.

She went out. 'Clare! Clare!' she hissed.

Clare appeared from the bushes, first two hesitant steps, then one. She halted. 'What have you done with him?'

Helen gripped her by both her arms, she put her face close to hers. 'An intruder killed him. An Indian. Or it may have been a gang. It doesn't matter. You slept through it all. Heard nothing. You'd taken those pills, remember? You woke – late. He was gone. Gone. A mystery. That's all. That's all you have to remember.'

'But I can't! Can't! Can't!' Clare was sobbing.

'You've got to. Now do what I say. Sleep or pretend to sleep till morning. Then look for him. Then say he's vanished. You had a migraine. Those pills. You slept heavily. You heard nothing, know nothing. Got it?' Clare only whimpered. Helen shook her even more violently, her nails digging into her quailing flesh. Clare nodded, her body still racked with gulping sobs which sounded like an endless retching.

'All right. Now let's get back to the house. Come on. Move!' She gave Clare a shove. Clare went down the zigzag path ahead of her, silent now, a hand over the mouth. Once, her silk wrap caught on a bush and she gave it a sharp tug, so that there was a sound of ripping silk. 'Oh, oh!' she wailed; but she went on.

'Take off those galoshes.' Outside the French window, Clare stooped and removed first one and then the other. Her teeth were chattering. Helen had already kicked off her boots. Holding them in one hand, she pushed Clare ahead of her, one arm holding the galoshes against her breast, into the moonlit drawing room. Clare pointed: 'Blood!'

Helen looked down. There was a darkening stain at her crotch. Strange. She had felt neither its dampness nor its warmth. She gave herself a shake. 'It'll wash out. And I'll have to wash these boots.' There was no blood on them but they were caked with soil from the floor of the privy. 'All right. Let me see the galoshes.' Clare handed them to her. 'They seem no different.' Helen thrust them back. 'Put them back in the cupboard exactly where you found them and then get upstairs. Upstairs!'

They went out into the hall. Clare crossed to the cupboard and thrust the galoshes far back to the rear.

'I think I'm going to be sick.' Shoulders hunched, a hand to her mouth, Clare stood there, unmoving.

'No, you're not. Upstairs. Hurry.'

Clare, stooped like an old woman, her shadow humped and huge beside her, clutched the banister rail and began to haul herself upwards, as though her strength were ebbing with each step. Boots in one hand and knife in the other, Helen followed her, erect and calm. They reached the landing. Helen indicated the door to Clare's and the child's bedroom with an inclination of the head. Clare turned the handle, went in, let out a choking gasp.

Toby stood there.

Again rockets fizz, this time in extravagant profusion, one after another, up in the sky. The show has reached its climax. 'Ah!' It is like the sigh of some universal orgasm. Then someone begins to clap and in a second everyone is clapping, as the rockets crackle and splutter all over the indigo sky.

. . . Toby stared at Clare, not at Helen. Helen might not have been there. 'Clare. What's happened to him? Where is he?' He was in his pyjamas and slippers, his face freshly shaved and still stinging from the eau de cologne which he had just rubbed into it.

Clare sank on to the child's bed. Helen closed the door.

'He's dead,' Helen said with flinty calmness.

Toby merely stared at her.

'It was a mistake, it wasn't intended to happen. We were together, he woke up. He was going to scream, we tried to stop him. He suffocated.'

No shock, horror or grief appeared on Toby's face. It was

impassive in its rigidity, the muscles of the neck and uptilted jaw stretched taut.

Then: 'But where is he now? Where?'

Clare began to rock herself back and forth on the bed, her hands to her stomach, as though in some attack of excruciating colic.

'Clare.' He went and sat on the edge of the bed beside her. 'Who did this? Did she do it? Did you do it?' He put an arm around her shoulder but she at once pulled away.

Helen replied with the same flinty calmness: 'We both did it. We didn't mean to do it. An accident. But no one will believe that. Now listen, Daddy. Listen.'

She stood over the two of them and told him, in a voice which never faltered or trembled, of all the events of the night – except for the reasons for her presence in Clare's room at such an hour and for a reaction so violent to the crying out of a child from his sleep. Toby never looked up at her throughout her account. His gaze was fixed on Clare, who was now absolutely motionless, as though unconscious or in a deep sleep, her legs drawn up and a hand over her eyes, on the bed beside him.

Helen finished. That Thing within her told her that she had the power to make him do what she wanted. He would go back to his dressing room, he would say nothing, it would all have happened as she willed it to have happened. There had been an intruder or intruders. An act of terrorism. An act of revenge. Hideous. Horrendous. But what could you expect of such people in such a country?

'Yes,' Toby said at the end. 'Yes. We'll say first that someone must have stolen him. Then someone – someone will find the body. We must make ourselves believe that someone has stolen him. We must forget all the rest. We must believe it, behave as if we believed it. Stolen him.' He rose from the bed but he still looked down, as though in thrall to some unbreakable spell, at the motionless body outstretched on the bed. Then he raised his eyes to Helen, gave a dazed, squinting frown, pointed. 'Nightdress. Blood.' Again he pointed.

322

She nodded, herself peering down at her crotch. 'I'll wash it.'

'Give me.' He held out a hand.

She looked around her, pulled the bedspread off the child's bed. She dropped the bedspread to the floor, turned her back to him, raised her arms, clumsily pulled off the nightdress. She threw it to him, not now caring if he saw her naked, and then picked up the bedspread and wrapped it round herself.

'Knife.' The knife lay on the chair across which the brassière had been thrown. Then he himself stooped, as though aching in every bone, and picked it up.

'What are you going to do with them?' she asked.

'Destroy them.' He hesitated. It was almost an interrogative, as though he were seeking her advice. Then he said more firmly: 'Throw them into the lake.'

Knife in hand, he moved back close to Clare's bed. Again he looked down. 'Oh, Clare, Clare, Clare.' He spoke with terrible anguish. He also spoke with terrible remorse, as though it had been he and not the two girls who had been responsible for the death of the child. Though he must have noticed the omissions in Helen's story, he had not once asked why Helen and Clare had been together so late in the night, what they had been doing to wake the child and cause him so much terror or why, in panic, they had silenced him in so horrific a fashion. He knew. Helen knew that he knew, just as she knew why he had come to Clare's room.

Toby left the room and Helen, the boots in one hand while the other hand held the bedspread around her, also left it. He did not look back at her as she crept up the stairs. She went along to the bathroom, washed her hands, washed them over and over, scrubbing them so violently with a nailbrush under the cold tap – there was no running hot water in the house – that at the end they were red and raw. She wet a flannel and rubbed vigorously at her cheek, where the sludge of the privy had splashed it, as though to remove an indelible mark. She ran the same flannel over her belly, where the child's blood was smeared, and then used it to scrape and dab at the boots.

She rinsed the flannel, rinsed it again and yet again, before she wrung it out and placed it beside her towels on the towel-stand. She returned to her room, unwound the bedspread which she had again wound about her naked body, and slipped into a clean nightdress taken from the same drawer from which she had taken the knife. The sheath! The sheath was still in the drawer.

The house was completely silent as she crept down the stairs again, the bedspread bundled under an arm and a hand clutching the sheath. Would she be able to slip into the dressing room and give Toby the sheath without waking Isabel? She dropped the bedspread to the floor of the landing, gently turned the handle of his door and pushed it open. She heard him give a startled gasp. He was by the open window, leaning against its frame, a hand holding up the net curtain as he looked out and down to the lake. Without a word, she held out the sheath to him. He hesitated, then took it from her. Not for a moment did he look at her. Turning back from the window, he muttered: 'Tomorrow morning. In the lake. I'll ride there. From The Bluff.'

She slipped out, leaving the door ajar. If Isabel woke when he shut it, then he could tell her that he had been along to the bathroom. She opened the door to Clare's room with the same stealth. The Eurasian girl still lay motionless on her bed, her knees drawn up and her face, eyes staring in shock, turned to the wall. Helen spread the bedspread over the child's bed, smoothed it with both her hands, patted a pillow. Then she went over to Clare.

'Remember what you have to say tomorrow.'

A little whimper bubbled up from between Clare's lips.

'Nothing ever happened, none of this. We know nothing about it. Nothing. Remember?' She leant over and shook Clare roughly by a shoulder. 'Make yourself believe that. Nothing.'

Clare made no reply. Had she taken in what Helen had told her? Helen did not know.

Helen went out of the room, again leaving the door ajar.

324

She started to mount the stairs. All at once an ineluctable weariness had sapped all her movements and thoughts. She wanted only to sleep, sleep, sleep.

The fireworks are over. People are beginning to wander back into the 'Castle'; but the glow of two cigarettes shows that the young couple, passengers in the same car as Helen, are still lying out together on the grass. Helen looks up. The immense sky is crowded with stars beyond stars. Her sight dazzles, her brain tingles with them. She begins to walk round the castle and up the slope, retracing the journey which she made with Laurel.

There are lights burning in some of the bungalows and shacks and from one of them – which she cannot be sure – there comes the insistent thud of pop music. That thud, over so much distance, is all that she can hear. It seems to be in time to a thudding within her, here – she touches the place with the fingertips of her right hand – just behind the breastbone. Some nocturnal creature scuttles in the bushes beside her.

Outside that corrugated-iron shed a naked bulb dangles, encrusted with dead flies as though with beads. The chair is still out in front of it but there is no person in the chair, only a cat. The cat, a tabby, stares at her, ears pricked and eyes glinting, as she approaches, then arches it back and slips off the chair and away into the darkness. She can hear voices but they are the voices, metallic and jumbled, which come from a television set or a wireless.

Slowly she goes up to the door and stands there for a long time, listening to those American voices, the staccato rattle of shots, the roar and screech of a car being gunned into action. There is no bell. Eventually she raises a hand and knocks. No answer. Again she knocks, now loud and peremptory.

'Who is it?' The door does not open. The voice is in no way frightened, only irritated and bewildered that so late in the evening someone should disturb her while she is watching television.

'Helen.'

'Who?' It is the question of someone going deaf, not of someone surprised.

'Helen. From – .' She adds the name of that far-off place in that far-off time.

A key turns, a bolt is withdrawn. Clare clutched her silk wrap close about her beautiful neck with a trembling hand. This old woman, her face almost the colour of a walnut, clutches an ancient dressing-gown about her raddled neck with a hand like a claw. She stares up, with misty eyes, into Helen's face. 'You,' she says. No shock. No surprise. She holds the door open.

Helen enters.

'I saw you. Earlier today.'

'Yes. With Laurel.' But how can Clare have seen her? Her eyes were shut.

Helen edges into what she now realizes is the only room, kitchen and bathroom apart, which this woman owns. 'I couldn't believe it. To have come so far, so many thousands of miles, and then – there – you!'

'It would have been even more unbelievable if you had found me in the street next door to the one in which you live.' Clare's voice is hoarse and dry as though, in the intense heat of that paved space in which she sits out in her rocking-chair, doing nothing, day after day, the vocal cords had withered.

. . . On the bench by the lake, the Eurasian girl examined her stocking, holding her elegantly shod foot out before her. There was a small snag, which might soon become a ladder. She licked the tip of her forefinger and then touched the snag. 'Does that stop it laddering?' Helen asked. 'Of course.' The answer was scornful. Satisfied, the Eurasian girl went on: 'How I hate mess. They live in such a mess. You should see the kitchen. We have an icebox and we have a pantry but the food lies out there on the kitchen table – just rotting, rotting away! And the cockroaches – as big as rats.' She laughed. 'Well, as big as mice. And the silverfish – as big as fish.' Again she laughed. Then she frowned in angry remembrance: 'And I tried so hard to keep at least that room of mine clean and tidy. But those boys would litter it with their magazines and their clothes and their – their *mess*. That's why I took this job, really. I wanted to get away to a house where things were clean and orderly and – and nice.'

The low-ceilinged room, lit by a single naked electric light bulb, similar to that outside the shack, is in an unbelievable state of dirt and disorder. Not nice, at all. There is a sagging unmade bed, with a tawny cat, so still that it might be dead, stretched out across it like a discarded fur. There are cardboard boxes piled in one corner and a litter of paperback murder mysteries, trashy magazines and used Kleenex tissues over the threadbare linoleum of the floor. Pushed to one end of a plain deal table are the remains of a meal. A newspaper is spread out over the rest of it, open at the page which lists the television programmes. Some clothes have been flung, haphazard, over an armchair sprouting horse-hair. An old-fashioned brassière lies on the ground. There is a terrible din from the black-and-white television set, until Clare goes over and turns down the sound. The pictures have the blurred, grainy quality of early photographs transmitted by radio.

'Sit.' Clare picks up the clothes off the chair and stoops, groping for the brassière. Then she flings the whole bundle over on to the bed. The cat, startled, squawks and leaps to the floor, to slink through a half-open door, presumably to bathroom and kitchen. Helen sits. Clare goes over to the straight-backed chair from which she had been watching the television and lowers herself on to it, as though her joints were stiff. One arm goes over its back and her body leans forward, as she stares at the silent people flickering on the screen.

'You vanished,' Helen said. 'No one knew what had happened to you.'

Still staring at the screen, Clare shakes her head. Contradiction? But no one in India, not even her own family, had known what had happened to her. She had met this man, she had gone away with him. Some kind of artist, a good-for-nothing. That was all they could tell to the police. Suddenly

Clare laughs, as though to herself, her visitor forgotten. 'I wanted to make a new life,' she says. 'I made many new lives. Day by day.'

Helen is puzzled.

'He became a famous painter. You know that? Painted me, painted me often. No, not me, not this me, but all those – all those others. Paintings lost, destroyed, who knows? Those different others lost, destroyed. Gone.' While she speaks in this jerky manner, still with that chichi accent – that, at least, has not been lost, destroyed, that remains – Helen wonders if perhaps she has had a stroke. Clare turns her head from the screen. 'You. You went to prison. Many years.'

She knows. Helen nods. 'Yes. I went to prison.'

'Why?'

'Why? Because I confessed.'

This strange, dishevelled, skinny woman, who was once the Clare whom Helen held in her arms, stamps irritably with her slippered foot on the floor. 'Why confess? Why?'

So many people have asked Helen that question and only Ilse and the Bishop, both now dead, were certain that they knew the answer. Atonement. Ilse used that word. The Bishop used it. 'Atonement,' Helen now says, but tentatively, as though, in some infinitely complicated card game with this woman, she was unsure what to play.

'I thought it was for him.'

Does she mean the dead child? Does she mean Toby?

'Him?'

'Your father.'

'Perhaps.'

Helen does not yet know. He wandered aimlessly from room to room of the house at the top of the estuary. He tapped the barometer in the hall with a swollen knuckle. He sat out on the lawn, doing nothing, as the water ebbed and the mud glistened in wider and wider rings. He avoided her. He hated her. Yes, he hated her. She sees that now.

Clare stares back at the television. A commercial. A tot, her hair fastened with ribbons on either side of her plump, freckled face, opens her mouth wide and bites off a piece of chocolate from a bar. Clare turns again, that thin, sinewy arm, almost black from the sun, still hanging over the back of her chair. 'Atonement,' she murmurs. Then louder: 'Anyway, you were atoning for someone else. You were not that one, I am not that one. And so you are not the one who atoned. And I am not the one who read of your atoning. Simple.' She smiles and repeats: 'Simple.' Then she puts hands to the white hair on either side of her temples, rakes her crooked fingers through it. There is suddenly an expression of horror on her face. 'Terrible,' she says.

They stare at each other.

Helen glances at her watch. Babs told her that they would be leaving at about eleven. Soon, someone will come looking for her. She gets up from the chair. 'I must go. I just wanted . . .'

Clare appraises her, her red-rimmed eyes going up and down, up and down. 'Beautiful,' she says at last. 'You're still beautiful. Clean. Neat. Nice.' She does not rise.

'Goodbye, Clare.'

Clare does not answer.

Helen goes out of the shack, raising a hand in a quick farewell. At the sound of her closing the door behind her, a dog begins to bay. Other dogs take up the sound. They all seem far, far off.

Helen stands listening to them, her head on one side and her hands clasped before her.

In the beginning was the Word (*die*) and the Word (*die, die*) was with God and the Word (*die, die, die*) was God. The girl sat facing her stepmother, who had her hands over her ears, her eyes screwed up and her shoulders hunched, as though in expectation of a blow. The lightning darted from one hilltop to another. *The girl watched it strike, like some huge golden snake, at the woman before her.* The woman removed the hands from her ears, opened her eyes, straightened herself, straightened her skirt over her knees. She looked up gratefully at the red-haired man whose fingers were caressing the nape of her neck.

329

The girl opened the letter. She was seated on the edge of the iron bedstead in the dormitory into which she was not allowed to go except at night-time. She began to read, her lips moving silently. 'Mama has had a mysterious fever for several days. Dr McGregor has been baffled. It's not malaria, not enteric, not flu.' *The headmistress said 'Sit down, dear. I have some bad news for you, I'm afraid. Your mother – stepmother . . .' The girl walked into the schoolroom and all the other girls looked up from their prep and stared at her. The mistress in charge called the girl over to her. 'Come and sit over here with me.' She put an arm round the girl's narrow shoulders, hugging her closer to her.* The girl read on. 'Fortunately last night her temperature fell and, having eaten nothing for several days, she announced that she was ravenous!'

The servants had carried her father into his darkened dressing room and the girl had come back with Dr McGregor, whom she had ridden off to summon. Dr McGregor went into the dressing room, with the battered Gladstone bag of which the girl's stepmother once remarked contemptuously: 'Even an Indian doctor would be ashamed of going around with a bag like that.' Girl and stepmother stood motionless outside the dressing-room door, then the stepmother led the way down the stairs, groping the banister with her plump right hand, as though there were no light shining down on them from the skylight. The stepmother said: 'It could have been us too. It could have been any of us.' The girl did not answer. 'Couldn't it? Dangerous country.' *The stepmother sprawled threshing, like some huge, pale fish, her mouth agape, on the flags of the kitchen floor, while the poison glided, a corrosive snake, within her.* At the bottom of the stairs the old woman looked up at her daughter-in-law and her grand-daughter, her eyes screwed together against the light which flooded down from the skylight. 'Oh, poor Toby, poor Toby! Poor angel! But thank God that, at any rate, you both are all right.'

On the calm lake, the boat rocked from side to side as the Eurasian girl rowed it with a jerky clashing of oars on rowlocks. The girl sat in the stern, the rudder in her hand. A long, twisted stick, covered in a silvery slime, bobbed past them and then circled, caught in a lethargic eddy. The boy leaned over the side, reached, lost his balance. *He let out a shrill cry, as he tumbled downwards. The Eurasian screamed: 'Do something, do something!' She lurched to her feet in the rocking boat. 'I can't swim, I can't swim!' Almost overbalancing herself, she held out one of the oars over the water, the other abandoned, while the boat drifted away. The girl stared at an arm flailing, a head emerging and disappearing. 'Oh, do something!' At last, kicking off her shoes and diving over the side of the boat, the girl did something, when it was too late for anything effective to be done.* The girl shot forward and grabbed the boy by the back of his jumper. 'You little fool! Be careful! You might have been drowned. Your mother'd never forgive us.'

The boy pointed to a vast snake, grey mottled with green, uncoiling itself sleepily from a branch. Its eyes glittered. 'Isn't he beautiful?' he said. Then he cried out, 'Let me down, let me down!' *Stooping, she lowered him in her grasp and then let him go. He raced towards the snake, first smiling, then laughing. The old woman screamed, his father shouted, the servants rushed forward, abandoning their burdens. The snake reared up, its tongue flickered, it struck.* The girl, her fingers pressing him so tight against her midriff that she felt that she had only to exert a little more strength to crack him open like an egg, restrained him. 'Don't be silly! It's poisonous, it could kill you.'

The Eurasian snatched up the brassière off the back of the chair in the moonlit room and with frantic, red-nailed fingers thrust it downwards into the open mouth. The girl did not at once hiss at her, 'Clare, Clare, don't, *don't*!' A second passed. Two seconds. Three seconds. 'Clare, Clare, don't, *don't*!' The girl at last said it. Too late.

At the end there was the Word (*atone*) and the Word (*atone, atone*) was with Aunt Sophie and the Word (*atone, atone, atone*) was Aunt Sophie. A sudden intensity kindled in the dying eyes under the heavy lids, as she squinted up at her niece. 'Who would want to do such a thing? Who? Who?' But Aunt Sophie, with that piercing simplicity of hers, knew who would want to do such a thing and who had wanted to do it for years and years. She knew and she held out the gift of forgiveness,

331

even without atonement. But the gift was like those beads which Aunt Sophie had dreamed that the murdered boy had snapped with a tug – beads rolling, rolling everywhere. It was a gift unuseable, unless the girl went on her knees and collected them up, with infinite patience, one by one, and restrung them, as once, long ago, that child had strung beads together with infinite, pathetic patience to make her a bookmarker.

Atone, at one. Looking up into the wide sweep of the sky above her, her head tilted and her eyes dazzled by stars and tears, Helen is now at one not only with Aunt Sophie but with Ilse, who was part of her atonement, with Clare, who was the fragile implement of her will, with her dead father, who was another such implement, with Isabel, implacable in her grief, and even with the child, his small palm scored with two brief gashes and his head lolling back at that other, deep, long gash which had all but severed it from its neck.

Helen shudders. The dogs have ceased to bark, it is now very still. Momentarily, as she once again feels that knife in her hand and that warm body beneath it, something dark and terrible, the undying worm in a constantly dying world, stirs again within her. Then: 'Dr Eliot! Dr Eliot!'

It is Laurel or Babs or Hank or someone calling to her. Once again from the bald slope stretching away in front of her and from the dark, humped hill beyond it, the dogs begin, one by one, to set up their barking. They sound demented with terror.

'Dr Eliot?'

'Yes. Yes, it's me.'

MORE ABOUT PENGUINS, PELICANS
AND PUFFINS

For further information about books available from Penguins please write to Dept EP, Penguin Books Ltd, Harmondsworth, Middlesex UB7 0DA.

In the U.S.A.: For a complete list of books available from Penguins in the United States write to Dept DG, Penguin Books, 299 Murray Hill Parkway, East Rutherford, New Jersey 07073.

In Canada: For a complete list of books available from Penguins in Canada write to Penguin Books Canada Ltd, 2801 John Street, Markham, Ontario L3R 1B4.

In Australia: For a complete list of books available from Penguins in Australia write to the Marketing Department, Penguin Books Australia Ltd, P.O. Box 257, Ringwood, Victoria 3134.

In New Zealand: For a complete list of books available from Penguins in New Zealand write to the Marketing Department, Penguin Books (N.Z.) Ltd, P.O. Box 4019, Auckland 10.

In India: For a complete list of books available from Penguins in India write to Penguin Overseas Ltd, 706 Eros Apartments, 56 Nehru Place, New Delhi 110019.

THE ENGLISHMAN'S DAUGHTER
Peter Evans

Lord Henry's defection sent deadly shock waves through Whitehall and the Kremlin. Ten years later – and this time it's his daughter, beautiful, talented and vulnerable, who is trapped in the vortex.

As the action switches from London and Venice to Moscow and Leningrad, Peter Evans's brilliant and surprising thriller traces out a grey landscape of treason and sexual duplicity. As the enormity of Lord Henry's action is revealed, so too is the sinister world of international intrigue, dominated by the brooding darkness of the Cold War.

'A Discovery! Peter Evans is an exciting new talent. *The Englishman's Daughter* is as fast-moving as *Gorky Park*' – Len Deighton

THE WATCHER
Charles Maclean

There was no warning of any kind. No discernible pattern of events leading up to the incident ... Martin Gregory's unremarkable life explodes into a nightmare when he commits an atrocity so unexpected that it stuns everyone – including himself ...

'Original, horrific and compulsively gripping' – *Sunday Express*

'A thriller that riveted my attention. It is quite remarkable how dextrously Mr Maclean manipulates us' – *The New York Times*

'I'm something of an insomniac. I read *The Watcher* and stopped sleeping altogether' – Paul Newman

WHITE MISCHIEF
James Fox

'A story which is as compelling and violent as a thriller, but which also happens to be one of the most dazzling feats of reportage in recent years' – *Time Out*

When the body of Josslyn Hay, 22nd Earl of Erroll, was discovered with a bullet through his handsome head just outside Nairobi in January 1941, the resulting scandal revealed a hornet's nest of upper-class decadence and misbehaviour ...

'Marvellously entertaining' – Auberon Waugh

'Eccentric settlers and shady aristos, neurotic wives and sad drunks, *morphineuses* and lounge-lizards. The cast and setting are unique' – William Boyd

SCANDAL
A.N. Wilson

A rising star in the political firmament, Derek Blore has a reputation that is boringly impeccable. But is it?

When Bernadette Wooley entertains every week the man she knows as Billy Bunter, she does not realize that her client is tipped as a future leader of his Party. Nor does she attach much importance to the hidden camera and tape recorder ...

'Mr Wilson is a wonderfully funny writer in his wry, downbeat way' – Francis King in the *Spectator*

'Drily witty, deliciously nasty ... rich entertainment' – *Sunday Telegraph*